Palgrave Studies in Nineteenth-Century Writing and Culture

Palgrave Studies in Nineteenth-Century Writing and Culture is a new monograph series that aims to represent the most innovative research on literary works that were produced in the English-speaking world from the time of the Napoleonic Wars to the *fin de siècle*. Attentive to the historical continuities between 'Romantic' and 'Victorian', the series will feature studies that help scholarship to reassess the meaning of these terms during a century marked by diverse cultural, literary, and political movements. The main aim of the series is to look at the increasing influence of types of historicism on our understanding of literary forms and genres. It reflects the shift from critical theory to cultural history that has affected not only the period 1800–1900 but also every field within the discipline of English literature. All titles in the series seek to offer fresh critical perspectives and challenging readings of both canonical and non-canonical writings of this era.

Titles include:

Eitan Bar-Yosef and Nadia Valman (*editors*)
'THE JEW' IN LATE-VICTORIAN AND EDWARDIAN CULTURE
Between the East End and East Africa

Heike Bauer
ENGLISH LITERARY SEXOLOGY
Translations of Inversions, 1860–1930

Laurel Brake and Julie F. Codell (*editors*)
ENCOUNTERS IN THE VICTORIAN PRESS
Editors, Authors, Readers

Colette Colligan
THE TRAFFIC IN OBSCENITY FROM BYRON TO BEARDSLEY
Sexuality and Exoticism in Nineteenth-Century Print Culture

Dennis Denisoff
SEXUAL VISUALITY FROM LITERATURE TO FILM, 1850–1950

Stefano Evangelista
BRITISH AESTHETICISM AND ANCIENT GREECE
Hellenism, Reception, Gods in Exile

Laura E. Franey
VICTORIAN TRAVEL WRITING AND IMPERIAL VIOLENCE

Lawrence Frank
VICTORIAN DETECTIVE FICTION AND THE NATURE OF EVIDENCE
The Scientific Investigations of Poe, Dickens and Doyle

Yvonne Ivory
THE HOMOSEXUAL REVIVAL OF RENAISSANCE STYLE, 1850–1930

Colin Jones, Josephine McDonagh and Jon Mee (*editors*)
CHARLES DICKENS, A TALE OF TWO CITIES AND THE FRENCH REVOLUTION

Jarlath Killeen
THE FAITHS OF OSCA
Catholicism, Folklore

Stephanie Kuduk Weiner
REPUBLICAN POLITICS AND ENGLISH POETRY, 1789–1874

Kirsten MacLeod
FICTIONS OF BRITISH DECADENCE
High Art, Popular Writing and the *Fin de Siècle*

Diana Maltz
BRITISH AESTHETICISM AND THE URBAN WORKING CLASSES, 1870–1900

Catherine Maxwell and Patricia Pulham (*editors*)
VERNON LEE
Decadence, Ethics, Aesthetics

Muireann O'Cinneide
ARISTOCRATIC WOMEN AND THE LITERARY NATION, 1832–1867

David Payne
THE REENCHANTMENT OF NINETEENTH-CENTURY FICTION
Dickens, Thackeray, George Eliot and Serialization

Julia Reid
ROBERT LOUIS STEVENSON, SCIENCE, AND THE *FIN DE SIÈCLE*

Anne Stiles (Editor)
NEUROLOGY AND LITERATURE, 1860–1920

Caroline Sumpter
THE VICTORIAN PRESS AND THE FAIRY TALE

Sara Thornton
ADVERTISING, SUBJECTIVITY AND THE NINETEENTH-CENTURY NOVEL
Dickens, Balzac and the Language of the Walls

Ana Parejo Vadillo
WOMEN POETS AND URBAN AESTHETICISM
Passengers of Modernity

Phyllis Weliver
THE MUSICAL CROWD IN ENGLISH FICTION, 1840–1910
Class, Culture and Nation

Paul Young
GLOBALIZATION AND THE GREAT EXHIBITION
The Victorian New World Order

Palgrave Studies in Nineteenth Century Writing and Culture
Series Standing Order ISBN 978–0–333–97700–2 (hardback)
(outside North America only)

You can receive future titles in this series as they are published by placing a standing order. Please contact your bookseller or, in case of difficulty, write to us at the address below with your name and address, the title of the series and the ISBN quoted above.

Customer Services Department, Macmillan Distribution Ltd, Houndmills, Basingstoke, Hampshire RG21 6XS, England

---

Robert Louis Stevenson, Science, and the *Fin de Siècle*

Julia Reid

palgrave
macmillan

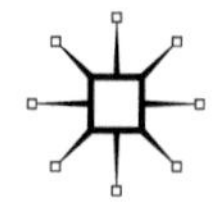

First published in hardback 2006
First published in paperback 2009 by
PALGRAVE MACMILLAN

Palgrave Macmillan in the UK is an imprint of Macmillan Publishers Limited, registered in England, company number 785998, of Houndmills, Basingstoke, Hampshire RG21 6XS.

Palgrave Macmillan in the US is a division of St Martin's Press LLC, 175 Fifth Avenue, New York, NY 10010.

Palgrave Macmillan is the global academic imprint of the above companies and has companies and representatives throughout the world.

Palgrave® and Macmillan® are registered trademarks in the United States, the United Kingdom, Europe and other countries

ISBN-13: 978–1–4039–3663–9 hardback
ISBN-10: 1–4039–3663–3 hardback
ISBN-13: 978–0–230–23032–3 paperback
ISBN-10: 0–230–23032–6 paperback

This book is printed on paper suitable for recycling and made from fully managed and sustained forest sources. Logging, pulping and manufacturing processes are expected to conform to the environmental regulations of the country of origin.

A catalogue record for this book is available from the British Library.

Library of Congress Cataloging-in-Publication Data

Reid, Julia, 1974–
Robert Louis Stevenson, science, and the fin de siècle / Julia Reid.
p. cm.—(Palgrave studies in nineteenth-century writing and culture)
Includes bibliographical references and index.
ISBN 978: 1–4039–3663–3 (cloth) ISBN 978: 0–230–23032–3 (pbk.)
1. Stevenson, Robert Louis, 1850–1894—Criticism and interpretation.
2. Evolution (Biology) in literature. 3. Literature and science—Great Britain—History—19th century. I. Title. II. Series.

PR5496.R45 2006
828′.809—dc22 2005056411

10 9 8 7 6 5 4 3 2 1
18 17 16 15 14 13 12 11 10 09

Printed and bound in Great Britain by
CPI Antony Rowe, Chippenham and Eastbourne

For my parents, Janet and Walter, and for Dan and Callum

Contents

List of Figures ix

Acknowledgements xi

Textual Note xiii

Introduction: Stevenson, Evolution, and the 'Primitive' 1

Part I '[O]ur civilised nerves still tingle with . . . rude terrors and pleasures': Romance and Evolutionary Psychology **13**

1 Stevenson and the Art of Fiction 15

2 Romance Fiction: 'stories round the savage camp-fire' 31

Part II 'Downward, downward lies your way': Degeneration and Psychology **55**

3 'There was less *me* and more *not-me*': Stevenson and Nervous Morbidity 59

4 'Gothic gnomes': Degenerate Fictions 77

Part III Stevenson as Anthropologist: Culture, Folklore, and Language **107**

5 'The Foreigner at Home': Stevenson and Scotland 111

6 '[T]he clans disarmed, the chiefs deposed': Stevenson in the South Seas 138

Conclusion 174

Notes 178

Works Cited 216

Index 234

List of Figures

2.1 Map of Treasure Island, from Robert Louis Stevenson, *Treasure Island* (London: Cassell, 1883), ii. Reproduced courtesy of The Bodleian Library, University of Oxford. Arch.AA e. 149. 36

2.2 Illustration from serial version of Robert Louis Stevenson and Lloyd Osbourne, *The Ebb-Tide, To-Day* 1 (11 November 1893), 4. Reproduced courtesy of The Bodleian Library, University of Oxford. Per.3974e.34. 46

3.1 Annotated copy, from Stevenson's library, of Francis Galton, *Records of Family Faculties* (London: Macmillan, 1884), 16. Reproduced courtesy of the Beinecke Rare Book and Manuscript Library, Yale University. 66

6.1 Nan Tok', Fanny Stevenson, Nei Takauti, and Robert Louis Stevenson on the Gilbert Islands. Reproduced courtesy of the Edinburgh Writers' Museum. 138

6.2 Map showing Stevenson's travels, from *In the South Seas* (London: Heinemann, 1924), ii. Reproduced courtesy of the English Faculty Library, University of Oxford. 144

Acknowledgements

I have incurred many debts during the writing of this book. First, I should like to thank Helen Small for her expert and enthusiastic supervision of my doctoral research, and her unfailing generosity with her time and scholarship. I also wish to express my gratitude to Sally Shuttleworth, whose work first inspired my interest in the intersections between Victorian literary and scientific discourses, and who has been a much-appreciated source of intellectual support and practical advice ever since.

I am indebted to Kate Flint, Dinah Birch, and Lyn Pykett for their erudite criticism, encouragement, and guidance over the years. My thanks are also due to Kathryn Sutherland, Roslyn Jolly, and James Buzard, who have commented perceptively on early drafts or versions of my work, and to Scott Ashley, Ralph Parfect, Claire Harman, and Roger Ebbatson for their input and insights.

I owe an important debt to Joseph Bristow, and one which I am glad to be able to acknowledge here. I have been exceptionally fortunate in having him as series editor, and the book has benefited enormously from his rare blend of critical rigour, encouragement, and support.

I am grateful for the assistance of the librarians in the Bodleian Library, Oxford University, the British Library, and the National Library of Wales. The staff of the Beinecke Rare Book and Manuscript Library, Yale University, gave me expert help, and unpublished material from the Stevenson Collection is reproduced with thanks. Every effort has been made to seek permission to quote from materials which may be in copyright, but the publisher would be grateful if notified of any omissions. Sections of the present book have appeared, in somewhat different form, in Louise Henson et al., eds, *Culture and Science in the Nineteenth-Century Media* (Aldershot, Hampshire: Ashgate, 2004), *Journal of Victorian Culture* 10.1 (spring 2005), and Richard Dury and Richard Ambrosini, eds, *Robert Louis Stevenson: Writer of Boundaries* (Madison, Wisconsin: University of Wisconsin Press, 2006). The revised chapters appear in the book with the permission of Ashgate, Edinburgh University Press, and the University of Wisconsin Press.

The process of completing the book has been enriched by my colleagues at the University of Wales, Aberystwyth, and the University of Liverpool, and by lively seminar discussions with students at both institutions. The support of my friends has also been very important to me: over the years, Gillian Hamilton, Muna Reyal, Claire Squires, Kirstie Blair, Karen Stöber, Damian Walford Davies, and Matt Houlbrook have provided encouragement and diversion in equal measure. I am especially grateful to my parents-in-law, Dick and Jeanette Scroop, for making me so welcome in their family, and to Bryony Reid for being a great sister and friend, and an admirably efficient research assistant.

The book is dedicated to my parents, Walter and Janet Reid, and to Dan Scroop and our baby son, Callum. My parents' love and support, and their enthusiasm for this project, have meant much more to me than I can express; their childhood present of Stevenson's *A Child's Garden of Verses* no doubt laid the seeds of my later research interests. Dan has been here since the earliest stages of my research, and his love and intellectual engagement has helped to shape the book in more ways than he will ever realize. Callum has yet to discover the joys of Victorian literature, but he has contributed to the book in his own way, principally by spurring me on to finish it before his joyful but disruptive arrival.

Textual Note

When quoting unpublished manuscript sources, I have maintained original spelling, punctuation, italicization, and capitalization. I have used the following symbols:

/ \ (around the word or words affected) denotes that this text has been inserted.

—— (through the characters or words affected) denotes that the text has been scored through.

⊔⊓ (between the words affected) denotes that this text has been transposed.

Introduction: Stevenson, Evolution, and the 'Primitive'

Cruising between the Pacific islands in the late 1880s, Robert Louis Stevenson gathered ideas for an ambitious work of travel writing, which he hoped would capture the essence of the South Seas.[1] In May 1889, his wife Fanny confided her fears to their friend, Sidney Colvin: 'Louis', she wrote, 'has the most enchanting material that any one ever had in the whole world for his book, and I am afraid that he is going to spoil it all'.[2] Instead of entertaining his readers with all 'the extraordinary adventures that befell us', she lamented, he had 'taken into his Scotch Stevenson head, that a stern duty lies before him, and that his book must be a sort of scientific and historical impersonal thing'.[3] Fanny's complaint opposes the domains of dry, 'impersonal' science, and a romantic literature steeped in authorial personality. Twenty months later, she recalled her frustration over the 'South Sea book':

> [m]any times I was almost in despair. He had got . . . [Darwin's] *Coral Reefs*; somebody else on Melanesian languages, books on the origin of the South Sea peoples, and all sorts of scientific pamphlets and papers . . . Instead of writing about his adventures in these wild islands, he would ventilate his own theories on the vexed questions of race and language. He wasted much precious time over grammars and dictionaries, with no results, for he was able to get an insight into hardly any native tongue.[4]

Fanny Stevenson's disdain for her husband's mastery of linguistic science was matched, and exceeded, by her ridicule of his meagre expertise in marine biology. His perverse decision to 'study the coral business', she continued, 'would have ruined the book but for my brutality'.[5] Relating an incident which took place on an atoll in the Gilbert Islands, she cast her husband as the blundering British man abroad, the artist unskilled in practical or scientific matters. Having gone ashore on the island, she and her son parted company with, and soon lost sight of, Stevenson. They finally found him gathering coral specimens

> on the reef, halfway between the ship and shore, knee-deep in water, the tropical sun beating on his unprotected head, hammering at the reef with a big hatchet. His face was purple and his eyes injected with blood . . . [He] showed me the fragments that he wished me to take to the ship for dinner, fatigue, nothing should get him away from the important discoveries he was making. I looked at his specimens with contempt. 'Louis,' I said, 'how ignorant you are! Why, that is only the common brain coral. Any schoolboy in San Francisco will give you specimens if you really want them.' [6]

In Fanny's anecdote, Stevenson's scientific pretensions are ludicrous, and he is a figure of fun – fun, indeed, which betrays her exasperation, if not a hint of malice.[7] Yet her disparagement of his scientific interests also stems from her belief in Stevenson's literary powers. Her perception of her husband as 'the man of genius' (the phrase is at once tongue-in-cheek and entirely in earnest) involves an absolute separation between artistic and scientific spheres of human thought.[8] She explains her resistance to Stevenson's 'fight[ ] to keep his book impersonal, that he might feel free to fill up with scientific interests' by exclaiming, 'oh, my dears, he is an artist, and he knows nothing about science'.[9]

The conception of divided realms, artistic and scientific, had received unprecedented publicity a decade before Fanny Stevenson wrote. In the early 1880s, the notion was popularized by the exchange between T. H. Huxley, pugnacious advocate of a more scientific education, and Matthew Arnold, defender of the faith of literary humanism. Resisting Huxley's assertion that science was an integral part of culture, Arnold declared that literature satisfied human desires in ways that science could not.[10] This debate established the lines along which commentators discussed the notion of cultural division over the next century and more. Famously recapitulating its terms in 1959, C. P. Snow diagnosed European intellectual society as suffering from a division into 'two cultures', and called for more recognition of science, a plea that F. R. Leavis resolutely rejected.[11]

In the years since Snow mourned the loss of a common culture, however, scholars in the social sciences and humanities have undermined his thesis of cultural schism. An increasingly relativist and externalist approach to the history of science, fostered by Thomas Kuhn's *The Structure of Scientific Revolutions* (1962), has encouraged the recognition that science is a product of culture rather than simply a transcription of nature, and that scientists are subject to multifarious socioeconomic, ideological, and linguistic constraints.[12] The acceptance that science as much as literature is culturally bounded has generated since the 1980s sustained critical investigation of the interactions between science and literature. Stefan Collini describes this academic phenomenon as a field of scholarly endeavour in its own right, an 'interdiscipline'.[13] Questions about the dynamics of influence between literature and science, about the translation of ideas between different discourses, are central to this analysis. It is now widely (though not universally) accepted that influence flows in both directions: there is, Gillian Beer demonstrates, no 'one-way traffic' from scientific to literary discourses.[14] Yet at the same time, the current of influence – in either direction – is not smooth or unproblematic; ideas, that is, are not simply transferred from one realm to, or reflected in, the other.[15] Ideas originating in one discourse are resisted, challenged, creatively modified, as often as they are assimilated in another realm: 'transformation', Gillian Beer suggests, is a more helpful concept than 'translation'.[16]

Studies of nineteenth-century science and literature have been particularly valuable. Inspired by Beer's seminal work, *Darwin's Plots* (1983), critics have investigated how literary figures engaged with scientific discourses, both affirming and resisting the tales they told.[17] Active engagement rather than passive digestion, indeed, marked cultural interactions between nineteenth-century scientists and literary figures. George Levine explores how novelists variously questioned or espoused Darwinian ideas; his interpretation, however, emphasizes *unconscious* processes of absorption, examining writers who did not necessarily read Darwin's writings, but were part of a common culture in which Darwinism was a powerful force.[18] By contrast with this notion of generalized cultural influence, Sally Shuttleworth, Peter Allan Dale, Laura Otis, and others focus on the precise mechanisms of literary writers' encounters with scientific ideas and people: the periodicals, books, and newspapers they read, and the scientists with whom they enjoyed intellectual relationships.[19] Shuttleworth, for example, examines Charlotte Brontë's involvement in local intellectual and cultural transactions, and demonstrates her ability to expose contradictions inherent within contemporary psychological theories. Critical work on scientific engagement with literary genres, too, emphasizes resistance as much as assimilation. Helen Small suggests, for instance, that literary representations of madness influenced medicine in complex and discontinuous ways: scientists did not simply appropriate literary images and narratives, but responded according to specific professional pressures.[20]

Robert Louis Stevenson has received little attention from scholars working in the 'interdiscipline' of literature and science, despite possessing suggestive credentials in the shape of his scientific background and interests. Born in 1850 to a family of lighthouse engineers, Stevenson was educated to follow in the family profession. He embarked on an engineering degree at Edinburgh University, and even delivered a paper entitled 'On a New Form of Intermittent Light for Lighthouses' to the Royal Scottish Society of Arts in 1871, before, only a few days later, abandoning engineering.[21] He lost his faith as a young man following his exposure to Herbert Spencer's scientific naturalism, and his early interest in the relations of evolutionary science and ethics endured, prompting him to describe his essay, 'Pulvis et Umbra' (1887), as 'a Darwinian Sermon'.[22] References to Darwin, E. B. Tylor, and Spencer appear throughout his notebooks and letters, and evolutionist rhetoric informs his essays on literary appreciation and creativity.[23] During his final years in the South Pacific, he was a member of the Society for Psychical Research, and an enthusiastic student of Polynesian anthropology, contributing to debate in London periodicals about the evolution of religious worship.[24]

The neglect of Stevenson's scientific interests by interdisciplinary critics is perhaps not surprising, as it forms part of a pattern of critical denigration which began soon after his death. Literary critics came to view his literary talents as shallow and juvenile, and his charming essay style as facilely imitative by comparison with, for example, George Eliot or Thomas Hardy (the two writers most commonly singled out for interdisciplinary study). Describing how Stevenson 'went in search of a style as Cœlebs in search of a wife', John Jay Chapman wrote that '[w]hether or not there was some obscure connection between his bodily troubles and the arrest of his intellectual development, it is certain that Stevenson remained a boy till the day of his death'.[25] During the early decades of the twentieth century, Stevenson was remembered predominantly for *Treasure Island* and *Kidnapped* – works which, in a climate of hostility to the 'romance' form, were treated as uncomplicated boys' adventure stories.

The scholarly rehabilitation of Stevenson's reputation, which began in the mid-twentieth century, is now well established. Yet, perhaps inevitably, the new-found critical interest has privileged certain topics, approaches and works. Consideration of his Scottish writings remains dominated by the question of Scottishness, with many critics focusing on his uneasy relations with nationalist concerns. Andrew Noble and Christopher Harvie interpret his historical fiction as escapist and backward looking, a sentimental recompense for his inability to deal with the social and political problems facing contemporary Scotland.[26] Stevenson's Pacific writings, meanwhile, have received increasingly positive attention, and are the subject of recent studies by Vanessa Smith, Rod Edmond, Barry Menikoff, and Robert Hillier.[27] They are regarded as prophetically tackling many issues now facing a postcolonial world, and thus seem to be in tune with current critical and political interests.[28] Clearly there is a need to reconcile the divergent interpretations of the Scottish and Polynesian Stevensons: to trace how an early interest in Scottish folklore developed into his valorization of Polynesian superstition, and how his celebration of 'romance' modulated into the grim psychological realism of his final Pacific fiction.

As suggested by the interpretation of his Scottish work as culpably nostalgic and his Polynesian work as admirably avant-garde, critics rarely depict Stevenson as a man of his time. Thus Alan Sandison interprets Stevenson – albeit in his Scottish as well as Polynesian œuvre – as an anticipator of modernism, or even postmodernism.[29] Barry Menikoff similarly observes that Stevenson's 'play with narrative/linguistic technique' in *New Arabian Nights* is 'unsurprising to the reader of late twentieth-century fiction . . . for whom Stevenson's method would appear wonderfully postmodern'.[30] In recent criticism, there has been a reluctance to situate Stevenson's work in its contemporary intellectual context, and limited attention, in particular, to his engagement with science. Certainly, the concern with degeneration in *The Strange Case of Dr. Jekyll and Mr. Hyde* has attracted much sophisticated analysis, by Stephen Heath, Stephen Arata, Robert Mighall, and others, but the narrow focus on this one work has obscured the range and complexity of Stevenson's transactions with late-Victorian science.[31]

Robert Louis Stevenson, Science, and the Fin de Siècle explores Stevenson's interest in evolutionist thought, arguing that an interest in the 'primitive' forms a unifying preoccupation across his work. Epithets such as 'savage', 'primitive', and 'civilized' are profoundly loaded terms, clearly referring not to realities, but to Western constructions. As Elazar Barkan and Ronald Bush note, '[a]s for "primitives," they never existed. Only Western "primitivism" did, invented in heated arguments about human society'.[32] While recognizing this, I employ the terms throughout my study in relation to their use by Stevenson and his contemporaries. Using them in this way enables me to scrutinize the deep investment in notions of the primitive which connected late-Victorian scientific and literary thought.

Stevenson, I contend, engaged seriously – and often ambivalently – with late-Victorian theories of evolution, and his relationship with science was much more dynamic than has hitherto been recognized. His critics often seem unaware that, in Beer's words, the 'traffic' between literature and science is not 'one-way', and that his work may resist as well as affirm, or may even *influence*, late-Victorian science.[33] Elaine Showalter, citing Stevenson's friendship with the psychical researcher F. W. H. Myers as possible inspiration for *Dr. Jekyll and Mr. Hyde*, perpetuates what Roger Cooter and Stephen Pumfrey characterize as the 'diffusion model of popularization' – the idea that science is always diffused downwards (usually in diluted terms) by professional scientists.[34] Ed Block also represents Stevenson's fiction as unquestioningly 'dramatizing' the scientific theories of evolutionary psychologists such as James Sully.[35] This interpretation privileges science as an authoritative discourse whose empirically discovered truths are merely reflected in literature: despite the friendship enjoyed by Sully and Stevenson, Block depicts the intellectual 'influence' as flowing in one direction only, from the scientist to the literary writer.[36] Elsewhere, Block deploys a different model, but one which equally figures scientific and literary discourses as inhabiting separate spheres. He asserts that Stevenson and other fictional writers 'anticipated the work of later psychologists' such as Freud, Carl Gustav Jung, and R. D. Laing, with *Dr. Jekyll and Mr. Hyde* forming 'an important foreshadowing of twentieth-century scientific research': creative literature, this suggests, can intuit truths which are as yet denied to science.[37] The notion of 'two cultures' clearly survives in this interpretation. Stevenson, it implies, absorbed contemporary currents of scientific thought in a merely passive manner, but artistic inspiration nonetheless enabled him to prefigure the next century's scientific preoccupations.

Yet, as the present study shows, Stevenson and the evolutionary scientists were engaged in a creative dialogue – one marked by dissonance as well as consonance. The chapters that follow focus on Stevenson's transactions with the new evolutionist sciences of psychology, degeneration theory, and anthropology. Common themes united the debates conducted by psychologists, degenerationists, and anthropologists, as they sought to understand the development, through time, of human life and thought. Nonetheless, evolutionary theories were ambiguously accented, and yielded multiple, often contradictory, interpretations. Stevenson's writings inquire into these ambivalences – about the nature and direction of change, the possibility of progress or degeneration, the relations of 'savagery' and 'civilization', the influence of environment and heredity, and the relations of the individual and the race. Much of the creative tension and imaginative power of Stevenson's work, I argue, derives from his ability to exploit – or expose – the friction and dissension between divergent theories of evolution.

The concept of evolution – whether of individuals, species, cultures, or societies – was central to Victorian science and culture.[38] In the subsequent century, evolutionism became exclusively associated with Charles Darwin, but Darwin's thesis was only one of many conflicting theories which collectively exerted such influence.[39] At the beginning of the nineteenth century, evolutionism was largely the legacy of Scottish Enlightenment thought, which emphasized the gradual, developmental progress from primitive to refined society.[40] From mid-century, new life was injected into the idea of evolution by two contemporaneous developments. In 1859, Darwin's *The Origin of Species* disseminated his belief that evolution worked through the 'natural selection' of spontaneously occurring variations. Independently, sociocultural evolutionists including Spencer and Tylor presented secularizing accounts of humankind's mental and cultural evolution, exploring how language, religion, science, and morality had developed as part of a natural progression from savagery to civilization.[41] Spencer and Tylor became the founding fathers of the new sciences of evolutionary psychology and anthropology.[42]

Although these models of evolution were *collectively* influential in the late-Victorian period, they were certainly not *consensually* so. Unresolved questions plagued evolutionist thought: was the current direction of change progressive, and could it be reversed? Was evolution teleologically directed, or a process of random change? How far did the past survive into the present? At the heart of these uncertainties lay the contested nature of the evolutionary mechanism. In the early nineteenth century, the French naturalist Jean-Baptiste Lamarck elucidated his theory of the 'inheritance of acquired characteristics': organisms, he claimed, responded to environmental stimulus by self-development, and passed the characteristics acquired to subsequent generations. Lamarck's model of evolution had a notably progressive momentum. Darwin's rival hypothesis of the 'natural selection' of random variations, by contrast, was subject to multiple, conflicting interpretations: progress and direction existed alongside unpredictability and extinction. As Peter Bowler demonstrates, until the late twentieth century historians exaggerated Darwin's influence, suggesting that his hypothesis had been generally accepted in the late nineteenth century.[43] Yet far from discrediting Lamarck, an 'ironic result of Darwinism's success', Martin Fichman notes, 'was that Lamarckism seemed more plausible after *The Origin of Species* had given evolutionism greater, and more widespread, credibility'.[44] Spencer's evolutionism was dependent on Lamarck's model of self-development in response to environmental challenge, and through Spencer Lamarckism remained influential throughout the nineteenth century.[45]

As the turn of the century drew nearer, the strains within evolutionary thought intensified. Commentators increasingly focused on the darker implications of the Darwinian narrative: as Beer describes, Darwinism's 'disturbing elements', its emphasis on 'extinction and annihilation', 'gradually accrued a heavier and heavier weight in consciousness'.[46] Even the fundamentally progressivist traditions of evolutionary psychology and anthropology harboured unspoken tensions – while celebrating the advance of the human mind, they were nonetheless preoccupied by the *survival* of the past within the present, the endurance of savage psychologies. The new theory of degeneration, moreover, which haunted *fin-de-siècle* Europe, increasingly challenged the meliorist narratives of evolutionist psychology and anthropology. Advanced by British scientists, including Henry Maudsley and Edwin Ray Lankester, along with their Continental counterparts, the theory of degeneration recognized that life did not always move from the simple to the complex, and envisaged instead a future characterized by arrested development, atavistic throwbacks, and the disintegration of overly evolved civilizations. Degenerationist theories drew on and fed into *fin-de-siècle* concerns about racial decline, but were ultimately hesitant about the relative influence of heredity or environmental pathologies.

Stevenson's work negotiates and exposes these evolutionist uncertainties, undermining psychologists' and anthropologists' confident assumptions about inevitable progress. Dramatizing the endurance of savagery at the heart of *soi disant* civilization, his writing disturbs the hierarchical relations between the civilized and primitive. Stevenson's radical revaluation of the 'primitive' suggests that the genealogy of literary primitivism needs revision. Critics have customarily viewed primitivism's engagement with evolutionism as a modernist phenomenon, exemplified by T. S. Eliot's debt to J. G. Frazer, but Stevenson's equivocal response to evolutionist discourses of the primitive arguably anticipates the modernists' primitivism.[47] Furthermore, critics often read modernism as inaugurating, in Gregory Castle's words, 'a form of resistance both to anthropology and imperialism'.[48] For David Richards, Eliot and the modernists used the 'primitive' to challenge 'the panopticon disciplinary gaze of the Frazerian notion of science', and to 'cut the bands of imperial grand theory'.[49] Nicholas Daly similarly contrasts an allegedly imperialist Victorian primitivism, articulated in romances by Stevenson, Rudyard Kipling, and H. Rider Haggard, with a more subversive modernism: 'romance narratives work to make imperial expansion, and thus the destruction of the premodern, an adventure', whereas modernist '[w]riters position themselves outside the modern, on the side of the "primitive"'.[50] This distinction between a pro-imperialist Victorian primitivism and a more critical modernism is clearly overdrawn, if only because, as this book shows, Stevenson's interrogation of evolutionism destabilized colonialism's hierarchical vision of savagery and civilization.

Not only did Stevenson engage ambivalently with evolutionist theories; his relationship with scientists including the anthropologist Andrew Lang and the psychologist James Sully was also characterized by *mutual* intellectual influence. Late-Victorian literary London made these associations possible: Lang, Sully, and Stevenson were all members of the Savile Club, and their articles shared space in periodicals such as the *Cornhill Magazine*, *Longman's Magazine*, and the *Academy*. Indeed, Lang's commissioning of work by Stevenson for *Longman's* and the bond between Stevenson and Sully as fellow *Cornhill* contributors are an important part of the cultural context in which evolutionism was debated in the 1870s and 1880s. Recent work by Peter Broks and Paul White is illuminating in this context, interpreting the mainstream Victorian periodical press as the site not merely for the dissemination of science, but for the active construction of scientific meaning and authority.[51] Stevenson was able to engage productively with Myers, Lang, and Sully about the questions exercising evolutionary psychology and anthropology largely because these nascent disciplines were still unprofessionalized, enjoying only an insecure academic and institutional standing.[52] He also, moreover, possessed recognized expertise in these fields – first through his supposed access, as creative writer, to the unconscious mind, and later through his direct knowledge of Polynesian cultures.

My book discusses Stevenson's engagement with evolutionary sciences across a wide range of his writings, unpublished as well as published: essays, romance narratives, letters, memoirs, neo-Gothic tales, fables, historical novels, and Pacific travel writing and fiction. I have selected those works which interrogate Victorian evolutionist discourses most cogently; had space permitted, I would also have considered Stevenson's celebration of what he understood as primitive poetic tradition in *Underwoods* and *Ballads*, the burlesque tales of *New Arabian Nights* and *The Dynamiter*, the subversion of heroic masculinities in *The Black Arrow*, and the confrontation with other cultures and other selves in his American and European travel writing. I examine Stevenson's transactions with evolutionism thematically: Part I considers evolutionary psychology, Part II degenerationist theory, and Part III anthropology. In all three parts, I show how Stevenson's writings coalesce around the contested meaning and value of 'primitive' instincts, energies, and cultures.

Part I investigates how Stevenson engaged critically with evolutionary psychology, unsettling complacent assumptions about inevitable progress from savage to civilized psychologies. In Chapter 1, I reveal how Stevenson's romance polemics and other essays drew on evolutionary psychology to celebrate precivilized states of consciousness, but also undermined its confident narrative of evolutionary advance. Throughout the 1880s, his essays on romance, childhood make-believe, oral culture, and the creative imagination valorized the endurance and resurgence of primitive memories, their ability to regenerate an impotent modernity. His ideas elicited conflicting evolutionist responses, illustrating the disquieting nature of his deployment of evolutionist psychology, his capacity to read it against the progressivist grain. Chapter 2 argues that Stevenson's adventure novels negotiate ideas about the evolutionary appeal of romance in more equivocal ways than the essays, evincing a heightened mistrust of resurgent states of primitive consciousness. Even *Treasure Island,* a classic of the romance revival, examines adventure's darker side – its implication with aggressive imperialism and violent masculinities; and, under the pressure of his South Seas experiences, Stevenson increasingly sensed that the energies unleashed by romance might be destructive rather than invigorating. Rejecting the idea that the cult of heroic manliness might rejuvenate an ailing modernity, Stevenson rewrites the romance in *The Ebb-Tide,* scrutinizing critically its implication both with oppressive discourses of class and masculinity and with a brutal evangelical imperialism.

Part II demonstrates that, while his romance writings negotiated the progressivist tradition of evolutionary psychology, Stevenson was equally fascinated by its dark side, the theory of degeneration. It discloses how his work deals ambivalently with contemporary theories of atavism. In Chapter 3, I consider Stevenson's representation of his own nervous morbidity in his letters, essays, and memoirs. His concerns – about childhood, loss of faith, and masculinity – resonate with degenerationist psychiatry. Interrogating the causes of his psychological morbidity and raising disquieting questions about how far individuals could control a degenerative heritage, Stevenson explores and reveals the tensions within late-Victorian degenerationism – tensions over the relative influence of nature and nurture. Chapter 4 investigates how the preoccupation with psychological degeneracy articulated in Stevenson's letters and his interest in questions about heredity, will, and environment find fictional form in the cluster of neo-Gothic tales which he wrote in the early 1880s: 'The Merry Men', 'Olalla', 'Markheim', and *Dr. Jekyll and Mr. Hyde.* Inhabited by characters whose mental pathologies drive them to savage bestiality, insanity, or death, these tales figure the irruption of primitive states of mind in the supposedly civilized present. Yet, I contend, they also reveal the tacit conflict between hereditary and environmental explanations of degeneration, undercutting the emphasis on biological inheritance, and suggesting that degeneration stems rather from the *denial* of savage instincts.

Part III turns from Stevenson's engagement with individual psychology to his interest in anthropology's broader evolutionary narrative. Tracing the development from his early Scottish fiction to his final South Seas work, this part of my discussion demonstrates that Stevenson was centrally concerned with anthropological debates about primitive culture, cultural change, and the possibility of progress. Indeed, Grant Allen recognized this, hailing his novels, along with Haggard's, as a new class of fiction – the 'romance of anthropology'.[53] In Chapter 5, I explore how, despite Stevenson's interest in secularizing anthropology, even his early fiction such as 'The House of Eld' and 'Thrawn Janet' is hesitant about a confident evolutionary narrative, dramatizing instead the resurgence of superstitious states of mind. The scepticism deepens in *Kidnapped* and *The Master of Ballantrae*, which question Scotland's progress towards modernity and evoke the intertwining of primitive and civilized cultures, unsettling the possibility of an objective ethnographic enterprise. Chapter 6 shows how Stevenson's Pacific experiences intensified his perception of the savagery lurking at the heart of so-called civilization. The celebration of traditional, oral cultures in 'The Beach of Falesá' and *In the South Seas* destabilizes racial and cultural hierarchies, underscoring the brutal effects of European imperialism. Pointing forward to a new cultural relativism, these works illuminate late-Victorian anthropology at a pivotal point, as an appreciation of plural cultures gradually eroded hierarchical evolutionism. More fundamentally still, their questioning of the viability of cross-cultural sympathies undercuts the anthropological enterprise. These concerns in turn feed into Stevenson's final Scottish fiction, informing *Catriona* and *Weir of Hermiston*'s heightened awareness of vulnerable cultures and languages, and of individual helplessness in the face of the cultural struggle for survival.

Running through Stevenson's work, as all three parts of this book show, is his scepticism about evolutionary hierarchies. Unsettling the binary relations between savagery and civilization, the unconscious and the conscious, and past and present, his writings portray the persistence and irruption of precivilized states of consciousness in the modern world. The book aims to demonstrate the ambivalence, centrality, and continuity of his transactions with evolutionist thought, and thus to reconcile the Scottish and Polynesian Stevensons. His involvement in evolutionist debates also illuminates the creative intersections and complex interweavings between late-Victorian literary and scientific discourses: Stevenson was able to engage critically and dynamically with evolutionist thought, both affirming and – importantly – challenging its assumptions. At the heart of this challenge was his revaluation of contemporary evolutionist notions of the 'primitive', and his belief in the enduring heritage of savagery in modern life.

Part I
'[O]ur civilised nerves still tingle with . . . rude terrors and pleasures': Romance and Evolutionary Psychology

> The fortune of a tale lies not alone in the skill of him that writes, but as much, perhaps, in the inherited experience of him who reads; and when I hear with a particular thrill of things that I have never done or seen, it is one of that innumerable army of my ancestors rejoicing in past deeds.[1]

In this essay, 'Pastoral' (1887), one of his most compelling explorations of heredity and literary pleasure, Stevenson attributes the reader's enjoyment to 'inherited experience', to a resurgence of unconscious, ancestral memories. Creating a psychological narrative which spans the generations, he breaks down barriers between past and present and unsettles the notion of a unified identity. He imagines ancestry as an irresistible force (an 'innumerable army'), but one which is joyous and exhilarating. Throughout his life, Stevenson was fascinated by what he saw as the unconscious roots of artistic appreciation and creation. In essays written during the 1880s, he used an evolutionist vocabulary of primitive 'survivals' and 'organic memory' to examine the meaning and value of romance, oral culture, the childhood imagination, and creative inspiration. This interest in unconscious inheritance also informed his fiction. From his early children's novels to his final Pacific work, Stevenson's adventure narratives explore the idea that romance represents the revival of what he understood as savage human psychologies. In both essays and fiction, he was preoccupied by questions about resurgent ancestral forces: how important was the influence of heredity? How far did the past live on, consciously or unconsciously, within the present? What were the relations of primitive and civilized life? Were the energies associated with the savage past rejuvenating or destructive?

These questions, which stood at the heart of much of Stevenson's writing, tapped into late-Victorian debates that were taking place within the new field of evolutionary psychology. Across the 1850s, 1860s, and 1870s, scientists advanced important evolutionist readings of psychology and culture. In *Principles of Psychology* (1855), Herbert Spencer seminally interpreted psychology in terms of racial as well as individual development.[2] The theory of 'organic memory', formulated by Spencer, Samuel Butler, and others, enshrined the belief that a primitive past persisted within the present. It held that individuals remembered their ancestral and racial experiences unconsciously, through their instincts: Spencer described how 'conscious memory passes into unconscious or organic memory'.[3] Equally influential was the anthropologist E. B. Tylor's notion of 'survivals', proposed in *Primitive Culture* (1871). Examining the stages of humankind's progressive intellectual development, Tylor viewed modern 'savages' as examples of 'an early condition of mankind', and noted the endurance, even in modern Europe, of cultural 'survivals . . . carried on by force of habit into a new stage of society'.[4] These evolutionist treatments of psychology and culture were alike in looking simultaneously backwards and forwards: preoccupied by questions about the legibility of the past in the present, they were nonetheless also fundamentally progressive in their interpretation of evolution, celebrating what they viewed as the upward movement of the human mind, its development from savagery to civilization. Spencer memorably hailed evolution as 'that grand progress which is bearing Humanity onwards to a higher intelligence and a nobler character'.[5]

Stevenson's engagement with this essentially meliorist evolutionary psychology was ambivalent. As I reveal in Part I of the present study, his essays and adventure fiction negotiated the new science somewhat equivocally, raising questions about the nature and direction of the evolutionary process, and about the relations between savage and civilized psychologies. In Chapter 1, I argue that while Stevenson's essays draw on evolutionist rhetoric to celebrate literature's instinctual appeal, they also destabilize many of its confident assumptions about inevitable psychological progress, suggesting instead that civilized modernity is ailing. Chapter 2 explores how *Treasure Island* (1881–82) and *The Ebb-Tide* (1893–94) engage with Stevenson's valorization of romance in consistently thoughtful and sometimes highly critical ways, evincing much more wariness about the notion of primitive inheritance than the essays. It demonstrates that even *Treasure Island*, often seen as the archetypal romance narrative, is hesitant about the allegedly savage charm of adventure, and it examines why this uneasiness hardened into the later novel's outright scepticism about the rejuvenating powers of romance.

1
Stevenson and the Art of Fiction

In a cluster of essays written during the 1880s, Stevenson explored – and celebrated – the persistence of precivilized states of consciousness in the modern world, in the guise of romance, oral narratives, childhood make-believe, and the literary imagination. These essays, which appeared in popular journals and enjoyed a wide readership, mark Stevenson's engagement with the emergent evolutionist approach to literature. A new school of psychologists, following Herbert Spencer, examined the imagination as a connection between modern individuals and humanity's collective past. The psychologist James Sully and others used an evolutionary model of the mind to explore the affinity between dreaming, myth-making, and literary inspiration. An increasing interest in the unconscious mind also informed the writings of psychical researchers including F. W. H. Myers and the new sciences of comparative mythology and physiological æsthetics, as practised by Andrew Lang and Grant Allen. Similarly, contemporary writers often expressed evolutionist understandings of creativity: for Kipling, the artist's imagination represented his memory of past lives and, for Wilde, 'concentrated race-experience'.[1]

Stevenson moved in the same social circles as many prominent evolutionary scientists – most notably Sully, Myers, and Lang – and he repeatedly discussed with them ideas about the unconscious basis of literature. Sully recollected how he 'wrote an article for an American Review on the connection between imaginative writing and dreaming – a subject I was no doubt led to think about by a talk I had recently enjoyed with R. L. Stevenson'.[2] Late-Victorian literary London, its clubs and periodicals, made these interdisciplinary associations possible. As Sully wrote, '[a]lthough I was [Stevenson's] senior, the fact of our having joined the Savile [Club] at about the same time, and still more the synchronizing of our series of contributions to the *Cornhill*, made him seem in a curious way a brotherly companion'.[3] Lang, Sully, and Stevenson all joined the recently founded and intentionally informal Savile Club in the early 1870s, as did Myers's brother, the physician A. T. Myers; and Stevenson made it his London headquarters. His articles also appeared alongside contributions from these scientists in the *Cornhill Magazine, Longman's Magazine,* and the *Academy*. The *Cornhill,* with its innovative and inexpensive combination of important serial novels and critical essays, was a particularly significant vehicle for debates about the nature of literature.[4]

Ed Block has represented Stevenson's work as unquestioningly 'dramatizing' the scientific theories of evolutionists, yet, as Sully's remarks indicate, Stevenson's intellectual relationship with evolutionary scientists was clearly dynamic and reciprocal.[5] Indeed, he was able to resist as well as affirm the tales told by evolutionary psychologists. While the psychologists recognized the instinctual basis of literary pleasure, they did so within a framework which emphasized the passage towards a more civilized art: with increasingly peaceful social conditions, Spencer had explained, art appealed to ever more refined and sympathetic feelings.[6] By contrast, Stevenson (despite his acknowledgement of Spencer's influence on his early intellectual development) questioned the meliorist accent on gradual imaginative refinement, and suggested the vitality of primitive states of consciousness.[7]

Stevenson's ambivalence towards evolutionist psychology emerges most clearly in the well-known, transatlantic literary debate about 'romance' and 'realism'. The clash between the supporters of romance and the defenders of realism was not a new contest of values, but it took on renewed urgency in the 1880s, in the context of arguments about the new 'mass readership', the advance of literature, and the intellectual growth of contemporary readers. The disagreement drew on conflicting evolutionary narratives. Thus the realist confidence in literary progress chimed with the evolutionist belief in psychological development. The American author, editor, and advocate of realism, W. D. Howells, defended Henry James's psychological realism as a 'new kind of fiction': 'the stories were all told long ago', he wrote, and now readers wanted analytic studies and should surrender the 'childish ... demand' for 'finished' tales.[8]

The champions of romance, however, led by Andrew Lang, a dedicated Tylorian folklorist and friend of Stevenson, saw psychological realism as a mark not of intellectual progress but of morbid overcivilization. Lang's celebration of popular tastes in fiction was firmly rooted in evolutionary psychology. Only adventure novels, he believed, could exert a truly popular appeal, reaching out beyond an effete intellectual élite. He maintained that the renascent romance form appealed to savage 'survivals' within human psychology:

> [t]he Coming Man may be bald, toothless, highly 'cultured', and addicted to tales of introspective analysis. I don't envy him when he has got rid of that relic of the ape, his hair; those relics of the age of combat, his teeth and nails; that survival of barbarism, his delight in the last battle of Odysseus, Laertes' son . . . Not for nothing did Nature leave us all savages under our white skins; she has wrought thus that we might have many delights, among others 'the joy of adventurous living,' and of reading about adventurous living.[9]

Lang's scorn for the unhealthy, emasculate reader of realist fiction was central to the romance revival. He used his de facto editorial position at *Longman's Magazine* to foster 'reading about adventurous living', promoting authors such as Stevenson, H. Rider Haggard, Rudyard Kipling, Arthur Conan Doyle, and Anthony Hope.[10] With fellow crusaders, including Haggard and the journalist and literary critic George Saintsbury, Lang envisaged the romance as heralding a reinvigorating return to the heroic masculinity and conservative social ideals which he felt had been betrayed by an effete modern world.[11] Stevenson's romance polemics were much more measured and subtle, but they have been tainted by Lang's cruder advocacy, and by romance's steady deterioration into shrill imperialist apology: its 'gradual debasement', Peter Keating alleges, can be 'traced back' to Stevenson's 'unguarded critical assertions'.[12] As a result, there has been little serious critical attention to his romance polemics, and still less to their challenging negotiation of evolutionist science.[13]

In 'A Gossip on Romance' (1882) and 'A Humble Remonstrance' (1884), Stevenson uses evolutionist psychology, paradoxically, to collapse the forward-moving narrative of evolution, unsettling the hierarchical relations between unconscious and conscious mind, senses and intellect, and low and high culture. 'A Gossip on Romance', published in *Longman's Magazine*, calls for a genuinely popular literary art. Declaring that 'romance' summons up 'in the mind an army of anonymous desires and pleasures', Stevenson affirms its ability to tap the deep, unconscious memories within humankind, and contrasts this with what he saw as realism's preoccupation with the 'clink of teaspoons and the accent of the curate'.[14] He thus pits the artificial and cultured world of genteel manners against natural, instinctual, and even inarticulate forces. Readers' 'nameless longings', Stevenson suggests, are all-important: 'the great creative writer shows us the realisation and the apotheosis of the day-dreams of common men'.[15] His evolutionist rhetoric, with its accent on the popular, fitted in well with the anti-élitist philosophy of *Longman's Magazine*. The magazine cultivated an overtly demotic ethos: it was founded in 1882, in the wake of the 1870 Elementary Education Act and the 1880 Education Act, with the avowed aim of providing reading matter for the newly literate classes.[16]

'A Humble Remonstrance', Stevenson's rejoinder to Henry James in the famous 'Art of Fiction' exchange, also valorizes the denigrated realms of the unconscious and popular. Walter Besant's April 1884 lecture to the Royal Institution, 'The Art of Fiction', had opened the debate. James's essay of the same name, published in *Longman's* in September, ostensibly answered Besant's realist manifesto, but it was also an indirect riposte to Lang's disparagement of psychological realism: as N. N. Feltes suggests, James intentionally made his case before Lang's popular audience.[17] The essay was a nuanced defence of literary realism, of novels which attempted to produce the 'illusion of life'.[18] Stevenson entered the fray with 'A Humble Remonstrance', published in *Longman's* in December, which opposed James's claim that 'art . . . can successfully "compete with life" ', and contended that its value lay in its *difference* from life.[19] James, whose admiration for Stevenson was not compromised by his contempt for the 'Philistine' Lang, consequently amended the 1888 edition of his essay, removing the offending phrase 'compete with life'.[20] Stevenson's essay overturned the hierarchy between intellectual and sensual literature, suggesting that the romance was just as valuable as the 'novel of character'.[21] His celebration of novels which appealed to the 'sensual and quite illogical tendencies in man' was partly a strategic move of self-defence against James's criticism of *Treasure Island*, but also indicated a revaluation of unconscious dreams and desires.[22] Whether a novel touched a reader, James had claimed, depended largely on whether it touched one's experience: 'I have been a child', he wrote, 'but I have never been on a quest for a buried Treasure'.[23] Stevenson countered what he saw as this narrow definition of experience, exclaiming that, in dreams at least, every child had hunted treasure, had 'been a pirate, and a military commander, and a bandit of the mountains'.[24] *Treasure Island*, he claimed, stirred atavistic instincts: '[t]he luxury, to most of us, is to lay by our judgment, to be submerged by the tale as by a billow'.[25] The 'romance', this suggests, has a deeper and broader resonance than the realist novel, pleasing not just the highly cultured, but potentially a mass readership.

Throughout the 1880s, Stevenson's essays returned, as if compulsively, to this central theme: the appeal of romance to the evolutionary unconscious. Readers' responses, he believed, were often beyond the reach of critical speculation. He was not alone in attributing literature's charm to the survival of barely discernible memories. Sully, whose writings were among the first evolutionist treatments of æsthetics, held that some emotions were irrecoverable because they were part of a racial memory.[26] Stevenson stands out, however, for his delight in the unfathomable nature of artistic experience. In 'On Some Technical Elements of Style' (1885), he declares that the writer's 'artifices', 'if we had the power to trace them to their springs, [are] indications of a delicacy of the sense finer than we conceive, and hints of ancient harmonies in nature . . . We shall never learn the affinities of beauty, for they lie too deep in nature and too far back in the mysterious history of man'.[27] For Stevenson, literature's instinctual gratification is no less important than its appeal to the allegedly higher intellectual and moral faculties. Describing the fascination of alliteration, 'this barbaric love of repeating the same sound', he notes that 'such a trick of the ear is deeper-seated and more original in man than any logical consideration'.[28]

'Pastoral' (1887) and 'The Manse' (1887) suggest more forcefully the potentially disturbing aspects of Stevenson's evolutionist rhetoric, its paradoxical ability to unsettle the narrative of smooth psychological progress from savagery to civilization. In both essays, Stevenson deploys 'organic memory' theory to subversive effect. 'Pastoral', published in *Longman's* in 1887, recollects Stevenson's childhood delight in a shepherd's stories, and ponders the importance of heredity in narrative pleasure. Linking the shepherd's talk and 'romance', Stevenson affirms the importance of unconscious memories, explaining that a 'trade that touches nature, one . . . in which we have all had ancestors employed, so that on a hint of it ancestral memories revive, lends itself to literary use, vocal or written'.[29] This invocation of 'ancient memories' draws on the theory of 'organic memory', developed by Spencer, Butler, and others. Stevenson inflects this theory with a democratic rhetoric, an emphasis on the latent capacities of the common reader: thus the tale's fortune 'lies not alone in the skill of him that writes, but . . . in the inherited experience of him who reads'.[30] He hails the romance as a truly popular form, judging that

> novels begin to touch not the fine *dilettanti* but the gross mass of mankind, when they leave off to speak of parlours and shades of manner and still-born niceties of motive, and begin to deal with fighting, sailoring, adventure, death or child-birth; and thus ancient outdoor crafts and occupations, whether Mr. Hardy wields the shepherd's crook

> or Count Tolstoi swings the scythe, lift romance into a near neighbourhood with epic. These aged things have on them the dew of men's morning; they lie near, not so much to us, the semi-artificial flowerets, as to the trunk and aboriginal taproot of the race.[31]

The sense of decadence conveyed by the metaphor of 'semi-artificial flowerets' and vigorous 'aboriginal taproot' suggests how Stevenson's use of 'organic memory' theory undercut its conventionally progressivist assumptions. Spencer and Butler, despite their emphasis on the potency of the unconscious, retained an assured belief in the upward movement of the human mind. Indeed, 'organic memory' theory rested on the French naturalist Jean-Baptiste Lamarck's model of evolution as the 'inheritance of acquired characteristics': a much more confidently progressive vision than Darwin's, this theory held that organisms adapted to their environment, and passed the traits acquired to subsequent generations.[32] Butler's *The Way of All Flesh* (1903) dramatizes this process, envisaging the hero's unconscious as an internal power, one which has been shaped by antenatal experiences but which adapts to and is taught by the environment.[33] By contrast with this teleological and meliorist narrative, Stevenson uses 'organic memory' theory to celebrate the primitive forces still potent within the apparently civilized. With a mischievous glee, he describes his most admired literary critic, 'a certain low-browed, hairy gentleman, at first a percher in the fork of trees, next (as they relate) a dweller in caves', and identifies him, in Darwin's phrase, as 'Probably Arboreal'.[34] In a deterministic move that scorns the pretensions of the 'fine *dilettanti*', Stevenson reduces literary appreciation to ancestral influences: 'Probably Arboreal' tops every family tree, and 'in all our veins run some minims of his old, wild, tree-top blood; our civilised nerves still tingle with his rude terrors and pleasures; and to that which would have moved our common ancestor, all must obediently thrill'.[35] These 'rude terrors and pleasures', Stevenson suggests, can be rekindled by romance. Yet while this resurgence of inherited forces appears to be a revitalizing experience, it also advances a disturbing sense of the helplessness of the individual, as readers are in thrall to imperative and bewildering hereditary predispositions ('all must obediently thrill').

'The Manse', published in *Scribner's Magazine* in 1887, suggests, like 'Pastoral', the equivocal nature of Stevenson's use of evolutionary psychology. While it does not so directly address debates about romance, its concern with dormant primitive memory provides a comparable, if oblique, comment on what Stevenson saw as the function of romance – namely, the arousal of primitive instincts. The article reflects on his ancestry, again using the trope of 'organic memory' to link the individual present with a collective past. Recalling childhood visits to his grandfather's manse, Stevenson wonders what he has 'inherited from this old minister', and imagines unknown ancestral influences: 'even as I write the phrase, he moves in my blood, and whispers words to me, and sits efficient in the very knot and centre of my being'.[36] He invokes the importance of 'our antenatal lives', explaining that '[o]ur conscious years are but a moment in the history of the elements that build us'.[37] This observation plays down the importance of conscious, rational elements in human life, strikingly echoing Butler's judgment that the 'history of man prior to his birth is more important . . . than his surroundings after birth'.[38] Stevenson's evocation of 'antenatal lives' works to erode barriers between individuals, connecting them together in a cross-generational psychological narrative. Thus he imagines joining in his grandfather's childhood games: 'that, too, was a scene of my education. Some part of me played there in the eighteenth century'.[39] Indeed, he continues whimsically,

> this *homunculus* or part-man of mine that walked about the eighteenth century with Dr. Balfour [his grandfather] in his youth, was in the way of meeting other *homunculos* [*sic*] or part-men, in the persons of my other ancestors . . . as I went to college with Dr. Balfour, I may have seen the lamp and oil man taking down the shutters from his shop . . . and from the eyes of the lamp and oil man one-half of my unborn father, and one-quarter of myself, looked out upon us.[40]

The sense that the line between individual and collective memory was blurred, and that the unconscious was not just a personal but a racial phenomenon, was a fundamental belief in late-nineteenth-century psychology.[41] But whereas Spencer and others usually saw the evolutionary past as prelude to an ever more civilized present, Stevenson viewed it as *compensation* for the present. It affords, in 'The Manse', a heady exhilaration, and translates personal identity from an impotent and effete present into a heroic past. Stevenson asks, '[a]re you a bank-clerk, and do you live at Peckham? It was not always so. And though to-day I am only a man of letters . . . I was present when a skipper, plying from Dundee, smuggled Jacobites to France after the '15'.[42] Tracing his 'antenatal' self further into the past, he lists all his vicarious experiences, declaring that 'parts of me have seen life, and met adventures'.[43] The process moves from the individual, through the family, nation, and human race, to the animal kingdom, culminating 'in the still cloudier past'. Returning to his favourite Darwinian phrase, Stevenson asks '[w]hat sleeper in green tree-tops, what muncher of nuts, concludes my pedigree? Probably arboreal in his habits'.[44]

This quest for ancestral origins conveys a thrilling sense of immortality; yet underneath the excitement lies a potentially more unsettling perception of mysterious and uncontrollable hereditary forces. The anxiety is particularly evident in the essay's final depiction of Stevenson's grandfather, a 'grave, reverend' minister who is at the mercy of 'an aboriginal frisking of blood that was not his; tree-top memories, like undeveloped negatives, lay dormant in his mind; tree-top instincts awoke and were trod down; and Probably Arboreal . . . gambolled and chattered in the brain of the old divine'.[45] It is a revealing passage, identifying the primitive forces still alive in the civilized figure of the 'old divine'. Outbreaks of unconscious memory figure as arbitrary primitive resurgences ('tree-top instincts awoke and were trod down'). The metaphor of 'undeveloped negatives' evokes the unpredictability of inherited instincts. This uncertainty about what triggered latent memory undermines Spencer's progressivist evolutionary model of organic memory, bringing Stevenson's vision closer to Darwin's picture of irregularity and instability. Darwin described the latent propensities harboured within organisms: written in 'invisible characters', they are 'ready to be evolved whenever the organization is disturbed by certain known or unknown conditions'.[46] Stevenson's clerical grandfather is similarly at the mercy of 'unknown conditions': not only is his individuality threatened by 'an aboriginal frisking of blood that was not his', but he is also subject to the capricious forces which catalyse these 'dormant' memories.

Nonetheless, despite the uneasy frisson occasionally generated by the survival of a savage inheritance, both 'The Manse' and 'Pastoral' clearly celebrate the capacity of primitive memories to invigorate an impotent modernity, one characterized by an artificial and sterile realism, and by the prosaic Peckham 'bank-clerk'. This perception of contemporary enfeeblement and the need to renew humankind's instinctual desires similarly underlies Stevenson's essays on orality and the childhood imagination. 'Talk and Talkers' and 'Talk and Talkers: A Sequel' (1882), 'Child's Play' (1878), and 'The Lantern-Bearers' (1888) demonstrate Stevenson's belief that oral narratives and childhood make-believe were primitive forms of narrative. This comparative evolutionist approach is implicit in 'Popular Authors' (1888), which views children and 'readers of the penny-press' as representative of an earlier stage of evolutionary development, and links popular fiction with ancient, spoken narratives, claiming that cheap novels are 'unhatched eggs of Arab tales; made for word-of-mouth recitation'.[47]

Throughout his life, Stevenson admired – and often sought to emulate – preliterate, oral culture. He composed poetry in Scottish dialect, published a volume of Scottish and Polynesian ballads, wrote many folk tales, and towards the end of his life praised Haggard's *Eric Brighteyes*, a romance inspired by the Icelandic sagas, confiding his desire to 'try *my* hand at a saga', and requesting 'any volumes that are out' in the Saga Library.[48] As this enthusiasm indicates, Stevenson shared the *fin-de-siècle* desire for a literary return to the 'speaking voice' – a desire encapsulated in Wilde's declaration that 'writing has done much harm to writers. We must return to the voice'.[49] This movement drew on new scientific insight into the nature of language. Scientists, as Linda Dowling shows, increasingly believed that spoken dialects represented an active, vital language, whereas written language was always to an extent atrophied.[50] This new principle underlay contemporary folklore, with its deep nostalgia for folk literature: Lang and Stevenson typically hailed poems or tales notable for their artlessness or simplicity as evidence of a vitally popular artistic tradition.[51]

Stevenson's essays in the *Cornhill* on 'Talk and Talkers' contrast spontaneous and original orality with debilitated modern print culture. Written literature, he argues, is the product of degeneration rather than progress:

> [l]iterature in many of its branches is no other than the shadow of good talk; but the imitation falls far short of the original in life, freedom and effect . . . Talk is fluid, tentative, continually 'in further search and progress;' while written words remain fixed, become idols even to the writer, found wooden dogmatisms.[52]

As Penny Fielding perceives, Stevenson 'consistently identifies speech with the natural', and 'the natural with the plural and the disruptive'.[53] His emphasis is on the free, untameable nature of the voice, its power to liberate men and women from modernity's deadening daily grind: 'speech runs forth out of the contemporary groove into the open fields of nature'.[54] Significantly, Stevenson associates orality not only with outdoor life and the natural world, but also with the physical passions and fears of 'battle'.[55] Good talk, his aggressively masculine imagery suggests, is an invigorating struggle. The exhilaration afforded by debate is like 'the fencer's pleasure in dexterity displayed and proved': '[t]he aboriginal man within us, the cave-dweller, still lusty as when he fought tooth and nail for roots and berries, scents this kind of equal battle from afar; it is . . . a return to the sincerity of savage life from the comfortable fictions of the civilised'.[56]

The opposition is between authentic, primitive, and ferocious orality, and feeble and insincere modern literature (the 'comfortable fictions of the civilised'). Vigorous primitive consciousness, Stevenson intimates, is in danger of being muffled by the civilized accretions of modern life. This perception of a degenerate modern literary scene clearly informs Stevenson's romance polemics. The revived romance form, for him, heralds at least a partial return to an unaffected oral culture: the 'real art', according to 'A Humble Remonstrance', is that 'of the first men who told their stories round the savage camp-fire'.[57] Undoubtedly, Nicholas Daly is right to point out that 'the definition of romance as a vigorous "primitive" form dissimulates the extent to which it is a specifically modern and commercially successful form'.[58] Nonetheless, Stevenson casts romance as a cultural curative, the restorative for a modernity whose sickness stems from its repressed instinctual life. His diagnosis anticipates Freud's more famous analysis, in 'Civilization and Its Discontents' (1930), of how civilization's 'restrictions of instinct' and of 'aggressivity' cause unhappiness, and his concern that such repression may have produced a 'neurotic' modernity.[59]

Stevenson's interest in the capacity of 'primitive' psychology to rejuvenate an etiolated and prosaic modernity also inspired his essays on the childhood imagination. 'Child's Play' (1878), as Glenda Norquay judges, figures the child's imagination as 'both a paradigm of what fiction should offer, and a point of entry into the workings of the creative processes'.[60] Stevenson also envisages childhood make-believe, however, as a literal archetype of adult creativity, drawing on the evolutionist belief that children recapitulated the developmental stages passed through in the evolution of the race. Psychologists, Sally Shuttleworth observes, increasingly saw children as bearers of elemental 'passions'.[61] For evolutionists, the childhood imagination was – like oral culture – representative of an earlier stage of evolutionary development: as E. B. Tylor wrote, 'in our childhood we dwelt at the very gates of the realm of myth'.[62] Tylor, who considered animism the mark of 'primitive' psychology, noted that '[e]ven in civilized countries, it makes its appearance as the child's early theory of the outer world'.[63] Stevenson's essay advances a similar model of childhood psychology, recalling that when 'my cousin and I took our porridge' they imagined that his cousin's sugar-topped bowl was 'a country continually buried under snow', and that his own milk-filled bowl was 'a country suffering gradual inundation'.[64] Echoing Tylor's vocabulary, Stevenson ruminates on children's 'frame of mind', and finds himself quite disconcerted, exclaiming, '[s]urely they dwell in a mythological epoch, and are not the contemporaries of their parents'.[65] He strengthens the analogy between children and 'primitive' peoples by suggesting that children see their parents as 'bearded or petticoated giants' or 'deities' who 'move upon a cloudy Olympus'.[66] In a later essay, '"Rosa Quo Locorum"' (1896), Stevenson also views the child as an embodiment of archaic human life, noting that 'there is more history and philosophy to be fished up [from the child's mind] than from all the printed volumes in a library'.[67] Just as he regrets the passing of societies which tell stories 'round the savage camp-fire', Stevenson suggests that the modern child takes a 'great and dangerous step', one which impoverishes the imagination, in passing 'from hearing literature to reading it'.[68]

Like Sully, Tylor, and Lang, then, Stevenson believed that much of this primitive psychology was sloughed off on reaching adulthood (for Lang, children 'trail their clouds of glory no further than the Lower Fourth').[69] Yet while it was an evolutionist commonplace to represent 'the mythologic stage of thought' as having survived only in the 'poet of our own day', Stevenson saw this primitive heritage as much more prevalent, suggesting that the imaginative impulse itself was not lost, but merely redirected.[70] Childhood make-believe, he declares in 'Child's Play', prefigures the adult's romance: '[i]t is when we make castles in the air and personate the leading character in our own romances, that we return to the spirit of our first years'.[71] This description strikingly foreshadows Freud's later portrayal of the 'growing child' ('instead of *playing*, he now *phantasies*. He builds castles in the air and creates what are called *day-dreams*').[72] Stevenson's analogy between childhood play and adult romance draws on Spencer's belief in the similarity of the 'play-impulse' and the 'æsthetic sentiments'.[73] Spencer's narrative, however, has a progressive impetus, figuring the 'æsthetic sentiments' as a 'higher' version of the 'play-impulse', whereas Stevenson affirms the enduring vitality of the child's consciousness within civilized adults.[74] In 'The Lantern-Bearers', for instance, Stevenson contests the popular belief that 'a poet has died young in the breast of the most stolid' and declares that the imaginative impulse lives on unseen: '[h]is life from without may seem a rude mound of mud; there will be some golden chamber at the heart of it, in which he dwells delighted'.[75]

For Stevenson, the *Arabian Nights* symbolized the invigorating survival of primitive consciousness. They were at the heart of his childhood games (in 'Child's Play' he remembers imagining with his cousin that 'the treasures of the *Forty Thieves*' were buried inside the 'secret tabernacle' of their calves' feet jelly), and were often the hallmark of romance in his fiction.[76] His comments on the tales undercut the progressivist picture of the increasing delicacy and selflessness of æsthetic pleasures. Like Spencer, Grant Allen considered literature which exercised aggressive feelings as outdated, and wrote that '[d]epth, earnestness, tenderness, all our higher feelings, must be gratified by art, unless it wishes to sink to the level of Eastern tales or children's stories'.[77] By contrast, Stevenson destabilized the idea of gradual imaginative refinement, denying that readers outgrew the *Arabian Nights*:

> [t]here is one book . . . that captivates in childhood, and still delights in age – I mean the 'Arabian Nights' – where you shall look in vain for moral or intellectual interest. No human face or voice greets us among that wooden crowd of kings and genies, sorcerers and beggarmen. Adventure, on the most naked terms, furnishes forth the entertainment and is found enough.[78]

In this passage, Stevenson celebrates the *Arabian Nights* as the archetype of romance, and is unabashed by the absence of 'moral or intellectual interest'. The continuing ability to enjoy these tales points to an instinctual life which endures not only in the modern child but also in those adults who are fortunate enough to retain an exhilarating connection with their savage past.

'A Chapter on Dreams' (1888), which brought Stevenson's own experience of creative inspiration to bear on evolutionist psychology, was his most influential contribution to evolutionist debate about literature. According to Lang, its illustration of 'the involuntary elements in imaginative creation' was 'full of interest for students of the human mind'.[79] The essay demonstrates again Stevenson's ability to read evolutionist psychology against the grain and dramatize the endurance of pre-civilized states of consciousness. Exploring the affinities between dreams, myth-making, and literary creativity, it depicts the young Stevenson as composed of two distinct consciousnesses, a waking and a dreaming self. The third-person narrative describes how he began 'to dream in sequence and thus to lead a double life – one of the day, one of the night – one that he had every reason to believe was the true one, another that he had no means of proving to be false'.[80] Although evolutionary psychology increasingly pathologized 'divided consciousness', the essay attests to the beneficent nature of Stevenson's dreams, showing how they inspired him with ideas for *Jekyll and Hyde* and 'Olalla'.[81] He describes his conscious self when asleep as the audience at a play, entertained by 'the little people who manage man's internal theatre' and provide inspiration for his tales.[82] He exclaims gratefully, 'how often have these sleepless Brownies done him honest service, and given him, as he sat idly taking his pleasure in the boxes, better tales than he could fashion for himself'.[83] For Stevenson, literary inspiration clearly occurs below the surface of consciousness. He later made this belief explicit, explaining that

> [I] sit a long while silent on my eggs. Unconscious thought, there is the only method: macerate your subject, let it boil slow, then take the lid off and look in – and there your stuff is, good or bad . . . the will is only to be brought in the field for study, and again for revision. The essential part of work is not an act, it is a state.[84]

While the will, in this quotation, is able to exert itself as and when it chooses, nonetheless Stevenson figures involuntary thought as the root of creativity. His Brownies, personifying his creative unconscious, have resonances with the literary critic E. S. Dallas's 'good fairy': in *The Gay Science* (1866) Dallas compared the obscure workings of the unconscious imagination to 'the lubber-fiend who toils for us when we are asleep'.[85]

Yet Stevenson's Brownies are not as well behaved as Dallas's sprite. Nor do they signify untainted Romantic genius: they weave their tales for financial gain as much as creative pleasure.[86] Rather, they represent the savage myth-making instincts which survive within a civilized human exterior: as Stevenson laments, 'I do most of the morality, worse luck! and my Brownies have not a rudiment of what we call a conscience'.[87] The essay suggests that the human psyche harbours traces of many different developmental stages: Stevenson awkwardly distinguishes his Brownies from 'myself – what I call I, my conscious ego, the denizen of the pineal gland unless he has changed his residence since Descartes'.[88] This hesitancy over 'myself – what I call I' intimates that there is no such thing as a fully rational, conscious ego, and that his Brownies may be in control more often than he imagines. He admits, 'my Brownies . . . do one-half my work for me while I am fast asleep, and in all human likelihood, do the rest for me as well, when I am wide awake and fondly suppose I do it for myself'.[89]

The equivocal nature of Stevenson's deployment of evolutionist psychology emerges most clearly from the conflicting evolutionist responses to 'A Chapter on Dreams'. Sully and Myers both welcomed the essay as a recognition of the wide compass of the unconscious. Myers's reaction was one of whole-hearted enthusiasm. Critics have usually seen Stevenson as drawing inspiration from Myers, rather than engaging in creative dialogue. Thus Elaine Showalter speculates that their friendship may have been responsible for shaping the treatment of psychological themes in *Jekyll and Hyde*.[90] However, Myers was as much indebted to Stevenson, whose essay confirmed his belief in the liberating value of states of altered consciousness, its account of an independent dream life resonating with his theory of the 'subliminal Self'.[91] Myers responded excitedly to 'A Chapter on Dreams', sensing that Stevenson's experiences might illuminate the mysteries of the unconscious mind. In an unpublished letter, written to Stevenson in April 1892, he hailed the essay as a 'valuable ~~addition~~ /contribution\ to experimental psychology'. Urging that Stevenson record his psychic life for the sake of science, he inquired whether

> your Dreams are wholly imaginative or are ever *hypermnesic* . . . And I would earnestly ask you, – for your own sake as well as for the sake of Science – , to try the so-called 'crystal-vision', or gazing into some clear depth where no reflected image disturbs you, to *externalise* your dreams in waking hours . . . If you succeed in this expt I should greatly like to be allowed to read your expt, if in time, to the Congress whose name heads this paper; – wh. is composed of savants from many countries, – and embraces *all the field of Exp. Psych.*[92]

Myers also acknowledged his debt to Stevenson in *Human Personality and Its Survival of Bodily Death* (1903), which welcomed 'A Chapter on Dreams' as a 'description of the most successful dream-experiments thus far recorded'.[93] Myers claimed that Stevenson's essay demonstrated 'that helpful and productive subliminal uprush which I have characterised as the mechanism of genius', and proved that mental abstraction, even when it came close to divided consciousness, could be 'integrative' rather than 'dissolutive'.[94]

Myers's unqualified appreciation of Stevenson's essay clearly reflects his somewhat marginal position within British psychological thought. As a founding member of the Society for Psychical Research, Myers rejected the dominant evolutionist progressivism. He staunchly opposed evolutionary psychiatrists such as Henry Maudsley who pathologized 'abnormal' mental states such as reveries, dreams, and inspiration.[95] Instead, he emphasized the value of the unconscious mind: as he wrote in 1886, 'for some uneducated subjects' the hypnotic trance 'has been the highest mental condition which they have ever entered'.[96] Interestingly, Stevenson's early travel writing also flirted with the idea of liberation through altered mental states. He revelled in the 'ecstatic stupor' achieved through open-air exertion: '[t]he central bureau of nerves, what in some moods we call Ourselves, enjoyed its holiday without disturbance . . . the beasts that perish could not underbid that, as a low form of consciousness. And what a pleasure it was! . . . I was about as near Nirvana as would be convenient in practical life'.[97] Despite his flippant tone, Stevenson clearly conveyed the exhilaration derived from his supposed return to primitive consciousness, declaring himself 'the happiest animal in France'.[98] It was this celebration of the many layers within human consciousness which appealed to Myers, affirming his scepticism about the unified ego and about inevitable psychological progress.

Sully's response was more hesitant, although he too was stimulated by Stevenson's ideas about inspiration. He explained in his 1918 autobiography that, during a visit to Stevenson in the late 1880s, he was intrigued by his account of 'the part that dreams had played in the "Strange Case of Dr. Jekyll and Mr. Hyde" ', and began to investigate the nature of literary creativity.[99] Having collected 'personal testimonies' from many novelists, he concluded that 'there are two pretty clearly marked types of novelist. Howell's [*sic*] attempt to make all fiction "voluntary" activity . . . will not do in the face of Stevenson's account of how the little people, unknown to him, do all the weaving work'.[100] Sully also experimented with creative writing himself, and was intrigued to find it an unconscious and instinctive process: 'I could not say how it came to shape itself. Unlike my more serious writing, which was for the greater part a matter of fiercely conscious struggling towards the light, it spun itself out as easily and smoothly as a spider's thread'.[101] For Sully, this confirmed 'the view of Stevenson that – for some novelists at least – the fashioning of a story is largely a subconscious mental process'.[102] Yet here he reacted with less enthusiasm than Myers. His respect for 'the creator of fiction', he noted, was diminished (though not his esteem for Stevenson's work), and he decided that 'the art of story-weaving', rather than being the sign of a highly-evolved intelligence, was 'a sort of trick'.[103]

While Myers, then, viewed Stevenson's work as confirming that literary creativity was a valuable manifestation of the 'subliminal Self', for Sully Stevenson's account suggested the backward-looking nature of the creative unconscious. Yet despite its atavistic connotations, the creative imagination was obviously far from threatening to Sully: in 'Poetic Imagination and Primitive Conception' (1876) he had likened the 'pleasure of æsthetic fancy' to 'that of a good romp, in which we rejoice to throw off for a few moments the shackles of adult life, and to return to the condition of spontaneous childhood'.[104] As Shuttleworth notes, Sully offered 'a Wordsworthian, celebratory response to the primitive, imaginative qualities of the child mind'.[105] Clearly Sully was fascinated by Stevenson's account of literary creativity and dreaming, and accepted that both states amounted to a revival of instinctual life. Nonetheless, where Stevenson (and Myers) viewed this primitive resurgence as important and liberating, Sully cast it rather as a regressive but harmless indulgence.

These divergent evolutionist reactions to Stevenson's article illustrate the complex interweaving of late-Victorian literary and scientific discourses, and suggest that Stevenson was able to engage critically and dynamically with evolutionist thought. Sully's rather wary, and more conventional, reaction to the essay's depiction of instinctual revival indicates the ambivalence of Stevenson's evolutionism. While his essays draw on evolutionist belief in the unconscious origins of literary pleasure and deploy a scientific vocabulary of 'survivals' and 'organic memory', I have argued that they also undercut the progressive narrative of psychological development.

Stevenson's essays, celebrating the endurance of humankind's primitive heritage into an apparently refined contemporary world, unsettle the hierarchical evolutionary relations between savagery and civilization, past and present, low and high culture, and senses and intellect. Rejecting the evolutionist picture of gradual imaginative refinement, Stevenson applauds the revitalizing connection with the past offered by romance, childhood make-believe, oral narratives, and the creative imagination, and deems it their mission to revive and gratify humankind's instinctual desires. Despite occasional disquiet about the survival of unruly hereditary forces, Stevenson's essays clearly hail the invigorating excitement afforded by primitive psychology – an excitement which has the potential to rejuvenate an impotent, overcivilized modernity.

2
Romance Fiction: 'stories round the savage camp-fire'

In his essays on romance, literary pleasure, and the creative imagination, Chapter 1 has shown, Stevenson was fully engaged in scientific debate about the lingering primitive heritage in the modern world. Nonetheless, critics have been reluctant to examine how this depth of intellectual inquiry informs his own romance fiction, which – at least in its earliest 1880s manifestations – has typically been considered as childish, playful, and buoyantly unreflective. Ironically, the dismissive critical valuation of Stevenson's early romance fiction, and of late-Victorian romance more generally, is perhaps the legacy of the contemporary belief that romance appealed to primitive energies. This belief, of course, was encouraged by romance's supporters as much as its enemies: Stevenson hailed as 'the real art . . . that of the first men who told their stories round the savage camp-fire'.[1] Romance, according to this model of literary evolution, was the undeveloped form of realism. Thus realism became securely associated with the contemporary, the rational, the adult, and the literate, while romance, increasingly a residual cultural form, bore connotations of the primal, the instinctual, the immature, and the oral. W. D. Howells accordingly praised readers' graduation from the 'childish . . . demand' for romance to more sophisticated appreciation of the 'new kind of fiction' offered by realism, and H. Rider Haggard reluctantly viewed realism as 'the art of the future'.[2] These associations have proved resilient: even Gillian Beer's sympathetic analysis of the romance genre describes 'something "child-like" ' in its pleasures.[3]

More recently, critics have found the late-Victorian romance ideologically unpalatable, on the grounds of its reactionary gender politics and jingoistic imperialism. According to Elaine Showalter, the romance revival was rooted in misogyny and represented an escape from the pressures of heterosexuality.[4] For romancers including Haggard and Andrew Lang, the ideal of heroic masculinity promised to regenerate an effeminate modern world. The bellicose energies of New Imperialism also underlay this vision: as Stephen Arata judges, the romance revival offered imperialist 'fantasies of a revitalized masculinity'.[5] Indeed, Lang's belligerent rhetoric conveys this point: he hailed 'men of imagination and literary skill' as 'the new conquerors – the Corteses and Balboas of India, Africa, Australia, Japan, and the isles of the southern seas'.[6] With its code of heroic masculinity, the quest romance helped to sustain the imperialist ethos, providing, in Joseph Bristow's words, 'Reading for the Empire'.[7] In its most strident form, at the hands of Anthony Hope, G. A. Henty, Stanley Weyman, and others, the romance degenerated into conservative chauvinism and imperialist apology.[8]

Stevenson's adventure novels have long been tainted by association with the late-Victorian romance revival. In the early twentieth century, he was remembered only as the author of 'boys' stories'. Even his mid-twentieth-century critical rehabilitation, as Leslie Fiedler notes, assumed 'a derogatory evaluation of the Romance', showing him 'progressing from the lesser form of the Romance to the Novel proper'.[9] Thus David Daiches cast *Treasure Island* (1881–82) as a 'simple story' of conflict between good and evil, and argued that only with the unfinished *Weir of Hermiston* (1896) did Stevenson finally transcend romance's limitations.[10] Edwin Eigner first challenged this critical consensus, demonstrating the maturity of his early romance fiction.[11] Since then, his adventure fiction has attracted much positive attention, but the model of his graduation from romance to realism has persisted, and there has been little consideration of the continuities between his early and late romance fiction. Recent criticism has accordingly read his Pacific writings as marking a radical shift towards a realist mode of representation. Roslyn Jolly argues that 'The Beach of Falesá' (1892) reverses Stevenson's previous position on 'realism' and 'romance', and Patrick Brantlinger shows how the same narrative moves from 'ironic adventure tale into domestic problem story'.[12] This generic shift, critics have assumed, paralleled Stevenson's transition from an early jingoistic conservatism to his eventual radical anti-imperialism. Thus Brantlinger contends that 'The Beach of Falesá' and *The Ebb-Tide* (1893–94) – 'accounts of the contemporary results of empire' which are 'skeptical about the influence of white civilization on primitive societies' – are 'quite at odds with his romances of historical adventure'.[13]

This model of Stevenson's transition from romance to realism is partially true, as his early disparagement of realism gradually turned to admiration. Nonetheless, it obscures his longstanding ambivalence towards romance. Stevenson's adventure novels, like his essays, explore the idea that romance represents the revival of savage human psychologies. His fiction, however, engages with his romance creed more equivocally and subtly, evincing a heightened wariness about primitive resurgences, especially as embodied in violent codes of manliness. This chapter examines Stevenson's first children's novel, *Treasure Island*, and his final Pacific novel, *The Ebb-Tide*, written in collaboration with his stepson, Lloyd Osbourne. It explores his early scepticism about romance's revivifying promise: *Treasure Island*, I argue, despite its classic romance credentials, not only enacts the delights of romance but also meditates on some of its dangers. The chapter then charts Stevenson's growing sense, under the pressure of his Pacific experience, that romance's energies might be destructive rather than rejuvenating, showing how his doubts about adventure's heroic masculinities hardened into *The Ebb-Tide*'s committed anti-imperialism.

Treasure Island, serialized in *Young Folks* from 1881 to 1882, and published in volume form by Cassell in 1883, was invoked by all the leading defenders of romance as the harbinger of the romance revival. Yet ultimately the novel is surprisingly ambivalent about the promise of romance. Its prefatory matter intimates this duality and suggests the self-conscious nature of its engagement with romance. *Treasure Island* opens with a dedication to Stevenson's stepson and a poem. The dedication, a homage to Lloyd's 'classic taste' in adventure narrative, counterpoints the wryly self-deprecating poem 'To the Hesitating Purchaser', which proffers 'all the old romance, retold / Exactly in the ancient way', and hopes that this will 'please, as me [it] pleased of old, / The wiser youngsters of to-day'.[14] Echoing the language of Stevenson's romance polemics, the poem pits the rude appeal of the adventure tale against effete modern tastes:

> If studious youth no longer crave,
> His ancient appetites forgot,
> Kingston, or Ballantyne the brave,
> Or Cooper of the wood and wave:
> So be it, also! And may I
> And all my pirates share the grave
> Where these and their creations lie! (xxx)

The roll-call of authors – W. H. G. Kingston, R. M. Ballantyne, and James Fenimore Cooper – places *Treasure Island* in the tradition of boys' adventure stories, narratives of exploration and conquest, and frontier romances. Stevenson's desire to awaken 'ancient appetites', and the rueful worry that they may have withered, also informs his letter to W. E. Henley announcing the novel as 'The Sea Cook / or Treasure Island: / A Story for

Boys'.[15] Noting dryly that '[i]f this don't fetch the kids, why, they have gone rotten since my day', he signs himself off as 'R.L.S. / Author of Boys' Stories'.[16]

Stevenson's yarn is apparently faithful to his own romance polemics, which taught that the adventure novel was rooted in the senses, relying on physical effects and abjuring 'moral or intellectual interest': '[d]anger is the matter with which this class of novel deals; fear, the passion with which it idly trifles; and the characters are portrayed only so far as they realise the sense of danger and provoke the sympathy of fear'.[17] The narrative momentum, indeed, turns upon fear, and the characters' story-telling also demonstrates the pleasures of terror. Jim recalls the pirate Billy Bones's tales ('[d]readful stories they were; about hanging, and walking the plank, and storms at sea'), which frightened his listeners 'at the time, but on looking back they rather like it; it was a fine excitement in a quiet country life' (4). As befits an adventure hero, Jim seems to understand the psychology of romance better than his inn-keeper father, who fears that Bones will drive away his customers (4).

The novel also conforms to Stevenson's maxim that romance should bring alive 'youthful day-dreams'.[18] In 'A Humble Remonstrance', Stevenson attributes *Treasure Island*'s charm to the universal appeal of a 'quest for buried treasure': in dreams, every child has 'hunted gold, and been a pirate . . . and suffered shipwreck and prison, and imbrued its little hands in gore, and . . . triumphantly protected innocence and beauty'.[19] The romance æsthetic emphasizes the articulation not of a known world but of hidden dreams: 'the artist writes with more gusto and effect of those things which he has only wished to do, than of those which he has done. Desire is a wonderful telescope'.[20] *Treasure Island* describes a quest inspired by maps and dreams of unknown territories. The narrator, Jim Hawkins, recalls his emotions after his first sight of the map of Treasure Island: he was 'full of sea-dreams and the most charming anticipations of strange islands and adventures . . . Sitting by the fire in the housekeeper's room, I approached that island in my fancy . . . Sometimes the isle was thick with savages, with whom we fought; sometimes full of dangerous animals that hunted us' (36). Jim's fantasy of exploration is in the *Boy's Own* mould, the hero confronted by 'savages' and 'dangerous animals'. It closely resembles Stevenson's account of the novel's inspiration: he sketched a map for his stepson, and then, 'as I paused upon my map of "Treasure Island," the future character [*sic*] of the book began to appear there visibly among imaginary woods; and their brown faces and bright weapons peeped out upon me from unexpected quarters, as they passed to and fro, fighting and hunting treasure, on these few square inches of a flat projection'.[21] (Stevenson's sketch was later lost; a map drawn by draftsmen from his father's office was used to illustrate the Cassell edition [see Figure 2.1].)

Maps, for Stevenson, acted on the imagination, stimulating ancient predatory instincts. Jim Hawkins, cosily ensconced by the fire and 'full of sea-dreams and the most charming anticipations of strange islands and adventures', is a figure for the reader. It was, after all, the reader's day-dreams that Stevenson believed the romance should embody: 'the great creative writer shows us the realisation and apotheosis of the day-dreams of common men'.[22] As 'youthful day-dreams' of hunting and fighting were universal, Stevenson claimed, adventure novels enabled all readers to recapture the primitive, heroic spirit of their childhood dreams. Even his sombre father, listening to the story, 'caught fire at once with all the romance and childishness of his original nature'.[23] Stevenson stressed romance's ability to reawaken his father's juvenile – and therefore primitive – desires: 'I had counted on one boy, I found I had two in my audience'.[24] Like *King Solomon's Mines* (1885), which was dedicated by Haggard to 'all the big and little boys who read it', Stevenson's narrative was designed to gratify all those readers who retained traces of their 'original nature'.[25]

With its emphasis on reawakening bellicose 'youthful day-dreams', *Treasure Island* seems to celebrate the purifying value of masculine adventure, fitting relatively easily with Lang's championing of romance as, in Arata's words, 'an antidote to an effeminate modernity'.[26] The supposedly universal dream of a 'quest for buried treasure' embodied in Stevenson's novel is clearly a violent and aggressively masculine fantasy, and his belief that every child has, in dreams, 'imbrued its little hands in gore, and . . . triumphantly protected innocence and beauty' is unmistakably gendered. *Treasure Island,* however, is often equivocal about romance, and about the imperial heroism with which the genre was implicated. Its eighteenth-century setting, amid 'wild deeds and places on the Spanish Main', raises questions about patriotic Englishness, imperial aggression, and adolescence and the attainment of manhood (4). The 'youthful day-dreams' which underlie the narrative are revealed to be not only attractively potent but also dangerous. Stevenson's suggestion that maps of unknown territories arouse primitive, brutal desires, especially in children, anticipates Conrad's more famous portrayal, in *Heart of Darkness* (1899, 1902), of the young Marlow, enthralled by the 'blank spaces' on the map.[27] Moreover, Jim's boyish imagination is fundamentally mistaken. It is not 'savages' or wild animals that haunt Treasure Island, but the more equivocal figure of the buccaneer – and Englishman – Long John Silver. The 'charming anticipations of strange islands and adventures' modulate into the more

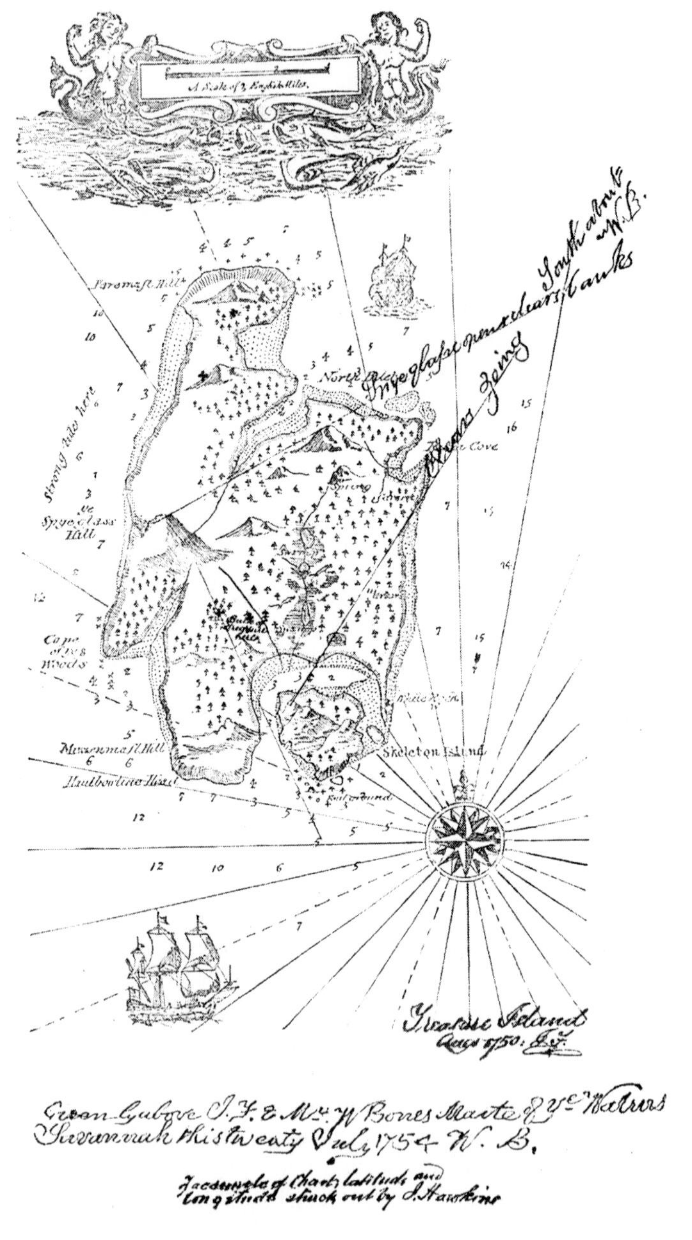

Figure 2.1 Map of Treasure Island, from Robert Louis Stevenson, *Treasure Island* (London: Cassell, 1883), ii. Reproduced courtesy of The Bodleian Library, University of Oxford. Arch.AA e. 149.

worldly-wise voice of Jim as narrator. When he confesses that 'in all my fancies nothing occurred to me so strange and tragic as our actual adventures', the repetition of 'strange', a marker no longer of the exotic but of alienation, evokes his disillusionment (36).

This hesitancy about romance is at the heart of *Treasure Island*, and may explain the novel's relative unpopularity in *Young Folks* where, unlike Stevenson's next children's novel, *The Black Arrow* (1883), it evoked little enthusiasm from its young readers.[28] Despite protestations to the contrary, the novel has many realist touches, including an interest in its characters' psychology. Retrospectively narrated by Jim, the action is focalized through the eyes of his younger self, who has to learn independence of action and maturity of judgment. The tale is a *Bildungsroman* as much as a romance. Treasure Island – as with so many of Stevenson's islands (in *Kidnapped*, 'The Beach of Falesá', and *The Ebb-Tide*) – becomes a psychic space in which the hero must complete his *rite de passage* to adulthood. Moreover, despite Stevenson's belief that a 'quest for buried treasure' impels the narrative, many critics have noticed the lack of sustained emotional investment in the treasure hunt.[29]

The treasure may initially provide the focus of desire, but it is soon displaced – to be replaced, I shall argue, by the idea of romance or adventure. Squire Trelawney and Doctor Livesey, who significantly constitute the lawful party, ranged against the illicit power of the pirates, are carried away by the romance of the enterprise. In 'A Gossip on Romance', Stevenson aligned romance and make-believe, judging that 'the triumph of romantic story-telling' is accomplished 'when the reader consciously plays at being the hero'.[30] Trelawney's romance credo is thus rooted in fantasy. He kits himself out as a naval officer, and insists that he be addressed as admiral (40, 34). As he exclaims, 'Hang the Treasure! It's the glory of the sea that has turned my head' (38). The theme of romance as make-believe runs strongly through the narrative, uniting the consummate actor Silver with Livesey, who brings the unruly pirates to heel by assuming a familiar bedside manner (164). *Treasure Island*, Joseph Bristow observes, is 'self-conscious' romance fiction, with a reflexive interest in story-telling.[31] Indeed, the thespian Silver represents the compelling but ultimately amoral glamour exerted by adventure: in Stevenson's words, he is 'that smooth and formidable adventurer'.[32] Jim's quest is to learn to resist Silver's seductive offer of partnership in heroic romance.

Stevenson's essay 'The English Admirals' (1878) associates national identity, heroism, and the romance genre in a glorious triumvirate. It shares *Treasure Island*'s interest in awakening primitive appetites by means of romance, invoking the renascent 'sense of hereditary nautical experience' in a 'man from Bedfordshire, who does not know one end of the ship from the other'.[33] The exploits of England's heroic admirals, Stevenson teaches, 'stir English blood like the sound of a trumpet; and if the Indian Empire, the trade of London, and all the outward and visible ensigns of our greatness should pass away, we should still leave behind a durable monument of what we were in these sayings and doings of the English Admirals'.[34] A defensive anxiety about Britain's waning imperial and military might informs the rousing, martial diction, and the romance genre becomes the catalyst for national regeneration, in terms which recall Lang's championing of a revitalizing masculine adventure: '[i]t is not over the virtues of a curate-and-tea-party novel, that people are abashed into high resolutions . . . to stir them properly they must have men entering into glory with some pomp and circumstance. And that is why these stories of our sea-captains . . . [are] full of bracing moral influence'.[35]

The essay has intriguing resonances with *Treasure Island*, whose 'Admiral Benbow' inn is named after the famous British naval commander celebrated in the essay. But where the essay is uncomplicatedly affirmative, the novel is more problematic (as is so often the case with Stevenson) and insinuates a measure of doubt about patriotic endeavours. Invocations of Englishness are playfully undermined almost as soon as they are voiced. Captain Smollett, rightly fearing a mutiny, is branded 'unmanly' and 'un-English' for his caution by the Squire, yet it is not long before his fears are vindicated, and the Squire then exclaims of the seditious crew, 'to think that they're all Englishmen' (50, 67). The novel also collapses the distinction between heroic admirals and dastardly pirates. The villainous Long John Silver, who lost a leg as a companion of the notorious adventurer Flint, claims to have 'lost it in his country's service, under the immortal Hawke' (38). Edward Hawke, the eighteenth-century naval commander, appears in 'The English Admirals' as an exemplar of national greatness, and yet *Treasure Island* questions the distinction between naval heroism and piratical feats.[36] Not only does Silver falsely claim Hawke's mantle but also Flint himself receives a ringing acclamation from the patriotic Squire. 'He was the bloodthirstiest buccaneer that sailed', the Squire enthuses, 'Blackbeard was a child to Flint. The Spaniards were so prodigiously afraid of him, that, I tell you, sir, I was sometimes proud he was an Englishman' (31–2). Bones's piratical tales likewise stir jingoistic fervour: the customers at the inn feel that 'there was the sort of man that made England terrible at sea' (4). The narrative structure too, in which the pirates and cabin-party mirror each other's actions, questions apparent moral distinctions. 'What were these villains after but money?' asks Trelawney, only to vow that 'I'll have that treasure if I search a year' (32).

Silver's own ambiguity, the duplicitous cruelty which coexists with so much charm, is of course at the root of the novel's uncertainty about romance. Prefiguring Stevenson's later villains, James Durie in *The Master of Ballantrae* and Case in 'The Beach of Falesá', Silver has many conversational registers at his command, and is able to adapt his tone and vocabulary variously to his fellow pirates and to the genteel Squire and Doctor. It is Silver's mastery of the middle-class language of duty (albeit pronounced 'dooty') which leads the Squire to pronounce him 'a perfect trump' (45–6). His subversion of middle-class codes also emerges from the mischievous echoes he sets up between 'gentleman' and 'gentleman of fortune' (the euphemistic term, Jim realizes, for 'a common pirate') (58–9). Despite all his double-crossing, Silver has a real attraction, grounded in the verve with which he conducts his play-acting. Trelawney's make-believe is a matter of externals (the sea-officer's dress, and the 'capital imitation of a sailor's walk'), but Silver has an inner conviction (41). Recalling Silver 'giving such a show of excitement as would have convinced an Old Bailey judge or a Bow Street runner', Jim ruefully comments that 'he was too deep, and too ready, and too clever for me' (44–5). In the whimsical fable 'The Persons of the Tale' (1895), Silver declares that he rather than Smollett is Stevenson's favourite character – and he may well be right.[37] This sketch, in which Silver and Smollett take a break, after the thirty-second chapter of *Treasure Island*, for a stroll and a smoke, forms a theatrical meditation on the artificial nature of art.[38] Whereas Smollett believes in 'a future state' for fictional characters, Silver's scepticism resonates with Stevenson's own belief in the distinction between art and life (he tells Smollett, 'we're off dooty now; and I can't see no call to keep up the morality business . . . I'm on'y a chara'ter in a sea story').[39] A complex and alluring villain, Silver is a far cry from the pirates in R. M. Ballantyne's *The Coral Island* (1858). Ballantyne, a favourite author of the young Stevenson, renders a much more clear-cut moral world, one where a dying pirate repents of his wild ways as a member of a 'crew of desperadoes', and longs for the consolations of the Christian faith.[40]

Nor is Jim Hawkins, for all his 'sea-dreams', an untroubled empire hero in the making. Robert Crawford emphasizes *Treasure Island*'s affinities with the works of Ballantyne and Henry Mayne Reid, judging that the novel represents masculinity as a cheerful game.[41] Indeed, Jim's part is characterized by a sportive curiosity and lively zest. In his struggle with Israel Hands, he takes possession of the ship, insists on being addressed as captain, strikes the Jolly Roger, and exclaims, 'God save the king!' (133). His assumption of the captaincy recalls Stevenson's essay on childhood make-believe, 'Child's Play' (1878). Jim is, undoubtedly, playing at manhood: '[i]t was such a game as I had often played at home about the rocks of Black Hill Cove; but never before, you may be sure, with such a wildly beating heart as now. Still, as I say, it was a boy's game' (141). However, he has not yet achieved a state of self-sufficient adulthood – gulled by flattery, he does not anticipate Hands's treachery, and is wounded – and his experience instead forms a more disturbing process of adolescence.

Despite Robert Kiely's belief that the novel is structured by a 'principle of "clean" adventure virtually unblemished by good or evil', Jim himself is a far from spotless character.[42] His complicity with the pirates is foreshadowed at the very beginning of the novel by his reaction to Billy Bones's fear of fellow seamen: despite his youthful innocence, Jim is 'a sharer in his alarms' (3). His affinity with Silver is still more pronounced. Bristow observes that Silver 'has the daring but not the moral fibre of the altogether untainted young Jim'.[43] Yet Jim quickly believes himself a favourite of Silver, and his actions significantly mirror Silver's. Twice he deserts the cabin-party. Although he acts to help their cause, in retrospect he recognizes that his behaviour is morally dubious, amounting to 'desertion' or 'truantry' – words which intriguingly align his actions with those of the mutineering pirates – and muses that 'I would have carried it out, I believe, in the teeth of Captain Smollett himself' (135, 119). Like Silver, Jim has an untameable quality. He acts as a free agent, often reluctant to knuckle down to authority. It is perhaps for this reason that Smollett tells him, 'I don't think you and me'll go to sea again. You're too much of the born favourite for me' (185).

Moreover, if Jim's passage to independent adulthood is marked by an unsettling kinship with the pirates, it also proves more unnerving than he had anticipated. Initially, his 'ancient appetites' are undoubtedly aroused, and he is eager for adventure, imagining going 'to sea in a schooner, with a piping boatswain, and pig-tailed singing seamen; to sea, bound for an unknown island, and to seek for buried treasures!' (40). The 'delightful dream', however, is gradually displaced, as the bloody narrative unfolds, by Jim's dawning sense of his story as a 'strange and tragic' tale. His experience of the slippery Silver undermines his belief in a clear-cut morality, teaching him the cruelty and treachery of heroic masculinities, and the ambiguities of patriotic Englishness.

Jim's dreams are ultimately exposed as illusory, and the nightmares to which his adventures give rise prove more enduring. Even before he meets Silver, his sleep is 'haunted' by the one-legged sailor about whom he has been warned, and he recalls that 'I would see him in a thousand forms, and with a thousand diabolical expressions' (3). Ironically, the narrative reverses the opposition between cosy life and adventurous dreams as

Jim, tossed at sea in his frail coracle, falls asleep 'in the midst of my terrors . . . and dreamed of home and the old "Admiral Benbow." ' (125). The novel, moreover, closes with Jim's description of his recurrent nightmares: '[o]xen and wain-ropes would not bring me back again to that accursed island; and the worst dreams that ever I have are when I hear the surf booming about its coasts, or start upright in bed, with the sharp voice of Captain Flint [Silver's parrot] still ringing in my ears: "Pieces of eight! pieces of eight!" ' (191). Horror at the prospect of returning to Treasure Island has replaced the initial 'youthful dreams'. For Jim, 'romance' has ultimately proved disturbingly uncontrollable, just as 'The Manse' hints that, once unleashed, ancestral forces, for all their revivifying promise, may be unpredictable and alarming. As the parrot's echoing voice intimates, Jim is never quite able to shake off Silver's unsettling memory, and his response to him remains to the last ambivalent. He is eventually 'revolted' by his duplicity, yet still feels beholden to him (181, 188).

Jim's journey has been a rite of passage from childhood to a disillusioned maturity. Edwin Eigner describes the life that faces Jim on his return as one of 'quiet and inglorious retirement'.[44] Indeed, while he tells us what happens to Smollett, Gray, and Gunn, Jim lets slip no word of his own fate. At the heart of late-Victorian romance was a belief in the British boy's natural leadership qualities: for Bristow, *The Coral Island* and *Treasure Island* are populated by boys who can effortlessly 'lead and command'.[45] Jim's retirement thus raises implicit questions about the imperial mission with which the genre was so closely implicated. Yet while he renounces a life of adventure, its verve and appeal remain. Jim describes his memento, the Black Spot: 'I have that curiosity beside me at this moment; but not a trace of writing now remains beyond a single scratch, such as a man might make with his thumb-nail' (162). The fading of the writing evokes Jim's diminished life: there is an enduring sense of sadness and loss in the relinquishing of adventure's delights. The relish and gusto with which the narrative opens ('I remember him as if it were yesterday') convey the vivid endurance of his memories of adventure (1). Jim's trajectory, ironically, reverses the voyage that Stevenson envisaged for his adult readers. On reading *Treasure Island,* Stevenson hoped, readers of all ages would emulate Jim as he appeared at the tale's opening, rediscovering 'ancient appetites', and experiencing the thrills and fears of a 'quest for buried treasure'.[46] As these contrary journeys suggest, *Treasure Island* is an equivocal work, celebrating and enacting the resurgence of primitive romance, but at the same time exploring its darker side – its implication with bellicose imperialism and a ruthless creed of heroic manliness.

If *Treasure Island*'s historical setting obliquely discloses late-Victorian concerns about imperial aggression and the formation of national masculinities, Stevenson's final, Pacific fiction brings these anxieties more explicitly to the fore. The South Seas were strongly associated with adventure in the British imagination. As the setting for boys' stories such as Ballantyne's *The Coral Island,* for tales of heroic explorers including Captain Cook, and for narratives of missionary and colonial endeavour, the region exerted a popular fascination. Ballantyne, indeed, was an idol of the young Stevenson and 'the first author whom it was [his] destiny to meet': he describes meeting this 'ideal' and 'superior being' and being 'tongue-tied' and 'sick of thwarted adoration'.[47] Ballantyne played a significant part in Stevenson's early literary development, and the encounter 'greatly strengthened an inborn partiality for authors'.[48] Fuelled by tales of romance and adventure, Stevenson's dreams of living in the South Seas were typically Victorian. In 1875, after hearing about the South Sea islands from a New Zealand civil servant, he pronounced himself 'sick with desire to go there'.[49] In 1888, seven years after he wrote *Treasure Island,* Stevenson embarked on a series of cruises around the Pacific islands, and in 1890 his poor health led him to settle in Samoa. Soon afterwards, he wrote of his 'delight' in the landscape around him:

> I could not but be reminded of old Mayne Reid; as I have been more than once since I came to the tropics; and I thought, if Reid had been still living, I would have written to tell him that, for me, *it had come true*; and I thought, forby, that, if the Great Powers go on as they are going, and the Chief Justice delays, it would come truer still; and the war conch will sound in the hills, and my home will be inclosed in camps, before the year is ended.[50]

In this letter, Stevenson conveys his exhilaration at the prospect of war – war mediated *via* Captain Mayne Reid's boys' adventure tales.

Stevenson's experiences in the South Seas, however, rapidly led to an intensification of his doubts about adventure. While his earlier romances, including *Treasure Island,* figure imagined violence, in his Pacific work romance confronts actual violence. Faced with the realities of imperialism, Stevenson found himself disabused of his illusions about exotic adventure. His disenchantment was part of a wider *fin-de-siècle* 'disillusionment in adventure fiction', a response, in Bristow's judgment, to the 'decline of empire'.[51] Stevenson deplored the damaging effects of European and American imperial rivalries, and the incursions of foreign traders and missionaries into traditional island life.[52] His radical displacement in the

South Seas also led him to overturn conventional readings of savagery and civilization. In his account of Samoan current affairs, *A Footnote to History* (1892), he makes it clear that the true savages are not the native Polynesians but the white colonists, who 'fell to on the street like rival clansmen. And the little town . . . had fallen back in civilisation about a thousand years'.[53] Stevenson's fiction mirrors this transition from dreams of adventure to disenchantment. The meaning which he attributes to the romance genre shifts: adventure becomes increasingly dystopic, and a much more politicized reality begins to emerge. His fiction now offers an overtly subversive racial politics, and is newly concerned with the present. In 'The Beach of Falesá', he claimed, 'almost all that is ugly is in the whites', while *The Wrecker* (1891–92) 'is certainly well nourished with facts; no realist can touch me there; for by this time I do begin to know something of life in the XIXth century'.[54]

The Ebb-Tide (1893–94), written in collaboration with Lloyd Osbourne, marks Stevenson's sense of the horrifying irony that romance bears with the real conditions of imperialism.[55] Those who expected a cheerful escapism did not welcome Stevenson's engagement with contemporary times in *The Ebb-Tide*: his friend Sidney Colvin upbraided him for the novel's 'general revoltingness, in which you are but one with your age'.[56] The novel evinces a politicized disenchantment with adventure, as Stevenson interrogates with a jaded eye romance's affiliations with an imperialist and homosocial code of heroic masculinities. Moreover, in *The Ebb-Tide* romance is challenged by new narrative modes. Earlier novels including *Treasure Island* and *The Black Arrow* may have exhibited scepticism about romance, but they usually ended on a note of regret for the past, for the lost dreams of adventure.[57] By contrast, in *The Ebb-Tide* Stevenson moves beyond the adventure genre, deftly weaving together naturalistic realism with political allegory and a proto-modernist symbolism.

In *The Ebb-Tide*, the once-mistrusted realism confronts romance – and it is a realism which has affinities with its *fin-de-siècle* progeny, naturalism. In Stevenson's letters, he constantly deprecates the novel's grimness and griminess, in terms which recall his condemnation of Zola many years earlier ('[r]omance with the smallpox', he diagnosed: 'diseased anyway and blackhearted and fundamentally at enmity with joy').[58] Zola becomes a surprising touchstone for Stevenson's new novel. Writing to Henry James in June 1893, he declared of *The Ebb-Tide* that

> [m]y dear man the grimness of that story is not to be depicted in words. There are only four characters to be sure, but they are such a

> troop of swine! . . . If the admirers of Zola admire him for his pertinent ugliness and pessimism, I think they should admire this; but if, as I have long suspected, they neither admire nor understand the man's art, and only wallow in his rancidness like a hound in offal, then they will certainly be disappointed in *The Ebb-Tide*. Alas! Poor little tale, it is not *even* rancid.[59]

Stevenson persists with the imagery of rottenness and decay, but here he applies it to Zola's followers; Zola himself is revalued, and respected for his 'pertinent ugliness and pessimism'.

This new respect for a disheartening art, an art which is faithful to the unattractive aspects of human life, forms part of the wider *fin-de-siècle* debate about pessimism in modern culture.[60] Stevenson's appreciation of Zola distances him from the romancers' insistence that literature be a bracing restorative to healthy, manly virtue. It is a far cry from the resolute cheerfulness he enjoined in 1885:

> [i]n my view, one dank, dispirited word is harmful . . . a piece of acquired evil; every gay, every bright word or picture . . . is a piece of pleasure set afloat; the reader catches it and, if he be healthy, goes on his way rejoicing; and it is the business of art so to send him, as often as possible.[61]

For the champions of the romance revival, realism was pathological. Lang imagined a typical Jamesian novel as set in a 'gloomy, new, bleak, white hotel', populated by 'consumptive inmates', and filled with 'the pulmonary talk at the *table d'hôte*'.[62] Adventure promised to restore this effete world to healthy virility. Lang proclaimed that, thanks to Haggard and Stevenson,

> King Romance hath won his own,
> And the lands where he was born!
>
> Now he sways with wand of gold
> Realms that honoured him of yore.[63]

The Ebb-Tide radically undermines this belief in the curative value of adventure. The narrative's dominant image is of decay and sickness. It opens memorably, representing the contaminating influence of Europeans in the Pacific: they 'carry activity and disseminate disease'.[64] The image undermines the *fin-de-siècle* trope of native degeneracy, drawing on the countervailing nineteenth-century notion, popularized by Herman Melville, that Europeans were corrupting a prelapsarian Pacific. It also resonates with Stevenson's reason for settling in the Pacific – his ill health. The opening of *In the South Seas* (1896) strikingly conveys the morbidity of his exile:

> [f]or nearly ten years my health had been declining; and for some while before I set forth upon my voyage, I believed I was come to the afterpiece of life, and had only the nurse and undertaker to expect. It was suggested that I should try the South Seas; and I was not unwilling to visit like a ghost, and be carried like a bale, among scenes that had attracted me in youth and health.[65]

Stevenson's illness and anticipated death underlie not only the preoccupation with dying cultures in *In the South Seas* but also *The Ebb-Tide*'s concern with disease and corruption. Indeed, although he soon found his health somewhat restored, the novel's composition was punctuated by others' illness. As he finished writing it, he told Colvin that

> [a]ll the house are down with the iffluenza [*sic*] in a body, except Fanny and me: The iffluenza appears to become endemic here, but it has always been a scourge in the islands. Witness the beginning of *The Ebb-Tide*, which was observed long before the Iffle had distinguished himself at home by such Napoleonic conquests.[66]

The novella's first part – 'The Trio' – challenges the idea that romance can be a tonic. The three protagonists are beachcombers, existing on the fringes of white society. Their aliases indicate not so much fresh beginnings as 'moral bankruptcy' (126). The most likeable, Herrick, through whom the narrative is focalized, has fled to the Pacific to escape his own weakness, but has little expectation that adventure will reinvigorate him or invest him with a sense of manly purpose. The narrator observes that Herrick 'had struck his flag; he entertained no hope to reinstate himself or help his straitened family; and he came to the islands (where he knew the climate to be soft, bread cheap, and manners easy) a skulker from life's battle and his own immediate duty' (126). A recurrent symbol in the novel, the flag signifies Herrick's ignominious surrender to a life of degenerate drifting. Davis, the Captain, is also driven to the Pacific by shame, after his 'drunken orders' have lost six lives (139). Meanwhile, the Cockney clerk Huish's 'dwarfish person . . . pale eyes and toothless smile', and the influenza which racks his body, symbolize his moral degeneracy (127). The characters' regression is not an exhilarating return to primitive vitality, but a degrading experience. They eke out a living by begging: Davis performs to the native islanders for his breakfast like a dancing bear (135). This is an inversion of what was seen as the natural racial hierarchy in Victorian adventure fiction – in *The Coral Island*, whose narrative *The Ebb-Tide* ironically recasts, Peterkin confidently predicts that 'we'll rise, naturally, to the top of affairs. White men always do in savage countries'.[67] By contrast, *The Ebb-Tide* opens by describing the atavistic existence of Europeans in Polynesia, 'dressed like natives, but still retaining . . . some relic (such as a single eye-glass) of the officer and gentleman' (123) (see Figure 2.2).

The narrative repeatedly raises the prospect of bracing, therapeutic adventure, only for it to be undermined. When the three 'co-adventurers' set sail in the *Farallone*, the ravaged Huish is fraudulently 'shipped A.B. [able-bodied] at eighteen dollars' (153). Disease and moral decay pervade the *Farallone*, which flies the yellow plague-flag. The previous captain and

DRESSED LIKE NATIVES, BUT WEARING PERHAPS AN EYE-GLASS.

Figure 2.2 Illustration from serial version of Robert Louis Stevenson and Lloyd Osbourne, *The Ebb-Tide, To-Day* 1 (11 November 1893), 4. Reproduced courtesy of The Bodleian Library, University of Oxford. Per.3974e.34.

mate have died of smallpox, and their infected bedclothes remain in the cabin (153). This scepticism about the escapist or restorative function of foreign adventure, and by extension romance fiction, intensifies as the narrative develops. As the boat approaches the island at the end of 'The Trio',

> the excitement of the three adventurers glowed about their bones like a fever. They whispered, and nodded, and pointed, and put mouth to ear, with a singular instinct of secrecy, approaching the island underhand like eavesdroppers and thieves. (188)

The feverish nature of their excitement casts adventure's pleasures as morbid, while their guilty approach suggests the compromised consciences of European intruders in the Pacific world.

Patrick Brantlinger observes that, like Conrad's fictions, *The Ebb-Tide, The Wrecker,* and 'The Beach of Falesá' are 'botched romances in which adventure turns sour or squalid, undermined by moral frailty'.[68] Indeed, an unheroic weakness characterizes the three men's 'adventures'. Herrick constantly deplores his own unmanly irresolution. His highly-strung nerves feminize him – he is subject to shameful fits of hysteria, and expresses a recurrent wish to die, but lacks the tenacity to carry it through (138, 148, 160). His characterization is informed by the psychological realism whose 'introspective analysis' Lang so deplored, and the novel's naturalist concern with moral frailty and squalor, with Zola's 'pertinent ugliness and pessimism', distances it from the buoyant adventure ethos (Ralph Rover's exuberant preface to *The Coral Island* advises anyone 'who loves to be melancholy and morose' to shut the book).[69] Herrick's 'co-adventurers' dramatize the corrosion of heroism and adventure in a still more sordid manner. They drink the ship's cargo of champagne and abandon any pretence to pilot the ship, the captain passing his days 'in slavish self-indulgence or in hoggish slumber' (165). Their plan to hijack the ship's cargo and sell it in 'the wild islands of Peru' associates them with islands inhabited by pirates and escaped convicts, where natives are kidnapped and sold into slavery; Davis also compares the trio to the notorious buccaneers and slave traders, Pease and Hayes (151, 148).

The analogy with slave traders indicates the novella's anti-imperialist racial politics, and measures its distance from the confident imperialism of the Victorian romance. The native Polynesian crew members are dutiful, loyal, and righteous, reading their Bibles and singing missionary hymns, and Herrick soon learns their 'simple and hard story of exile, suffering, and injustice among cruel whites' (167). The Captain's renaming of the native crew exemplifies the whites' cruelty: declaring Taveeta's name 'gibberish', he christens him Uncle Ned (156). The ship is a microcosm of colonial society, and Herrick is ashamed to see the Polynesians, whom he assumes were once cannibals, 'so faithful to what they knew of good': it is 'a cutting reproof to compare the islanders and the whites aboard the *Farallone*' (168).

The whites' lawlessness is not liberating but marked by a lack of will and vigour. The narrative construction underlines this, mirroring the characters' dissolute vagrancy. It challenges the conventions of romance: here there is none of the 'incident' so beloved by the Stevenson of 'A Gossip on Romance'. Instead, the novel's first part is characterized by an attenuated narrative momentum, as suggested by the 'ebb-tide' of the title. The narrative – like much *fin-de-siècle* naturalist fiction – inscribes the characters' gradual degeneracy (indeed, as Part II will show, Stevenson shared late-Victorian anxieties about degeneration, pessimistically reassessing an earlier belief in evolutionary progress). The frequent invocations of fate and doom, as in the references to Beethoven's Fifth Symphony, cast the trio's degeneration as inevitable (144). The repetitive narrative patterning, as well as the imagery of contamination, conveys the sapping of vigour: Davis's alcoholism reiterates past behaviour, while one botched fraudulent endeavour succeeds another. The comrades discover that even the *Farallone*'s cargo is a sham: beneath the top layers, the champagne bottles contain water. In a caustic allusion to Daniel Defoe's tale of staunch British manhood and endurance against the odds, the narrator describes how 'each stared at the bottle in its glory of gold paper as Crusoe may have stared at the footprint' (176). Davis resolves to profit from the fraud, by losing the schooner and claiming insurance; but, as the novella's first part ends, this scheme in turn falls through as the ship's provisions run out.

Romance itself, it appears, is degenerate: the ironic invocations of romance literature suggest that adventure's energies are depleted. Its bankruptcy is established by Herrick's failure to exchange his Virgil for a meal (the 'dead tongues' were not in demand in the South Seas) (124). The *Arabian Nights*, as so often in Stevenson's fiction the touchstone of romance, likewise symbolize its decadence. Herrick spins a yarn in which he summons up an Arab magician, but even he – with his debilitating cough – shares in the universal frailty and contamination. His magic carpet transports Herrick not to exotic climes, but to his parents' house in London, indicating his inability to escape the past (130). Sea yarns too are sterile and unproductive: addressing the native crew, Herrick 'racked his brain, and overhauled his reminiscences of sea romance for some appropriate words', but to no avail (155). For Vanessa Smith, the novel's presentation of reading and writing indicates the 'exhaustion of narrative possibility'.[70] Indeed, even the father of South Seas romance is associated with the dominant imagery of decay and imprisonment – the three beachcombers shelter in the prison which had once incarcerated Melville and his fellow mutineers, its doors now 'rotting before them in the grass' (143). In *The Wrecker*, Stevenson invoked Melville to significantly different effect: in this narrative, the hero Dodd reads *Omoo* and is enchanted by the Pacific islands.[71] Indeed, Stevenson's earlier novel portrayed romance and adventure narratives much more positively, with its playful epilogue showing that Dodd successfully published his own tale.[72] In *The Ebb-Tide*, by contrast, story fails the protagonists. When Herrick is asked for a story, he speaks 'not like a man who has anything to say, but like one talking against time' (129). Nor is Davis or Herrick any more adept at producing written narratives. Attempting to compose letters home, they scribble out words, bite their pencils, and stare out to sea; only the abominable Huish writes with facility, and when the others see his letter, a far-fetched tale of South Seas romance, their outrage compels him to destroy it (139–42).

Just as the trio's luck – and the narrative possibilities – appear spent, however, the adventurers come upon a mysterious and unexpected island (182). The narrative finds a new lease of life, and is injected with much more explicitly political energies. In the novel's second part, 'The Quartette', Stevenson acerbically rewrites the narratives of *Robinson Crusoe* (1719–20) and *The Coral Island*, whose islands are stages for the enactment of a providential colonialism. Attwater, the island's enigmatic missionary, trader, and authoritarian ruler, represents the sinister and intertwined forces of Empire, the Church, Commerce, and the Law. The story of Attwater's severe mission forms a parable of evangelical colonialism. The 'red ensign of England' flying from the pierhead denotes his assumption of an imperial authority, which he enforces in a brutal and patriarchal fashion – forcibly marrying off an attractive native woman to avoid temptation and executing insubordinate natives (190). The narrative's most arresting image is the ship's figurehead, the 'ensign and presiding genius of that empty town', distinguished by its colour, a 'leprous whiteness' (190). Alastair Fowler reads the statue as an emblem of European capitalism, while for Roger Ebbatson it represents the 'lives destroyed by European imperial conquest'.[73]

The figurehead seems most potent, nonetheless, as a symbol of the degeneracy of adventure, an adventure which is tainted by its association with colonialism. Herrick feels that she 'confronted him in what seemed irony' and wonders whether this 'was . . . the end of so many adventures' (200). Looking up at her 'with singular feelings of curiosity and romance . . . he could have found it in his heart to regret that she was not a goddess, nor yet he a pagan, that he might have bowed down before her' (200). The adventure ethos, indeed, sustains Attwater's malign imperialism: he recalls that he was brought to the South Seas by '[y]outh, curiosity, romance, the love of the sea, and . . . an interest in missions' (203). Trade also underwrites the imperial missionary endeavour, and the parallel between Attwater's and the trio's money-making schemes suggests that religion merely offers a veneer of decorum to the fraudulent appropriation of property. A messianic fervour and providentialism underlies his ruthless and bloody subordination of the natives: 'I was making a new people here; and behold, the angel of the Lord smote them and they were not!' (204). As the Old Testament vocabulary indicates, Attwater's is an unforgiving religion. In his words, Christianity is 'a savage thing, like the universe it illuminates; savage, cold, and bare, but infinitely strong' (204). He is undoubtedly implicated, as Fowler claims, in Stevenson's 'quarrel with God', and is a troublingly ambiguous character.[74] His transition from tender saviour (he 'spread out his arms like a crucifix; his face shone with the brightness of a seraph's') to 'easy, sneering gentleman' compellingly figures his duality (206–7). In many ways he prefigures Kurtz in Conrad's *Heart of Darkness*. Marlow's hesitation over whether Kurtz is an 'angel or a fiend' echoes kindred doubts about Attwater: Davis not only imagines him as Herrick's 'god', but also associates him with hell, mistaking his armoured native servants for demons (223, 244).[75] Confronted by Davis and Huish's plan to kill Attwater, Herrick vacillates between pity for his murderous companions' 'helpless victim' and his growing horror of Attwater as an 'angel of the Lord's wrath'; he eventually deserts his fellow sailors and offers himself piteously to the missionary (211).

Attwater's power over the trio is girded by discourses of class and masculinity. Class prejudices and ideals of manliness underwrite his oppressive evangelical imperialism, and cast him as a sinister father figure for the three men. In much *fin-de-siècle* adventure fiction, the journey from metropolis to colonial margins afforded an escape from social problems, but *The Ebb-Tide* offers no such optimism that domestic malaises may be transcended. Social prejudice and stratification continue to taint life in the colonies. The 'copper-bottomed aristocrat' Attwater spurns the friendly advances of the 'vulgar wolves', Davis and Huish, distinguishing the Oxford-educated Herrick alone as worthy of attention (197, 205). Herrick feels a reluctant affinity with the missionary, one based in a shared classical education, accent, and code of manners, which frequently overrides his moral revulsion. Against his will he is pleased 'that he should be accepted as an equal, and the others thus pointedly ignored'; and his completion of Attwater's quotation from the *Aeneid* testifies to the power of a shared cultural heritage (193, 202). An opposition between written and oral languages articulates these class tensions. Attwater takes as his disciple Herrick, who shares his taste for 'dead tongues', and he despises Huish for his affiliations with a lower-class oral culture, its music-hall songs, slang, and colloquialisms.

The Ebb-Tide also exposes the creed of manliness which ensures Attwater's sinister dominance. The novella undoubtedly excludes women, and in these terms conforms to Showalter's model of the romance as representing a flight from heterosexuality. However, Stevenson rejects the idea that the cult of heroic masculinity might regenerate a feminized modernity, and he rewrites the romance by scrutinizing critically the homosocial bonds that sustain life at the colonial margins. In addition, he uncovers romance's latent homoeroticism (there is a suggestively sexual element in Herrick's response to Attwater: he stammers, blushes, and thrills) (205).[76] For all three beachcombers, Attwater embodies an ideal of manliness. Their approbation is ironically represented: the missionary's ruthless enforcement of his law provokes Davis's admiring response, 'you're a man' (216). Attwater is an authoritarian but charismatic father figure, a type that recurs throughout Stevenson's fiction. The vexed issue of paternity famously haunts his writings, surfacing dramatically in the final, uncompleted *Weir of Hermiston* (1896). Like Attwater, Hermiston is a brutal lawgiver and unforgiving father, his justice founded in Old Testament notions of retribution. The link between Attwater and Hermiston is strengthened by Stevenson's references to Tembinoka, the King of Apemama in the Gilbert Islands. Attwater takes Tembinoka as model for his own summary justice (he recalls that the King 'used to empty a Winchester all around a man', killing his victim only with the last ball), and in *In the South Seas* Stevenson compares the 'tyrant' Tembinoka to the 'conscientious Braxfield', the Scottish judge who was the original for Hermiston (209).[77] Both *The Ebb-Tide* and *Weir* articulate the same tensions: the brutally authoritarian yet engaging father figure, and the other characters' contradictory needs, both to submit and to rebel.

Davis's and Herrick's weaknesses draw them to Attwater. The missionary's charm is presented, Ebbatson notes, as an occult power (the captain is 'mesmerized', and Herrick is 'attracted and repelled') (214, 197).[78] The metaphor suggests that they are in mysterious, unwilling thrall to the enigmatic missionary. What underlies Herrick's attraction to Attwater is an embattled masculinity, rooted in lack of self-belief – or indeed of any belief. The faith which animates the missionary fascinates Herrick but is 'only folk-lore' to him (207). Herrick's ironic quotation from Henley's

'Invictus' evokes his sense of powerlessness: he thanks '"whatever Gods there be" for that open door of suicide' (227). His helplessness contrasts strikingly with the poem's resounding declaration, 'I am the master of my fate; / I am the captain of my soul', and the sardonic allusion measures Stevenson's distance from the conservative jingoism of *fin-de-siècle* New Imperialism.[79] The need to believe in something, even an illusion, underlies Herrick's desolation when he fails to commit suicide: 'that also was only a fairy tale, that also was folk-lore', he realizes, and now 'told himself no stories . . . even the process of apologetic mythology had ceased' (229). Davis's need for Attwater also stems from shattered self-esteem. When Attwater spares his life, Davis succumbs to the missionary's evangelism, and in a symbolic baptism 'his late executioner now laved his face' (248). The transformation is far from a redemption. It is equivocally presented: 'his countenance brightened and was deformed with changing moods of piety and terror' (250). The conversion perhaps embodies another retreat from life, a further betrayal of the children whom he has abandoned but longs to regain. When escape from the island is finally possible, he prefers to remain behind, declaring 'I found peace here, peace in believing. Yes, I guess this island is about good enough for John Davis' (252). The protagonists' ambivalent responses to Attwater point to the sinister allure of the code of heroic masculinity – an allure which sustains and buttresses the malign forces of adventure, mission endeavour, and capitalist imperialism.

The Ebb-Tide thus charts Stevenson's transition from romance to a radicalized disillusionment with adventure – a transition impelled by his confrontation with the brutal energies of imperialism. Its imagery of disease and corruption questions the curative value of romance, undermining the notion that it might restore a morbidly overcivilized world to a bracing and primitive virility. Instead, the novel represents the forces unleashed by romance as pitiless and destructive. Many contemporaries were surprised that the erstwhile champion of King Romance had produced this naturalist and modernist parable from the edges of empire. Yet the disenchantment inscribed by the narrative of *The Ebb-Tide* is prefigured – albeit in more muted terms – in Stevenson's earlier romances: Davis's reflection on the 'nightmare end' to his 'golden expectations' echoes Jim Hawkins's passage from dreams of romance to nightmares (232). And just as Jim's fear of 'savages' and 'dangerous animals' gives way to terror of the glamorous adventurer Silver, Davis comes to feel that 'perish[ing] at the hands of cannibals' might be preferable to the implacable antagonism of the gentleman missionary (232). As this suggests, the truly threatening savagery lies not – as romance would have it – in the colonial native, but closer to home, in the violent energies tapped by the romance code itself.

This belief in humankind's enduring primitive heritage, I have argued, is at the heart of Stevenson's essays and romance fiction. His romance polemics and other essays written in the 1880s engage creatively with evolutionist psychology. They deploy a strikingly evolutionist vocabulary, but undermine the confident belief in an inevitable transition from savagery to civilization, dramatizing instead the revival of primitive states of consciousness in the modern mind. Romance was not the only realm in which Stevenson believed primitive desires might be gratified: literary creativity, dreams, the childhood imagination, and oral culture likewise embodied a revivifying resurgence of instinctual life. Notwithstanding the occasional moments of anxiety, the essays clearly celebrate the revitalizing exhilaration offered by this savage inheritance.

Whereas Stevenson's essays are predominantly affirmative, I have shown that his adventure fiction dramatizes the resurgence of primitive appetites in more problematic terms. It engages critically with the romancers' claim that heroic adventure might rejuvenate an overcivilized, effete contemporary world, and suggests instead the troubled nature of the masculine adventure creed. The conventional picture of Stevenson's transition from romance to realism obscures his longstanding ambivalence towards adventure. Even the classic adventure narrative of *Treasure Island* evinces doubt about romance's rejuvenating potential, demonstrating its dangerous savagery. Nonetheless, the doubts about adventure's restorative promise clearly intensified under the pressure of Stevenson's experience in the South Seas, and *The Ebb-Tide*, his most 'grim and gloomy tale', registers the destructive realities of an oppressive evangelical imperialism.[80] *Treasure Island* may ultimately depict the rejection of romance, but its world is thereby diminished, and it ends on an elegiac note. *The Ebb-Tide*, by contrast, moves beyond romance. Embracing new literary modes including a naturalistic realism, it undertakes a radical politicization of the romance genre, as it identifies adventure's primitive energies with the brutal imperialist creed of heroic masculinity.

Part II
'Downward, downward lies your way': Degeneration and Psychology

> I wish I could write to you, but it isn't me who holds the pen – it's the other one, the stupid one, who doesn't know French, who doesn't love my friends as I love them, who doesn't appreciate things of art as I appreciate them; he whom I disavow, but whom I control sufficiently to make him take up a pen and write this twaddle. This creature, dear Rodin, you do not like; you must never know him. Your friend, who is asleep just now, like a bear, in the depths of my being, will awaken before long. Then he will write to you in his own hand. Wait for him. The other one doesn't count; he is only a poor unfaithful secretary with a cold heart and a wooden head.
>
> He who is sleeping is always, my dear friend, yours; he who writes is commissioned to inform you of the fact and to sign under his trade name
>
> Robert Louis Stevenson and Triple-Brute.[1]

In this letter to Auguste Rodin, written almost a year after *Dr. Jekyll and Mr. Hyde* was published, Stevenson weaves the novella's motif of divided personality into a description of his own state of mind, playing with the contrast between a true inner self – intellectual and artistic – and the 'stupid' self who is compelled to execute everyday chores, and signing off with a double signature. For all the surface of wry comedy, Stevenson's dual consciousness appears frustrating and wearisome. He uses the language of evolutionist psychiatry to articulate his sense of alienation and dislocation. The depiction of an insensible inner consciousness ('asleep just now') and an alter ego 'whom I disavow, but whom I control sufficiently' unsettles the notion of a unified will and identity. This theme of dual consciousness is pursued, with varying accents, across Stevenson's fiction and non-fiction. The bear sleeping 'in the depths of my being' is related to Dr Jekyll's 'brute that slept within', although here it represents the true rather than degenerate self. Earlier in the year, Stevenson invoked the novella more explicitly, reporting that his father subjected him to a 'dose of Hyde at breakfast . . . (Jekyll has been in the ascendant till now)', and two days later signing himself, 'Yours – (I think) Hyde – (I wish) Jekyll'.[2]

Multiple personality, moreover, is only one of many psychological spectres which stalk his writings, traversing the genres of fiction and non-fiction. Stevenson's autobiographical self and his fictional characters are prey to nervous degeneration, depression, emasculation, morbid introspection, and primitive resurgences. As this suggests, he entered uneasily into contemporary anxieties about mental instability and divided identity. While his romance writings engaged with the progressivist tradition of evolutionary psychology, Stevenson was equally fascinated by its dark side, the theory of degeneration. His autobiographical writing and neo-Gothic narratives engage ambivalently with the preoccupations of degeneration theory, exploring contemporary ideas about savage resurgences and raising unsettling questions about the relative influence of heredity and environmental pathologies.

Fin-de-siècle Europe was famously haunted by the fear of degeneration. With its roots in pathological medicine and biology, and drawing on the Darwinian mechanism of natural selection, the theory of degeneration amounted to a reassessment of progressive narratives of evolution, and a recognition that life did not always advance from the simple to the complex. Elaborated by scientists including Bénédict-Augustin Morel and Théodule Ribot in France, and Henry Maudsley and Edwin Ray Lankester in Britain, degeneracy was variously envisaged as disintegration of the highest levels of nervous organization, as arrested development, or as atavistic reversion.[3] Theorists of degeneration understood it as a morbid condition of the nervous system, and one which could be biologically transmitted to one's offspring. Yet for all their vehement insistence on heredity, scientists were uneasily dependent on the notion of environmental influence. Herbert Spencer was an important influence on degeneration theory. Even his *Principles of Psychology*, second edition (1870–72), which delineates a confident narrative of progressive mental evolution, addresses mental pathologies, often attributing these to the morbid effect of the environment, while later writings lamented the devolutionary potential of social welfare policies.[4]

These worries about racial and cultural reversion were shaped by the social and political conditions of 1880s and 1890s Europe. In Britain, the rhetoric of degeneration was used to articulate middle-class fears about the emergent forces of democracy, socialism, and mass society.

Degeneration theories traversed literary, social, cultural, and political as well as scientific discourses. As is well known, they responded to and fed into concerns about racial decline, focusing on the atavistic potential of modernity, the city, and the rapidly multiplying urban working classes.[5] For conservative cultural commentators, the New Woman and homosexual, decadent artist and genius, madman and criminal, and immigrant and colonial native were also evidence of modernity's degeneracy. Theories of degeneration were not uncontested: the Hungarian physician Max Nordau's popularizing work was challenged and derided in the mid-1890s, most notably by George Bernard Shaw, who branded it a 'sham-scientific vivisection'.[6] Nonetheless, degeneration theory enjoyed considerable influence. Criminologists, sexologists, and psychiatrists developed a complex set of diagnostic criteria – often focusing on visible stigmata – designed to identify and pathologize behaviour and identities which disturbed dominant middle-class norms. Despite this emphasis on 'visible vice', scientists also fostered a belief in psychological 'borderlands'. Maudsley articulated the growing sense that there was a continuum between sanity and insanity: '[t]here exists no . . . separating boundary on the one side of which lies positive disease and on the other side not'.[7] The belief that one might imperceptibly slip into madness, or might harbour insanity without this being visible to others, contributed to the anxious foreboding present in, and exploited by, much *fin-de-siècle* Gothic writing.

Perhaps under the pressure of a new *fin de siècle*, the 1980s and 1990s saw a resurgence of critical interest in the subject of degeneration. William Greenslade and Daniel Pick, among others, have offered perceptive studies of the responses of writers including Thomas Hardy, George Gissing, Arthur Conan Doyle, Stevenson, and H. G. Wells, showing that these authors engaged with degenerationism in multifarious ways, both affirming and resisting the narrative of decay.[8] Stevenson has been a central figure in this recent interest in fictional treatments of degeneration. Critics, however, have concentrated almost exclusively on *The Strange Case of Dr. Jekyll and Mr. Hyde*: in compelling readings, Stephen Arata and Robert Mighall have argued that the novella lays bare the middle-class creation of deviancy.[9] In Part II, I develop this interpretation, but examine a range of Stevenson's other fictional and non-fictional works. Stevenson's interest in psychological instability forms a unifying preoccupation across his writing. He grapples with degenerationist anxieties directly in his letters, and invokes the language and concepts of psychopathology throughout his neo-Gothic fiction. Chapter 3 considers his representation of his own psychological 'borderlands' in his autobiographical writings, and Chapter 4 examines his ambivalent engagement with degenerationism in his 'gothic gnomes', 'The Merry Men' (1882), 'Olalla' (1885), 'Markheim' (1885), and *Dr. Jekyll and Mr. Hyde* (1886).[10] In my discussion, I contend that his autobiographical and neo-Gothic works are centrally concerned with questions about heredity, environment, and will. They illuminate the tensions within late-Victorian degenerationist thought, caught as it was between biological and cultural explanations of atavism.

3

'There was less *me* and more *not-me*': Stevenson and Nervous Morbidity

Stevenson's autobiographical writing, in letters, memoirs, and essays, shares degeneration theorists' interest in psychological pathologies. His preoccupation with his own nervous morbidity runs through his writing, uniting his adolescent outpourings to his cousin with his final letters from Samoa, and demonstrating his enduring concerns about mental instability and fractured identity. His study of his own 'borderlands' coalesces around three areas of degenerationist apprehension: childhood, loss of faith, and masculinity. Like the neo-Gothic tales which he wrote in the 1880s, his autobiographical writing focuses on the causes of morbid psychologies, scrutinizing the relative influence of heredity, environment, and volition, and questioning whether degenerative tendencies can be controlled.

Stevenson represents his childhood as sickly, nervous, and overimaginative. By the *fin de siècle*, Jenny Bourne Taylor notes, the nervous child had become the emblem of fears about Britain's degenerate future.[1] For Stevenson too, the juvenile nervous system was particularly vulnerable. In 'Memoirs of Himself', he describes the 'high-strung religious ecstasies and terrors' which subjected him to an unrelenting succession of nightmares:

> I would not only lie awake to weep for Jesus, which I have done many a time, but I would fear to trust myself to slumber lest I was not accepted and should slip, ere I awoke, into eternal ruin. I remember repeatedly . . . waking from a dream of Hell, clinging to the horizontal bar of the bed, with my knees and chin together, my soul shaken, my body convulsed with agony.[2]

This passage chimes with concerns about children's psychiatric health, which often focused on troublingly liminal states of consciousness: doctors urged parents to watch for warning signs of impending trouble, from insomnia, nightmares, and somnambulism to trance-like waking states.[3] 'Night terrors' became a commonplace in medical commentaries on childhood, with writers often blaming overstimulated imaginations.[4] Stevenson holds his nurse, Cummy, responsible for his nervous woes. Describing himself as 'morbidly religious', he blames 'Cummy's overhaste to make me a religious pattern'. Rather than amusing him with 'healthy [stories] about battles' (Stevenson characteristically views bloodthirsty tales as wholesome fare), she 'defiled' his mind with stories about 'dismal and morbid devotees'.[5] Children, he teaches, should be protected from adult concerns: they 'should dwell by shallow, sunny water, plucking the lilies of optimism . . . to go down into the great deep is not for these unused and trembling sailors'.[6] His strictures echo the psychiatrist James Crichton-Browne's criticism of parents or nurses 'who compel timid, nervous children to sleep alone in the dark, and who amuse them by narrating horrific tales'.[7] Yet although Stevenson believes Cummy corrupted his childhood innocence, he also hints at a hereditary predisposition to religious gloom. The songs which he composed as a child on Satan and the Fall of Man, he declares, unwittingly followed traditional Scottish rhythmic patterns which must have been 'a trick of the ear, inherited from eighteenth century ancestors'.[8] Stevenson's diagnosis of his childhood nerves, then, locates danger both in environmental influences and in heredity, clearly identifying childhood as a vulnerable time.

While Stevenson interpreted religious fervour as a symptom of childhood nervous disorder, he also saw his loss of faith as a young man in terms of psychological disintegration. He lost his faith in the early 1870s after reading Herbert Spencer's works and talking with his free-thinking cousin, Bob.[9] His frank confession of religious doubt led to a painful rift with his orthodox family and disaffection with a stiflingly religious Edinburgh culture – an experience reflected in 'The Misadventures of John Nicholson' (1887), where the hero is alienated from his severe father, 'that iron gentleman', and the 'tight little theological kingdom of Scotland'.[10] Stevenson suffered immediate nervous prostration, and was sent to the Riviera on medical advice. His letters attribute his nervous trouble largely to family conflict. He wrote soon after reaching the south of France in 1873 that

> I am awfully weary and nervous; I cannot read or write almost at all and I am not able to walk much . . . However . . . I am free now from the horrible worry and misery that was playing the devil with me at home.[11]

Stevenson's anguish stemmed from his recognition that he could not abandon inherited beliefs without wounding his father: he judged his actions as tantamount to parricide.[12] The Oedipal note suggests that, for Stevenson as for many nineteenth-century doubters, religious uncertainty and the painful process of achieving emotional independence from the family were intimately entangled.

By the late 1870s, Stevenson's family conflict was resolved, but one legacy of his crisis was an enduring anxiety about the absence of moral purpose or meaning to life. In Stevenson's fiction, loss of faith causes psychological and ethical disorientation: in *New Arabian Nights* (1878), one young man joined the 'Suicide Club' after reading Darwin (he could not bear to be 'descended from an ape'), while in *The Ebb-Tide* (1893–94) Herrick's crisis of faith underlies his neurotic sense of futility.[13] As in so many Victorian autobiographies and novels of doubt, Stevenson's letters articulated a persistent need to impose human meaning on a universe which now seemed unintelligible. Desiring to salvage a system of ethics from the debris of Christianity, Stevenson confessed that '[e]thics are my veiled mistress; I love them, but I know not what they are'.[14] He was determined to 'give a good example before men and show them how goodness and fortitude and faith remain undiminished, after they have been stripped bare of all that is formal'.[15] The strain in these letters reflects a wider tension within late-Victorian thought, as eagerness to build a new foundation for ethics was tempered by apprehension that no new system could measure up to the old Christian ideal. This is the reason why, for many late Victorians, loss of faith threatened to cast society adrift from its moral and psychological moorings.[16]

The disorientation associated with religious crisis is explored most expansively in 'Pulvis et Umbra' (1888). This essay is Stevenson's most sustained attempt to come to terms with a universe stripped of Christian meaning, order, and purpose: it is, as he informed Sidney Colvin, 'a Darwinian Sermon'.[17] The essay opens with a bleak vision of a world unfitted for humans. Evincing the *fin-de-siècle* sense that scientific and human meaning is radically opposed, Stevenson even warns that a scientific view of the world threatens human sanity: 'that way madness lies; science carries us into zones of speculation where there is no habitable city for the mind of man'.[18] He flees to the more congenial sphere of human life, only to find there a 'mountain mass of the revolting and the inconceivable'.[19] Humanity appears no longer as a divine creation, but as a 'disease of the agglutinated dust'; yet it has noble aims, which are at odds with 'barbarous' instincts.[20] In this double bind, human idealism is ill fated: 'it is not alone their privilege and glory, but their doom; they are condemned to some nobility; all their lives long, the desire of good is at their heels, the implacable hunter'.[21] This vision of a universe where human morals are accidental to the larger evolutionary drama resonates with Hardy's judgment that '[t]he emotions have no place in a world of defect, and it is a cruel injustice that they should have developed in it'.[22] Stevenson seeks, rather hesitantly, to draw comfort from human 'kinship' with all forms of animate life: all are united in being 'crucified between that double law of the members and the will'.[23] Will was central to debates about evolutionism, with anti-Darwinian commentators such as the Duke of Argyll teaching that free will marked a fundamental distinction between humans and animals.[24] While Stevenson critiqued Argyll's *The Reign of Law* (1867) as a student, the essay retrieves the concept of will, using it to reassert some meaning for life, both human and animal.[25] He concludes, albeit uneasily, by yoking Darwinism with Christian rhetoric: '[l]et it be enough for faith, that the whole creation groans in mortal frailty, strives with unconquerable constancy: Surely not all in vain'.[26] Confronting apparent ethical and psychological collapse, the essay offers at best a strained and embattled optimism.

Stevenson soon recovered from his religious crisis, rebuilding his relationship with his parents and even returning towards the end of his life to some sort of Christian faith or at least observance, but his sense of emasculation persisted.[27] His decision to renounce the family faith, soon after abandoning the family profession, engineering, perhaps contributed to his sense of his own decadence, his lack of manly purpose. *Fin-de-siècle* degenerationist discourse was centrally concerned with the figure of the unmanly male, and few writers shared contemporary misgivings about masculine nerves more fully than Stevenson. The trope of degeneration recurs repeatedly in his letters and papers. He uses it to depict his own life as a regression from the active vigour of his ancestors' lives, not only in physical but also in psychological and moral terms. In a succinct, if flippant, unpublished note, he summarized his life:

> [b]orn 1850 at Edinburgh. Pure Scotch blood; descended from the Scotch Lighthouse Engineers, three generations. Himself educated for the family profession . . . But the marrow of the family was worked out, and he declined into the man of letters.[28]

His reverence for his ancestors, the 'Scotch Lighthouse Engineers', contrasts with his sense of his own deficiency in both steadfast will and determination. Stevenson finds in his family's past, as suggested in Chapter 1, an exhilarating connection with his ancestral inheritance, which offers some compensation for his own perceived degeneracy: in 'The Manse' (1887), he declares that, 'though to-day' he is 'only a man of letters', his forebears played an adventurous and heroic part in Scottish history.[29]

By contrast with his swashbuckling ancestors, Stevenson travelled in search of health throughout his life. He also diagnosed himself as suffering from numerous psychological malaises. In the years of his adolescent and youthful turmoil, he described himself as 'melancholy mad', suffering 'attacks of morbid melancholy', of an 'introspective humour', 'wretchedly nervous', 'under the influence of opium', and prone to 'hypochondria'.[30] In the 1880s, he was diagnosed with 'brain exhaustion', and wrote of his 'anaemia and paltriness', having just surfaced from 'three months of black depression'.[31] In 1889, when the French neurologist Jean-Martin Charcot treated his friend Sidney Colvin (of whom Kipling caustically remarked, he 'suffers from all the nervo-hysterical diseases of the 19th Century'), Stevenson wrote that 'I gather I have had a touch of the same'.[32] At the end of his life, he speculated that he might be suffering from 'softening of the brain'.[33] Throughout his life he suffered from recurrent bouts of dual consciousness, from the out-of-body experiences described in *An Inland Voyage* (1878) to the feverish struggles between '*myself*' and '*the other fellow*' recounted in his 1892 letter to F. W. H. Myers.[34]

Stevenson's nervous invalidism was hard to reconcile with Victorian ideals of manliness which, by the *fin de siècle*, called for physical as well as moral health.[35] Nervous disorders, moreover, were increasingly interpreted as psychological rather than somatic. Invalidism, Janet Oppenheim notes, 'underscored' men's 'lack of purpose, initiative, energy, and will [and] thus denied their very claim to manhood'.[36] While British psychologists still diagnosed hysteria as an almost exclusively female disorder, there was a growing tendency to pathologize cases of male nervous susceptibility, and to brand the nervous male effeminate.[37] Stevenson's reverence for feats of physical and military prowess and his ambivalent attraction to romance, adventure, and heroism in, for example, *Treasure Island* (1881–82) and *The Black Arrow* (1883) owes much to his own perceived effeteness. His so-called 'War Correspondence', written while he was convalescing in Switzerland in the early 1880s, makes telling reading: Stevenson played elaborate games of tin soldiers with his stepson, Lloyd Osbourne, and wove them into equally involved war reports. Osbourne described the campaigns as

> an intricate 'Kriegspiel,' . . . mimic war indeed, modelled closely upon real conditions and actual warfare, requiring, on Stevenson's part, the use of text-books and long conversations with military invalids.[38]

As the allusion to 'military invalids' suggests, Stevenson's obsessive fascination with the smallest detail of military lore is ironically juxtaposed with his physical incapacity. Throughout his life, whether planning to martyr himself for the cause of Anglo-Irish Union, or exerting himself in the Samoan conflict, Stevenson's attraction to the glamour of war reflected his yearning for a virility he felt he lacked.[39]

Stevenson's scrutiny of his morbid psychology interrogates the respective influence of nature and nurture, and raises the question of how far degenerative tendencies can be exacerbated – or indeed controlled – by the cultural environment. In doing so, his writing exposes the tensions within late-Victorian degenerationist theory. The conflicting claims of inheritance, environment, and volition formed the principal fault line of *fin-de-siècle* degenerationist discourse. Earlier in the century, the psychiatric discourse of 'moral management' had taught that the active exercise of the 'will' might halt the onset of insanity, but by the 1860s this had been cast in doubt. In 1867 Henry Maudsley emphasized hereditary patterns of mental decay, claiming that 'the acquired ill of the parent becomes the inborn infirmity of the offspring'.[40] Yet the phrase 'acquired ill', which draws on Lamarck's theory of the inheritance of acquired characteristics, intimates that Maudsley's strict hereditarianism was tempered by an emphasis on environmental influence. Moreover, he later advocated exercising the will in order to control mental aberration – evidence of the enduring legacy of 'moral management', with its rhetoric of self-discipline.[41] So degeneration theory, despite its hereditarian bent, was paradoxically dependent on Lamarckian notions of will and environmental influence.[42]

Stevenson often treated his nervous morbidity deterministically, usually looking to the influence of heredity. While he often viewed himself as the degenerate offspring of an active, vigorous line, he also acknowledged a family strain of melancholy. He concluded a particularly wretched letter in 1873 by admitting that 'I have written to you in all the deformity of my hypochondriasis . . . remember that I come of a gloomy family, always ready to be frightened about their precious health'.[43] Most late-Victorian doctors and patients, Oppenheim observes, interpreted psychological problems as a hereditary affliction: autobiographers such as J. A. Symonds painstakingly scanned their ancestors' characters for warning signs of a nervous temperament.[44] Stevenson's letters evoke his father's gloomy irritability, and his own susceptibility to these moods.[45] His obituary of his father, published in 1887, portrayed Thomas Stevenson's tendency to depression, his 'morbid sense of his own unworthiness . . . [and] of the fleetingness of life'.[46] In an intellectual climate which increasingly interpreted individual psychology in terms of race, the notion of 'Celtic gloom' had become fashionable currency, popularized by Gaelic revivalists such as William Sharp.[47] Stevenson played with these ideas of racial character, interpreting his father's tendency to 'emotional extremes' as a 'Celtic trait', describing how 'his thoughts were ever tinged with the Celtic melancholy', and likening his expressiveness to 'what we read of Southern races'.[48] Reading his father's temperament as stamped by the hereditary mark of race had, of course, implications for himself: Stevenson was all too aware of his own morbid tendencies, and the admonitions to his father not to succumb to self-indulgent gloom often read like memoranda to himself.[49]

As nervous disorders were increasingly attributed to heredity, Francis Galton, Darwin's cousin, attempted to trace the scientific laws of inheritance, setting forth the principles of the nascent eugenics movement in his *Inquiries into Human Faculty and Its Development* (1883). In 1884, he published *Records of Family Faculties*, a book designed 'for those who care to forecast the mental and bodily faculties of their children, and to further the science of heredity'.[50] Urging the male reader to fill in his family's data, Galton promised that the research would

> lay bare many far-reaching biological bonds that tie his family into a connected whole, whose existence was previously little suspected . . . no man stands on an isolated basis, but . . . is a prolongation of his ancestry in no metaphorical sense.[51]

Stevenson and his wife, Fanny, had a copy of Galton's *Records* in their library in Samoa, in which the Stevenson family data have been entered in Fanny's hand (see Figure 3.1).[52] The categories devised by Galton construct bodily and mental powers in terms of norm and deviation: they include 'Bodily strength and energy, if much above or below the average', 'Keenness or imperfection of sight or other senses', and 'Mental powers and energy, if much above or below the average'. Fanny has filled out records for Stevenson's parents, and the entry for Thomas Stevenson gives a revealing glimpse of an excessively talented and volatile individual, with 'energy somewhat below [average]; except in anger, when far above', possessing the 'temperament of genius' and 'much interest and odd opinions in theology', and in character 'choleric, hasty, frank, shifty'.[53] Fanny's language chimes with contemporary pathologizations of genius, associating exalted mental powers with nervous excitability and even madness. The Italian criminal psychologist Cesare Lombroso notoriously linked genius and madness.[54] English psychiatrists too emphasized the hereditary dangers of genius. James Crichton-Browne,

2 FATHER Thomas Stevenson

1. Date of birth. July 22 1818 — Birthplace. Edinburgh

2. Occupation. Civil Engineer — Residences. Edinburgh.

3. Age at marriage. — The place for this entry is at 4 in next page.

4. do. of wife — The place for this entry is at 3 in next page

5. Mode of life so far as affecting growth or health. healthy, much outdoor exercise, much travelling

6. Was early life laborious? why and how? no

7. Adult height. 5·10 — Colour of hair when adult. dark brown — Colour of eyes. grey

8. General appearance. stout, broad-shouldered, florid, strongly-marked features

9. Bodily strength and energy, if much above or below the average. strength above the average, energy somewhat below; except in anger, when far above

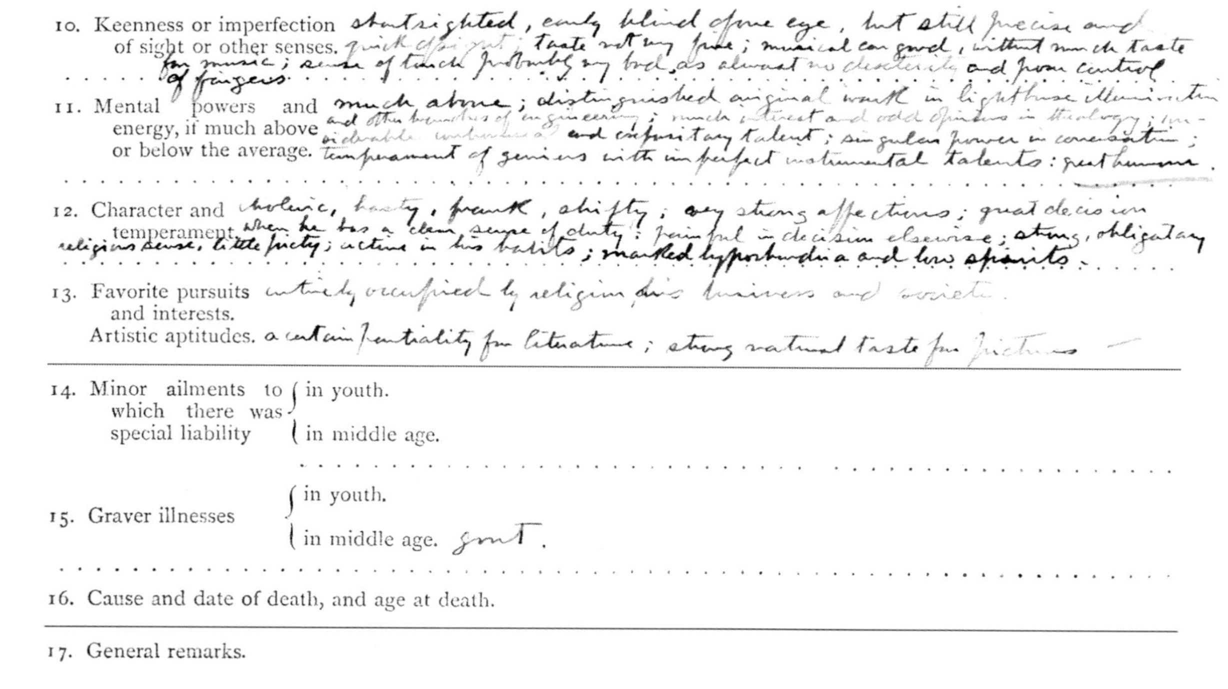

10. Keenness or imperfection of sight or other senses. shortsighted, early blind of one eye, but still precise and quick of sight; taste not very fine; musical ear good, without much taste for music; sense of touch probably very bad, as almost no dexterity and poor control of fingers

11. Mental powers and energy, if much above or below the average. much above; distinguished original work in lighthouse illumination and other branches of engineering; much interest and odd opinions in theology; considerable [illegible] and expository talent; singular power in conversation; temperament of genius with imperfect instrumental talents: great humour.

12. Character and temperament. choleric, hasty, frank, shifty; very strong affections; great decision when he has a clear sense of duty; painful indecision elsewise; strong, obligatory religious sense, little piety; active in his habits; marked hypochondria and low spirits.

13. Favorite pursuits and interests. entirely occupied by religion, his business and society.
Artistic aptitudes. a certain partiality for literature; strong natural taste for pictures —

14. Minor ailments to which there was special liability { in youth. / in middle age.

15. Graver illnesses { in youth. / in middle age. gout.

16. Cause and date of death, and age at death.

17. General remarks.

Figure 3.1 Annotated copy, from Stevenson's library, of Francis Galton, *Records of Family Faculties* (London: Macmillan, 1884), 16. Reproduced courtesy of the Beinecke Rare Book and Manuscript Library, Yale University.

for example, warned in 1859 that the 'legacy left by a genius to his family' was often 'mental weakness in the child. Thus the children of the great and the eminent are frequently below mediocrity, and a race of distinguished men is quite exceptional'.[55] Stevenson himself, so proud of his ancestors and so sensitive to his own perceived failure to live up to their tough and manly standards ('I ought to have been able to build lighthouses and write *David Balfours* too'), shared these common anxieties about the running down of a family's hereditary stock.[56]

The reasons which Stevenson envisaged for his nervous disorders turn, therefore, on his inborn character, on nature rather than nurture. He looked for explanation, however, not only to the racial legacies which so intrigued him, but equally to the peculiar propensities of the artist. Stevenson shared widespread *fin-de-siècle* apprehensions about the essential unhealthiness of the writer. Throughout his life, he suspected that writing was a decadent vocation, and the man of letters unpractised in that manly vigour which he admired. It was a misgiving which exercised Stevenson even as an adolescent, shaping his taste for tales of manly derring-do: he condemned Keats who 'lulls where he should arouse and relaxes where he should brace', and exclaimed of the cult of beauty, '[w]hat a grovelling ideal! What an enervating atmosphere!'.[57] Significantly, this outburst occurs during a soul-searching letter to his cousin Bob, in which he acknowledges his 'unhealthy state of [mental] agitation', and reviles his literary aspirations as a 'dead pandering to the senses'.[58] His declaration of his literary vocation is uneasily counterpointed to a Christian ideal of service by the acknowledgement that '[w]hat I should prefer would be to search dying people in lowly places of the town and help them; but *I cannot trust myself* in such places'.[59] With this rueful admission, Stevenson contrasts what he views as the noble commitment of a Christian life with the vanity of the literary calling. Nor, despite the overwrought language, was his mistrust of literature merely an adolescent phase. In the last few months of his life he speculated about the 'possibility that literature is a morbid secretion, and abhors health'.[60]

The artist, indeed, was the archetypal *fin-de-siècle* degenerate, and the concept of artistic decadence was entangled with scientific theories of degeneration: Max Nordau notoriously represented æsthetic decline as both cause and symptom of modernity's degeneracy.[61] Yet scientific representations of the creative imagination were often conflicting. Psychiatrists, as noted, were increasingly determinist in their treatment of degeneration, usually attributing nervous pathology to the dictates of heredity. The theory that higher levels of nervous organization, being the most recently developed, were those that succumbed first to decay, threatened exalted and sensitive natures with a nervous breakdown which would return them to the lower levels of consciousness.[62] Thus those believed to have highly evolved, overrefined nervous systems were seen as predisposed to degeneration. As J. M. Fothergill wrote in a popular medical work, '[a] mind at once powerful and coarse of fibre has a great advantage, as regards sheer endurance, over another mind of finer fabric'.[63]

However, this hereditary reading of the degenerative propensities of the artistic temperament coexisted with a contrary emphasis on the impact of habit and volition. Artistic inspiration, for many scientific commentators, involved altered mental states, and seemed fearfully close to pathological conditions such as the hypnotic trance or dual consciousness. Maudsley characterized Dickens's vivid imagination, for example, as hallucinatory, warning that 'too frequent exercise of the power is full of peril to the mind's stability . . . He is like the sorcerer who has called spirits from the vasty deep, and has forgotten the power by which to lay them again'.[64] While he acknowledged that an intense imagination was 'consistent with perfect sanity of mind', Maudsley clearly implied that excessive indulgence of the imagination led to an atrophy of will.[65] States of altered consciousness were viewed as lapses from a healthy norm, when the psyche lost its power of self-determination, and the mind fell prey to delusion.[66] As this suggests, the moral – even Lamarckian – emphasis on volition continued to play a critical part in degenerationist discourse, despite the increasing importance of heredity. Maudsley, Galton, and Sully stressed the dangers attendant on mental states where the will was in abeyance. Sully noted that the intensity of the genius's vision made 'the severest demands on the controlling and guiding forces of volition'.[67]

The writer was seen as particularly vulnerable. Dual consciousness, Karl Miller notes, became a figure for the authorial imagination at the *fin de siècle*.[68] Crichton-Browne tapped into these concerns about artistic neurosis, in an 1895 lecture which drew on the experience of Tennyson, Wordsworth, Dickens, and J. A. Symonds.[69] The psychological condition of the 'dreamy mental state', Crichton-Browne said, consisted 'in a feeling of being somewhere else – in double consciousness – in a loss of personal identity – in supernatural joyousness or profound despair – in losing touch of the world – in a deprivation of corporeal substance'.[70] Crichton-Browne viewed these states as pathological evidence of resurgent primitive impulses, explaining that they provided access to a realm beyond conscious life, and were 'revivals of hereditarily transmitted or acquired states'.[71] Sully too warned that if the modern poetic imagination, with its 'primitive' inheritance, were not restrained by will or external orientation, it would fall into pathological dual consciousness.[72] These claims invested mental pathology with a significantly moral content. They drew attention to the question of whether inherited – and less evolved – psychologies could be triggered by lack of restraint, and how far they could be contained, whether by internal resolve or by external, cultural influence.

Stevenson's reflections on creativity and imagination expose this evolutionist uncertainty about whether the imagination could be controlled. In many writings, especially his 'romance' polemics, he undoubtedly attested to the rejuvenating effects of creativity, but he also had a darker understanding of its possible consequences. In 'Ordered South', written after his dispatch as a nervous invalid to the Riviera in 1873, Stevenson sought to understand his predicament, and the article's depiction of mental pain brought his mother to tears.[73] Evoking the hazards of an over-evolved artistic temperament, Stevenson warns that

> the possession of a brain that has been . . . improved and cultivated, and made into the prime organ of a man's enjoyment, brings with it certain inevitable cares and disappointments. The happiness of such an one comes to depend greatly upon those fine shades of sensation that heighten and harmonise the coarser elements of beauty. And thus a degree of nervous prostration, that to other men would be hardly disagreeable, is enough to overthrow for him the whole fabric of his life.[74]

Stevenson finds himself returned to the lower levels of consciousness: his spirit is 'numbed', and he 'cannot recognise that this phlegmatic and unimpressionable body with which he now goes burthened, is the same that he knew heretofore so quick and delicate and alive'.[75] He characterizes this trance-like state by the figure of divided consciousness: knowing intellectually that the scenery he inhabits is beautiful, 'in his heart of hearts he has to confess that it is not beautiful for him . . . He is like an enthusiast leading about with him a stolid, indifferent tourist'.[76]

In certain contexts, Stevenson clearly wanted to redeem the notion of dual consciousness from the charge of pathology. Elsewhere in his travel writing, for example, he revels in what he represents as a return to a pre-civilized state: he celebrates the 'ecstatic stupor' achieved through open-air exertion, likening it to the Buddhist state of Nirvana, and suggesting that it is '[a] pity to go to the expense of laudanum, when here is a better paradise for nothing!'.[77] Stevenson describes his paradise in terms of dualism:

> [t]here was less *me* and more *not-me* than I was accustomed to expect. I looked on upon somebody else, who managed the paddling . . . my own body seemed to have no more intimate relation to me than the canoe.[78]

This passage, which echoes Crichton-Browne's rendering of trance-like symptoms in 'On Dreamy Mental States', stresses the joyfulness of the out-of-body experience. In 'Ordered South', however, the accent is mournful, with 'numbness of spirit' and 'dulness of the senses' seen as 'a gentle preparation for the final insensibility of death'.[79]

Duality is at the heart of the creative process as understood by Stevenson. 'A Chapter on Dreams' (1888) clearly characterizes the writer as split between a dreaming and a waking self, leading 'a double life – one of the day, one of the night'.[80] The essay betrays Stevenson's characteristic uncertainty about whether the literary imagination is liberating or morbid. Thus while he welcomes unconscious inspiration, as demonstrated in Chapter 1, he also appears uneasy about the 'primitive' nature of the mental powers which his 'Brownies' embody, noting ruefully that they 'have not a rudiment of what we call a conscience'.[81] The pathological aspects of the writer's imagination indeed weighed on Stevenson, and he was more troubled than Myers or Sully by the prospect of psychological disintegration. Stevenson portrayed a disordered dual consciousness in a letter written to Myers in 1892.[82] Recounting his experiences while in a fever, Stevenson described his divided consciousness as '*myself*' and '*the other fellow*', and explained how, despite being awake, he found his rational self unable to control '*the other fellow*'.[83] Myers published the letter in the 1894 *Proceedings of the Society for Psychical Research*, and subsequently in *Human Personality and Its Survival of Bodily Death* (1903), where he acknowledged that, while 'A Chapter on Dreams' had shown the healthy workings of genius, this letter demonstrated that 'under morbid conditions, this temperament of genius – this ready permeability of the psychical diaphragm' might lead to mental disintegration.[84]

Underlying Stevenson's celebration of the writer's art lurks a fear that undue exercise of the creative faculties might be mentally debilitating. Indeed, he warned in an unpublished manuscript that immersion in the imagination to the exclusion of real life, though pleasant, could lead to a quasi-primitive state of enervation and torpor:

> all this is attained by the undue prominence of purely imaginative joys, and consequently the weakening and almost the destruction of reality. This /is\ buying at too great a price. There are seasons when the imagination becomes somehow tranced and surfeited, as it is with me this morning; and then upon what can we fall back? The very faculty that we have fostered and trusted has failed us in the hour of trial; and we have so blunted and enfeebled our appetite for the other that they are subjectively dead to us . . . I am vacant, unprofitable: a leaf on

> a river with no volition and no aim: a mental drunkard the morning after an intellectual debauch. Yes I have a~~n~~ more ~~opium~~ subtle opium in my own mind than any apothecarys drug; but it has a sting of its own, and leaves one as flat and helpless as the other.[85]

The imagery of intemperance and addiction ('appetite', 'debauch', 'opium', 'drug') chimes with contemporary insistence on mental hygiene. Stevenson's mistrust of the writer's 'tranced and surfeited' imagination and the 'undue prominence of purely imaginative joys' is reminiscent of Maudsley's and Sully's writings on mental pathology. Seeing in his disordered mental state both lack of 'volition' and the 'weakening . . . of reality', he shares their emphasis on the need for the will and external orientation to restrain the irrational parts of the mind. The passage figures the influence of habit, and consequently of the cultural environment, on the individual mind, thereby undercutting a purely hereditary conception of artistic temperament.

The fear of self-absorption resonates with more general Victorian anxieties, explored by Stefan Collini, about 'sinking into a state of psychological malaise or anomie' through immersion in 'purely selfish aims'.[86] Stevenson perceived psychological danger not only in literary creativity, but also in the cultivation of any imaginative or introspective mental state. In self-flagellating letters to his cousin from 1868, he pitted his self-centred brooding against the healthy call of the external world: '[w]hat an egotistical brute I am! self! self! self!', he lamented.[87] Only duty, he confessed, could rescue him from his solipsistic prison: 'I am almost drifting back into my old introspective humour, perhaps opportunely, as I am now again thinking seriously of my duty'.[88]

These worries about the enervating psychological effects of imagination also, importantly, tempered his celebration of reading. Stevenson clearly hailed romance as affording a rejuvenating connection with primitive life. Yet he also demonstrated a more sinister understanding of literary transactions, one in which reading disturbed humankind's fragile mental stability, rather than simply gratifying instinctual desires. Reading might, he feared, become an alternative to real life and to human contact, a mark, indeed, of that 'undue prominence of purely imaginative joys' which he deplored in his discussion of the 'tranced and surfeited' imagination. In 'The Day After Tomorrow' (1887), Stevenson condemns all literary experience as an artificial substitute for active life, claiming that literature fosters a passive introversion, and extending this mistrust to all games and play. The essay warns that '[p]lay in its wide sense, as the artificial induction of sensation, including all games and all arts, will, indeed, go far to keep [man] conscious of himself, but in the end he wearies for realities'.[89]

The readers who appear in Stevenson's fiction often conform to this pathological diagnosis, with their avid consumption of literature bespeaking their psychological isolation. The Reverend Mr Rolles in *New Arabian Nights* (1878) relies on books to preserve him from 'the petty shocks and contacts of the world'; the narrator in 'The Pavilion on the Links' (1880) describes himself and his companion as '[m]isanthropes', who spend months together, 'speaking little, reading much, and rarely associating except at meals'; and the minister in 'Thrawn Janet' (1881) is described, in a typical opposition, as 'fu' o' book-learnin' . . . [but] wi' nae leevin' experience'.[90] Stevenson displayed none of Sully's confidence that one might indulge in reading as a brief and harmless escapism. Sully talked approvingly of 'this age . . . when men purposely set themselves to escape for the nonce from the melancholy of years by trying to revive jaded sensation at the fount of boyish literature', but, for Stevenson, escapist reading was fraught with psychological hazard.[91]

His belief that fiction evoked a somatic response both primitive and pleasurable was undercut by concern about whether the contagious effects of this process could be controlled. The imagery of illness permeates his discussions of reading. Considering the psychological effects of an apparently momentary surrender to a powerful literary work, he judged that reading Dostoevsky was like 'having a brain fever', and advised his father against reading J. G. Lockhart's biography of Walter Scott, 'as it has made me very ill and would make you worse'.[92] His romance polemics imagine readers as susceptible to physical affect: the scene of 'Rawdon Crawley's blow', he asserts, forms 'the chief ganglion' of Thackeray's *Vanity Fair*, with readers being 'reward[ed]' by 'the discharge of energy from Rawdon's fist'.[93]

For Stevenson, popular literature is particularly dangerous, apt to release potentially contagious desires. Thus his valorization of the 'romance' is double edged, evoking its degenerate as much as invigorating effects: it appeals to the lower instincts, gratifying the 'sensual' and 'illogical' tendencies of the human mind.[94] The uncritical and sympathetic relationship to the narrative which Stevenson attributes to romance readers resonates with contemporary representations of the potential hazards of reading. It was a period when increasing emphasis was being laid on *how* to read, on the importance of thinking critically rather than reading addictively.[95] Commentators construed the physiological involvement of the reader with the text as a possible danger. Discussions of hysteria and nervous diseases frequently cite the harmful effect of reading, demonstrating the widespread belief in 'the affective qualities of print'.[96] As Kate Flint has shown, women were regarded as especially vulnerable to desires unleashed by the written word.[97] But the new readership for popular literature also attracted concern. Working-class reading habits, Kelly Mays demonstrates, were aligned with those of women, and seen as similarly susceptible to pathology.[98] Critics viewed mass literacy and education, cheap literature, and a growing newspaper press as both causes and symptoms of degeneracy.[99] Stevenson expressed some of these anxieties in an 1886 letter to Edmund Gosse: discussing the reading public, he lamented the 'bestiality of the beast whom we feed', and famously mused that '[t]here must be something wrong in me, or I would not be popular'.[100]

More so than his romances, which he often represented as an invigorating, healthful alternative to realism, Stevenson's 'gothic gnomes' prompted his worries about literary degeneracy. His neo-Gothic output was substantial: in addition to the tales considered in Chapter 4, it included 'The Body Snatcher' (1884), parts of *The Master of Ballantrae* (1888–89), Scottish tales such as 'Thrawn Janet' (1881), and South Seas fiction such as 'The Beach of Falesá' (1892).[101] Stevenson's feelings about his neo-Gothic tales were ambivalent: he dubbed them 'crawlers' or 'bogey tales'.[102] His apprehension that such works constituted a degenerate genre was rooted in concerns about their effect on the reader's morality, their æsthetic integrity, and their place in a commercialized literary market place.

Stevenson's misgivings about the harmful impact of uncanny stories on readers emerge in an exchange with his friend, Lady Taylor. Commenting on 'Markheim' and *Dr. Jekyll and Mr. Hyde*, Lady Taylor questioned whether it was healthy for Stevenson to enter into the 'diabolic thoughts of evil men', and 'whether in the course of your very *thorough* researches some evil may not stick to *your* soul'.[103] In reply, Stevenson wrote,

> I do not think it is a wholesome part of me that broods on the evil in the world and man; but I do not think that I get harm from it; possibly my readers may, which is more serious; but at any account, I do not purpose to write more in this vein.[104]

Importantly, Stevenson conceives the reader rather than writer to be at risk of psychological 'harm', although the author's vulnerability is also underscored by the vocabulary of illness ('not . . . wholesome') and moral resolution ('I do not purpose'). Indeed, his moral distaste led him to frequent declarations that he would renounce his 'crawlers': he wrote in July 1881 that 'The Body Snatcher' 'is laid aside in a justifiable disgust, the tale being horrid'.[105]

Æsthetic as much as moral considerations, however, underlay his aversion to Gothic supernaturalism. *The Master of Ballantrae*, he judged, was 'sound, human tragedy' for the most part, but the final sections 'are fantastic, they shame, perhaps degrade, the beginning'; and when he 'escaped' from using a 'supernatural trick' to conclude 'The Beach of Falesá', he proclaimed that 'the yarn is cured'.[106] Stevenson's aversion to the commercialization of literature underpinned his ambivalence towards his 'gothic gnomes'. This is captured in his greeting the morning after a dream brought him the inspiration for *Dr. Jekyll and Mr. Hyde*: 'I've got my shilling shocker', he told his doctor.[107] In an age when advertising became central to literary culture, he was outraged by the *Pall Mall Gazette*'s degrading and undignified advertisement of his forthcoming tale, 'Markheim', calling the manager Charles Morley 'a most desperate fellow'.[108] The *Pall Mall Gazette* had proclaimed that

> MR ROBERT LOUIS STEVENSON, one of the most powerful imaginative writers of the day, whose vivid picture of the 'Suicide Club' has frozen the heart's blood, whose *Treasure Island*, written for boys, has fascinated a Prime Minister, and become a classic, has consented to write for us a vivid GHOST STORY, and when ghosts are walking Mr Stevenson is at his weirdest.[109]

Stevenson deplored this as 'the most truculent advertisement I ever saw', complaining that 'the white hairs of Gladstone are dragged round Troy behind my chariot wheels'.[110]

Stevenson's thoughts on his 'gothic gnomes', then, form part of the *fin-de-siècle* debate about literature and degeneracy. Unleashing potentially contagious desires, depending on cheap supernatural tricks, provoking terror, dread, and shock, and belonging in a grubby literary market place, they are a far cry from the wholesome and invigorating romance code he championed elsewhere. While reading and writing figure as particularly hazardous, we have seen that the spectre of psychological degeneracy takes many shapes, haunting his letters and essays. His autobiographical work engages directly and anxiously with degenerationist concerns, focusing on his nervous and sickly childhood, the ethical and psychological disintegration attendant on loss of faith, and his embattled masculinity and nervous invalidism. The causes of psychological morbidity fascinated Stevenson. His writings explore and expose the tensions within late-Victorian degenerationism – tensions about the respective influence of nature and nurture. Searching for the causes of his own nervous troubles, he was preoccupied by hereditary and racial legacies. Yet he also focused on the influence of habit, cultural environment, and volition on the individual mind, raising troubling questions about how far these could either exacerbate or contain a degenerative heritage.

4
'Gothic gnomes': Degenerate Fictions

Stevenson's 'gothic gnomes' bring alive the same late-Victorian anxieties about degeneracy which haunt his autobiographical writings.[1] They incite, and depend upon, reactions of pleasurable fear and horror – reactions which embody the supposed degeneracy of popular literature, and point to the way that external environment and cultural habit could trigger degeneration. They also, most importantly, tell tales of atavism, figuring the resurgence of irrational states of mind. *Fin-de-siècle* fiction, as Robert Mighall argues, took up an earlier Gothic interest in the power of the past to haunt the present, and invested it with a newly evolutionist accent.[2] Thus these irrational resurgences were understood as the irruption of the primitive in civilized modern life. Stevenson's tales of horror are populated by characters whose mental disorders push them towards savage bestial conditions, insanity, or even death, but they also question biological notions of primitive resurgences. This chapter investigates how the interest in the psychological 'borderlands' of degeneracy evident in Stevenson's letters, and his preoccupation with questions about heredity, will, and environment, finds fictional form in his neo-Gothic tales, 'The Merry Men' (1882), 'Olalla' (1885), 'Markheim' (1885), and *Dr. Jekyll and Mr. Hyde* (1886).

In 'The Merry Men' (1882), the sea coast is a trope for mental breakdown: the setting, on Scotland's rugged west coast, suggests a savage psychology. Stevenson called the tale 'a fantastic sonata about the sea and wrecks'.[3] Set in the mid-eighteenth century and laced with archaisms and biblical phrasing, the tale creates a mood of ominous psychological suspense. It dramatizes one man's terrified obsession with the sea, and his gradual degeneration into insanity and death. 'The Merry Men' explores the resurgence of irrational states of mind. These insane states of mind are both provoked and symbolized by the wild landscape: Gordon Darnaway becomes complicit with the sea's cruel and fascinating power, probably murdering a shipwrecked sailor, and eventually driven mad by his fear of supernatural vengeance.

The tale's opening invokes degeneration through the idea of dying races: Darnaway married a young woman native to the area, 'the last of her family', who died in childbirth, while his own 'family was dying out in the lowlands'.[4] Darnaway's psychology is never described in explicitly degenerationist terms, however, as Ed Block mentions, the tale contains 'hints [pointing towards an] evolutionist explanation of events'.[5] For Block, Darnaway 'degenerates under the combined influences of drink and the maddening roar of the waters of Sandag Bay'.[6] Certainly, alcohol and the sea drive him further out of his mind, but religious obsession is clearly the origin of his degeneracy. Darnaway's religious fervour is morbid: with his 'black fits' and his fixation with hell, he is the true son of the Cameronians, the Scottish Covenanters among whom he was raised (72). He reminds his nephew, the narrator, of 'one of the hill-preachers in the killing times before the Revolution' (72). Stevenson frequently cast Calvinism as a negative, unhealthy version of Christianity. Comparing Scottish and French religious rebels several years earlier, he judged that

> [t]hose who took to the hills for conscience' sake in Scotland had all gloomy and bedevilled thoughts; for once that they received God's comfort they would be twice engaged with Satan; but the Camisards had only bright and supporting visions.[7]

Darnaway, in his puritanical equation of pleasure and sin, and his virulent anti-Catholicism, represents the dark side of Christianity.

Although Block's emphasis on alcohol and the savage sea suggests that Darnaway's wild instincts are to blame for his insanity, it is, rather, his fanatical repudiation of them which threatens his peace of mind. His horror of savagery is clearly inspired by Christianity. Indeed, for Edwin Eigner, the tale is a meditation on 'the mythic confrontation of man with his own conception of the powers of blackness'.[8] Thus his nephew is surprised by his drunkenness, feeling it was surely 'morally impossible in a man like my uncle, whose mind was set upon a damnatory creed and haunted by the darkest superstitions' (94–5). Yet, as Darnaway admits, his moral repulsion paradoxically increases the fascination: 'if it wasnae sin, I dinnae ken that I would care for 't' (98). His sins include gleeful joy at the sight of ships being wrecked, and salvaging costly ornaments from the wreck of the *Christ-Anna* (an operation that probably leads to the murder of a survivor). When his nephew returns from university, he finds that his uncle has decorated the family house with these 'braws' (72). They weigh on Darnaway's conscience: 'it's for the like o' them . . . folk daunton God to His face and burn in muckle hell' (72).

Darnaway's terror of supernatural retribution produces a horror of the sea, populated in his imagination by 'deils' and 'bogles', and forming a 'muckle yett [gate] to hell' (75, 74). His mental degeneracy is clear: he is affected by the elements ('when I hear the wind blaw in my lug, it's my belief that I gang gyte [mad]'), and tormented by illusions, seeing a fish following the boat as a supernatural omen (98, 75). He feels an intense sympathetic identification with the breakers called the 'Merry Men'. When he waits by the headland in the hope of witnessing a shipwreck, he admits that the stormy scene 'comes ower me like a glamour. I'm a deil, I ken't. But I think naething o' the puir sailor lads; I'm wi' the sea, I'm just like ane o' her ain Merry Men' (98). This sympathetic identification is a significant milestone on his degenerative journey. It marks a regression to animism, the tendency to invest natural elements with life, which the anthropologist E. B. Tylor believed was at the heart of 'primitive' culture.[9] James Sully, explaining how animism survived in the modern world, noted that external reality normally mediated the resultant delusion.[10] Darnaway, however, is at the mercy of his illusions: the isolation of his house, cut off from the Scottish mainland by the tides, underlines his mental imprisonment. He lacks external guidance to correct his psychological aberrations, and his superstitions are reinforced by his servant's local, pagan folklore. His nephew's mockery of his 'childish superstitions' suggests his regression along the hierarchical scale of cultural evolution, resonating with Tylor's view of contemporary spiritualism as a regression to a 'savage' state of mind, and with Henry Maudsley's view of religious enthusiasm as pathological evidence of degeneration (75).[11]

Under the pressure of his guilty terrors, Darnaway's mind finally gives way. His insane hysteria is indicated by his pallor, trembling, and shining eyes, and soon he degenerates further, into a bestial condition 'past the power of speech' (74, 88). As Block observes, the narrative engages with scientific interest in the degeneration of speech, associating 'speechlessness and madness' ('discarding speech', 'speechless', 'silent') (93, 96, 103).[12] Additionally, unnatural language pervades the narrative – from singing mermaids and talking seals to Darnaway's roaring in concert with the sea (his nephew describes, 'now shrill and thrilling and now almost drowned, the note of a human voice that accompanied the uproar of the Roost') (68, 105). In the 1882 serialization of 'The Merry Men' in the *Cornhill Magazine*, a scene omitted from the 1887 volume publication underlines the link between madness and disordered verbal communication. As he watches a ship go down, despite Puritan abhorrence of such behaviour, Darnaway drinks and dances, and sings 'a snatch of a sea-drinking song' interspersed with 'old Scottish psalm tunes' and 'such cries as young men utter in a reel'.[13] The incongruous medley conveys the conflicting and disintegrating state of Darnaway's mind, as his wild and raucous instincts vie with his religious obsession.[14]

The tale's ending dramatically illustrates the degenerative effect of religious mania. In a tense dénouement, Darnaway is confronted by a black stranger in the bay – evidently a survivor of a recent wreck, but in Scottish folklore the manifestation of the devil. Tragically, Darnaway assumes that this is the man whom he murdered, returned from the dead, and flees, 'silent, like a beast' (103). He is finally chased to a watery grave by this 'man in whom [he] found his fears incarnated' (105). Critics have often objected to the appearance of the black man. For J. R. Moore, the tale betrays a 'wavering of purpose between the psychological analysis of the elder Darnaway and the melodramatic appearance of the Black Man'.[15] Honor Mulholland regrets the emphasis on the stranger's 'natural existence', feeling that a supernatural reading would have yielded more moral significance.[16] Nonetheless, the stranger's 'natural existence' is crucial to a tale that illustrates the distorting effect of superstitious fear on perception. The point is made more strongly in the *Cornhill Magazine* version, where we are told that Darnaway was 'fed in youth . . . on tales of the devil appearing in the similitude of a black man, and, with cozening words and specious pretexts, luring men to ruin'.[17] Eigner judges that Darnaway, unable to accept the irrationality and wildness in himself, projects it onto the black man.[18] More specifically, it seems that it is Darnaway's morbid obsession with the devil and damnation which prompts his deluded interpretation of the black man. His reaction exemplifies how the damnatory creeds of Scottish folklore and Calvinism lead to degeneration: religious fixation and guilt trigger illusions, insanity, and finally death.

The narration of Darnaway's nephew, Charles, adds another layer of psychological drama to the story. Tom Shearer identifies the narrative's subjectivity as a 'problem', which complicates the 'attempt to make a coherent reading' of the tale.[19] Charles's narration, however, is a crucial part of the work's subtlety and power. His English diction contrasts with the other characters' Scottish dialect, while the solemnity and restraint of his narration counterpoint his uncle's hysterical ranting. Yet his account is marked by self-righteousness, and his protestations of rationality become increasingly desperate – as he acknowledges, 'I have said a thousand times that I am not superstitious' (99). Charles attempts to distance himself from the threatening return of the wild and superstitious past symbolized by the sea, welcoming the lights and buoys which are now being installed along the coast of 'our iron-bound, inhospitable islands' (68). He repeatedly avows his rationality, insisting that 'far from being a native of these parts', he is a university man (65). Indeed, his mentor is the famous Enlightenment historian and Principal of Edinburgh University, William Robertson. Robertson's tutelage of Charles is significant because his work cohered around an Enlightenment interest in superstition, and he traced the evolution of religious belief from primitive religions' basis in fear to the apparent progress of modern Christian societies towards tolerance and politeness (interestingly, though, he acknowledged that superstition persisted within Protestant as well as Catholic belief).[20]

Charles's rôle in the narrative's negotiation of primitive forces, nevertheless, emerges as highly compromised. While he piques himself on his education, the narrative renders the quest for knowledge, and specifically the act of reading, morally suspect. The attempts by both Charles and his uncle to read 'certain strange, undecipherable marks – sea-runes . . . on the surface of the bay' yield nothing more than reflections of their private obsessions (77–8). Alerted by historical documents he has read at university to the presence of a wrecked Spanish Armada ship, Charles dives for treasure from the wreck. Moore judges that this is 'an innocent adventure which merely distracts attention from his uncle's crime in plundering the vessel cast away before his eyes'.[21] Yet, far from being an irrelevant diversion, this sub-plot mirrors the elder Darnaway's story, emphasizing the theme of avarice. Charles yearns for 'ingots, ounces, and doubloons' to 'bring back our house of Darnaway to its long-forgotten dignity', although he soon repents of his 'sacrilegious' meddling with the 'treasures of the dead' (65, 69, 82, 85). When a group of Spaniards arrives to plunder the Armada wreck, it transpires that their leader has gained information from Robertson by representing himself as a historian – ironically underscoring the abuse and corruption of learning (69).

Charles is undoubtedly much more similar to his uncle than he cares to admit, united to him not just by greed but by religious morbidity. Despite his apparent intolerance of his uncle's regressive behaviour, he is himself, as Ed Block judges, 'swept toward a primitive state of consciousness'.[22] Like his uncle's, his religion is a denunciatory one. He speaks a punitive language of sin and guilt, interpreting natural events as supernatural omens ('I became the witness of a strange judgment of God's', 'a wreck is like a judgment', 'these were the decrees of God') (69,

72, 106). Although he dismisses most local folklore as 'old wives' stories', this in itself recalls his uncle who scorns Rorie's tales of mermen as '[a]uld wives' clavers!' yet listens 'with uneasy interest' (68, 76). And, despite his protestations of rationality, he gradually falls prey to the superstitious habit of mind which he repudiates: '[i]n spite of myself, I was infected with a measure of uneasiness' (70–1).

Initially Charles carefully distinguishes himself from those native to the area, but soon he betrays his belief in local folklore. Fearing for instance that the stretch of sea known as the 'Roost' is 'revolving mischief', he explains that 'all we dwellers in these parts attributed, if not prescience, at least a quality of warning, to that strange and dangerous creature of the tides' (80). His inclusion of himself in his description of indigenous beliefs ('all we dwellers in these parts') represents a significant shift in his attitude. His response to the Merry Men themselves is almost as marked as his uncle's in its animism: their noise, he claims, 'seemed even human. As when savage men have drunk away their reason, and, discarding speech, bawl together in their madness by the hour; so, to my ear, these deadly breakers shouted by Aros in the night' (93). The personification is vivid, portraying declining powers of speech and reason. Soon, Charles finds himself likewise returned to a lower level of consciousness, an irrational and hysterical state which mimics the drunkenness he detects in the Merry Men: '[t]hought was beaten down by the confounding uproar; a gleeful vacancy possessed the brains of men, a state akin to madness; and I found myself at times following the dance of the Merry Men as it were a tune upon a jigging instrument' (94). Like the 'ecstatic stupor' which Stevenson relished in *An Inland Voyage* (1878), Charles's 'gleeful vacancy' is construed as a joyful return to primitive consciousness.[23] The undignified 'jigging' connects Charles not just with the 'dance of the Merry Men' but also with his uncle's grotesque cavorting in the tale's serial publication – a connection which underlines the parallel psychological disintegration of uncle and nephew.

Although Block sees the tale as a straightforward narrative of degeneration 'toward a primitive state of consciousness', 'The Merry Men' arguably problematizes the idea of the 'primitive'. Charles's characterization as much as his uncle's suggests that it is human fear of savagery – rather than savagery itself – which causes degeneration. He is puritanically suspicious of pleasure, observing that 'I have always thought drunkenness a wild and almost fearful pleasure, rather demoniacal than human' (94). As Eigner points out, Charles may even imagine that his uncle is guilty of murder – he certainly leaps to that conclusion without substantive evidence.[24] Harsh and punitive, he contributes to his uncle's decline into insanity, sitting in judgment, accusing him of this terrible sin, and calling on him to repent in solemn, biblical language ('I ask you in the sight of heaven', 'God has warned you by this crime') (89, 99). Nor is his initial reaction to the sight of the black man much more measured than his uncle's: 'at that moment, with my mind running upon death and sin, the unexplained appearance of a stranger on that sea-girt, solitary island filled me with a surprise that bordered close on terror' (99–100). Soon he realizes, more rationally, that the stranger is the survivor of the shipwreck over which his uncle has just gloated, and manages a polite and hospitable reaction (100–1). But the rational solution to the 'mystery of his presence' does not appear entirely to satisfy him (102). Watching his uncle being chased into the sea by the stranger, Charles sees their deaths as 'decrees of God that came to pass before our eyes' (106). He is left psychologically scarred by his experiences. Like his uncle, whose superstitious illusions are inextricably entwined with his guilt, Charles admits that 'since I became the witness of a strange judgment of God's, the thought of dead men's treasures had been intolerable to my conscience' (69).

Religious obsession is clearly at the heart of the Darnaways' morbid psychology: the harm is caused not so much by wild or savage instincts *per se* as by their repudiation. For, although Charles shares degeneration theory's anxiety about primitive resurgences within the apparently civilized present, the narrative problematizes the attempt to distance oneself from the savage and superstitious past. While 'The Merry Men' traces these patterns of psychological disintegration without explicit reference to the interpretative framework of degeneration, Stevenson's later Gothic tale, 'Olalla' (1885), makes an interesting contrast, deploying degenerationist rhetoric throughout the narrative. A wounded English officer is sent to recuperate with a Spanish family ('once great people . . . now fallen to the brink of destitution'), and finds himself alone with the indolently sensual mother, the idiot son, Felipe, and the enigmatic daughter of the house, Olalla.[25] Critics have often neglected the tale's sophistication. Block judges that 'Olalla' uses degenerationist imagery to 'develop the sense of the family's evil', and that Stevenson himself was a proponent of Galton's eugenic theories, and Claire Harman claims that the story deals 'crudely' with racial degeneration.[26] Yet the narrative is in reality much more ambivalent in its handling of hereditary determinism, drawing attention indeed to the psychological dangers of a denial of free will. The story opens with a medical diagnosis, as the rather pompous doctor, in a tone of professional authority, brands the mother 'the last representative of a princely stock, degenerate both in parts and fortune' (158). Detached, scientific description is recommended as the appropriate register for the story: when the narrator anticipates 'strange experiences', he is gently rebuked by the doctor who says, 'I would not romance, if I were you . . . you will find, I fear, a very grovelling and commonplace reality' (158–9).

This opening suggests the possibility that tropes of madness traditionally found in Gothic romance may be re-interpreted within a scientific realist framework of degeneration theory. When the soldier reaches the *residencia*, his narrative seems to confirm the doctor's diagnosis. Felipe betrays unmistakable signs of arrested development, his depiction having affinities with representations of the animal and of what contemporaries called the savage: the narrator notes his 'imperfect enunciation' and dusky, hairy body, and explains that he 'was but a child in intellect; his mind was like his body, active and swift, but stunted in development' (159–60). Close to nature and animal life ('he would suddenly spring into a tree with a bound, and hang and gambol there like one at home'), alternately cruel and gentle, Felipe is a Pan-like figure (164–5). As Eigner notes, Stevenson's interest in the Pan myth was signalled in a poem written in 1881, 'Et Tu in Arcadia Vixisti'.[27] Recalling the rustic paradise of Arcady, Stevenson wrote,

> There hast thou seen
> Immortal Pan dance secret in a glade,
> And, dancing, roll his eyes; these, where they fell,
> Shed glee, and through the congregated oaks
> A flying horror winged; while all the earth
> To the god's pregnant footing thrilled within.
> Or whiles, beside the sobbing stream, he breathed,
> In his clutched pipe, unformed and wizard strains,
> Divine yet brutal.[28]

This vision conjures up the mingled 'glee' and 'horror' of the primitive which Pan symbolizes. Indeed, the figure of Pan – and those of other pagan deities – was increasingly used at the *fin de siècle* to signify the irruption of precivilized wildness and freedom in the modern world. In Arthur Machen's *The Great God Pan* (1894), Vernon Lee's 'Marsyas in Flanders' (1900), and Walter Pater's 'Apollo in Picardy' (1893), Pan, his fellow satyr Marsyas, and Apollyon are reborn, bringing a volatile mixture of creativity and destruction to the mediæval and modern worlds.[29] The horror embodied by the satyr was often sexual in nature – this is clear in Machen's novel, although a veil is drawn over the depravities practised. In Stevenson's narrative, while Felipe is not sexualized, this aspect of the Pan-figure is transferred to other members of his family.

Thus the Señora is described as having none but sensual pleasures: she 'lived in her body; and her consciousness was all sunk into and disseminated through her members, where it luxuriously dwelt' (167–8, 178). Her compulsive brushing of her abundant hair points to her uninhibited sexuality, while a local muleteer casts her as demonic femme fatale in his tale of her seduction and rumoured murder of his companion (168, 191). Stevenson's interest in the borderlands between human and animal articulation, evident in 'The Merry Men', also informs her characterization. Her 'savage and discordant' cries keep the narrator awake one stormy night, and, not yet knowing to whom they belong, he fears that 'some living thing, some lunatic or some wild animal, was being foully tortured . . . Who was the author of these indescribable and shocking cries? A human being? It was inconceivable. A beast?' (171). The Señora's 'bestial cries' accompany her most dramatic primitive resurgence, the vampire-like attack on the narrator after he has cut his wrist (183).

The narrative, however, undermines a simple hereditary determinism. For all the moral fibre possessed by the narrator (he is, after all, an Englishman, and boasts a heroic military record), his narrative is far from an objective, uninvolved commentary on these atavistic manifestations. He is 'unpleasantly attracted' as often as he is repelled by the degeneracy he finds around him, and is himself capable of sudden flashes of violence (163, 165). His wrist wound is self-inflicted when, 'like one in a dream', he thrusts his arm through the window pane (183). These primitive resurgences show that the narrator is not a rational onlooker. Moreover, the assumptions which he repeatedly makes about family members are so wide of the mark that doubt is cast on the interpretative framework of hereditary degeneration within which he makes his diagnoses. He does not meet the daughter of the house, Olalla, until halfway through the tale, and until then his speculations about her nature are wildly inaccurate. At first assuming that the inhuman cries must be hers, he is then surprised by the asceticism of her chamber and wonders 'that I should ever have attributed those shocking cries to one of whom I now conceived as of a saint, spectral of mien, wasted with maceration' (172, 174). When he finally meets Olalla, and witnesses the full bloom of her beauty, he admits that the 'pale saint of my dreams had vanished for ever' (176). Repeatedly breaking out of the stories which the narrator assiduously constructs for her, Olalla destabilizes his assumptions about the visibility of hereditary degeneration.

The narrator falls passionately in love with Olalla, yet his failure thus far to penetrate the family's mysteries raises doubts about his ability to understand her. He himself is confident: 'I had now her image by rote, and as I conned the traits in memory it seemed as if I read her very heart' (178). His responses to her continue to owe less, however, to any skilful reading of her 'image' than to his own preconceptions about degeneration and about the alternately alluring and threatening nature of the primitive and of sexuality. Thus he envisions Olalla as connecting him with an invigorating, precivilized world: '[h]er touch had quickened, and renewed, and strung me up to the old pitch of concert with the rugged earth, to a swelling of the soul that men learned to forget in their polite assemblies' (182). Yet the horror which he feels for the sensual, instinctual life awakened in him is also evident: Olalla seems to him 'a thing brutal and divine, and akin at once to the innocence and to the unbridled forces of the earth' (182). These words echo Stevenson's description of Pan's music as '[d]ivine yet brutal', in 'Et Tu in Arcadia Vixisti'. Again, the narrator's judgment reveals less about Olalla than about himself, conveying his horror of animal passion, and particularly of female sexuality (180). His views chime with the contemporary scientific belief that women were at once more spiritual than men and more wholly at the mercy of their bodies (as the physician J. G. Millingen expressed it, '[w]oman, with her exalted spiritualism, is more forcibly under the control of matter').[30] Moreover, the narrator's concern is ultimately for himself rather than Olalla: although he worries about the possible degeneracy of her pitying moans as she tends his wound ('[y]es, they were beautiful sounds, and they were inspired by human tenderness; but was their beauty human?'), his chief anxiety seems to be about his own attraction to these primitive sounds (184).

The narrator's reactions to the family portrait hanging in the *residencia* are as intriguing as his responses to Olalla. The ancestral portrait, a Gothic trope for the family curse, was reinvigorated by *fin-de-siècle* ideas about atavism, figuring most famously in Oscar Wilde's *The Picture of Dorian Gray* (1890, revised 1891) and Arthur Conan Doyle's *The Hound of the Baskervilles* (1901–2).[31] Robert Mighall argues that Stevenson, like Wilde and Doyle, uses the ancestral portrait to convey the power of hereditary determinism.[32] Certainly, the painting is central to the tale's exploration of Galtonian notions of hereditary degeneration. Stevenson's interest in heredity and knowledge of Galton's work has already been noted. The portrait of Olalla's ancestor, in which the painter 'had not only caught the image of one smiling and false-eyed woman, but stamped the essential quality of a race', recalls Galton's notion of the common physiognomic image of a family (167). In Stevenson's essay 'Pastoral' (1887), he remembers how in 'those composite photographs of Mr. Galton's, the image of each new sitter brings out but the more clearly the central features of the race'.[33] The narrator undoubtedly experiences the portrait's intimations of heredity as uncanny and preternatural (he has 'a half-lingering terror that [the sitter] might not be dead after all, but re-arisen in the body of some descendant') (163). Nonetheless, we have seen that the narrator is not portrayed without irony, and there is no indication that the narrative endorses his reading of the portrait.

Block contends that Stevenson uses the portrait as a 'typically Victorian frame of reference to develop the sense of the family's evil', and that he deploys degenerationism in order to 'suggest a truth even more vivid than [his] Calvinistic meditations on original sin' – the idea that a 'transpersonal' evil connects Olalla to her ancestors.[34] Yet the narrative in fact questions the validity of degenerationist diagnosis. While Dorian and Stapleton in *The Picture of Dorian Gray* and *The Hound of the Baskervilles*, respectively, do embody their ancestors, as conveyed in striking recognition scenes (Stapleton's face, for example, 'had sprung out of the canvas'), it is Olalla's mother rather than Olalla herself who is the portrait's reincarnation (167).[35] Although Block interprets Olalla as the 'symbolic equivalent' of the Señora, Olalla is set apart from her relatives by her perfect speech, strong will, and strict morality, and the local priest exclaims against the notion that she resembles her mother (189).[36] The narrative seems, rather, to convey a more complex warning about the self-fulfilling power of fatalistic beliefs such as the theory of degeneration. Olalla's long, quasi-Galtonian speech, in which she renounces the narrator despite their mutual love, on account of what she perceives as her degeneracy, points up the punitive nature of determinism. Mighall interprets Olalla's disavowal of love and procreation as wise: '[w]hen the family taint turns out to be a form of vampirism, one does well to take such scruples seriously'.[37] However, her understanding of heredity condemns her to helplessness, and denies her any sense of individual, rational self-governance. She imagines herself

> an impotent prisoner ... The hands of the dead are in my bosom; they move me, they pluck me, they guide me; I am a puppet at their command; and I but reinform features and attributes that have long been laid aside from evil in the quiet of the grave ... Shall I bind another spirit, reluctant as my own, into this bewitched and tempest-broken tenement that I now suffer in? (186–7)

The narrator, despite intermittent attempts to break down Olalla's resistance, shares her sense of personal impotence in the face of irresistible forces and her horror at the bodily nature of all experience, and he rebels too against the idea of their love being 'a mere brute attraction . . . Of me she knew nothing but my bodily favour; she was drawn to me as stones fall to the earth' (180).

The story ends in an act of painful renunciation which suggests the oppressive force of evolutionary determinism. Begged by Olalla to leave, the narrator journeys to a nearby village, where he hears the peasants' tales of horror about the *residencia*, 'that house of Satan's' (191). Indeed, the narrator's description of these 'savage notions' as 'but a new edition, vamped up again by village ignorance and superstition, of stories nearly as ancient as the race of man' indicates the possibility that Olalla's own deterministic beliefs may be in turn merely a more sophisticated version of this 'primitive' folklore (190, 191). The narrator finds Olalla praying by the crucifix on the lonely mountainside, and this comparison with a retributive Christianity, symbolized by the 'ghastly daubed countenance' and 'painted wounds' of the crucified Christ, again intensifies the harsh cruelty of Olalla's Galtonian creed (192). Her final forswearing of love draws on biblical ideas of sin and suffering: '[w]e are all such as [Christ] was – the inheritors of sin; we must all bear and expiate a past which was not ours' (192–3).

Hereditary determinism, then, emerges as a warped version of Christianity, where *all* must be expiators of the past, and its affinities seem less with Catholicism than with Calvinist theories of predestination.[38] Block's argument that Stevenson utilizes science as an explanation for original sin is unconvincing, as the narrative suggests rather that the deterministic denial of free will has tragic, self-fulfilling consequences. The narrator accepts Olalla's embrace of pain and suffering. He acts fairly unheroically, his 'ardour' restrained as much by the 'savage notions' of the peasantry as by respect for Olalla's beliefs (190). The tale ends in isolation and silence: he leaves, and looking back 'for the last time before the wood closed about my path . . . [sees] Olalla still leaning on the crucifix' (193). Thus 'Olalla' discloses typically Gothic ambivalence towards science, tapping into evolutionary determinism, but ultimately undermining its claims to human truth. The notion of degeneration is used to suggest not so much the past's control of the present as the human *fears* of a resurgent primitiveness.

Mental disintegration and debates about the rôle of free will in human psychology are also at the core of 'Markheim' (1885). Like 'Olalla', it was shaped by the commercial imperatives of the Christmas number.[39] The tale was written in response to the manager Charles Morley's desire for a gruesome addition to the 1884 Christmas number of the *Pall Mall Gazette*.[40] Having seen the previous issue's 'truculent advertisement', Stevenson wrote to Morley, 'I see you desire the blood to be curdled: be it so'.[41] According to Colvin, the story was 'advertised in the streets of London by sandwich-men carrying posters so horrific that they were suppressed, if I remember aright by the police'.[42] A convoy of corpses armed with coffin lids also paraded the streets.[43] Stevenson had, rather dryly, agreed to this, writing to Morley, 'My dear Sir, I am afraid I cannot put a skeleton into my story, but I will say nothing against one!'.[44] But, as Stevenson's sardonic and slightly embarrassed tone throughout the correspondence indicates, he found Morley's brand of horror banal and demeaning. The tale is much more interested in mental terrors, and is, as Stevenson remarked of Edgar Allan Poe's tales, 'an important contribution to morbid psychology'.[45]

The tale opens with Markheim's murder of a pawnbroker, and traces his mental breakdown under the pressure of guilt. Its focus on the psychological tumult following a murder recalls Poe's 'The Tell-Tale Heart' (1843), a story which demonstrates what Stevenson lauded as Poe's 'insight into the debatable region between sanity and madness'.[46] There are also close similarities with Fyodor Dostoevsky's *Crime and Punishment* (1866).[47] Like Markheim, Dostoevsky's murderer is distracted at the crime scene by imagined footsteps and knocking at the door, and the remainder of the narrative traces his guilt-induced mental torture.[48] Most significantly, 'Markheim' engages with contemporary scientific interest in mental pathology, dramatizing the protagonist's gradual descent into multiple consciousness. Stevenson's frequent meditations on dual consciousness, as discussed in Chapter 3, betrayed uncertainty about whether it was liberating or morbid. While 'A Chapter on Dreams' (1888) evokes the largely beneficent nature of fissured consciousness, 'Markheim' dramatizes its terrifying and bewildering aspect. The shop where the action unfolds becomes a projection of Markheim's mind, with the play of light and dark paralleling the fluctuations of his good and evil impulses: the light penetrates the shadows 'like a pointing finger'.[49] The narrative conveys the dissolution of Markheim's identity: 'he was now so pulled about by different alarms that, while one portion of his mind was still alert and cunning, another trembled on the brink of lunacy' (135). Time and space are weirdly skewed (the shop's many clocks tick away at different rates, and its many mirrors reflect the protagonist at divergent angles), undermining the possibility of a traditional, unified ego, and of unilinear character development (133–4).

Dual consciousness is at the heart of the narrative. 'Markheim' develops and literalizes the pathological self-division explored more tentatively in 'The Merry Men'. Adopting a device to become more famous in *Dr. Jekyll and Mr. Hyde*, the narrative externalizes Markheim's psychic division. His disintegration into multiple identities is initially suggested by the Gothic trope of doubling: he gradually becomes 'inexplicably conscious of some presence . . . to every room and corner of the house his imagination followed it; and now it was a faceless thing, and yet had eyes to see with; and again it was a shadow of himself' (136). Markheim's sense of multiple consciousness intensifies, and the feeling 'that he was not alone grew upon him to the verge of madness' (138). This shadowy perception of duality presages the arrival of Markheim's 'visitant' or alter ego, whose dialogue with him occupies the remainder of the tale.

The visitant is an enigmatic presence, seeming variously tempter or moral guide, devil or angel. Joseph Egan reads him as Markheim's 'better self', and certainly it is significant that he first appears when the protagonist's thoughts revert to his innocent childhood: hearing a hymn, he recalls 'church-going children and the pealing of the high organ' (139).[50] Yet Markheim responds with uneasiness to the stranger's uncanny familiarity, and fears him as satanic: 'at times he thought he knew him; and at times he thought he bore a likeness to himself; and always, like a lump of living terror, there lay in his bosom the conviction that this thing was not of the earth and not of God' (140). This distrust fits into a tradition of misrecognition in the literature of *Doppelgänger*. In James Hogg's *The Private Memoirs and Confessions of a Justified Sinner* (1824), Wringhim takes his alter ego Gil-Martin, at least initially, as 'an angel of light'.[51] Conversely, in Poe's 'William Wilson' (1839), the protagonist sees his double as his 'tormentor', only realizing too late that he is in fact his conscience.[52] Markheim's visitant, although symbolically close to Wilson's alter ego, is more inscrutable. He plays devil's advocate (leading Jenni Calder to interpret him as representing 'the sheltering power of the Devil').[53] Only at the end do we recognize that he represents Markheim's alienated conscience.

It is hypocrisy which causes Markheim's disintegration into multiple consciousness. He has denied his participation in evil and stifled his conscience (symbolically, he refuses to look at himself in a mirror, reviling it as a 'hand-conscience') (132). As Irving Saposnik judges, 'the ultimate act of murder . . . releases his pent-up conscience'.[54] Markheim's repudiation of conscience also amounts to a denial of free will. He evinces a self-serving disbelief in free will, justifying his crimes by his powerlessness: 'giants have dragged me by the wrists . . . the giants of circumstance' (141). As he explains to the visitant, he is not afraid of God's judgment, as his 'excuses' are 'exceptional'; having 'lived to belie [his] nature', he denies any 'control' over his life or actions (139, 141).

The visitant taunts and baits Markheim, showing him the hypocrisy of his belief in his essential goodness. As Markheim responds, it becomes evident that the duality is harboured within his own mind: he confesses that '[e]vil and good run strong in me, haling me both ways' and asks desperately, 'are my vices only to direct my life, and my virtues to lie without effect like some passive lumber of the mind?' (143–4). The image of hidden furniture recalls scientific metaphors of the mind: for the physician Forbes Winslow, memories were 'stored away' in 'obscure recesses of the mind', which he imagined as 'mysterious . . . chambers' or a 'cerebral treasure-house'.[55] Markheim's memories seem twofold, chiming with contemporary medical explanations of divided consciousness as originating in the splitting of strands of memory.[56] The existence of different trains of memory undermines the possibility of a coherent, single self; for, as Stevenson recognized elsewhere, memory was the basis of individual identity: 'conceive that little thread of memory that we trail behind us broken at the pocket's edge; and in what naked nullity should we be left! for we only guide ourselves and only know ourselves, by these air-painted pictures of the past!'.[57] Markheim vacillates between appalled memories of his vices and nostalgic recollections of his childhood, which he sees as representing an alternative, virtuous life: 'there lies my life; I have wandered a few years, but now I see once more my city of destination' (143). The decision to confess his crime and accept arrest is the outcome of Markheim's resolution to embrace the side of his personality which has long lain fallow: '[s]omething comes over me out of the past; something of what I . . . forecast when I shed tears over noble books, or talked, an innocent child, with my mother' (143).

Like 'Olalla', 'Markheim' is ultimately a story about free will, exploring its value in the face of determinism. Its ending, however, is ambiguous. The visitant deterministically mocks Markheim's resolution to reform: '[d]ownward, downward, lies your way . . . you will never change; and the words of your part on this stage are irrevocably written down' (144). Markheim's eventual decision to surrender to the police apparently disproves this 'moral horoscope', and he clearly sees it as an assertion of free will (charged with 'a fresh resolve to be myself', 'I become in all things a free actor in this world') (144, 143). Yet it gives evidence of only a very limited, negative form of choice. Rather than deciding in favour of good, Markheim acts on his 'hatred of evil', goaded by the visitant's feigned advice to kill the returning maid (145). Moreover, by surrendering himself to probable capital punishment, Markheim chooses to opt out of the struggle represented by life: '[i]f I be condemned to evil acts . . . there is still one door of freedom open – I can cease from action. If my life be an ill thing, I can lay it down' (145). Unlike Raskolnikov's surrender to redemptive imprisonment, Markheim's capitulation amounts to a suicidal rejection of life: '[l]ife, as he thus reviewed it, tempted him no longer; but on the farther side he perceived a quiet haven for his bark' (145).[58] For Eigner, Markheim's decision represents 'life-desertion', while for Saposnik it amounts to a 'death-wish'.[59]

Yet despite the renunciatory streak which links Markheim with Stevenson's other self-denying heroes and heroines (Jim Hawkins, Gordon Darnaway, Olalla, et al.), the narrative arguably portrays his decision in a more positive light. As soon as Markheim understands the 'lessons from [his] soul', he proclaims that 'my eyes are opened, and I behold myself at last for what I am' (144). With this rejection of hypocrisy, his dual consciousness too begins to disappear: thus the visitant's features 'brightened and softened with a tender triumph', then gradually 'faded and dislimned' (145). As Egan observes, with Markheim's confession to the maid, the tale 'moves from an interior to an exterior level of consciousness'.[60] More essentially, the shift back to external reality mirrors the fading of the visitant, and thus of the disordered consciousness which he symbolizes.

The interest in the disintegrative tendencies of the human mind evident in Stevenson's 'gothic gnomes' culminated in the publication of *The Strange Case of Dr. Jekyll and Mr. Hyde* in 1886, in which again, and much more famously, the dissolution of individual identity leads eventually to suicide. Described by Stevenson as a 'shilling shocker', 'gothic gnome', or 'bogey tale', *Jekyll and Hyde* is informed by his wariness about mass-produced popular literature. Indeed, for Richard Boyle and Patrick Brantlinger, *Jekyll and Hyde* is 'an unconscious "allegory" about the commercialization of literature'.[61] Longmans intended the tale for the Christmas 1885 market (though publication was delayed until January), and it was indeed received as an – albeit somewhat unseasonal – Christmas 'crawler': ' "Jekyll and Hyde" ', the *British Weekly* critic opined, 'is the greatest triumph extant in Christmas literature of the morbid kind'.[62] Stevenson's comments on the tale in his letters reflect his unease with its commercial impetus: 'I drive on with *Jekyll*, bankruptcy at my heels', he wrote to his wife, while to Colvin he sardonically proclaimed, 'I am pouring forth a penny (12 penny) dreadful; it is dam dreadful'.[63] Even favourable reviewers (and most were highly favourable) contrasted its superficially popular format with its profundity. For Julia Wedgwood,

Jekyll and Hyde was 'a shilling story, which the reader devours in an hour, but to which he may return again and again, to study a profound allegory and admire a model of style'.[64] The *Academy* reviewer was even more struck by the incongruity of the novella's packaging: '[it] is not an orthodox three-volume novel; it is not even a one-volume novel of the ordinary type; it is simply a paper-covered shilling story, belonging, so far as external appearance goes, to a class of literature familiarity with which has bred in the minds of most readers a certain measure of contempt'.[65] Yet 'in spite of the paper cover and the popular price', he judged, 'Mr. Stevenson's story distances so unmistakably its three-volume and one-volume competitors, that its only fitting place is the place of honour'.[66]

The contrast between popularity and serious intent which reviewers emphasized exemplifies the duality which is at the core of *Jekyll and Hyde*. In 'A Chapter on Dreams' (1888), Stevenson described how he had 'long been trying to write a story on this subject, to find a body, a vehicle, for that strong sense of man's double being, which must at times come in upon and overwhelm the mind of every thinking creature'.[67] The tale externalizes psychic division even more strikingly than 'Markheim'. Doubleness, indeed, marks all aspects of the narrative, even the tales of its inception. Stevenson's 'Brownies', 'A Chapter on Dreams' suggested, inspired him with the central scene, and thus the novella stemmed from his unconscious as much as his conscious mind.[68] The same essay evokes, in the third person, Stevenson's own experience of dual personality: how he began 'to dream in sequence and thus to lead a double life – one of the day, one of the night'.[69] Intriguingly, his description echoes Jekyll's situation – he dreamt of spending a 'long day in the surgical theatre', and his double life eventually 'sen[t] him, trembling for his reason, to the doors of a certain doctor; whereupon with a simple draught he was restored to the common lot of man'.[70] Fanny Stevenson's account of the tale's origin similarly emphasizes its twofold nature, again invoking the opposition between popular and serious literature. Recalling her original dissatisfaction with the story, she explained that Stevenson had written a merely sensational tale; her criticisms apparently induced him to burn the first draft and rewrite the story as an allegory.[71]

It is perhaps this emphasis on the tale's allegorical significance which has led to its simplification in popular culture, where the 'Jekyll and Hyde personality' has come to symbolize a battle between good and evil. This process began almost immediately – in sermons such as the Reverend Dr Nicholson's, reported in the *Leamington Spa Courier* in 1888, and in Graham Balfour's account of how Stevenson came to write the tale.[72] 'A subject much in his thoughts at this time', Balfour wrote, 'was the duality of man's nature and the alternation of good and evil; and he was for a long while casting about for a story to embody this central idea'.[73] Balfour clearly echoes Stevenson's words in 'A Chapter on Dreams' but recasts them in terms of a more clear-cut morality. The tale was thus interpreted in terms of a timeless struggle between good and evil, or read as a Christian parable of God and devil. In the last forty years, however, and especially from the 1980s, critics have resolutely rehistoricized the novella, examining how its imagination of psychological disintegration engages with a host of *fin-de-siècle* concerns.

Jekyll and Hyde's contemporary resonances are clear. While his other 'gothic gnomes' are set in a past which is distanced according to Gothic convention, *Jekyll and Hyde* is firmly set in the modern metropolis. Its portrayal of seedy Soho life clearly relates to contemporary concerns about 'Outcast London'. Stevenson's Soho (its 'dingy street . . . gin palace . . . ragged children huddled in the doorways . . . [and] women of many different nationalities') is a version of the East End, its threat intensified by its proximity to the West End (48). The horror unfolds within a self-consciously civilized and modern milieu: that of a comfortably middle-class, professional, and male London. The novella, moreover, belongs to a nascent, thoroughly modern genre, the detective story, although its narrative form – an assemblage of collated testimonies – is also shaped by Gothic generic conventions. The first two-thirds of the narrative recount the lawyer Utterson's attempts to fathom Jekyll's secret; Dr Lanyon's first-person narrative follows, in the form of a letter to Utterson; and finally Jekyll's own testimony unveils the origins of the horrors witnessed by the other characters. The narrative's presentation as a 'Case' indicates its affiliation with modern legal and medical discourses as well as detective fiction, and indeed Utterson and Lanyon approach Jekyll's predicament with the diagnostic tools of their respective professions.

Most importantly for my analysis, Stevenson's novella engages with the 'new sciences' of the degenerationist *fin de siècle* – criminology, criminal anthropology, evolutionist psychiatry, and sexology. Critics have increasingly recognized the importance of these sciences to Stevenson's novella.[74] Stephen Arata and Robert Mighall have compellingly examined *Jekyll and Hyde*'s subversive participation in degenerationist discourses, interpreting Hyde as representing the threat of deviance, returned to haunt the middle-class psyche which constructed it.[75] I shall draw on this reading, but argue that *Jekyll and Hyde*'s depiction of degeneration is shaped by a central tension between inheritance and environment. Despite its apparent allegiance to hereditary models of atavism, the tale goes beyond even 'Olalla' in questioning the hereditary nature of degeneration, and explains individual and cultural malaise in terms of environmental influence. The narrative exposes the residual Lamarckianism at the heart of degeneration theories. As discussed in Chapter 3, degenerationism, despite its emphasis upon heredity, was tacitly reliant on Lamarck's theory of use-inheritance. Even such a strict hereditarian as Maudsley wrote that a 'tendency to mimicry is a natural instinct of the human nervous system', warning that children 'assimilate unconsciously what they feel and see around them', and are thus vulnerable to contracting diseases from their surroundings.[76] This unspoken conflict within degenerationist discourse between heredity and external infection surfaces in Stevenson's novella.

The portrayal of Jekyll's predicament undoubtedly invokes evolutionist ideas about biological inheritance. When Utterson first meets him, Hyde's atavistic appearance is described in terms which echo the criminology and criminal anthropology pioneered by Lombroso and purveyed to British audiences by Havelock Ellis: he 'shrank back' and 'snarled aloud into a savage laugh'; and Utterson sees him as 'hardly human' and 'troglodytic' (39–40). For Jekyll's servant Poole, Hyde is also degenerate: a 'dwarf' and a 'monkey' (97–8). Lanyon, meanwhile, deploys the language of psychiatry. He is 'convinced' by Jekyll's behaviour that he is 'dealing with a case of cerebral disease', and treats Hyde as a 'patient', diagnosing 'hysteria' (77, 78). Interpreting Jekyll/Hyde's behaviour in terms of mental pathology, these characters offer an evolutionist, hereditarian ætiology.

Jekyll's own testimony adheres to a similarly evolutionist explanation. He depicts the human brain as complex and disunified, consisting of different layers of mental organization, developed sequentially over the long evolutionary past. Jekyll rebels against this mixed heritage. He longs to 'reconcile' his psychological drives or at least to attempt the 'separation of these elements', and laments it as the 'curse of mankind that these incongruous faggots were thus bound together'.[77] Jekyll's 'war among my members' has Christian resonances, echoing St Paul's 'law of sin . . . in my members', which 'war[s] against' the 'law of God' (82).[78] Nevertheless, whereas 'Pulvis et Umbra' (1888) tentatively accepts this simple binary model in its depiction of the 'double law of the members and the will', the novella deconstructs it.[79] As Jekyll explains, 'man is not truly one, but truly two. I say two, because the state of my own knowledge does not pass beyond that point . . . man will be ultimately known for a mere polity of multifarious, incongruous and independent denizens' (82).

Jekyll portrays a chaotic *mêlée* of psychological drives. This reading chimes with evolutionist understandings of identity, evoking what F. W. H. Myers would slightly later call 'the multiplex and mutable character of that which we know as the Personality of man'.[80] Although John Herdman sees Stevenson's tale as dependent on 'crude scientism' or 'pseudo-science', and deficient in earlier writers' understanding of the 'reality of the spiritual world', Hyde clearly emerges from Jekyll's incoherent psyche.[81] The drug he compounds, Jekyll insists, does not *create* anything; it only unleashes the constituent elements of his psychological disposition (85). Myers captured this point in the series of excited letters he fired off to Stevenson, hailing *Jekyll and Hyde* as a modern masterpiece (but noting errors committed 'for want of familiarity with recent psychophysical discussions').[82] Myers glossed Hyde's 'permanent state' as the 'stabler and intenser reproduction' of Jekyll's moments of lawlessness.[83]

Jekyll's account resonates powerfully with cases of multiple consciousness, which in the 1870s and 1880s were being explored in French evolutionist psychiatry and discussed for British audiences by Myers and others.[84] Stevenson's familiarity with psychological debates about 'multiplex personality' is questionable. Fanny Stevenson wrote that her husband first encountered the idea for *Jekyll and Hyde* in a 'French scientific journal on sub-consciousness', but Stevenson claimed not to have heard of multiple personality until Myers sent him a paper after *Jekyll and Hyde*'s publication.[85] Despite his denial, it is perhaps likely that he read the scientific popularizer Richard Proctor's 'Dual Consciousness' (1877), which appeared in the same *Cornhill Magazine* volume as an article by Stevenson, at a time when he was a regular contributor.[86] Whether or not he knew of these developments, his novella certainly engages with the same issues, taking up for instance the question of moral responsibility raised by Proctor.[87] Jekyll attempts to avoid responsibility for Hyde's murder of Carew, alluding to 'the infamy at which I thus connived (for even now I can scarce grant that I committed it)' – an evasion which taps into vexed debates about criminal responsibility and insanity (87).[88] Moreover, some contemporary scientists used Stevenson's work to validate a hereditarian ætiology of dual consciousness. Discussing an otherwise respectable gentleman troubled by an apparently inexplicable urge to steal, the American writer Smith Baker invoked the tale, noting, 'I find that he was born of a parentage representing on the one hand, honor, and probity and trustworthiness; but on the other hand, just a generation back, a number of petty thieves, sexual perverts and dandified mediocres – giving a typical ground field for the Jekyl-Hyde [*sic*] personality'.[89]

Jekyll's narrative also follows hereditary models of atavism, which saw the most recently acquired functions, less firmly embedded in the mind, as the first to disintegrate.[90] As Hyde gradually gains predominance, Jekyll fears an atrophy of the will, which alone can control the lower instincts, and the consequent danger that 'the power of voluntary change be forfeited' (89). He confesses that 'I had voluntarily stripped myself of all those balancing instincts by which even the worst of us continues to walk with some degree of steadiness among temptations' (90). He also reads Hyde's murder of Carew as evidence of moral insanity – a frequent diagnosis within *fin-de-siècle* degenerationist discourse (90).[91] Jekyll's account is a devolutionary narrative. He portrays Hyde as atavistic, twice referring to his behaviour as 'ape-like' (96, 97). Indeed, he imagines Hyde as having regressed even further down the evolutionary ladder, describing him as 'inorganic' (95). This imagery resonates with contemporary evolutionist visions of the origin of life. T. H. Huxley, peering 'beyond the abyss of geological recorded time', had pictured the 'evolution of living protoplasm from not living matter'.[92] Jekyll's words convey his horror at the materialist explanation of descent: '[t]his was the shocking thing; that the slime of the pit seemed to utter cries and voices; that the amorphous dust gesticulated and sinned; that what was dead, and had no shape, should usurp the offices of life' (95). Interestingly, it is evolutionary progress as much as degeneration that is seen as grotesque: the 'slime of the pit . . . utter[ing] cries', the inorganic becoming organic. This vision of evolution – and devolution – as monstrous recurs throughout neo-Gothic fiction. In H. Rider Haggard's *She* (1887), Ayesha shrivels up like a 'monkey', and in Machen's *The Great God Pan* the anti-heroine's body 'descend[s] to the beasts', then plunges into 'the abyss of all being', before finally becoming 'a substance as a jelly'.[93]

Thus Stevenson's tale represents the atavism unveiled by evolutionist psychiatry, which focused on the survival of primitive elements in human consciousness. Savage instincts, or what Jekyll calls 'lower elements', endure amid civilization, and Jekyll's repudiation of Hyde ('[h]e, I say – I cannot say I') amounts to a refusal to countenance the mixed human condition (83, 94). His loathing of the 'thought of the brute that slept within' is not so far from the response of the young man in *New Arabian Nights* (1878) who cannot live knowing that he is 'descended from an ape' (94).[94]

Yet despite the novella's apparent evolutionism, it also highlights tensions within degenerationist theory, between heredity and infection by others. Implicitly questioning the power of heredity, the tale explains devolution rather in terms of environmental influence. Jekyll's environment is imperative. Reversionary dangers are located within the urban, professional world. For while many degenerationists found atavism in the brutalized working classes of 'Outcast London', others such as Edwin Ray Lankester focused on the dangers of overcivilization.[95] In his essay 'The Day After Tomorrow' (1887) Stevenson attributes degeneration to modernity's attempts to stifle the savage elements which have survived in the modern psyche. The essay shares with some degeneration theorists a belief that humanity needs the galvanizing effects of fear if it is not to stagnate, with the picture of the bourgeois 'too much cottoned about for any zest in living' anticipating H. G. Wells's Eloi in *The Time Machine* (1895).[96] (The essay's politics, though, diverge from those of Wells: Stevenson is sceptical about socialism as well as capitalism, fearing it will offer the 'stall-fed life of the successful ant-heap'.)[97] Stevenson condemned modernity as enervating because it provided too much security and comfort. Humanity, he argued, needed to be subjected to risk and danger: '[i]t is as old . . . as man. Our race has not been strained for all these ages through that sieve of dangers that we call Natural Selection, to sit down with patience in the tedium of safety; the voices of its fathers call it forth'.[98] For Stevenson, the need for insecurity was part of humankind's 'primitive' heritage, and fear and hazard were life enhancing.

Jekyll's problems, like those of the essay's modern city dwellers, stem not from his savage instincts *per se*, but from his culturally informed anxiety to deny this biological heritage, his desire to 'wear a more than commonly grave countenance before the public' (81). Even before Hyde's emergence, his concealment of his pleasures leads him to 'a profound duplicity of life' (81). Jekyll is at pains to stress the relative innocence of his misdemeanours, claiming that his 'dual nature' is caused by 'the exacting nature of my aspirations, [rather] than any particular degradations in my faults' (81). Stevenson uses Jekyll's dilemma to exemplify the hypocrisy of a professional class whose idol is reputation, and whose business it is to deny the primitive or animal side of human nature. The threat of blackmail stalks the narrative. When Hyde buys off threats of scandal with Jekyll's cheque, Utterson betrays his allegiances by sympathizing with 'an honest man paying through the nose for some of the capers of his youth' (33). The men's gender politics are clear. As Arata points out, '[t]he homosocial bonding' is 'intensified by its overt misogyny': after Hyde attacks a young girl, Enfield concentrates on shielding Hyde from the 'harpies' who threaten him (32).[99] Throughout the narrative, the professional men close ranks to protect Jekyll's reputation: even after the discovery of Hyde's body, Utterson's main concern, rather absurdly, is 'to save his credit' (73).

The question of whether Jekyll/Hyde's misdemeanours are specifically sexual in nature has long exercised critics. Stephen Heath has explored the novella's affinities with contemporary sexology, arguing that by excluding women *Jekyll and Hyde* directs attention to a problematic male sexuality.[100] Certainly, for some contemporary readers, the sexual implications were clear. The American sexologist Edward Charles Spitzka, describing a patient who, '[a]s his appearance suggested', was an 'inveterate masturbator', wrote that 'I could not resist the impression that the author of that ingeniously absurd romance, "Dr. Jekyll and Mr. Hyde," had some such person as my patient in his mind when he described the repulsive influence exerted by the latter on persons passing him in the street'.[101] For Spitzka, Stevenson's tale gives fictional authority to the notion that sexual 'deviance' was identifiable by physiognomic signs. Indeed, contemporaries often assumed that sexual pathology was at the heart of Jekyll's dysfunction. Thus in the article on multiple personality discussed above, Smith Baker, describing his patient's 'Jekyl-Hyde [*sic*] personality', notes that he numbered 'sexual perverts' among his ancestors. Later in the same article, Baker – like Stevenson – interprets St Paul's words for an evolutionist age, relating them to the sexological work of the Viennese psychologist Richard von Krafft-Ebing.[102] The new *fin-de-siècle* science of sexology was centrally concerned with the classification of homosexuality, and many critics have read *Jekyll and Hyde* as, in Elaine Showalter's words, 'a fable of . . . homosexual panic, the discovery and resistance of the homosexual self'.[103] Showalter claims that the narrative's frequent references to blackmail indicate its homosexual 'meaning': indeed, the Labouchère Amendment to the 1885 Criminal Law Amendment Act, which criminalized homosexual acts of 'gross indecency', became known as the 'Blackmailer's Charter'.[104]

The history of *Jekyll and Hyde*'s composition, however, suggests a more complex interpretation. Two principal drafts survive: the earliest surviving draft, known as the Notebook Draft, and the manuscript used by Stevenson's London publishers, known as the Printer's Copy.[105] In both, the sexual nature of Jekyll's misdemeanours was more explicit. The Printer's Copy contains a couple of deleted passages in which Utterson speculates that Hyde may be Jekyll's illegitimate son (suggesting that Stevenson envisaged heterosexual rather than homosexual 'deviance').[106] In the earlier Notebook Draft, Jekyll referred to his 'vices' as 'criminal in the sight of the law and abhorrent in themselves' and described himself as 'the slave of disgraceful pleasures'.[107] The latter phrase became 'the slave of certain appetites' in the Printer's Copy; it was omitted altogether from the published version.[108] These changes amount to a toning down of the sexual content, indicating an attempt either to offer more respectable, family reading, or to increase the tale's imaginative reach by making Jekyll's sins less specific, or to bring thematic unity to the tale. The last explanation is most convincing: removing the emphasis on sexual misdemeanour allowed Stevenson to stress instead the dangers of denying primitive instincts. This interpretation is endorsed by Stevenson's own comments in response to a review of Richard Mansfield and T. R. Sullivan's New York stage adaptation of *Jekyll and Hyde*: '[t]he harm was in Jekyll, because he was a hypocrite – not because he was fond of women; he says so himself; but people are so filled full of folly and inverted lust, that they can think of nothing but sexuality. The Hypocrite let out the beast'.[109] There is frequent scepticism about this disavowal. Heath claims that Stevenson's logic is specious, with his description of people full of 'lust' amounting to an admission that Hyde represents sensuality.[110] Nonetheless, Stevenson's phrasing is significant: he refers to 'inverted lust', implying that lust itself is not so problematic as its obsessive disavowal, and its censure in others. Indeed, as Jekyll intimates, his 'morbid sense of shame' is more destructive than his harmless 'irregularities' (81). The process of revision thus shifted the emphasis towards the dangers of hypocrisy, and the harm caused by the stifling and pathologization of sexual desire.

Stevenson's sense, then, that primitive survivals are less threatening than the culturally constructed responses to them shapes the portrayal of Jekyll. Hyde's representation also questions pathological science's focus on savage instincts. His alleged atavism evades explanation by professional classificatory discourses. Thus while Poole, Jekyll, and Utterson echo criminological diagnoses, feminizing Hyde, and affiliating him with the lower classes and non-European natives ('[w]eeping like a woman', 'corded, knuckly [hand]', 'troglodytic'), this tells us more about contemporary fears than about Hyde himself (69, 88, 40). As Arata observes, attention is turned back from Hyde to the 'interpretive procedures' by which the other characters construct him.[111] Legal and medical discourses are also brought to bear on Hyde's pathology. Utterson, as a lawyer, seeks natural, reasonable explanations: he is one 'to whom the fanciful was the immodest', and rejects an account which 'doesn't commend itself to reason', looking rather for one that 'is plain and natural, hangs well together and delivers us from all exorbitant alarms' (35, 65, 66). Along with Dr Lanyon, who is – according to Hyde – 'bound to the most narrow and material views', Utterson is of course balked of his desire for a natural explanation (80). Hyde famously eludes both language (onlookers are haunted by a sense of 'unexpressed deformity') and the gaze (he has never been photographed) (50). For M. Kellen Williams, this elusiveness indicates Stevenson's doubts about what he saw as the parallel projects of literary realism and pathological science, and their doomed attempts to represent the deviant body.[112] Utterson's attempt to put Hyde's menace into words has affinities with what Stevenson castigated as realism's compulsion to render 'all charactered and notable, seizing the eye'.[113]

Not only does Hyde evade professional classification, but descriptions of his supposed atavism in fact represent his observers' degeneracy. The intriguing nature of Hyde's atavism, as Arata and Mighall have recognized, is that it resides in the eye of the beholder.[114] This accounts for what Stephen Heath describes as the unsatisfactory nature of Hyde's violence (though for Heath this is because it elliptically expresses the 'sexual drive').[115] The focus is hardly ever on Hyde himself, but rather on his observers, and it is they who become subject to what contemporaries understood as primitive emotions and intuitions. Utterson, lying in wait for Hyde, hears the footsteps which herald his approach 'with a strong, superstitious prevision of success' (38). Hyde has an overpoweringly physical effect on those who witness him: the unemotional Edinburgh doctor turns 'sick and white with the desire to kill him' (31). Lanyon, trying to treat Hyde as a patient, feels so unwell that, in Mighall's words, he is 'forced to attend to his own "symptoms"', and '[m]orbidity is transferred from the "patient" to the doctor'.[116]

It is clear that those who experience these feelings mimic Jekyll's own pangs on turning into Hyde, his 'horrid nausea and the most deadly shuddering', indicating the reversionary nature of the reaction (92). As Lanyon judges of his own symptoms of loathing, 'I have since had reason to believe the cause to lie much deeper in the nature of man' (77). Although he claims that this cause 'turn[s] on some nobler hinge than the principle of hatred', his failure to accept the multiplicity of human nature ('I shall die incredulous') undercuts this interpretation, suggesting that his reaction is indeed an atavistic response (77, 80). The instinctive rather than rational nature of responses to Hyde is captured by the butler Poole when he affirms that he has seen Hyde in Jekyll's laboratory. He reminds Utterson of the peculiar feelings Hyde arouses, and then describes how, on catching sight of a 'masked thing', a feeling 'went down my spine like ice. O, I know it's not evidence . . . I'm book-learned enough for that; but a man has his feelings; and I give you my bible-word it was Mr Hyde!' (68). In common with Utterson and Lanyon, Poole experiences in Hyde's vicinity a regression from the realm of reason to that of powerful yet inarticulate feeling. The shrinking aversion which onlookers allegedly displayed in the company of a criminal was also a theme of contemporary criminal anthropology.[117] As described in Havelock Ellis's *The Criminal* (1890), this feeling of intuitive disgust is a hereditary memory, an echo of the ancestral fear of predators.[118]

While Havelock Ellis attributes this aversion to the fear of predators, the narrative suggests that it stems from the characters' fear of their own inner savagery. Thus some characters are relatively unaffected by Hyde. As Eigner observes, Hyde disturbs most seriously those who cannot accept their own duality or multiplicity: whereas the shock kills Lanyon, it 'merely provides an anecdote for Enfield, the man about town'.[119] Utterson, Lanyon, and Poole are unsettled by Hyde because they reject the savage side of their own nature (the dry rationality of both Utterson and Lanyon underscores their repudiation of the wild and irrational). Their atavistic responses therefore spring not from heredity but from cultural beliefs – about the importance of denying savagery. Significantly, atavism also needs to be activated by external influence. The almost infectious aspect of primitive resurgence, evident in these characters' responses to Hyde, underpins much late-Victorian psychology. Increasingly, contagion was privileged over heredity as the trigger for degeneration.[120] Sully and the physician Daniel Hack Tuke both believed that sympathetic identification could spark suffering and illness.[121] Early crowd theory was notably indebted to this model: Gustave Le Bon's *The Crowd: A Study of the Popular Mind* (tr. 1896) held the allied action of heredity and contagion to determine the behaviour of crowds.[122] The narrative shares this new emphasis: as the focus on Hyde's antagonists indicates, it is preoccupied by the contagious nature of his atavism rather than by Hyde himself.

Thus *Jekyll and Hyde* suggests that atavism is prompted by external influences, destabilizing a reading of degeneration based in hereditary determinism. Hyde's effect on his onlookers, his ability to awaken their latent primitive inheritances, taps into Stevenson's uneasiness about the contaminating nature of popular literature and Gothic 'crawlers'. Indeed, the physical response to Hyde which is experienced by Utterson, Lanyon, et al. is undoubtedly envisaged as being shared by the novella's readers, who are construed as interpreting the narrative in similar ways to those in which these characters read Hyde's body. For Stevenson and his contemporaries, reading 'shilling shockers' such as *Jekyll and Hyde* was itself an atavistic experience: as *The Times* reviewer judged, the novella was 'supremely sensational'.[123] For the *Birmingham Daily Post* reviewer, Stevenson's tale was 'a mere bit of catch-penny sensationalism' which demeaned both author and readers: '[i]t is as though a great sculptor should spend his time in making bogie turnip-lanterns to frighten children'.[124]

Jekyll and Hyde was published during what amounted to a moral panic about sensational literature and delinquency. Some of this concern coalesces in *Jekyll and Hyde*, where popular literature is associated with deprivation and crime: 'a shop for the retail of penny numbers' features alongside gin-palaces in Stevenson's Soho, and Utterson hears 'news boys . . . crying themselves hoarse along the footways: "Special edition. Shocking murder of an M.P." ' (48, 53). Most intriguingly, commentators on the gruesome murders of East End prostitutes in autumn 1888, attributed to the shadowy figure of 'Jack the Ripper', frequently invoked Stevenson's tale. For Mighall, this shows how quickly *Jekyll and Hyde* became 'a part of popular legend'.[125] Indeed, on 8 September the *East London Advertiser* described Jack the Ripper as 'another Hyde', while a month later it proposed the 'Jeckyll [*sic*] and Hyde theory, namely, that the murderer is a man living a dual life, one respectable and even religious, and the other lawless and brutal'.[126] More broadly, links drawn between Jekyll/Hyde and the Ripper demonstrate anxiety that fiction and drama could corrupt readers and viewers, and trigger their primitive desires. During the West End run of the Mansfield–Sullivan production of *Jekyll and Hyde*, which opened in August 1888, *Punch* condemned the lurid advertisements for 'certain dramas', deploring their effect on 'the morbid imagination of unbalanced minds', and blaming them for the 'horrible crimes in Whitechapel'.[127] Eventually, in October, the Ripper hysteria led to the production's closure. As the *Daily Telegraph* opined, 'there is no taste in London just now for horrors on the stage. There is quite sufficient to make us shudder out of doors'. Announcing Mansfield's intention to appear in a comedy, the paper applauded his 'determination to show us, before he leaves England, a pleasant side of human nature in contrast to the monsters he has conjured up'.[128] One terrified drama-goer even suspected that Mansfield was guilty of the murders – in a letter to the police, this correspondent cited the actor's murderous fury on the stage as evidence that he was Jack the Ripper.[129]

If the novella's embroilment in the Ripper hysteria illustrates some contemporaries' fears about sensationalizing crime, others feared that the very process of reading the book might be degenerative. Stimulating supposedly primitive emotions of fear and horror in its readers by portraying Jekyll's increasingly attenuated power of volition, the narrative ironically appeared to run the risk of weakening their own willpower and self-control. J. A. Symonds protested that the novella's denial of the human dignity embodied in free will 'left . . . a deeply painful impression on [his] heart'.[130] The secret duality of Jekyll's life no doubt struck a particularly raw nerve in Symonds, whose *Memoirs* record his attempts to repress his homosexuality, but his letter makes clear that the tale distressed him more generally because of its potential effect on individual willpower. Symonds berated Stevenson for writing 'a dreadful book, most dreadful because of . . . a shutting out of hope'.[131] Interestingly, Symonds believed that art should offer a defence against despair, and consequently felt let down by Stevenson:

> [p]hysical and biological Science on a hundred lines is reducing individual freedom to zero, and weakening the sense of responsibility. I doubt whether the artist should lend his genius to this grim argument. Your Dr Jekyll seems to me capable of loosening the last threads of self-control in one who should read it while wavering between his better and worse self.[132]

Feeling that 'human dignity' has been undermined by Stevenson's art, Symonds counter-attacked by branding Stevenson a 'sprite', and suggesting that 'there is something not quite human in your genius'.[133] Symonds's bitterness illustrates just how much he feared that works such as *Jekyll and Hyde* could trigger a desuetude of will which would return humankind to a quasi-bestial condition.

As Symonds's emphasis on the questions about willpower raised by '[p]hysical and biological Science' suggests, *Jekyll and Hyde*'s portrayal of psychological disintegration engages with *fin-de-siècle* degenerationist sciences. Highlighting the tensions between nature and nurture, *Jekyll and Hyde* questions the hereditary nature of degeneration even more forcefully than 'Olalla', and draws attention to the rôle of the cultural environment in triggering degeneration. Jekyll's tragedy stems not from his savage instincts but from his culturally informed attempts to deny them, to stifle his 'lower elements'. Equally, Hyde's representation unsettles the degenerationist emphasis on inherited, 'visible vice', pointing instead to the importance of cultural beliefs and to the contagious nature of degeneration.

Stevenson's concerns about degeneration, I have argued, provide a focal point around which his writings coalesce. His autobiographical writing resonates with *fin-de-siècle* apprehensions about mental disintegration. His letters, memoirs, and essays evoke an overimaginative childhood, the psychological turbulence caused by his loss of faith, and an embattled masculinity. More broadly, his representation of his own 'borderlands' explores the tensions within degenerationist theory over the respective influence of inheritance and environment. Throughout his life, Stevenson was fascinated not only by racial and inherited psychologies but also by the degenerative potential of culture and habit. Raising questions about how far inherited pathologies could be triggered by a lack of restraint, or by external, cultural infection, these writings illuminate the uncertain and internally contested nature of late-Victorian degenerationism.

The same concerns about psychological disintegration that haunt his letters reverberate through the cluster of neo-Gothic fictional narratives which Stevenson wrote in the first half of the 1880s. These 'gothic gnomes' disclose a central ambivalence about the idea of savage resurgences. Apparently tales of biological atavism, they actually problematize the idea of the 'primitive'. In 'The Merry Men', degeneration stems not from wild instincts but from their fanatical repudiation. While critics have often interpreted 'Olalla' as a tale of degeneration proving Stevenson's eugenicist credentials, the narrative is deeply ambivalent about hereditary determinism, drawing attention to the psychological dangers of denying free will. Stevenson's handling of psychological themes became increasingly confident and overt. Thus 'Markheim' externalizes the pathological self-division which was explored more tentatively in 'The Merry Men', and *Jekyll and Hyde* develops this still further. Indeed, the novella, with its contemporary, medical milieu, was widely recognized as engaging with debates about psychological pathology: as Vivian remarks in Wilde's 'The Decay of Lying' (1889), 'the transformation of Dr. Jekyll reads dangerously like an experiment out of the *Lancet*'.[134] Recent criticism has focused on *Jekyll and Hyde*'s questioning of degenerationist discourses. More specifically, I have argued, the narrative exposes the unspoken conflict between hereditary and environmental explanations of degeneration, undermining the emphasis on biology, and suggesting that degeneration stems rather from the refusal to accept savage instincts and from the construction of models of pathology and deviance. The novella's emphasis on cultural contagion invests literature with a grave responsibility, and chimes with contemporary anxieties about popular fiction. Symonds's charge that Stevenson had created a character 'capable of loosening the last threads of self-control' encapsulates fears – fears shared by Stevenson – that Hyde's atavism, and more broadly the neo-Gothic 'crawler', might provoke degenerate responses in vulnerable readers.

Part III
Stevenson as Anthropologist: Culture, Folklore, and Language

> I hit upon a means of communication which I recommend to travellers. When I desired any detail of savage custom, or of superstitious belief, I cast back in the story of my fathers, and fished for what I wanted with some trait of equal barbarism . . . the black bull's head of Stirling procured me the legend of Rahero; and what I knew of the Cluny Macphersons, or the Appin Stewarts, enabled me to learn, and helped me to understand, about the Tevas of Tahiti. The native was no longer ashamed, his sense of kinship grew warmer, and his lips were opened. It is this sense of kinship that the traveller must rouse and share.[1]

In this passage from *In the South Seas* (1896), Robert Louis Stevenson famously evokes a 'sense of kinship' between Scottish traveller and Polynesian native – a bond which he suggests is engendered by the affinities between Scottish and Polynesian legend. Stevenson, who elsewhere mocks the glib condescension of many European travel writers, clearly believes that his recitation of Scottish lore has banished the 'shame' inherent in the cross-cultural encounter, and that his own Scottishness thus renders him a more enlightened observer of native cultures. Yet the connection is not straightforward. As Vanessa Smith observes, the 'apparently even exchange remains weighted in favour of the materially stronger culture', while for Rod Edmond it is an opportunistic analogy, a strategic move to 'settl[e] the unease provoked by strangeness'.[2] Most importantly, it is ambivalent because the parallel is not one between contemporaneous cultures. Stevenson must 'cast back in the story of [his] fathers' to find folk tales which match those of contemporary Polynesia: it is the Scottish past which allows him to enter imaginatively into modern Pacific culture. This interest in the endurance of savagery in the modern world is at the heart of much of his work, forming a unifying thread running through his Scottish and Polynesian writings.

Stevenson's fascination with folklore has long been recognized, but critical specialization has often led to divergent readings of his Scottish and Polynesian work. Critics have convincingly positioned his engagement with Scottish folklore within a specifically Scottish literary tradition.[3] Frequently, his concern with the Scottish past has been read rather negatively, as sentimental recompense for an inability to deal with contemporary Scotland.[4] Meanwhile, Stevenson's Pacific writings attract increasingly positive attention, and are held to articulate a productive dialogue between local legend and metropolitan narrative.[5] They are regarded as prophetically tackling many issues now confronting a postcolonial world, and thus seem to be in tune with the critical and political interests of the late twentieth and early twenty-first centuries.[6] Clearly there is a need to reconcile these conflicting interpretations of the Scottish and Polynesian Stevensons, to trace his enduring interest in cross-cultural encounter and explore how his early enthusiasm for Covenanting legends modulated into his later interest in Tahitian ballads. Stevenson's lifelong interest in Scottish and Polynesian folklore was the mark of a deeper intellectual preoccupation, a concern with the evolution of cultures and religions, with the relations between past and present, savagery and civilization. The first two parts of this book have considered Stevenson's engagement with evolutionary psychology; this final part turns to his interest in the broader narratives favoured by anthropologists. His concern with the evolution of cultures, I shall argue, tapped into the central concerns of the new evolutionist anthropology. An illuminating figure for the history of the discipline, he exemplifies the intertwined nature of anthropology and creative literature at the *fin de siècle*.

At the beginning of the nineteenth century, evolutionism was largely the legacy of Scottish Enlightenment interpretations of society: Adam Smith, John Millar, Adam Ferguson, and others had emphasized the gradual, developmental progress from primitive to civilized culture, from rudeness to refinement.[7] From mid-century, new life was injected into this idea by the emergence of a secularizing sociocultural evolutionism, as Herbert Spencer, E. B. Tylor, J. F. McLennan, and others examined humankind's mental and cultural evolution, exploring how language, religion, science, and morality had developed as part of a natural progression from savagery to civilization.[8] Often indebted to the Scottish Enlightenment tradition, these thinkers shifted the emphasis from economic explanations to the mental and social factors which determined a society's progress through the evolutionary hierarchy.[9]

The nascent discipline of evolutionary anthropology sprang from this sociocultural evolutionism. Its founding work, Tylor's *Primitive Culture* (1871), proposed a unilinear evolutionary model of culture, where humankind passed inevitably from savagery, through barbarism, to civilization, and where the modern 'savage state' represented 'an early condition of mankind'.[10] Tylor advanced the influential notion of 'survivals', the idea that vestiges of cultural habits and beliefs might be 'carried on by force of habit into a new stage of society'.[11] 'Survivals' were anomalies in his resolutely progressive model of social evolution: he significantly called his work a 'development-theory of culture', and his analysis is marked by an optimistic, quasi-Enlightenment belief in the progress towards an emancipated rationalism.[12] He described the 'science of culture' as pre-eminently a 'reformer's science', and examined different religions, including Christianity, as stages in the natural, upward movement of human spiritual life, claiming that belief in the soul 'unites, in an unbroken line of mental connexion, the savage fetish-worshipper and the civilized Christian'.[13] Tylor's confidence in the forward-moving narrative of cultural evolution set the agenda for the next half-century of anthropological research. Andrew Lang applied Tylor's theories to folklore, proclaiming it his mission to study 'the evolution of [myth, ritual, and religion] from the savage to the barbarous, and thence to the civilised stage'.[14]

The anthropologists' belief in a single evolutionary scale and their confidence in humankind's advance set them apart from Darwin's reading of evolution (as an uncertain and often random process). While some historians have assumed that Darwin inspired 'the science of anthropology', anthropologists were allied more closely with Spencer.[15] Initially prone to erroneous ideas, Spencer's 'primitive man' slowly but surely reached an ever greater correlation between external nature and his own representations.[16] As George Stocking judges, Spencer envisaged an exhilarating narrative of rational emancipation: humankind, though 'natural rather than divine in origin, was nonetheless subject to rational moral purpose; evolution, which linked us to brute creation, enabled us also to transcend it'.[17] By contrast, Darwin's work depicted an evolutionary process which was neither directed, nor progressive, nor unilinear: in Gillian Beer's words, it 'emphasised extinction and annihilation equally with transformation'.[18] Anthropologists fashioned a narrative which was strikingly at odds with Darwin's tale of uncertainty. Evoking the transition from what they deemed traditional to modern culture, they took little account of the bewildering and disruptive nature of the process.

The present discussion traces Stevenson's anthropological concerns chronologically, exploring his central engagement with late-Victorian anthropological debates about primitive culture, cultural change, and the possibility of progress. It argues that he contested the relentlessly progressivist accent of evolutionary anthropology, just as previous chapters showed how he undermined evolutionary psychologists' assumption that the modern European mind had outgrown primitive instincts. Chapter 5 scrutinizes his engagement with distinctively Scottish anthropological concerns, from his early encounters with secularizing anthropology, through the short stories 'The House of Eld' (written in the 1870s but not published until 1895) and 'Thrawn Janet' (1881), to his historical novels, *Kidnapped* (1886) and *The Master of Ballantrae* (1888–89), suggesting that his scrutiny of Scottish culture and history questioned anthropology's vision of a steady progress from savagery to civilization. Chapter 6 shows how his experience of the South Seas heightened his scepticism about a confident evolutionary narrative, and his perception of the savagery lurking at the heart of *soi disant* civilization. It considers the engagement with South Seas folklore in *In the South Seas* (1896) and 'The Beach of Falesá' (1892), and examines how his concern about vulnerable, traditional cultures informs his final Scottish fiction, *Catriona* (1892–93) and *Weir of Hermiston* (1896).

5
'The Foreigner at Home': Stevenson and Scotland

Stevenson engaged eagerly with the new anthropological discourse. As a young man coming to maturity among the 1870s Edinburgh intellectual élite, he enjoyed a ringside seat as mental and spiritual evolution was debated. Indeed, despite the conventional impression that after the 1830s Scotland was unable to sustain a distinctive literary culture, Edinburgh remained a vibrant intellectual capital.[1] The new science of anthropology sprang largely from Scottish soil: J. F. McLennan, Andrew Lang, William Robertson Smith, and J. G. Frazer were all Scots. Robert Crawford describes the interweaving of 'literary and anthropological enterprises' in Scottish culture, and cites the friendship between Stevenson and Lang as exemplary.[2] In the early 1870s, though, Stevenson was yet to meet Lang, and his access to anthropological ideas would have been secured rather through attendance at the Edinburgh Evening Club (as well as through his reading).

The Club, whose members included Robertson Smith, McLennan, and P. G. Tait, Professor of Natural History at Edinburgh University, was described by Robertson Smith's biographers, John Sutherland Black and George Chrystal, as 'the last embodiment of the corporate intellect of Edinburgh'.[3] The Club 'reached the height of its prosperity in the early seventies', when its select membership, drawn from Edinburgh's 'literary and scientific' intelligentsia, included Stevenson's father, Thomas Stevenson.[4] Stevenson himself was a familiar member, his clubbability nostalgically extolled by Black and Chrystal: 'among the younger members there lingered traces of the old-fashioned and now almost obsolete Scotch conviviality, of which Robert Louis Stevenson (himself a junior member of the company) has given some curious glimpses'.[5]

During these years, an interest in the development of religion crystallized as anthropologists' central preoccupation.[6] McLennan, one of the

Club's founding members, developed his theory of totemism in the 1870s (tribes in the totem stage, McLennan explained, believed themselves to be descended from a particular species of animal or plant, which became the object of religious worship).[7] The theory gained many adherents, including William Robertson Smith. As Professor of Hebrew and Old Testament Exegesis at Aberdeen's Free Church College from 1870, Robertson Smith soon achieved notoriety for his biblical scholarship.[8] By the late 1870s, his belief that the biblical narrative was partly mythological and the Atonement was the refinement of a primitive totemic rite brought official censure. He was summoned to answer charges of heresy before the Church Assembly, and removed from his professorship in 1881; a successful career in the mellower theological climes of Cambridge followed. He became, indeed, a prominent figure in late-nineteenth-century anthropology, his theories about sacrificial ritual inspiring Frazer's epic work, *The Golden Bough* (1890). The dispute nonetheless illustrated the unsettling nature of evolutionist anthropology, closely echoing the controversy provoked by *Essays and Reviews* (1860).[9] As with *Essays and Reviews*, what prompted the outcry was not so much the doctrine of gradual spiritual progress as the implicit reduction of Christianity to the status of a myth. Interestingly, Stevenson was already familiar with Robertson Smith before the founding of the Edinburgh Evening Club: the latter was Tait's assistant at Edinburgh University's Physical Laboratory between 1868 and 1870, when Stevenson was a reluctant student. Tait's biographer recalled Stevenson's lively – and usually errant – intellectual interests: '[w]hen, as frequently happened, Stevenson got weary of reading thermometers or watching the galvanometer light-spot, he easily found some excuse to bring Robertson Smith within hearing and set him and John Murray arguing on the age of the earth and the foundations of Christianity'.[10]

Alongside these scientific naturalizers, the Edinburgh Evening Club harboured its own phalanx of Christian apologists. P. G. Tait and Thomas Stevenson mounted an intellectual defence of Christianity against the incursions of natural science. Black and Chrystal evoke the two friends' doctrinal pugnacity, recalling 'a memorable encounter'

> in which the merits of the theology of the Shorter Catechism were the issue of the battle. The antagonists sat, one on each side of the fireplace, smoking long clay pipes, – Tait, alert, aggressive, and Episcopalian; Stevenson grim, resistive, and Presbyterian, hurling taunts and logic at each other, till they parted, amicable but irreconcilable, in the small hours of the morning.[11]

The defences of a beleaguered Christianity offered by Tait and Thomas Stevenson suggest the tight intellectual nexus of the Evening Club and, more broadly, the professional world of Scottish physics. Adrian Desmond describes the debate between Darwin and William Thomson, later Lord Kelvin, over the origin of life and the age of the earth as a stand-off between 'London naturalizers' and 'the holier physicists of Scotland'.[12] In this controversy, Thomson relied on the support of Tait and his partner in his Atlantic submarine cable enterprise, Fleeming Jenkin.[13] Thomson and Tait, moreover, clearly hoped that their physics would offer the religious assurance which they felt Darwin's science was undermining. In 1875, Tait and the physicist Balfour Stewart published *The Unseen Universe*. An attempt to reconcile the incongruous claims of science and religion, the book deployed the laws of physics to undermine scientific materialism, and to prove the existence, in the 'unseen universe', of an immortal soul.[14] Significantly, Thomas Stevenson's own publication, *Christianity Confirmed by Jewish and Heathen Testimony and Deductions from Physical Science* (1877), drew heavily on *The Unseen Universe*.[15] His Christian apologetics rested on the study of physical phenomena as much as on historical evidence. Denying that biblical miracles 'either controverted or suspended natural laws', he appealed to human experience ('[w]e see, every day of our lives, that natural laws can be made subservient by man to his wishes'), and asked, '[m]ay the Deity not be expected to wield His laws so as to achieve much greater results than His creatures . . . ?'.[16]

Stevenson's religious doubt during the early 1870s is intriguing to consider in the context of this contradictory intellectual milieu – a club which was home both to advanced, secularizing free thinkers and to defenders of the faith.[17] Stevenson was tortured by his parents' charge of 'atheism or blasphemy', feeling that he was 'killing [his] father'.[18] His decision to 'read him some notes on the Duke of Argyll', in the hope of finding common ground, merely exacerbated the rift.[19] Argyll's *The Reign of Law* (1867), a counterblast against the scientific naturalism of Spencer and T. H. Huxley, claimed that evolution was inexplicable unless it were directed by divine will, and invoked humankind's quasi-divine capacity for free will.[20] Stevenson's 'notes' presumably related to his critique of Argyll, in a Speculative Society address entitled 'Law and Free Will – Notes on the Duke of Argyll'.[21] His assumption that his father would 'agree so far and that we might have rational discussion on the rest' was misguided, especially given the affinities between Argyll and Thomas Stevenson.[22] Deploying an argument which Thomas Stevenson echoed a decade later, Argyll insisted that the miraculous, rather than involving a 'violation of the laws of Nature', merely constituted evidence of a higher law, that of the 'Supreme Will'.[23] 'Our own experience', he argued, 'shows that the universal Reign of Law is perfectly consistent with a power of making those laws subservient to design'.[24] For Stevenson, loss of faith precipitated a wholesale realignment of intellectual values and wider loyalties. Frustrated by the vetoing of his proposal for a debate at Edinburgh University's Speculative Society on the topic 'Have we any authority for the inspiration of the New Testament?', he inveighed against the impossibility of 'free speech' in Scotland, 'this . . . country of Pharisees and whiskey'.[25]

During these months, Stevenson sought out, with increasing urgency, opportunities for free thought. By 1874, he was making periodic visits to London, where he enjoyed a liberating literary apprenticeship writing for periodicals, and moving in the same circles as noted evolutionists including Lang, James Sully, and W. K. Clifford. He later reminisced fondly of Clifford's

> noisy atheism . . . It was indeed the fashion of the hour . . . the humblest pleasantry was welcome if it were winged against God Almighty or the Christian Church. It was my own proficiency in such remarks that gained me most credit; and my great social success of the period, not now to be sniffed at, was gained by outdoing poor Clifford in a contest of schoolboy blasphemy.[26]

Although this passage treats his youthful atheism with levity, Stevenson's emotional conflict was serious and painful. An intellectual sympathy with the scientific naturalizers was at odds with deep-rooted family loyalties. This ambivalence emerges in his comments on Clifford's scathing review of *The Unseen Universe*: he enthusiastically hailed it as 'a fine article', while lamenting the sorrow it caused his father.[27]

This experience of family discord coloured Stevenson's attempts to understand cultural evolution, underlining for him the traumatic effects of religious emancipation. His considerations of the development of cultural and religious belief oscillated between the confident, secularizing line taken by anthropologists, and an awareness of the pain and loss embedded in the evolutionary process. Thus, in an undated notebook entry on mythology, Stevenson strikes a resoundingly Tylorian note, describing how

> [t]he old notion of offerings to the dead – of the necessity of a son to each man's body – of the Hindoo name for a son – a deliverer out of hell – of the old Hebrew practice of marrying a brother's widow in

> order to raise up seed to him – and the like, when taken all together and regarded as a universal, or almost universal, phase of human civilisation, may account for the first genesis of the messianic idea.[28]

The piling up of cognate beliefs, and the insistence on the 'universal', points to Stevenson's evolutionist belief in the psychic unity of humankind (evolutionist anthropology rejected the belief that the human races were originally distinct, attributing cultural difference rather to varying rates of evolution). He traces the origins of the Jewish faith not to divine revelation, but to primitive sacrificial ritual, and then figures Christianity itself as a step in the development of increasingly refined religious ideas:

> [t]he notion becoming gradually more and more abstract . . . might easily enough result in some abstract and refined dogmas as that of the Jewish Messiah, and in its further development into that of the world-saviour, Christ. This is no fanciful course for doctrine to follow; all religious dogma, without exception, tending finally to become ever more sublimated and more generalised, until like a circle in the waters, it dissipates itself into a non-existence . . . we find God gradually withdrawn from all nature to a mere residual mystery, and the Saviour sublimated out of a personality, into a mere type of self-suffering and thus self-redeeming mankind.[29]

The vocabulary of 'development', 'refinement', and 'sublimation' taps into Tylor's evolutionary progressivism, with the naturalistic interpretation of the 'genesis of the messianic idea' highlighting the mythological nature of Christian theology. The passage reveals the double-edged nature of the anthropological enterprise, its capacity to unsettle but also to reassure. Anthropology forges unexpected links between savagery and civilization, bringing Tylor's 'savage fetish-worshipper' and 'civilised Christian' into disturbingly close contact, but the emphasis on mental emancipation undoubtedly flatters the agnostic Victorian, situated at the top of the evolutionary ladder.

However, Stevenson's intellectual enthusiasm for the anthropological project, signalled by this notebook entry, was tempered by his sensitivity to the suffering and destruction inherent in the evolution of cultural belief. He found in Darwin's work authority for a bleaker reading of the struggle for survival, which emphasized the pain of cultural change. A brief, again undated, entry in Stevenson's notebook also underlines the Darwinian narrative's reliance on rupture and discontinuity. Selection, he observes, is not the only process implicit in the theory of Natural

Selection: 'Darwin is reminding us every page that he postulates "spontaneous variations" or "compensations of growth" or "correlated variations" . . . as the material which his selection is to weigh in the balance and keep and cast away as useless'.[30] If 'selection' was the benign side of Darwin's theory, with its suggestion of an anthropomorphic Nature honing and polishing its handiwork, the dark underside was represented by his insistence on inscrutable 'spontaneous variations' – these variations challenged the positive, rationalizing narrative which many interpreters discerned in his work. Stevenson's alertness to this aspect of Darwin's theory suggests the importance of irregularity and unpredictability in his own vision of the evolutionary process.

Stevenson, then, betrayed a fundamental ambivalence towards the secularizing project of evolutionary anthropology, responding to it with intellectual enthusiasm, but also with a mistrust of its overly confident narrative. This concern informs, in varying ways, his Scottish fiction of the 1870s and 1880s, 'The House of Eld', 'Thrawn Janet', *Kidnapped*, and *The Master of Ballantrae*. As Edwin Eigner formatively suggested, Stevenson's fiction portrays the primitive forces lurking beneath a veneer of civilization.[31] More particularly, I shall argue, he engaged with a specifically anthropological understanding of savagery as a survival from past times. Whereas 'survivals' are the exception in Tylor's theory, in Stevenson's fiction primitive impulses survive as a ubiquitous element of human nature, testifying to the stubbornly persistent force of savagery. Challenging anthropologists' confident and ethnocentric assumptions about the evolutionary process, and evincing scepticism about the belief that human nature evolved naturally along a hierarchical scale from savagery to civilization, Stevenson's Scottish fiction also emphasizes the anguish and uncertainty involved in relinquishing traditional beliefs.

'The House of Eld', an austere and moving fable, was probably written in 1874, the year after Stevenson's rift with his parents.[32] It has usually been read as an allegory of oppressive Puritanism, shaped by Stevenson's experience of a rigid and peculiarly Scottish Presbyterianism.[33] However, it is also informed by the more specific context of late-nineteenth-century debates about free thought. It is a parable of the attempt to escape the religion inculcated in childhood, and of the power of superstition over the human imagination. 'So soon as the child began to speak', it begins, 'the gyve [fetter] was riveted; and the boys and girls limped about their play like convicts' (287). When the young hero, Jack, glimpses fetterless strangers, he is warned by his uncle not to envy them: they are 'heathen . . . not truly human – for what is man without a fetter?' (287). Jack is told that he will be struck by a thunderbolt if he removes the fetter, but he questions the strangers, and they reveal that this is a superstition contrived by a sorcerer (287, 288). Jack is moved by pity for the limping, ulcerous children of his village, and feeling that 'he was born to free them' travels to kill the sorcerer (289). He accomplishes this heroically, but in a tragic dénouement discovers that he has killed his uncle, father, and mother, in whose shapes the sorcerer had materialized (292). The fetters fall from the villagers' feet, but they immediately start wearing a fetter on the other foot: 'that was the new wear, for the old was found to be a superstition' (292).

The fable's uneasy blend of reforming zeal and anxiety is resolved in the conservative 'Moral', a poem which underlines the tragic consequences of attempts at intellectual emancipation:

> Old is the tree and the fruit good,
> Very old and thick the wood.
> Woodman, is your courage stout?
> Beware! the root is wrapped about
> Your mother's heart, your father's bones:
> And like the mandrake comes with groans. (292)

The resonances with Stevenson's own family conflict are clear. The imagery of faith as roots entwined around the heart is strikingly prefigured in and reworks a letter written the previous year. Discussing his loss of faith with a confidante, Stevenson professes his desire to pull down 'the pillars of our sick world', but then pauses apprehensively, observing that

> this is no age for these blind, easy-hearted heroisms. One must nowadays be wary and considerate over all; there are fathers and mothers under this hideous roof and our heart-strings have been built in to the walls and buttresses of the infamous temple. The business is carefully to extricate these involved sentiments – tenderly to lead forth into the sunshine and the open air these misled imprisoned loved ones.[34]

The desire to emancipate, to 'lead forth into the sunshine and the open air', represented as a troublingly delicate operation in the letter, becomes even more problematic in the fable. The narrative's Oedipal note distils Stevenson's own anguish that, as he wrote in another letter, his apostasy was 'killing [his] father'.[35] More widely, it resonates with the feelings of a generation of secularizers, caught as many late Victorians were between a reforming impulse and reverence for the inherited fabric of social morality.

The fable celebrates the zealous altruism of Jack's mission, in terms which recall the earnest doubt of contemporary agnosticism: '[h]e was a grave lad; he had no mind to dance himself; he wore his fetter manfully, and tended his ulcer without complaint. But he loved the less to be deceived or to see others cheated' (288). The emphasis on deceit, and the uncle's denial of humanity to non-believers, suggests that religion is an illusion, its edicts not divinely ordained but based in fear. The symbolism is concise and potent: when he arrives at the sorcerer's house, Jack sees 'nowhere any living creature; only the bodies of some stuffed', and observes that 'the ground must be quaggy underneath for at every step the building quakes' (289–90). The house, with its lifeless inhabitants and precarious foundations, is a figure for religious creeds which are decayed and hollow.

Despite the narrative's secularizing impetus, however, it ultimately moves towards scepticism about free thought. By depicting one set of fetters discarded only to be replaced by another, the fable resists evolutionary belief in the progressive emancipation of the mind. The imagery of shackles and chains clearly engages with contemporary debate about the evolution of religious belief. Critics of evolutionary belief in intellectual emancipation often used the trope of superstition as an inescapable shackle. T. H. Huxley, for example, took issue with the idea that the passage from Catholicism to Protestantism marked a milestone on the road to intellectual liberty, noting ruefully that '[o]ne does not free a prisoner by merely scraping away the rust from his shackles'.[36] Stevenson's own father, in an unpublished letter to his son in 1877, castigated proponents of 'Atheistic Morality', including the evolutionary ethicist Leslie Stephen, for weakening Christian belief only to 'bind' humankind with 'chains of their forgery'.[37] He declared,

> I read today with much satisfaction a paper in the 19th. Century . . . against the Atheistic Morality taking very much my view of the subject. I afterwards read or rather glanced over a very unfair paper by L. Stephen who has come out as a *moral prig* . . . I don't like cant of any kind but it is rather too much for such writers to try forcing *their* religion for such they esteem their morality down people's throats . . . Such moral cucumbers as Mr J. Mill & his friends must please dish their cant about duty . . . / Such writers attempt to shake men's faith in Jesus Christ the son of glory & then try to bind them with chains of their forgery. I will have none of them. \[38]

'The House of Eld', while it celebrates the heroic zeal of Jack's mission, shares Thomas Stevenson's scepticism about free thought, using the motif of fetters to question the possibility of intellectual liberation. The implicit suggestion that superstition may be an inescapable element of human mentality is manifestly at odds with anthropologists' reformist confidence that, in Tylor's words, most superstition is 'survival, and in this way lies open to the attack of its deadliest enemy, a reasonable explanation'.[39] In Stevenson's fable, Jack's reforming motives are well intentioned but unavailing. His uncle's catechisms and moralizing parody missionaries' condescension towards 'benighted' heathen: '[a]h, poor souls, if they but knew the joys of being fettered!' (287). Yet, as Jack himself is constrained to use the same biblical language, his attempts to undermine the tyranny of convention are doomed to failure. The fable's opening figures the acquisition of language as imprisonment ('[s]o soon as the child began to speak, the gyve was riveted') (287). Human thought, this suggests, is limited by language, unable to escape its cultural heritage.[40] The fable is clearly shaped by conspicuously contemporary anxieties about proselytizing free thought. It articulates a central tension between the desire to emancipate humankind from the superstitious shackles of outworn creeds, and an uneasy apprehension of the traumatic – and even futile – nature of such an enterprise.

'Thrawn Janet' (1881), a Scottish horror story, dramatizes a similar conflict between enlightenment and an ineradicable supernaturalism.[41] It has conventionally been interpreted as shaped by peculiarly Scottish historical concerns: Stevenson himself set this critical trend, dismissing the tale as 'true for a hill parish in Scotland in old days, not true for mankind and the world', and even Kenneth Gelder's sophisticated analysis makes no mention of the narrative's late-Victorian context.[42] A tale about witchcraft and persecution, set in a Scottish moorland parish and written largely in dialect, it represents the struggle between superstition and tolerance in the early eighteenth century, as memories of the Covenanters and their persecutions at the hands of royalists several decades earlier were gradually fading. In this period, the Covenanters' religious fanaticism and obsession with damnation loosened their hold on Scottish society, and the intensity of the witch-hunts began to ease.[43] The tale, with its interest in the enduring legacies of the supernatural past, is in a literary tradition which we might call Calvinist Gothic, and recalls 'Wandering Willie's Tale' in Walter Scott's *Redgauntlet* (1824), and James Hogg's *The Private Memoirs and Confessions of a Justified Sinner* (1824). The tale also draws on Scott's representation of an untamed female orality: in Penny Fielding's analysis, 'Thrawn Janet' dramatizes the vanquishing of male literacy by the forces of female orality.[44] Yet it is also emphatically late Victorian (published, indeed, in Leslie Stephen's *Cornhill Magazine*), informed by a peculiarly evolutionist interest in the resurgence, or persistence, of primitive states of mind. Like much neo-Gothic fiction of the *fin de siècle*, it engages with a quasi-anthropological vision of savage survivals.

'Thrawn Janet' evokes the beginnings of the new, moderate eighteenth century. Reverend Soulis, the minister who comes to Balweary parish, represents the modern, enlightened spirit. But the narrative, in which Soulis is chastened by what he believes to be a supernatural encounter, figures the power of the irrational, primitive past to haunt the present. The narrative form also enacts this resurgence of superstition on both linguistic and generic levels. The introduction is narrated in English rather than Scots, and in an elevated and educated diction, by a character who appears unfamiliar to the district (205). Caroline McCracken-Flesher observes that this 'tempts the reader to adopt his superior linguistic and cultural perspective and to perceive only a colorful tale of provincial terror'.[45] The introductory narrator describes Soulis's demeanour after the events recounted in the main narrative. No longer a tolerant moderate, the minister now resembles the stern, forbidding Covenanter of old: 'it seemed as if his eye pierced through the storms of time to the terrors of eternity', and his sermons, on the torments of hell, frighten the children into fits (205). When the first narrator hands over to a local resident, 'one of the older folk', to relate the tale, it gradually becomes evident that the rationalist narrative cannot contain the events described (206). Nor, however, is the 'old narrator's account', as Fred Warner argues, simply 'lucid and objective'; rather, the tale dramatizes the conflict between these two perspectives.[46] The narration embodies the return of the primitive past, in the shape of a vigorously oral Scots dialect ('eh! Gude guide us', 'heavy as leed', 'the dunt-dunt-duntin' o' his ain heart') (212, 214). And whereas the first narrator emphasized the fear and uncertainty underlying Soulis's new religious severity, the second narrator offers an alternative moral centre: for him the minister learns a salutary lesson in the reality of Hell and damnation.

The tale of Soulis's experiences offered by the Scots dialect narrator is significantly cast in terms of generational conflict. When the minister arrives in the parish, the 'younger sort were greatly taken wi' his gifts and his gab', while the 'auld, concerned, serious men and women were moved even to prayer for the young man', whom they viewed as 'fu' o' book-learnin' an' grand at the exposition, but, as was natural in sae young a man, wi' nae leevin' experience in religion' (206). They disapprove of the rationalism and scepticism associated with his wide reading and university education, and feel that 'the lads that went to study wi' [college professors] wad hae done mair an' better sittin' in a peat-bog, like their forbears of the persecution, wi' a Bible under their oxter an' a speerit o' prayer in their heart' (207). Braving his parishioners' censure, Soulis pursues his path of enlightened tolerance, and fights against the enduring power of the superstitious past. He engages Janet McClour as his housekeeper, condemning the folk belief that she is 'sib to the de'il' (a belief perhaps related to her liaison with a royalist dragoon quartered in the village during the crushing of the Covenanters): 'it was a' superstition by his way o' it . . . he wad threep it doun their thrapples that thir days were a' gane by, an' the de'il was mercifully restrained' (207). The local womenfolk persist in their fears, and eventually throw Janet in the river 'to see if she were a witch or no, soom or droun'; from that day forth she is struck dumb, and her figure is 'thrawn [twisted]' (208–9). The sense of the uncanny intensifies, with Janet's appearance providing a Gothic prefiguring of her eventual hanging: 'wi' her neck thrawn, an' her heid on ae side, like a body that has been hangit, an' a girn on her face like an unstreakit corp [a body that has not been laid out for burial]' (209). Soulis and his parishioners interpret her change through rival explanations, respectively naturalistic and supernatural. The local folk believe that Janet herself has gone to Hell, and the 'thrawn' figure that remains is the devil, but Soulis resolutely holds to his humane rationalism: 'he preached about naething but the folk's cruelty that had gi'en her a stroke of the palsy' (209). Yet for all his compassion, the minister's almost aggressive repudiation of superstition ('threep it doun their thrapples') perhaps suggests that he is wilfully blind to non-rational, savage energies.

At this stage, Soulis's battle against superstitious prejudice reaches its furthest point, and falters, and the narrow-minded suspicions of the provincial folk are progressively vindicated. Unsettled by his vision of a black man in the churchyard (the traditional appearance of the devil in Scottish folklore), the minister is awakened to the living power of folklore: 'Mr Soulis had heard tell o' black men, mony's the time; but there was something unco [uncanny] about this black man that daunted him' (210). He struggles to retain his enlightened outlook, resisting the 'cauld grue in the marrow o' his banes', and addressing the man in tones of civilized hospitality (210). But he is unable to halt the return of the superstitious past, which is figured as an intensely somatic experience: looking at Janet anew, he has 'the same cauld and deidly grue', and sits 'doun like ane wi' a fever, an' his teeth chittered in his heid' (211). He finds himself regressing to an irrational and hysterical state. His shrinking aversion and sense of the uncanny is a physical response, rooted in instinct rather than reason. Suddenly realizing that Janet was 'deid lang syne, an' this was a bogle in her clay-cauld flesh', he returns to the manse, and finds her hanging in her bedroom; her corpse follows him down the stairs (212–14). Echoing the words of bygone Covenanters, he invokes God's name against Janet, and 'the auld, deid, desecrated corp o' the witch-wife' rises up in flames and falls to the ground in ashes (215). The old folks' fear that Soulis is 'fu' o' book-learnin'' but has 'nae leevin' experience in religion' is borne out, and he is given an encounter which forces him to recognize the dynamic power of 'savage' energies (206).

Soulis's transformation into the austere cleric described in the introduction suggests that educational and religious progress, as embodied in his initial outlook, is illusory. It indicates the enduring potency of fanatical superstition. His conversion to the Covenanters' Manichæan vision of salvation for the Elect and Hell for the Damned figures the power of Scotland's intolerant past to haunt the present. The persistence of the past within a supposedly emancipated present is a recurrent motif within Stevenson's short stories. As discussed in Chapter 4, both 'The Merry Men' (1882) and 'Olalla' (1885) explore the resurgence of savage states of mind and are narrated by characters who, perhaps because they so firmly attempt to distance themselves from the primitive past, gradually succumb to irrational, superstitious behaviour. Like these tales, 'Thrawn Janet' bears the impress of late-Victorian debates about superstition and enlightenment. Stevenson himself was well aware of the contemporary resonances of the tale, recognizing that readers were likely to identify with Soulis's enlightened naturalism. 'Poor Mr. Soukis's [*sic*] faults', he wrote, 'we may equally recognise as virtues; and feel that by his conversion, he was merely coarsened'.[47] That these apparent 'faults' are evidently Soulis's initial, admirable tolerance and respect for Janet's liberty and dignity indicates the uncertain status of his 'conversion'. 'Thrawn Janet' is underpinned by this ambivalence towards a secularizing narrative of cultural evolution. Like 'The House of Eld', it invokes a rationalist progressivism only to undermine it by testifying to the stubbornly persistent force of superstition.

While 'Thrawn Janet' and 'The House of Eld' illuminate contemporary debates about cultural progress by focusing on the battle between superstition and religious tolerance, Stevenson's historical fiction of the late 1880s engages rather differently with the narrative of inevitable advance from savagery to civilization. His historical novels unsettle the progressivist anthropological narrative by exploring critically the effects of the 1707 Act of Union on eighteenth-century Scotland.

Nineteenth-century commentators – anthropologists, folklorists, ethnologists, and historians – often saw contemporary Scotland as a barbarous country compared with its more civilized neighbour. The characterization of the Scottish people, and especially the Highlanders, as uncivilized representatives of an earlier stage of development is familiar from the work of Enlightenment writers such as William Robertson, and from Walter Scott's Waverley Novels.[48] Scott was nostalgically attracted to Scotland's independent past. However, taking his cue from the Scottish Enlightenment writers, he celebrated the 1707 Anglo-Scottish Union as ensuring Scotland's increasing anglicization.[49] He figured his Highland chieftains as anachronistic survivals, valued indeed for their picturesque qualities and, often, their morality and valour, but sacrificed on the altar of Scotland's pacification.[50] Scott's emphasis on improvement meant that he largely avoided dealing with the Highland Clearances.[51] Paradoxically, his encouragement of 'Highlandism', a picturesque myth which was to be highly influential throughout the nineteenth century and beyond, took place while real Highland culture was being destroyed.[52]

Victorian anthropology endorsed this belief, rooted in Enlightenment developmentalism, that the Union helped to civilize the Scots, bringing modernity and prosperity to the Lowlands, and leaving only the Highlands as the 'desolate refuge of a primitive people'.[53] For Tylor, the Hebrides, 'remarkable for a barbaric simplicity of life', provided valuable clues about a largely bygone, savage age: its 'earthen vessels', he wrote, 'might pass in a museum as indifferent specimens of savage manufacture'.[54] He interpreted Gaelic culture as a 'survival' from earlier stages of evolutionary development:

> [s]o the appearance in modern Keltic districts of other widespread arts of the lower culture – hide-boiling, like that of the Scythians in Herodotus, and stone-boiling, like that of the Assinaboins of North America – seems to fit . . . with survival from a low civilization. The Irish and the Hebrideans had been for ages under the influence of comparatively high civilization, which nevertheless may have left unaltered much of the older and ruder habit of the people.[55]

As the analogy between modern Celts and Herodotus' Scythians suggests, Tylor used the Comparative Method, pioneered by Scottish Enlightenment writers and developed by Victorian anthropologists, to rank societies as higher or lower on an evolutionary scale of development.[56] Folklorists followed Tylor in searching Scottish culture for what he described as 'the unchanged survival of savage thoughts in modern peasants' minds'.[57] Lang claimed that 'the Celtic peoples' have 'not lost the old poetical beliefs', and that superstition was not dead, because 'the Highlander is still rich in legends of every sort'.[58] The portrayal of Scotland as anachronistic was strengthened during the nineteenth century by developments in racial science, which confirmed the Celts as a savage people. Where Scotland had achieved progress, ethnologists such as Cosmo Innes and Daniel Wilson suggested, it was due to the Anglo-Saxon population which had settled in the Scottish Lowlands.[59] Historians shared this progressivist emphasis on the Union's 'civilizing' effects, its 'Improvement' of 'backward' regions, and applauded the British government's attempt to integrate the Highlands more fully within the Union following the 1715 and 1745 Jacobite risings. They often treated 1745 as the end of Scottish history, as Scotland became successfully absorbed into an English narrative of steady, evolutionary progress.[60] J. H. Burton's *History of Scotland from the Revolution to the Extinction of the Last Jacobite Insurrection* (1853) ends in 1748 when Scotland became 'completely fused into the great British Empire'.[61]

In his non-fictional and fictional work, Stevenson offered a radical challenge to the dominant meliorist account of Scotland's development. Undercutting the prevailing nineteenth-century interpretation of the Union, he evoked its harmful and divisive effects on a vulnerable culture. His plan to write a history of the Highlands from the quashing of the 1715 Jacobite rebellion indicates the tragic note of the story he wanted to tell.[62] As he explained to Sidney Colvin in 1880,

> [i]t is a most interesting and sad story, and from the '45 it is all to be written for the first time . . . There will be interesting sections on the Ossianic controversy and the growth of taste for Highland scenery. I have to touch upon Rob Roy, Flora MacDonald, the strange story of Lady Grange, the beautiful story of the tenants on the Forfeited Estates, and the odd, inhuman problem of the great evictions.[63]

Stevenson's interest in 'the odd, inhuman problem of the great evictions' and in the neglected aftermath of the '45 ('it is all to be written for the first time') marks his distance from the progressivist interpretation. Sympathy for the dispossessed Highlanders and awareness of the Union's often tragic results may partly have prompted his censure of Scott. Six years earlier, he had criticized Scott's 'snobbery' and 'conservatism', accusing him of taking up 'the wrong thread in History and notably in that of his own land'.[64] Stevenson's position would have had inevitable political implications in the 1880s, when Highland crofters began a campaign of direct action for the return of cleared land.[65] His research even led him to take, albeit temporarily, a radical political position on Irish Home

Rule: '[t]he effect on my mind of what I have read', he wrote, 'has been to awaken a livelier sympathy for the Irish; although they never had the remarkable virtues, I fear they have suffered many of the injustices of the Scottish Highlanders'.[66]

The Scottish historical novels for which Stevenson is most famous, *Kidnapped* and *The Master of Ballantrae*, are similarly distinguished by an underlying pessimism. Stevenson's historical novels are frequently censured for their perceived nostalgic romanticism. Like Scott, he is routinely accused of producing historical fiction as an escapist compensation for his more prosaic accommodation with Unionism.[67] Despite their resonances with Scott's work, however, Stevenson's historical novels abjure the meliorist account of Scotland's gradual progress from a savage past to an enlightened and prosperous present, and of the Highlanders as barbarous remnants of primitive culture. Destabilizing the progressivist narrative, they portray a tragically divided nation – a nation whose divisions stem largely from the Union – and raise disquieting questions about the relations between savagery and civilization, and the possibility of an objective ethnographic enterprise.

Kidnapped (1886) advertised itself as an adventure novel: like *Treasure Island* and *The Black Arrow*, it was serialized in *Young Folks*. In the self-deprecating 'Dedication', Stevenson protested that the book was 'no furniture for the scholar's library', and that its purpose was merely to 'carry [its young reader] awhile into the Highlands and the last century, and pack him to bed with some engaging images to mingle with his dreams'.[68] Modern criticism has often concurred with this picture of *Kidnapped* as an escapist, anodyne novel. Noble argues that both *Kidnapped* and its sequel *Catriona* answer the Victorian 'need for Highland life as pagaentry'.[69] He claims that both novels have an 'essentially comic plot', and that this 'Scott-derived narrative form' thwarts the tragic 'Highland story Stevenson seemed to wish to tell'.[70] Contemporary opinion was interestingly divided. Some reviewers thought *Kidnapped* merely picturesque and charming. R. H. Hutton pronounced it 'delightful' for all 'lovers of Scotch scenery and Scotch character', praised its 'picture of Highland character' as 'worthy of Sir Walter Scott himself', and noted in relief, '[n]or is there in this delightful tale the least trace of [*Jekyll and Hyde*'s] evil odour'.[71] Other reviewers, however, recognized its darker and more politically charged side; as the *Saturday Review* critic wrote of one passage, '[n]o one can read this admirable, and no doubt essentially truthful, dialogue without thinking of Ireland, and making his own reflections'.[72]

In *Kidnapped*, Stevenson radically recasts the adventure novel. The hero's adventures in an alien culture destabilize the possibility of truly understanding 'other' cultures, and the narrative engages critically with anthropology, contesting the progressive narrative of cultural evolution. Set in the eighteenth-century Scottish Highlands, the novel uses a Lowland hero, David Balfour, to guide the reader through a territory which is remote historically, geographically, and – most important – ethnographically. Ethnographic novels, James Buzard contends, study a people's way of life, their narrative mode anticipating 'the method of "immersion" in extensive fieldwork' and raising questions about whether 'the outsider can become a kind of honorary insider in other cultures'.[73] *Kidnapped* is an ethnographic novel in this sense, with David's tour of the Highlands prefiguring Stevenson's self-conscious performance of the rôle of ethnographer in the South Seas. *Kidnapped* draws on Scott's use of a fictional hero to conduct the reader through an exotic Highland culture in *Waverley* (1814) but, by contrast with the Englishman Waverley, David is a Lowlander, an exile in his own land. His Lallans speech and Covenanting ways alienate him from Highlanders as much as Englishmen. This estrangement undercuts the myth of 'Highlandism', whereby all Scots could claim a tartan heritage and a Lowlander such as Scott could 'assert an *auto*ethnographic' authority over the Highlands.[74] *Kidnapped* suggests rather that the Lowland traveller is unable fully to understand the territory he explores. The novel contrasts with *Waverley*, which Buzard describes as 'mediated through, directed toward, and "translated into" England and English'.[75] *Kidnapped* does register metropolitan pressures: Stevenson regretted having to tone down David's Lallans for the sake of English readers, explaining that

> it's Scōtch: no strong, for the sake o' they pock-puddens, but jist a kitchen o't, to leeven the wersh, sapless, fushionless, stotty, stytering South-Scotch they think sae muckle o'.[76]

Nevertheless, despite the modulation of David's 'Scōtch', the central relationship is between Lowlander and Highlander, not between the English centre and Scottish periphery. While Stevenson pays attention to the linguistic barriers separating David from what he calls 'the right English speech' (he confesses himself still unused to 'the English grammar, as perhaps a very critical eye might here and there spy out even in these memoirs'), the crux of the narrative is the Lowlander's changing perception of the Highlander (141).

Kidnapped portrays a divided nation – a nation in which the Union exacerbates the conflict between Highlander and Lowlander. Stevenson had explored this gulf in an earlier essay, which characterized Scots as divided by race, language, and politics, 'foreigners at home', yet claimed that 'the Lowlander feels himself the sentimental countryman of the Highlander'.[77] As is usual in Stevenson's œuvre, the optimism is lost in the translation from essay to novel, and David struggles to find himself the Highlander's 'sentimental countryman'. At the novel's opening, the innocent young hero has no experience of Scotland beyond his small community of Lowland Whigs, loyal to the Hanoverian succession, the Presbyterian settlement, and the mercantile interests fostered by Union with England. Travelling into the Highlands after the 1745 Jacobite rising, he becomes embroiled in the 1752 'Appin murder' (the murder of the King's factor, Colin Campbell, while he was evicting tenants from the forfeited estate of a rebel chieftain).[78] David and the fiery Highlander Alan Breck Stewart become the immediate suspects; when they escape, Alan's kinsman James Stewart is arrested as a convenient scapegoat. David is slow to comprehend the harsh rules of the political world, where a vengeful Campbell clan will not scruple to secure the conviction of a Stewart, whether guilty or innocent. His naïvety concerns the idea of nationhood: he protests that 'I have no fear of the justice of my country' (124). Alan responds with exasperation, '[a]s if this was your country!'. Scorning David's belief that '[i]t's all Scotland', Alan explains, '[t]his is a Campbell that's been killed. Well, it'll be tried in Inverara, the Campbell's head place; with fifteen Campbells in the jury-box, and the biggest Campbell of all (and that's the Duke) sitting cocking on the bench. Justice, David?' (124).

The 'Highland Line' clearly marks a cultural as well as a geological frontier. Raised in a peaceful, law-abiding Lowland society which respects the values of religion, property, and a nascent capitalism, David initially objects to Alan's Highland morals, with their exclusive emphasis on clan loyalty, honour, and courage. As Stephen Shapiro contends, David's encounter with Highland society is 'about the historical cross-over from an older socio-economic system to an emergent one'.[79] The clash is nicely caught by David's introduction of himself as a landowner ('David Balfour . . . of Shaws'), and Alan's scornful response, '[m]y name is Stewart . . . A king's name is good enough for me, though I bear it plain and have the name of no farm-midden to clap to the hind-end of it' – a rebuke which pits dynastic and clan loyalties against the values of private property (62). David's ignorance of his own family history shocks the Highlanders and, as Shapiro notes, intimates that 'he will look to secure his inheritance through the English State's court-machinery rather than Scottish tribal honor'.[80]

During his adventures above the 'Highland Line', David gradually learns about the 'other', his immersion in an alien culture foreshadowing the method of 'participant observation' which was to be at the core of twentieth-century ethnography.[81] The obstacles to understanding and empathy are constantly emphasized, with David frequently insisting on his ignorance ('[i]f I had been better versed in these things, I would have known the tartan to be of the Argyle (or Campbell) colours') (116). Initially, he resists the rôle of committed ethnographer, preferring to portray himself as frivolous tourist, and he abandons his serious reflections on Highland society, noting that, '[t]o be sure, this was no concern of mine, except in so far as it entertained me by the way' (102). Most strikingly, David cannot understand Gaelic, although significantly he later translates Alan's Gaelic song into 'the king's English' (69). Indeed, the narrative highlights the importance of decoding and deciphering alien cultures and the rôle of the translator: David's Lowland minister translates hymn-books into Gaelic (111).

Yet slowly David does reach a more sympathetic understanding of Highland culture. His first lesson is that the Highlands, rather than existing outside history in some timeless mythic arena, are bloodily imbrued with contemporary politics. He still occasionally sees his journey as a passage backwards in time, a regression from civilized life to folklore. He seems to be in retreat from the modern – at first fearless of the 'justice of my country', his anxiety about the trial grows as he imagines a gallows 'as I had once seen it engraved at the top of a pedlar's ballad' (124–5). But the narrative also undercuts the conventional nineteenth-century perception of the Highlands as a lawless wilderness. *Kidnapped* makes it clear that the clan system no less than Lowland culture enjoins a strict code of authority and order. Robin Oig, a hunted criminal, is perfectly safe within the territory controlled by his clan: he was 'sought upon all sides . . . yet he stepped about Balquidder like a gentleman in his own walled polity' (178).[82] Indeed, David soon questions progressivist assumptions about the passage from savagery to civilization, reflecting of his hospitable hosts that '[i]f these are the wild Highlanders, I could wish my own folk wilder' (101). He even comes to respect the integrity of Alan's Highland morality, although he cannot agree with the sacrifice of justice to clan loyalty (Alan's morals, David muses, 'were all tail-first; but he was ready to give his life for them') (123–4).

David's immersion in Highland culture leads to a surprising degree of identification, as he begins to see the world through the eyes of his new companions: hunted Jacobites, evicted tenants, and emigrants bound for America. Indeed, David is affiliated with these outlaws and exiles by parallel dispossessions – his uncle's appropriation of David's inheritance and his kidnapping to be sold into slavery in the Carolinas (he visualizes himself 'slaving alongside of negroes in the tobacco fields') (55). At first, others begin to see him differently: Neil Roy Macrob advises him to avoid Whigs, Campbells, and Hanoverians, 'in brief, to conduct myself like a robber or a Jacobite agent, as perhaps Neil thought me' (110). Soon, David's self-identification as a loyal Hanoverian also shifts: his first 'sight of the redcoats' fills him with 'pleasure and wonder', but, watching the troops come in against the tenantry, 'although this was but the second time I had seen King George's troops, I had no good will to them' (12, 115). The Lowlander Henderland, an SPCK catechist, displays even more prominently the sympathy attendant on immersion in an alien culture. After unfavourably comparing the Lowland cult of respectability with a forthright if brutal Highland morality, he asks wryly, '[y]e'll perhaps think I've been too long in the Hielands?' (112). David, however, shortly agrees that 'we ourselves might take a lesson by these wild Highlanders' (123).

Nonetheless, David never quite loses his fear of 'going native'. His anxiety is indicated at the end of the novel by his relief to have crossed over from 'the wrong side of the Highland Line' and become respectably dressed, 'the beggar-man a thing of the past' (182, 202). His complicity with Alan often distresses him: Susan Gannon argues that David, who dislikes rebellion against authority, is '"criminalized" by the association'.[83] David's fears are so potent because the novel problematizes the notion of uncomplicated duality between civilized self and savage other. David's own name is a Gaelic one, indicating his Highland ancestry (165). Indeed, responding to reviews which saw the novel as dramatizing a duality between Highland Gael and Lowland Anglo-Saxon, Stevenson protested that 'Gaelic was spoken in Fife little over the century ago, and in Galloway not much earlier, [and] I deny that there exists such a thing as a pure Celt'.[84] Not only are racial heritages mixed; political allegiances are also shifting: Alan deserted his post in the Hanoverian army to join the Jacobites during the '45 (79). This blurring of the distinction between self and other, savage and civilized, threatens the progressivist vision of cultural evolution, unsettling the binary terms on which Britain's internal colonialism and the ethnographic enterprise both depended.

The novel's ending underlines this rejection of the meliorist account of Scotland's progress towards enlightened modernity. Critics have often interpreted *Kidnapped* as a symbolic reconciliation of romantic Jacobite and canny Lowlander: for Donald McFarlan it constitutes a '"birth of a nation" portrait'.[85] The conflict, however, is not resolved. *Kidnapped* portrays instead the extirpation of an outdated Jacobitism, and the increasing dominance of Whig loyalism. The friends part on unequal terms: Alan is an exile, David welcomed into the Whig establishment by the solicitor Rankeillor. Polite culture is measured by linguistic refinement: Rankeillor asks him to write his 'great Odyssey . . . in a sound Latinity when your scholarship is riper; or in English if you please' (200). Now a landowner, David is glad to talk to 'a gentleman in broadcloth' after 'so long wandering with lawless people' (200). The 'credit' which Rankeillor places to his name with the British Linen Company recalls *Rob Roy* (1818), in which Bailie Nicol Jarvie pits the decent values embodied in 'credit' against the savage energies of 'honour' (217).[86] But whereas Scott endorses the idea of moderation and loyalism, exemplifying them in the worthy Jarvie, *Kidnapped* evokes the triumph of a rather grubby form of opportunism; and the money, Shapiro reminds us, 'represents the pool of capital that destroyed Breck's world through its investment in the Scottish enclosures'.[87] Although David still plans to risk his own safety by testifying in James Stewart's trial, his entrance into a world of moral compromise is signalled by Rankeillor's political equivocations and subterfuge. As Gannon judges, David's attainment of 'adulthood on his world's terms may also be seen as a loss'.[88]

Stevenson's sympathies in *Kidnapped* seem to lie with the suffering members of a dying culture. In *Waverley*, the period after 1745 is depicted as one of national prosperity, and the birth of a new Scotland from the ashes of Jacobite conflict is celebrated with emblematic wedding festivities.[89] *Kidnapped*, by contrast, suggests a much harsher delineation of decaying Highland culture. Alan describes how, despite the government's attempts to crush the clan system, men support their proscribed and exiled chiefs ('[o]ne thing they couldnae kill. That was the love the clansmen bore their chief'), and are ready to rise against the oppressive attempts at pacification (81, 84). If Alan's is inevitably a partial account, it is borne out by other characters. Even Henderland, sent to 'evangelize the more savage places of the Highlands', is full of pity for the Highlanders, blaming Parliament for its severe strictures against traditional dress (111). The passage to modern, commercial life is thus evoked as a loss rather than a triumph. The desolation wreaked by the destruction of this culture, too, is conveyed by Stevenson's description of the sounds of mourning as an 'emigrant ship' prepares to leave Scotland, 'bound for the American colonies' (108). The Highland Clearances themselves were yet several decades away, but already in the mid-eighteenth century there was a gradual drift of the surplus Highland population towards the New World. The sound of 'the people on board and those on the shore crying and lamenting one to another' is disturbing (David describes how they 'pierce the heart'), forming part of the process by which David, and by extension Stevenson's readership, is educated in the distressing realities of Highland life (108).

Despite its picturesque credentials, then, *Kidnapped* is a bleak novel, charting the often frustrated attempts of the hero, an exile in his own country, to understand an alien culture, and undercutting the meliorist account of Scotland's gradual progress towards civilized modernity. *The Master of Ballantrae* (1888–89) renders the same theme of the divided nation in yet more sombre tones. Critics this time had no illusions that the novel offered a 'delightful', Scott-derived tale. As William Archer declared, the 'one quality to which it can lay no claim is cheerfulness . . . for a militant optimist, Mr. Stevenson indulges in singularly gloomy fantasies'.[90] Others talked of its 'pervading gloom' or 'unmitigated gloom'.[91] Scott was invoked, but by way of contrast: Stevenson's novel, W. E. Henley wrote, 'differs from the romances of Sir Walter as a black marble vault differs from a radiant palace'.[92] It is certainly darker and more sordid than *Kidnapped*. Whereas David at least attempted a sympathetic understanding of an alien culture, *The Master of Ballantrae*'s narrative is fragmented, the product of passionate partisans, and under the overall control of the fiercest partisan of all, Ephraim Mackellar.[93] The narrative evokes the tragic national heritage of the '45, undercutting the belief in Scotland's progress towards moderation and enlightenment. It also develops the interest in superstition evident in Stevenson's earlier tales, 'The House of Eld' and 'Thrawn Janet', and disrupts the optimistic anthropological vision of irrational savagery giving way to rational civilization.

Drawing on the case of the Marquis of Tullibardine, the novel relates how the 1745 Jacobite rebellion shatters the fictional Durie family.[94] The charming, sinister James sides with the rebels and flees the country, but his presence haunts his younger brother Henry, a stolid Hanoverian who has inherited the title and home. The apparent dualism is mediated through Mackellar, Henry's servant, whose severe exterior belies his stubborn loyalty to his master, and his turbulent feelings of hatred and attraction towards the elder brother. As Douglas Gifford notes, the brothers, 'dour Calvinist' and 'extrovert romantic', are extreme versions of David and Alan, emblematic of a ruptured Scotland.[95] Representing the distorted and incomplete nature of Whig and Jacobite psyches, they desperately need each other's complementary characteristics.[96] The novel ends with their bodies interred together, and for Gifford this 're-unification in death' signifies that 'what has been dissociated by warping Scottish experience is now once again whole'.[97] The conflict, however, has not been laid to rest. Writing after the brothers' death, Mackellar refers to fears that Henry's son 'would prove a second Master', and hints darkly at the events surrounding 'my own exodus from his employment'; in his editorial persona, Stevenson deepens the suggestion of continuing discord by cutting the manuscript at this point, and noting that Mackellar seems to have been an '*exacting servant*'.[98]

As in *Kidnapped*, the divided nation is figured by the motif of exile and emigration. The narrative follows James's adventures in India and North America. Yet the perspective is different from that embodied in *Kidnapped*: the earlier novel evoked the suffering of Highlanders at the hands of the Hanoverian government, whereas *The Master of Ballantrae* exposes the sentimental myths propagated by Jacobitism. James's decision to join the '45 is dictated by political expediency and sheer chance rather than principle: the family agrees 'to steer a middle course' (11). It is decided by the toss of a coin that James should join the Young Pretender, and Henry remain loyal to King George (12). When James returns home, he claims to be an attainted rebel, but this heroic mask is soon peeled away, and he is exposed as a government spy, the 'discredited hero of romance' (89). The novel further questions a romantic mythography, Adrian Poole discloses, by subverting Jacobite allusions to Virgil's *Aeneid*: Stevenson figures James as an antitype of Aeneas, his wanderings a degraded version of the hero's adventures.[99] The narrative spurns the motif of exile and triumphal return, and instead depicts ultimate banishment to the wilderness. James also symbolizes the noxious effects of Jacobite mythology: as Rory Watson observes, Stevenson reveals the Jacobite romance as a cancer at the heart of Scottish culture.[100] The heroic glamour attaching to those who 'went out' with the Young Pretender renders James dangerously fascinating, and encourages his erstwhile sweetheart, now his brother's wife, to brood over his memory. He exploits the allure conferred by Jacobitism, singing a traditional ballad about 'a poor girl's aspirations for an exiled lover' (83). His performance suggests the divisive nature of the partisan tales, songs, and myths generated by the '45: Mackellar describes how he manipulates the pathos of his own situation as a tragically proscribed admirer, 'play[ing] upon that little ballad, and on those who heard him, like an instrument' (83).

This dark vision of Scotland as an irreconcilably divided nation, in which divisions are not healed by the years, undermines the belief in Scotland's progress after the Union. On a deeper thematic level, the novel also disrupts anthropology's progressive narrative by questioning whether superstition inevitably succumbs to rationalism, savagery to civilization. It figures the gradual dislocation of Mackellar's narrative by the untameable and purportedly primitive forces of orality and superstition.

Mackellar's narrative bears all the hallmarks of a dry rationalism and a fierce dedication to the written word. Stevenson's 'Preface', deploying a fictional device familiar from Scott, describes how Mackellar had given his narrative – spliced with extracts from the Jacobite Chevalier de Burke's memoirs – into the safe keeping of an Edinburgh law firm, to be opened a century later.[101] From the outset, Mackellar is insistent on his desire to make matters 'plain', to 'narrate them faithfully', and on his possession of 'authentic' documents (9). Discussing the early history of the Duries, he cites traditional, superstitious oral sources uneasily ('I cannot say how truly', 'I dare not say with how much justice'), and is relieved to move on to what he deems '[a]uthentic history' (9, 10). He also mistrusts Burke's narrative, and cuts part of his manuscript because of doubts about his reliability (59–60). Underlying this suspicion is the generic clash between Mackellar's realist aspirations and Burke's debt to romance. Burke's fantastic narrative introduces the consummate romantic figure of the Master, and heralds a battle for authority, according to Penny Fielding and Alan Sandison, between Mackellar's logocentric narration and James's subversive oral performance.[102]

This conflict encapsulates the perceived opposition between written culture and orality, enlightened and primitive thought. Mackellar, his Edinburgh University MA signifying his Scottish Enlightenment values, is pitted against James Durie, the Master, who embodies the forces of rumour and superstition (he is introduced by the tale of his persecution of a weaver who thought he was 'Auld Hornie') (22).[103] Associated with a vigorous orality, James is the master of seductive songs, and his verbal facility is indicated by his command of different languages, dialects, and accents. Besides French and Hindustani, he makes an easy transition from refined English to 'rude' Scots: he lays aside 'his cutting English accent, and [speaks] with the kindly Scots tongue', talking to Henry 'with a broad accent, such as they must have used together when they were boys' (76, 77). The narrative associates superstition and oral culture not only with the Scottish folk but also with India, which is seen as the repository of fantastic and occult tradition. Burke's first impressions of India are filtered through the lens of the *Arabian Nights*, and Henry refers to the Master's Indian servant, Secundra Dass, as his 'familiar spirit' (129, 210). Mackellar, when he hears the Master and Dass speaking a language he cannot comprehend (Hindustani), recalls an 'old tale' of 'a fairy wife . . . that came to the place of my fathers some generations back', illustrating his view of the Indian as an irrational and supernatural 'other' (133). He later assumes that he cannot understand English (148). As J. M. Harris observes, Mackellar misreads Dass, an educated man who 'belies' his caricature as 'an inarticulate alien'.[104]

The idea of progress from exotic folk supernaturalism (whether Scottish or Indian) to educated rationalism, indeed, breaks down, as the novel figures the gradual invasion of Mackellar's narrative by the uncontrollable forces of irrational superstition. Faced by James's repeated uncanny revivals, Henry and Mackellar are gradually infected by supernatural fears. Henry becomes convinced that James is the devil and that 'nothing can kill that man. He is not mortal. He is bound upon my back to all eternity' – an obsession which eventually kills him (122, 118). Mackellar comes to share Henry's forebodings about James: 'sometimes my gorge rose against him as though from something partly spectral' (156). As the narrative progresses, this son of the Scottish Enlightenment becomes subject to visions, and prophesies doom, at which James mockingly calls him a 'warlock' (154, 152). With the foundering of his rationalism, Mackellar's mistrust of the spoken word also subsides. Left alone with the Master, he is beguiled by the 'brilliancy of the discourse' (149). Temporarily, his narrow nature is broadened. By his own admission he is 'not formed for the world's pleasures'; yet, overcome by the Master's 'insidious' charm, he finds himself becoming witty and expansive, symbolically 'copying his words' (158, 149, 148).

The ending most dramatically erodes the distinctions between enlightened rationalism and oral supernaturalism, crystallizing the novel's curious combination of realism and fantasy. This generic hybridity explains why many critics – as well as Stevenson himself – have been troubled by the novel's ending. Stevenson confessed to 'panic fear of the conclusion' during the final stages of writing: '[h]ow, with a narrator like Mackellar, should I transact the melodrama in the wilderness?'.[105] Mackellar's painstaking description of the Master's partial revival, accomplished through 'some Oriental habit of Secundra's', reveals the unresolved conflict between rationalism and supernaturalism (204). Witnessing the fluttering and opening of the Master's eyelids, Mackellar records that '[s]o much display of life I can myself swear to. I have heard from others that he visibly strove to speak, that his teeth showed in his beard, and that his brow was contorted as with an agony of pain and effort. And this may have been: I know not' (218). As Alexander Clunas observes, Mackellar testifies 'as if in a court of law', but these 'improbable' events 'cannot be contained by a discourse of the real'.[106] The scene recapitulates the way in which Mackellar's dry narration is overcome by the forces of 'romance', illustrating that superstition and rationalism are intimately entwined.

The narrative also questions the notion that savagery and civilization are at opposite ends of an anthropological hierarchy. The novel's characters undoubtedly interpret Scots, Native Americans, Indians, and Africans as sharing a common savagery, and occupying an earlier stage of evolutionary development than those whom they understand as more civilized peoples. James, priding himself on being a 'good tyrant', likens his relationship with Dass to that of a 'petty chieftain in the Highlands' or a 'king of naked negroes in the African desert' with his followers (167). This debt to the Comparative Method also informs Mackellar's treatment of Sir William Johnson, a leader of the British colonists in America who famously negotiated with the Iroquois, and who makes a fictional appearance at the end of the novel. Mackellar draws a significant analogy between Scottish Highlanders and Native Americans, describing how Johnson's 'standing with the painted braves may be compared to that of my Lord President Culloden among the chiefs of our own Highlanders at the 'forty-five . . . he was, to these men, reason's only speaking-trumpet, and counsels of peace and moderation, if they were to prevail at all, must prevail singly through his influence' (207). Burke's memoirs develop this link, applying the same discourse of savagery to the subjects of Britain's 'external' and 'internal' Empire. Defensively insistent on his own gentility, Burke displays an obsessive interest in barbarity (41). He despises Scotland's 'savage people', but also self-deprecatingly calls himself an 'Irish savage' (33, 31). In the country of the Adirondack Native Americans, he describes 'a large war-party of the savages . . . all naked to the waist, blacked with grease and soot, and painted with white lead and vermilion, according to their beastly habits' (59). Native languages, for Burke, are a sign of backwardness. He disparages the Master for 'his Scots accent, of which he had not so much as some, but enough to be very barbarous and disgusting, as I told him plainly', a verdict he echoes in India when he describes the Master speaking to Dass 'in the barbarous native dialect' (51, 130). With these contemptuous comments, Burke implicitly links Scotland, Ireland, and the colonial arenas of India and North America in a shared diagnosis of primitivism.

Yet the narrative unsettles this comparative anthropological approach, questioning the European characters' assumption that savagery is simply embodied by colonized or marginal peoples. As Fielding argues, the novel blurs class, national, and racial identities.[107] Perhaps most fundamental is the destabilization of racial boundaries. Mountain, a white trader with the Native Americans, 'had not only lived and hunted, but fought and earned some reputation, with the savages' (195). Johnson, an intriguing choice of historical figure, also suggests a blending of identities – unmentioned by the novel, he lived with an Iroquois woman, with whom he had eight children.[108] The narrative reveals, moreover, that France and Britain, who were engaged in imperial conflict in India and North America, were responsible for much of the savagery in these areas.

Colonialism, far from being a civilizing mission, is driven by predatory avarice and a desire for adventure. James travels to India with the 'design of a fortune', and Mountain's party comprises 'the dregs of colonial rascality' (85, 197). Although the Europeans see the American wilderness as a 'barbarous country', 'infested with wild Indians', the scalping which they attribute to 'Indian bravos' is the work of Dass, probably under James's instruction (145, 178, 205). The comparison of Johnson with Duncan Forbes of Culloden indirectly intimates a critique of harsh colonial or metropolitan rule, as each sought to temper his government's severity towards, respectively, Native Americans and Jacobite clans.[109] The narrative also suggests that colonial conflict directly fosters barbarity: much Native American savagery is carried out at the behest of France and Britain. Burke describes how the 'Indians on both sides were on the war-path', collecting scalps 'for which they were paid at a fixed rate' (54). Revealingly, he wonders whether a 'war-party of the savages . . . were French or English Indians' (59).

In place of an evolutionary hierarchy, then, the narrative envisages savagery as existing even in the most apparently refined cultures. This duality figures in James Durie's epitaph: a 'MASTER OF THE ARTS AND GRACES', he was renowned 'IN THE TENTS OF SAVAGE HUNTERS' (219).[110] The human condition, Stevenson suggests, is irrevocably mixed. Like his dryly rational servant, the dull and conscientious Henry is perversely attracted to wildness, yearning to join the smugglers, to 'ride and run the danger of my life with these lawless companions' (21). He denies this inner savagery with tragic consequences, symbolized by his fanatical and fatal rejection of James.[111] As this unsettling of the idea of evolutionary progress indicates, *The Master of Ballantrae* dislocates anthropology's confident narrative in which superstition succumbs to rationalism, savagery to civilization. Exploring the links between Britain's internal and external Empire, it overturns the complacent rendering of 'native' peoples as barbarous, and shows that colonial relations themselves foster violent conflict. The narrative depicts the legacy of the '45 as an irreconcilable division within the Scottish nation, a division which festers down succeeding generations. It etches a vision of eighteenth-century Scotland which is deeply pessimistic, at odds with the dominant belief in progress in the century after the Union.

Stevenson's engagement with anthropology in the 1870s and 1880s, I have argued, taps into questions about cultural change, the possibility of progress, and the value of primitive culture. Although he was attracted by the anthropologists' radical, secularizing line, even his early fiction such as 'The House of Eld' and 'Thrawn Janet' evinces ambivalence about the possibility of free thought, representing the resurgence or persistence of superstitious states of mind.

Kidnapped and *The Master of Ballantrae* deepen this scepticism about an ethnocentric, progressivist anthropology. Both novels portray the tragic consequences of the '45 for the Scottish nation. *Kidnapped* undermines the portrayal of contemporary Highlanders as 'survivals' from an uncivilized stage of development and questions Scotland's progress towards civilized modernity. Unsettling the relations between savagery and civilization, self and other, it casts doubt on the possibility of a truly objective ethnographic enterprise. *The Master of Ballantrae* also brings alive the rancour which pitted one section of the Scottish population against another, focusing less on Highland suffering than on the poisonous effects of Jacobite myth-making. Stevenson wrote *The Master* while visiting Saranac, in the Adirondack Mountains, and Tahiti and Honolulu (the 'Preface' styles the narrative's supposed editor, 'R.L.S.', as 'an old, consistent exile', frequenting 'foreign spots').[112] As befits its genesis, the novel demonstrates Stevenson's newly cross-cultural interest in the relations between colonizer and colonized, metropolitan and marginal cultures – an interest which points forward to his ethnographic writings in the South Seas. Scrutinizing the resonances between transcultural encounters in India, North America, and Scotland, the narrative dramatizes the intertwining of superstition and rationalism, and the endurance of savagery in the most ostensibly civilized societies.

6

'[T]he clans disarmed, the chiefs deposed': Stevenson in the South Seas

Stevenson's life in the South Seas, from 1888 until his death in 1894, exerted a powerful fascination for the late-Victorian literary public (see Figure 6.1). His compulsive writing of Scottish historical novels during these years inspired a romantic legend of the exile yearning for his native homeland. By contrast, his Polynesian fiction, travel writing, and letters were condemned for their perceived realism and grimily contemporary

Figure 6.1 Nan Tok', Fanny Stevenson, Nei Takauti, and Robert Louis Stevenson on the Gilbert Islands. Reproduced courtesy of the Edinburgh Writers' Museum.

concerns. As Henry James judged, '[f]or the absent and vanished Scotland he *has* the image . . . The Pacific . . . made him "descriptively" serious and even rather dry . . . and this left the field abundantly clear for the Border, the Great North Road and the eighteenth century'.[1] Oscar Wilde echoed this privileging of 'romance' over realism. 'I see that romantic surroundings are the worst surroundings possible for a romantic writer', he wrote, noting sardonically that '[i]n Gower Street Stevenson could have written a new *Trois Mousquetaires*. In Samoa he wrote letters to *The Times* about Germans'.[2] By the late twentieth century, new critical and political values had overturned this hierarchy. Commentators now deprecate his Scottish fiction for its perceived nostalgia (in Christopher Harvie's words, 'why didn't Stevenson tackle the social realities of Scotland of his own day?'), while celebrating his Pacific writings for their visionary concern with a multicultural world.[3] Recent interpretations have thus cast Stevenson in a dual identity: a romantic antiquarian in his Scottish fiction and a postcolonialist *avant la lettre* in his Pacific writings.

Yet despite the conflicting interpretations of Stevenson's Scottish and Polynesian work, a sustained ambivalence towards anthropology's progressive narrative unites his œuvre. It was a narrative often invoked to justify imperialism as a triumphant evolutionary advance: as Leslie Stephen observed, '[e]verywhere we see a competition between different races, and the more savage tribes vanishing under the approach of the more civilised'.[4] Stevenson's experiences in the South Seas, however, unsettled this complacent assumption of progress. There, he witnessed first hand international rivalries like those he had described in *The Master of Ballantrae*, and found the struggle for survival between races even more vividly exemplified than in eighteenth-century Scotland.

The South Pacific in the late nineteenth century was a crucial theatre of imperial conflict, as the great powers extended their informal and formal empires. Traders and missionaries changed the balance of island life, fostering a hybrid world of pidgin languages and cross-cultural encounters. France had annexed the Marquesas and Tuamotus in 1842, but most island groups remained formally independent until the late nineteenth century, when imperialist rivalries heightened.[5] In the 1880s, war broke out in Samoa, largely owing to Germany's aggressive interference, and in 1889 the Berlin Conference, convened by Germany, Britain, and the United States, established their tripartite rule over Samoa.[6] Incensed by the high-handed conduct of the great powers, Stevenson intervened in support of the native opposition chief, writing an exposé of Samoan affairs, *A Footnote to History* (1892), and frequent letters to *The Times*.[7] Yet Stevenson should not be depicted simply as a radical anti-imperialist: his paternalistic control over the Vailima household and his interest in holding the British Consulship indicate the ambiguities of his position.[8] Nevertheless, in the unfolding conflict Stevenson consistently identified with indigenous interests: as he protested to Colvin, '[t]he natives have been scurvily used by all the white Powers without exception'.[9]

This chapter reconciles the divergent readings of Stevenson's Scottish and Polynesian work, showing how an enduring scepticism about progressivist anthropology runs through his œuvre. Stevenson's experiences in the South Seas, I argue, amplified his mistrust of a confident vision of evolutionary progress, and intensified his perception of the savagery which endured at the heart of apparently civilized societies. His anthropological interventions also shed light on the early history of the discipline, exemplifying the fruitful interweaving of scientific and literary discourses at the *fin de siècle*. Here I examine Stevenson's engagement with South Seas folklore in his exchanges with British anthropologists, and in his Pacific writings, *In the South Seas* (1896) and 'The Beach of Falesá' (1892), before considering how his anxiety about the fate of weak, traditional cultures shaped his last Scottish novels, *Catriona* (1892–93) and *Weir of Hermiston* (1896).

British anthropological debates clearly remained an important intellectual context for Stevenson's work. While Robert Hillier attributes his South Seas writings simply to delight in the Pacific's 'rich oral tradition of chants, legends and folktales', it is nonetheless significant that Stevenson continued to follow and participate in anthropological controversy in London periodicals.[10] In 1890, for example, Grant Allen, writing in the *Fortnightly Review*, deployed Spencer's notion of ancestor-worship to argue for stone-worship as the foundation of modern religions.[11] Lang's riposte, 'Was Jehovah a Fetish Stone?', used evidence from the Pacific islands to deny that there was any 'single "key of all the creeds." '.[12] At this stage Stevenson joined the debate, writing to Lang that he 'observed with a great deal of surprise and interest that a controversy in which you have been taking sides at home, in yellow London, hinges in part at least on the Gilbert Islanders and their customs in burial'.[13] Citing evidence gathered in conversations with Tembinoka, King of Apemama in the Gilbert Islands, Stevenson judged that the standing stones had 'no connection with graves', thereby supporting Lang's position.[14] Stevenson closed by welcoming further inquiries, emphasizing not only his own familiarity with South Seas culture but also his possession of a network of anthropological informants ('I have hands, friends and correspondents almost all over. Shape your queries, and 'tis hard if I cannot get the answer').[15]

Stevenson's anthropological lore clearly gained wide recognition. In 1893, Joseph Jacobs, the editor of *Folk-Lore*, wrote asking him to shed light on a 'disputed point' of Samoan mythology.[16] In an unpublished letter, he requested information on the Samoan myth of Puapae and Siati,

> which resembles greatly even to minute details a folktale known to the Norsemen as *The Master Maid*, to the Celts as *The Battle of the Birds* and to the ancient Greeks as the lives of Jason (=Siati) and Medea (=Puapae). You have doubtless seen Mr. Lang's essay on 'A far-travelled Tale' in his *Custom and Myth* which deals with the subject.
>
> Now this instance is the most striking example of similarity in folk-tales in widely apart regions and this is a crucial specimen by which to determine whether such similarities arise casually and independently (owing to similarities of mental condition) or are due to transmission.[17]

Jacobs's letter taps into vexed questions about the origin of myths. Lang, Tylor, and other evolutionists explained the affinities between myths as proof of humankind's psychic unity, but here Jacobs invokes a theory which was increasingly challenging the dominant model of unilinear cultural evolution: the hypothesis that correlations were due not to 'similarities of mental condition' but to diffusion. Diffusionism, the insistence on 'transmission' of folklore by cultural contact, undermined the evolutionist belief in a hierarchy of cultural development. As the letter suggests, the issue was far from settled. It is not known whether Stevenson replied to Jacobs, but his anthropological lore was clearly valued. Jacobs excused his intrusion by claiming that Stevenson's 'evident interest in the native Ballads absolves me from the necessity of apologising'.[18]

Stevenson's engagement with scientific writers highlights the rôle of amateurs in the early anthropological enterprise: as Scott Ashley urges, '[t]he work of ethnographic *flâneurs* like [J. M.] Synge or . . . Stevenson, living among the people about whom they wrote over a space of years, learning the language, hoping for some kind of understanding from the inside, should be incorporated within the histories of anthropology, or the rich cultural context in which the discipline was founded risks being thinned'.[19] The part played by late-Victorian literary writers in anthropology's development owed much to its unprofessionalized nature, and its lack of (or freedom from) fixed institutional support.[20]

Anthropology was also at a transitional point in its ideological development. By the beginning of the twentieth century, the confident vision of hierarchical evolution was gradually being displaced by an increasing appreciation of cultural plurality. Historians of anthropology continue to debate just when this epistemic shift occurred – and if indeed it ever did.[21] In Stocking's celebratory account, Franz Boas and Bronislaw Malinowski emerge as the heroic vanquishers of evolutionary anthropology, and practitioners of a more enlightened participant observation.[22] It is, however, far from clear that either Boas or Malinowski adhered to anthropological relativism.[23] The allegedly twentieth-century notion of plural cultures, meanwhile, was often foreshadowed in the previous century, as Christopher Herbert explores.[24] Moreover, while Stocking claims that twentieth-century fieldworkers identified with their host cultures rather than colonial powers, this was perhaps truer of 'ethnographic *flâneurs*' like Stevenson than of many later professionals.[25] Malinowski, for all his championing of participant observation, was notoriously scathing in private about the Melanesians with whom he lived.[26]

By the early twentieth century, anthropologists were far from discarding their ethnocentric evolutionism, but they were at least embarking on a gradual and contested transition towards a new understanding of cultural plurality. Cultural relativism, of course, has attracted censure in recent decades, with critics charging that the relativist emphasis on difference obliterates notions of equality and indirectly sustains the idea of essential, biological difference.[27] Nonetheless, because in the late nineteenth and early twentieth centuries 'relativism' offered a novel principle of cultural tolerance, I retain the term to define, in an affirmative manner, the new style of anthropological inquiry: as James Buzard notes, although 'we are now exhorted to liberate ourselves' from the discourse of cultural plurality, that discourse was 'then struggling to liberate *itself* from the universalizing vision of ethnological comparativism'.[28]

Stevenson's South Seas writings, especially *In the South Seas* (1896) and 'The Beach of Falesá' (1892), illuminate the discipline at this pivotal moment, pointing forward to the new relativism. *In the South Seas*, an ambitious account of the Marquesan, Tuamotuan, and Gilbert Islands, marks an important – and deeply ambivalent – engagement with *fin-de-siècle* anthropology.[29] Critics have frequently objected to the lack of 'romance' in the work. Stevenson's wife, Fanny, complained that he had obtained Darwin's

> *Coral Reefs*; somebody else on Melanesian languages, books on the origin of the South Sea peoples, and all sorts of scientific pamphlets and papers. He has always had a weakness for teaching and preaching, so here was his chance. Instead of writing about his own adventures in these wild islands, he would ventilate his own theories on the vexed questions of race and language.[30]

For Neil Rennie, '[t]he fundamental problem . . . was that Stevenson wanted to transcend the personal travel narrative, and write an anthropological and historical work'.[31] The volume indeed provides little sense of a consecutive narrative, although the book's publishers attempted to remedy this by including a map of his travels (see Figure 6.2). The focus lies elsewhere, on the meaning and value of what Tylor would readily call primitive culture. Recent critics have compellingly explored Stevenson's engagement with evolutionary models of cultural development. Rod Edmond argues that although *In the South Seas* initially draws on conventional, scientifically validated images of Pacific cultures, it evinces an increasing 'independence' of dominant scientific and specifically Darwinian discourses, demonstrated by its 'growing historical interest in the region and its relations with western powers'.[32] Roslyn Jolly's incisive reading of Stevenson's account of Samoan history, *A Footnote to History* (1892), similarly stresses his antagonism towards contemporary science, suggesting that this narrative too rejects the 'Darwinian or Spencerian "scientific" account of imperial history'.[33]

Yet despite Stevenson's undoubted scepticism about progress, he was far from rejecting Darwinian models of evolution. I shall argue that *In the South Seas* enacts a more equivocal negotiation of contemporary evolutionary narratives. The work exploits and exposes the strains within nineteenth-century evolutionary thought, revealing the tension between a Spencerian narrative of progress and Darwin's 'natural selection' of random variations. By contrast with Spencer's belief in evolutionary advance through the 'survival of the fittest', Darwinism was subject to conflicting interpretations: progress and direction existed alongside unpredictability and extinction and, as Gillian Beer notes, its 'disturbing elements . . . gradually accrued a heavier and heavier weight in consciousness'.[34] *In the South Seas* draws on Darwinism to challenge the Spencerian *laissez-faire* evolutionism which underlay the new science of anthropology.[35] Furthermore, its insistence on the value of cultural difference destabilizes Victorian anthropology's unilinear model of cultural development, foreshadowing the twentieth-century movement towards relativism.

This complex negotiation of contemporary evolutionism is evident in Stevenson's treatment of cultural hierarchies. Intriguingly, the narrative often seems to endorse Tylor's belief that modern 'savages' were survivals from an earlier evolutionary stage. On reaching the Gilbert Islands, Stevenson notes that 'the impression received was not so much of foreign travel – rather of past ages; it seemed not so much degrees of latitude that we had crossed, as centuries of time that we had re-ascended;

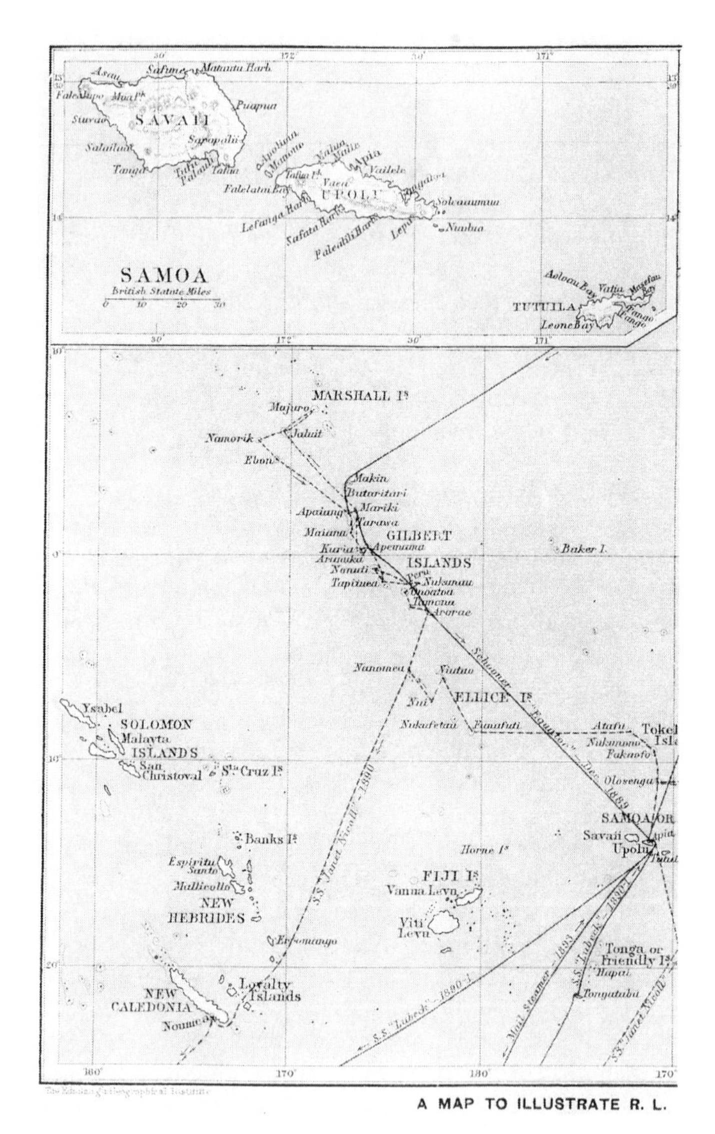

Figure 6.2 Map showing Stevenson's travels, from *In the South Seas* (London: Heinemann, 1924), ii. Reproduced courtesy of the English Faculty Library, University of Oxford.

leaving, by the same steps, home and to-day' (174). In Vanessa Smith's perceptive reading, Stevenson views the islands as 'a territory not yet penetrated by the European', and aspires to 'play first author', a rôle imbued with imperialist fantasy.[36] Indeed, the idea of time travel was a

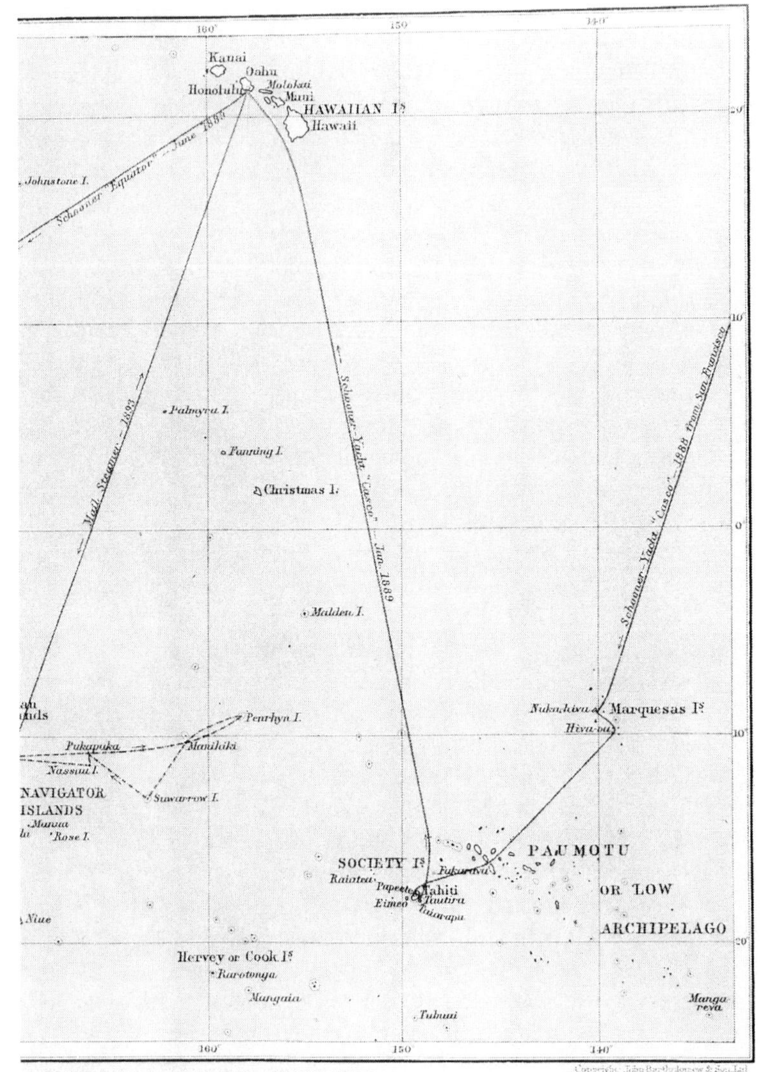

STEVENSON'S LIFE IN THE SOUTH SEAS

standard trope in evolutionist and imperialist treatments of 'primitive' culture. As the philologist Friedrich Max Müller wrote in a preface to W. W. Gill's *Myths and Songs from the South Pacific* (1876), the experience of finding oneself among 'a people who really believe in gods and heroes and ancestral spirits' was as if 'the zoologist could spend a few days among the megatheria, or the botanist among the waving ferns of the forests, buried beneath our feet'.[37] Yet despite apparently subscribing to the belief in hierarchical evolutionary development, *In the South Seas* steadily undoes the assumptions on which this model was based – assumptions about the inevitable progress from savagery to civilization.

Questioning the progressive narrative of cultural evolution, Stevenson condemns the effects of European imperialism in the Pacific, and evokes the vulnerability of colonized cultures and the pain involved in relinquishing traditional beliefs and customs. The work constantly draws comparisons between Pacific society and eighteenth-century Scotland, portraying both as traditional cultures at the mercy of stronger, allegedly more civilized societies. Recalling 'our Scots folk of the Highlands and Islands', Stevenson judges that '[n]ot much beyond a century has passed since these were in the same convulsive and transitionary state as the Marquesans of to-day. In both cases an alien authority enforced, the clans disarmed, the chiefs deposed, new customs introduced' (12). In both cultures, he describes a 'commercial age . . . succeeding . . . to an age of war abroad and patriarchal communism at home' (12). It is the same narrative of social evolution extolled by Scott as a story of triumph and progress but, for Stevenson, the 'commercial age' clearly brings to the region not so much peace and stability, as dishonest white traders who fleece the local rulers (214). French colonial politics are likewise explained by reference to eighteenth-century Anglo-Scottish relations, with the overthrowing of 'hereditary tyrants' in the Marquesas compared to the Hanoverians' exiling of 'Highland magnates' (36–7). There is no doubt that Stevenson's sympathies, as in *Kidnapped*, lie with the traditional culture which he believed was being destroyed.

This critique of the effects of European imperialism takes its place, as Rod Edmond observes, in a long tradition of representing Polynesian society as hovering on the brink of extinction.[38] Forty years earlier, Herman Melville's *Typee* (1846) and *Omoo* (1847) had depicted a Polynesian world where contact with Europeans brought sickness, immorality, and death.[39] Indeed, for contemporaries such as the journalist Arthur Johnstone, Stevenson's Polynesian sympathies indicated his outdated, eighteenth-century primitivism. Johnstone condemned Stevenson's adherence to a 'savage nativism' which he believed had been superseded by evolutionary thought, depicting him in thrall to 'that quaint school of philosophers who . . . before the awakening of science, dinned the world's ear with the assertion that man in a state of nature meant man in a state of savagery'.[40] Appealing to a *laissez-faire* evolutionism, he held that '[i]n politics . . . the contest between fitness and disability is severe', and that 'the extinction or absorption of the weaker race' would be 'inevitable' in the conflict between 'the unequal forces of savagery and civilization'.[41]

Although Johnstone represented Stevenson's thinking as anachronistic, his fierce opposition underlined its subversive potential, its capacity to unsettle contemporary evolutionism. For although Stevenson's analysis draws on conventional images of the dying race, it is also rooted in a Darwinian understanding of the necessarily gradual pace at which societies naturally evolve and change. Stevenson attributes the drastic depopulation of the Marquesas, which he and many others feared would soon lead to the extinction of the race, to the Europeans' brutal modernization of Polynesian tradition. 'Where there have been the fewest changes, important or unimportant, salutary or hurtful, there the race survives', Stevenson declares: '[e]ach change, however small, augments the sum of new conditions to which the race has to become inured' (33).

This passage closely echoes Darwin's judgment in *The Descent of Man* (1871) that 'the most potent of all causes of extinction' was 'lessened fertility and ill health . . . arising from changed conditions of life, notwithstanding that the new conditions may not be injurious in themselves'.[42] While Edmond contrasts the narrative's recourse to 'familiar types of explanation' such as Darwinism with its growing interest in imperialism, it appears rather that Stevenson deploys Darwinism precisely in order to censure the harmful effects of colonialism.[43] Dissenting from the evolutionary progressivist interpretation of imperialism, he finds in the less optimistic aspects of Darwin's work grounds for believing that the colonial overthrow of an existing culture is not simply the natural or lawful assertion of the might of a more advanced party. Stevenson's recognition that 'change of habit is bloodier than a bombardment' reinstates the violence and pain of evolution, an aspect of the evolutionary narrative which was increasingly emphasized in the *fin-de-siècle* climate of scientific pessimism (34). During these years, modern international rivalries came to be interpreted in terms of a ruthless process of natural selection. As the scientific writer O. Plumacher judged,

> [w]hen the earliest prehistoric races overcame their animal kindred . . . the pain of defeat in such rude struggles was no greater than now when we fight with lead and iron or the arts of diplomacy, or when by superior industry one nation compasses the ruin of another . . . The tearing teeth give way to the persuasive tongue and the skilful pen . . . But in every case those who succumb must suffer.[44]

The work's celebration of beleaguered Polynesian folk cultures also unsettles the imperialist ideology with which anthropology colluded. The indigenous cultures which Stevenson encounters emerge as much more than Tylor's anachronistic 'survival [from an] early condition of mankind'. Stevenson's interpretation also contrasts with J. G. Frazer's reading of myth as human misunderstanding and his disregard for material questions about property and government and for the realities of social life.[45] In Stevenson's sophisticated analysis, superstition, and especially taboo, is revealed not as an error made by unenlightened natives, but as integral to a complex system of government and belief. Far from being 'a meaningless and wanton prohibition, such as that which yesterday prevented any one in Scotland from taking a walk on Sunday', taboo 'is more often the instrument of wise and needful restrictions' (39–40). Stevenson's strongest invective is reserved for the missionaries who 'deride and infract even the most salutary *tabus*', and he condemns the unthinking drive to eradicate superstition, lamenting that 'so few people have read history, and so many have dipped into little atheistic manuals' (35, 65). Stevenson's analysis characterizes Polynesian customs and beliefs in terms not of irrational 'survival', but of their useful function within native society. In this respect, he prefigures the twentieth-century anti-evolutionary reaction in anthropology, and the new emphasis on the social value of superstition and ritual.

In the South Seas hovers on the edge of a new anthropological relativism. Stevenson describes the British 'absurdity of marriage presents', for example, as 'cognate' with Polynesian custom (61). Contemporaries often gestured towards this recognition. Grant Allen's novel, *The Great Taboo* (1890), set in the South Seas, concludes with the observation that '[t]aboos, after all, are much the same in England as in Boupari'.[46] Yet as Allen links a decorous English prohibition of unsupervised contact between young men and women with Polynesian taboos involving cannibalism and 'horrible bloodthirsty rites', the comparison is amusing rather than disturbing.[47] Unlike Stevenson, Allen does not seek to estrange self-confident readers from their own customs. *In the South Seas* unsettlingly contextualizes cultural norms – perhaps most provocatively in discussing cannibalism (the practice that, for British readers, put Polynesian society beyond the pale):

> [n]othing more strongly arouses our disgust than cannibalism ... And yet we ourselves make much the same appearance in the eyes of the Buddhist and vegetarian. We consume the carcases of creatures of like appetites, passions, and organs with ourselves ... We distinguish, indeed; but the unwillingness of many nations to eat the dog, an animal with whom we live on terms of the next intimacy, shows how precariously the distinction is grounded. (68)

At first identifying himself with his British readers, testifying to their shared 'disgust', Stevenson then chips away at the sense of an absolute standard of civilized behaviour.

Indeed, the work is impelled by a desire for increased tolerance, lamenting Christian missionaries' dogmatic belief in their cultural superiority, and their introduction of reforms which caused 'the dissolution of society' (162). Years before, Stevenson censured American missionaries who had come 'thousands of miles to change the faith of Japan, and openly professed their ignorance of the religions they were trying to supplant'.[48] Towards the end of his life, he warned a friend contemplating mission work that *'you cannot change ancestral feelings of right and wrong without what is practically soul-murder'*.[49] *In the South Seas* also ridicules the false authority claimed by European travel writers: Stevenson describes how a 'ship of war comes to a haven, anchors, lands a party, receives and returns a visit, and the captain writes a chapter on the manners of the island', and notes that he would be far more inclined to trust the testimony of 'an intelligent native' (35). This sense that native cultures must be understood from within connects with Stevenson's organic historicism, his conviction that each 'age must be measured of its own standard; seventeenth century actions must not be tried by the moral notions of nineteenth-century enlightenment'.[50] It also prefigures twentieth-century anthropologists' developing commitment to fieldwork, and its required immersion in the culture one was studying.[51]

Stevenson's representation of his own developing ethnographic consciousness is central to this drive towards cultural tolerance. His first contact with the Marquesans involves a disorientating perception of cultural difference. He describes the islanders as 'beyond the reach of articulate communication' (9). However, the narrative charts thereafter his gradual acclimatization, as he learns to respect native customs and, as we have seen, opens up lines of communication by volunteering Scottish legends in exchange for Polynesian lore. Indeed, what attracts Stevenson most about Polynesians is their cultural relativism – especially their acceptance of the 'local circumscription of beliefs' (the idea that a particular religion is only true for its own adherents) (42). Stevenson views this belief as the root of cultural tolerance: he claims that '[t]he Jews were perhaps the first to interrupt this ancient comity of faiths; and the Jewish virus is still strong in Christianity. All the world must respect our *tabus*, or we gnash our teeth' (42). Stevenson's valorization of the 'ancient comity of faiths', in this passage as throughout the work, amounts to a questioning of cultural hierarchies. Embracing a relativist view of culture, and drawing on a Darwinian narrative to emphasize the cruelty of evolution, Stevenson's work threatens, implicitly, to undermine the foundations of the late-Victorian anthropological enterprise.

In the South Seas also recognizes the difficulty – maybe even impossibility – of entering sympathetically into an alien culture, amplifying the doubts implicitly raised by David Balfour's ethnographic endeavours in *Kidnapped*. The change of title from *The South Seas* to *In the South Seas*, Kirsti Wishart has contended, destabilizes the ideal of scientific objectivity, acknowledging the subjective nature of the anthropologist's observations.[52] Stevenson is also alert to the obstacles to anthropological insight. Despite his efforts to elicit details of folklore from a Pacific islander, he admits to misgivings about the possibility of communication: 'I shall not hear the whole; for he is already on his guard with me' (140). An undated notebook entry illuminates his interest in cultural misunderstanding and the obscurity of linguistic exchange: Stevenson claims that 'our power of thinking is limited by our knowledge of words', which are no more than 'symbols' denoting 'different values' for each user.[53] Drawing on Tylor's description of native Brazilian belief, he explains that

> [w]e may see the difficulty in its highest terms, when a missionary asks a savage if he believes it is the virtuous who are to be happiest in a future state and receives an affirmative reply: the good man is much pleased with such incipient orthodoxy; while all the time they have been juggling it with each other with misunderstood symbols. The missionary had Christian virtue in his mind; while the Tupinamba means by the virtuous 'those who have well revenged themselves and eaten many of their enemies'.[54]

This recognition of the impediments to intercultural communication and sympathy was borne out by the hostile British reception of Stevenson's South Seas writings. Colvin objected to his letters for their disregard of 'our white affairs': 'you have not uttered a single word about anything but your beloved blacks – or chocolates – confound them; beloved no doubt to you; to us detested, as shutting out your thoughts . . . from the main current of human affairs'.[55] Stevenson's subsequent defence of his apparently 'remote' concerns turned on the notion of cultural sympathy: he urged the value of exercising imagination, of being 'able to enter into something outside of oneself'.[56]

The same questions about cross-cultural transactions are dramatized in Stevenson's Polynesian short stories, which evoke the confrontation between cultures in what Mary Louise Pratt styles the 'contact zone' or 'space of colonial encounter'.[57] Like the more famous 'The Beach of Falesá'

(1892), 'The Bottle Imp' (1891) and 'The Isle of Voices' (1893) depict multicultural societies whose *mores* are a concoction of traditional and modern, native and European. The texts are themselves shaped by cross-cultural contact: 'The Isle of Voices' is a patchwork of Polynesian folk-lore interwoven with realistic scrutiny of modern Pacific society, while 'The Bottle Imp' was published in a Samoan translation in *O Le Sulu Samoa*, the London Missionary Society magazine.[58] Tales of encounters between colonists and natives, they have an implicitly anti-imperialist edge. In 'The Isle of Voices', white characters are confronted with the validity of despised native creeds: warned about a poisonous fish, a 'fool of a white man, who would believe no stories but his own . . . cooked it and ate it, and swelled up and died'.[59]

'The Beach of Falesá' uses its fictionalization of hybrid Pacific cultures to offer a more explicit critique of imperialism than is afforded by these folk tales.[60] On one level it is a conventional tale of colonial adventure. It follows the attempts of a British trader, Wiltshire, to establish his station on a Polynesian island, efforts which are thwarted by the malevolent Case, another British trader. Case plays on native superstitions to drive his rivals from the island; Wiltshire soon finds that his own store is 'taboo', because Case has fomented fear of Wiltshire's native wife, Uma. In true *Boy's Own* style, Wiltshire ventures into the woods, where he discovers an apparently haunted temple rigged up by Case to keep the natives in terrified submission. In a dramatic showdown, Wiltshire destroys the shrine and kills Case. Despite dreams of returning to England, he now settles down with Uma in the South Seas.

Yet, as many critics have recognized, the seemingly gung-ho narrative actually works towards a demystification of imperial adventure. Patrick Brantlinger observes that the tale evinces a Conradian scepticism about the influence of white imperialism on indigenous societies.[61] Indeed, 'The Beach of Falesá' is the tale of Wiltshire's gradual awakening to the value of Polynesian society, encapsulated in the transfer of his loyalties from the white traders to Uma. In a compelling reading, Roslyn Jolly relates Wiltshire's increasing allegiance to Uma to the tale's generic shift away from the imperial adventure story, and towards the realistic and 'feminine realm of the domestic novel'.[62] Rod Edmond too focuses on the anti-imperialist implications of the romance plot, reading the narrative as a 'rewriting of the transcultural romance'.[63]

The imperial adventure and transcultural romance genres, of course, were sustained by colonial understandings of primitive culture. Critics have recently turned their attention to the central rôle of superstition in Stevenson's narrative: Jolly considers how the tale negotiates different modes of the 'South Sea Gothic', and J. M. Harris analyses Stevenson's deployment of folklore to subvert notions of racial difference.[64] As these critics suggest, superstition is used to undermine the idea of European cultural superiority. More specifically, I shall argue, Stevenson directly engages with a particularly evolutionist understanding of superstition and with an anthropological interest in savagery and civilization. The tale destabilizes anthropology's belief in racial and cultural hierarchies, rendering ironic its vocabulary of degeneration and survivals. Eschewing a belief in gradual progress from irrationality to enlightenment, and orality to literacy, the narrative – and to some extent the narrator – moves towards a relativist view of culture.

Wiltshire's personal journey inscribes this challenge to the evolutionist belief in a unilinear racial hierarchy. Initially, he accepts unquestioningly the imperialist notion of European evolutionary superiority. He views Polynesians as representing a less evolved stage on the evolutionary ladder, likening Uma to 'a child or a kind dog' (12).[65] Resistant to indulging any sentimental 'nonsense about native women', he deceives Uma with a fraudulent marriage certificate (11). His indignant reaction to the taboo further underlines his adherence to racial ideologies: he objects that 'I'm a white man, and a British subject, and no end of a big chief at home; and I've come here to do them good, and bring them civilization [and] . . . if they think they're going to come any of their native ideas over me, they'll find themselves mistaken' (23–4). Of course this protestation is ironically undermined by the narrative. Initially opposed to 'native ideas', Wiltshire learns much from his island experiences, coming to appreciate Uma's individuality, and to side with her against Case, despite the latter's rhetoric of racial solidarity (Case appeals, for instance, to 'the White Man's Quarrel') (22).

The gradual subversion of evolutionist hierarchies involves a questioning of contemporary fears about degeneration. These anxieties formed a common motif within *fin-de-siècle* anthropology and imperialism. In Patrick Brantlinger's delineation of 'Imperial Gothic', one of its central themes is the idea of going native.[66] At the outset, Wiltshire is haunted by the spectre of European reversion to native barbarism, describing with horror

> old Captain Randall, squatting on the floor native fashion, fat and pale, naked to the waist, grey as a badger, and his eyes set with drink. His body was covered with grey hair and crawled over by flies . . . Any clean-minded man would have had the creature out at once and buried him; and to see him, and think he was seventy, and remember

> he had once commanded a ship, and come ashore in his smart togs, and talked big in bars and consulates, and sat in club verandahs, turned me sick and sober. (8)

But the fear of degeneration is ironically deployed in 'Falesá', which figures most of the island's savagery as introduced by Europeans. Wiltshire dislikes white missionaries because 'they're partly Kanakaized' (Kanaka was the derogatory European term for Polynesian natives), 'and suck up with natives instead of with other white men like themselves'; the missionary, however, significantly emerges as the only honourable white man on the island (34).

By the story's end, Wiltshire's condescension towards natives has been moderated by a wiser recognition of their common humanity: talking of native superstition, he judges that '[t]his is mighty like Kanakas', but concedes that 'it's mighty like white folks too' (54). Nonetheless, he remains an equivocal character, whose enlightenment is only ever partial. In Jolly's words, he is 'partly complicit with, partly critical of, and not fully conscious of his own place within, imperialism'.[67] Though poised on the threshold of a new tolerance, Wiltshire is constrained by the traditional vision of hierarchical evolution. Thus he remains convinced that Polynesians represent a less advanced stage in the evolutionary process, claiming that '[i]t's easy to find out what Kanakas think. Just go back to yourself any way round from ten to fifteen years old, and there's an average Kanaka' (55). Belief in a racial hierarchy continues to dominate his mental world, and the narrative ends revealingly with his worry about his daughters: although they are 'only half-castes', he confesses anxiously, 'I can't reconcile my mind to their taking up with Kanakas, and I'd like to know where I'm to find the whites' (71).

The tale's scepticism about evolutionary hierarchies coalesces around the portrayal of superstition. The narrative undermines the evolutionist understanding of superstition as proper to a childlike indigenous culture. Case advances this patronizing interpretation, explaining the taboo on Wiltshire as 'one of their tomfool superstitions', while Wiltshire himself also associates natives with the occult, detecting shades of the spiritualist, Mme Blavatsky, in 'all island women' (25, 36). Yet, as Harris observes, the reference to modern European spiritualism ironically reveals the similarity between European and Polynesian culture.[68] Indeed, it implicitly undermines evolutionist belief in progress from superstition to enlightenment. Many evolutionists regarded contemporary European spiritualism as an atavistic resurgence. For Tylor, it was an exception to the usual pattern of intellectual advance, 'a truly remarkable case of degeneration', suggesting 'how direct and close the connexion may be between modern culture and the condition of the rudest savage'.[69]

Indeed, the Tylorian reading of superstitions as survivals from a primitive stage of culture is gradually destabilized. As the narrative unfolds, it transpires that many superstitions are recent imports, deployed by Europeans to control the native population. In addition to instigating the taboo on Wiltshire's store, Case has manipulated native fears in order to drive out a paralysed rival trader, Underhill. The missionary relates how '[w]ord was started that the helpless old man was now a devil, and this vile fellow Case worked upon the natives' fears, which he professed to share'; Underhill is eventually buried alive by the villagers (40). Unlike Soulis, who as a civilized outsider promotes a scientific explanation for paralysis in 'Thrawn Janet' (1881), Case encourages irrational superstition. What emerges here is a radical recognition that superstition is used by white men against the natives, as an instrument of social control.[70] Case's temple, with its smoking devils and eerily singing harps, most overtly symbolizes this strategy; and its destruction is consequently more than an exciting plot device. Notably, Christianity itself is aligned with the supernatural illusions by which natives are subjugated. Thus when Case discredits the missionary as mercenary by magically plucking a dollar from his head, his antagonist laments that '[t]he thing was a common conjuring trick . . . but how was I to convince the villagers of that? I wished I had learned legerdemain instead of Hebrew' (42).

Indigenous superstitions, by contrast, are portrayed much more positively. The narrative emphasizes their potency and validity, and the sophistication of folk cultures. Thus Wiltshire's education involves coming to respect local folklore. At first he ridicules Uma's grasp of 'theology' and listens to her tales of Polynesian folklore with studied indifference (48). Soon, though, as he himself feels the pangs of superstitious fear, he moves towards a more tolerant appreciation of cultural variation, noting that '[w]e laugh at the natives and their superstitions; but see how many traders take them up, splendidly educated white men . . . It's my belief a superstition grows up in a place like the different kind of weeds; and as I stood there and listened to that wailing I twittered in my shoes' (52). The passage is intriguingly ambivalent, an incipient recognition of the local validity of cultural beliefs jarring with the assumption of European superiority which is implicit in the degenerationist rhetoric. Wiltshire's superstitious susceptibilities echo Stevenson's own feelings alone in the jungle: 'only the other day', he wrote in a letter, 'I was lamenting my insensibility to superstition! Am I beginning to be sucked in? shall I become a midnight twitterer like my neighbours?'.[71] Indeed, this experience of supernatural dread inflects the narrative of 'Falesá', whose genesis the same letter explains: 'a new story . . . shot through me like a bullet in one of my moments of awe, alone in that tragic jungle'.[72]

As well as indicating the force of superstitious fears, 'Falesá' also suggests the sophistication and intricacy of local belief-systems. The narrative affirms the legitimacy of native folklore, as against imported traditions. Critics have conventionally read the narrative as depicting the triumph of realistic over fantastic modes: Edmond judges that in this tale 'the realist mode must win'.[73] It is true that Case's temple is destroyed, but Uma's stories significantly retain an undiluted power. Moreover, as Jolly maintains, Uma's scepticism towards European beliefs – her refusal to accept that Queen Victoria, whom Wiltshire claims as his protectress, has any sway over Falesá – amounts to an assertion of the authority of local cultures.[74] Like *In the South Seas*, 'The Beach of Falesá' indicates that indigenous superstitions should be understood as part of a complex system of government and belief. Thus Wiltshire comes to reassess his view of natives' childlike credulity. Recognizing that the island chief, Maea, cooperated with the taboo on Uma simply to shore up his influence with Case, he implicitly acknowledges that political savoir-faire rather than naïvety dictates native acceptance of taboos (58). The realignment marks a recognition of the functional value of superstition and its importance within a sophisticated and coherent society.

Like other European imports, the written word, introduced to the predominantly oral cultures of the South Seas, is also represented critically by the narrative of 'Falesá', as an instrument by which European colonists manipulate and exploit native cultures. Wiltshire deceives Uma by a sham marriage certificate, drawn up by Case. Innocently fetishized by Uma, it declares that she is 'illegally married to Mr John Wiltshire for one night, and Mr John Wiltshire is at liberty to send her to hell next morning' (11). As Barry Menikoff shows, this marriage certificate so shocked Stevenson's editors that it was omitted altogether from the 1892 *Illustrated London News* serial version, and when the tale was published in *Island Nights' Entertainments* (1893) the contract's duration was extended to one week.[75] By contrast with its caustic portrayal of the written word, 'Falesá' valorizes the oral cultures and spoken languages of the Pacific. Stevenson was enthralled by these. His regard for Herman Melville's South Seas writings was tempered by dismay at what he considered Melville's insensitive hearing: his copy of *Typee* is marked by annotations querying his rendering of Marquesan language.[76]

Stevenson's fascination with the spoken word had long shaped his writing. In essays such as 'Talk and Talkers' (1882) and 'A Humble

Remonstrance' (1884), he celebrated the revived romance form and linked it to a natural and spontaneous orality. Stevenson shared the late-Victorian interest in the origins of literature and in primitive forms of narrative – an interest which Linda Dowling compellingly relates to new scientific insight into language, and to the interpretation of spoken dialects as active, vital tongues, and of written languages as moribund.[77] This new understanding of speech underlay a developing tension within anthropology, as the traditional hierarchy of written and oral culture was increasingly disrupted. Andrew Lang, whose characteristically progressivist evolutionism was tempered by his attraction to older cultural forms, was influential in fostering recognition of the sophistication of oral culture.[78] Stevenson clearly found this appreciation of the spoken word liberating, but others were disquieted. The double-edged impact of the new esteem for orality, on a nation which often identified itself by its great written literature, is caught well in a contemporary anecdote about a clash between the young Stevenson and his father. Debating 'the subject of word-coinage', Stevenson countered his father's Johnsonian 'doctrine of a "well of English undefiled" ', rattling off

> whole sentences composed of words of foreign origin taken into our language from all parts of the world – words of the East, of classical Europe, of the West Indies, and modern American slang. By a string of sentences he proved the absurdity of such a doctrine . . . It was a real feat in the handling of language . . . The father was silenced; but for a moment he had been almost tearfully in earnest. One could see it was not a matter of mere vocabulary with him.[79]

While his father might deplore it, the spoken voice was always at the heart of Stevenson's interest in language and writing, in early stories such as 'Thrawn Janet' as much as in his later work.

Moreover, the political context of his Pacific writings gives the engagement with Polynesian orality in 'Falesá' an additionally subversive edge. Much of the story's dialogue is written in 'Beach-la-Mar', a pidgin of traders' English and native languages. As Stevenson noted in *In the South Seas*, it 'may be called, and will almost certainly become, the tongue of the Pacific'.[80] In Katherine Linehan's reading, the use of Beach-la-Mar infantilizes the Polynesian characters.[81] However, this pidgin is represented approvingly: less rigid than written language, it allows Wiltshire and Uma to negotiate a linguistic middle ground between their distinct cultures.[82] It is a miscegenated language whose liminal status provides a vivid and positive parallel for Wiltshire and Uma's children. Indirectly challenging the contemporary condemnation of biological miscegenation, the language is portrayed affirmatively, as characterized by hybridity and exchange.[83]

Stevenson's valorization of Beach-La-Mar, a language that might have been seen as regressive or infantile, and his mistrust of imperialist written culture, thus implies a subversion of progressivist evolutionary anthropology. Barry Menikoff traces the proofreaders' conscientious anglicization of unfamiliar idioms, and suggests that these changes work to 'contain' Stevenson's anti-imperialism.[84] Indeed, the toning down of the Polynesian vernacular indicates the threat posed by the narrative's use of dialect, which may have tapped into fears, endemic to *fin-de-siècle* imperialism, about the potential for the colonial centre to regress to savagery.[85] Stevenson's narrative, of course, was far from depicting any triumph for native Polynesians, whether in terms of the linguistic power struggle or of the larger drama of cultural conflict which it symbolizes. It is true that, as Jolly observes, Uma's fertility resists the conventional trope of the dying Pacific.[86] The tale also depicts Case's elimination from the island, and the increasing dominance of 'Beach-la-Mar'. Nonetheless, the uncertain ending underlines the resilience of imperialist ideologies and racial hierarchies. Stevenson's South Seas writings celebrate the value and sophistication of indigenous folk culture, but they also evince anxiety about the ability of a dominant culture or race to extinguish its weaker rival.

The same preoccupation with cultural and linguistic 'contact zones' informs Stevenson's Scottish historical novels, which were shaped by his experience of the clash of imperial and indigenous cultures in the South Seas. *In the South Seas*, as I have shown, traces similar patterns of confrontation and subjugation in eighteenth-century Scotland and the modern Pacific. Stevenson was apprehensive about the withering of a distinctive Samoan race and culture under European pressure: he warned Samoan missionary students not to sell their land to foreigners, or else

> your race will die – and in these islands, where your children might have lived for a hundred centuries, another race will sit. /and they will ask themselves, What were the Samoans? and may find word of you in ancient books.\[87]

Stevenson's concern about Polynesian extinction imbued his writings on Scottish history. The process by which he carried over these anxieties can be witnessed in *In the South Seas*, where he considers the universal insecurity of racial fortunes ('so much a matter of the day and hour, is the pre-eminence of race') (13). Reflecting on the Marquesas' depopulation,

Stevenson contemplates the possibility that all races will eventually die out: 'in a perspective of centuries I saw their case as ours, death coming in like a tide, and the day already numbered when there should be no more Beretani [Britons], and no more of any race whatever' (22–3). In an apocalyptic vision, he imagines a day when human life is obliterated from the British landscape. Describing the two sole survivors of the Marquesan Hapaa tribe, he suggests that '[a] similar Adam and Eve may some day wither among new races, the tragic residue of Britain' (23). Echoing Richard Jefferies's recent novel, *After London* (1885), Stevenson conjures up an alienating vision of the familiar British world threatened by extinction. More specifically, the allusions may recall the theory of the 'death of the sun' developed by William Thomson, later Lord Kelvin.[88] The image of the last Marquesans 'huddl[ing] about the embers of the fire of life', like a dwindling party of 'old Red Indians . . . the kindly tribe all gone, the last flame expiring', invokes this vision of inevitable extinction, playing on contemporary fears about racial decline (29).[89]

Stevenson's new sense of human evanescence underlies the energy with which he turned, in the 1890s, to research for a family history, published in 1896 as *Records of a Family of Engineers*. He described the thrill of his genealogical discoveries, in a letter to his cousin:

> I wish to trace my ancestors a thousand years, if I trace them by gallowses. It is not love, not pride, not admiration; it is an expansion of the identity, intimately pleasing, and wholly uncritical . . . I suppose, perhaps, it is more to me who am childless, and refrain with a certain shock from looking forwards. But I am sure, in the solid grounds of race, that you have it also in some degree.[90]

Evoking the uncomfortable and insecure nature of 'looking forwards', Stevenson looks to ancestry to construct a sense of personal and national identity. Indeed, his letters repeatedly assert the enduring importance of Scotland's Celtic heritage. 'I have changed my mind progressively', he wrote: 'practically the whole of Scotland is Celtic, and the western half of England, and all Ireland'.[91] Through this affirmation of Celticism, Stevenson contests the conventional view that Scotland's Lowland population was ethnically closer to its English neighbours than to its Highland compatriots – a view he denounces as 'the Anglo-Saxon heresy'.[92] However spuriously, he is able to create a reassuring sense of continuity with the past, connecting his family with Celtic mythology ('you are Cymry on both sides', he tells his cousin, 'and I Cymry and Pict. We may have fought with King Arthur and known Merlin').[93] The tenuous nature of his claimed genealogy suggests that Stevenson used this narrative to keep a sense of evanescence at bay. As Gillian Beer shows, late-Victorian narratives 'set great store by those signs and traces, those acts of decipherment that relieved oblivion'.[94]

Telling stories about his family history which provided a consoling sense of connection with the past, Stevenson also wrote his final historical novels in a seemingly compulsive manner, betraying similar apprehensions about cultural and racial obsolescence. Between 1892 and 1894 he was engaged on four Scottish novels. Of these he only finished *Catriona* (1892–93), leaving the unfinished *Weir of Hermiston* (1896), and fragments of *Heathercat* (1897) and *The Young Chevalier* (1897). The remainder of this chapter will focus on *Catriona* and *Weir of Hermiston*, arguing that they are informed by Stevenson's experience of contemporary encounters between European and native cultures in the South Seas, and evince a heightened awareness of the vulnerability of traditional cultures and languages.

Catriona, which resumes the tale of David Balfour's adventures where *Kidnapped* ended, has often been seen as an essentially light-hearted reprise of the earlier novel's themes. 'Many of the incidents of *Kidnapped*', Eigner judges, 'repeat themselves in more extended and more highly comic forms in *Catriona*'.[95] Andrew Noble too interprets the novel as a comedy. For Noble, the romance ending represents a failure of political nerve on Stevenson's part, an abandonment of radical intentions: the 'conflict between two civilizations and . . . the tragic collapse of one of them' cannot be 'embodied in an essentially comic plot'.[96] Certainly, the novel's structure lends support to these charges. Like *Kidnapped*, *Catriona* initially charts David's education in the cruel divisions between Whig and Jacobite, as he attempts to intervene in James Stewart's trial for the murder of the king's factor. However, the novel pivots on the Whigs' suppression of David's evidence in an unfair trial, and after this defeat for justice and idealism the narrative shifts from Scotland to Holland, and from public to private concerns. The second part traces David's growing love for the Highland heroine Catriona, Rob Roy's granddaughter and an ardent supporter of the Young Pretender, and ends with their marriage.[97]

Yet despite the romance ending *Catriona* is arguably a much more sombrely political novel than *Kidnapped*, delineating the ruthless machinations of the Hanoverian establishment. As Sir Arthur Quiller-Couch noted in the *Speaker*, 'the wordy, politic intrigue of "Catriona" is at least five years older than the rough-and-tumble intrigue of "Kidnapped"'.[98] David himself, in the few hours ostensibly elapsed since *Kidnapped* concluded, appears to have matured remarkably. Stevenson recognized the change of register, confessing that 'Davie seems to have changed his style'.[99] He displays not only a new interest in women, albeit one portrayed as both gauche and condescending, but also – as he attempts to find his way in a world of conspiracy – a new moral uncertainty and awareness of political corruption. Emma Letley attributes the shift in tone to Stevenson's Pacific experiences. 'The sober note of the opening chapters of the Scottish novel', she contends, registers 'Stevenson's disquiet at the colonial carve-up of the South Sea islands'.[100] She finds evidence of 'cross-fertilization' in the echoes of the colonial injustice exposed in *A Footnote to History*.[101] Certainly, *Catriona*, which dramatizes the destruction of a traditional, Highland culture at the hands of the royalists, evokes what Stevenson saw as a parallel process to the imperialist aggression in Samoa. In both cases a supposedly more civilized party exploits its legal and military expertise to crush ancient habits and customs.

The novel's Lowland hero, having cut the traces of his narrowly Whig upbringing, guides the reader through the decaying world of Highland society, as he shares the fortunes of the Jacobite Stewart and Macgregor clans. Catriona's father, James More Macgregor, reflects upon the changes since the '45, depicting himself as an anachronism in a society which no longer values the sword.[102] This appeal to a nostalgic romanticism initially recalls Scott's description, in the 1829 introduction to *Rob Roy*, of James More Macgregor's penurious exile in France: '[i]t is melancholy to look on the dying struggles even of a wolf or tiger, creatures of a species directly hostile to our own; and, in like manner, the utter distress of this man, whose faults may have sprung from a wild system of education, working on a haughty temper, will not be perused without some pity'.[103] Nonetheless, Scott's tone is ultimately confident that society is outgrowing violence and instability: the 'pity' is crucially dependent on feelings of superiority towards the benighted Highlanders (feelings which he undoubtedly expected his Lowland and English readers to share).[104] Scott's assessment of Rob Roy's appeal encapsulates his belief in the disparity between Highland ferocity and Lowland refinement: '[i]t is this strong contrast betwixt the civilized and cultivated mode of life on the one side of the Highland line, and the wild and lawless adventures . . . on the opposite side of that ideal boundary, which creates the interest attached to his name'.[105]

Catriona's narrative dynamic is much less progressive. Noble claims that Stevenson's novel shares Scott's vision of 'the historical discontinuity of the atavistic from the commercial, civil life of his age', and he contrasts this apparent complacency with his Pacific stories, which display 'the contemporary presence of the bestial'.[106] Yet *Catriona* clearly undermines the belief that Highlanders represented an earlier, more brutal stage of evolution, and that Scotland after the '45 was an increasingly peaceful society, as its Lowland leaders gradually extended the rule of law and order.[107] Instead, it reveals that the justice dispensed by a supposedly emancipated and unprejudiced Edinburgh legal élite is ruled by clan hatred. The Campbells, representative as they are of the ruling Hanoverian culture, disguise a ruthless vendetta in judicial trappings, condemning the innocent James Stewart to death in a trial marked by suppressed evidence and wrongfully imprisoned witnesses: as Charles Stewart declares, '[t]his is not a case, ye see, it's a conspiracy' (283). The mid-trial sermon is on Romans 5 and 13, texts on divine law which cast the ruling power as 'minister of God', and thus draw ironic attention to questions of legal authority and legitimacy (344).[108] Despite the façade of justice, David recognizes that 'James was as fairly murdered as though the Duke had got a fowling-piece and stalked him' (358). The Duke of Argyll, the Campbell chief who presides as judge, implicitly acknowledges that the verdict amounts to savage clan vengeance: had the '45 been successful and positions been reversed, he tells the condemned man, 'you might have been satiated with the blood of any name or clan to which you had an aversion' (357). Subverting the picture of a triumphant passage from savagery to civilization, the Lord Advocate Prestongrange cynically recognizes that the Campbells 'are still barbarians, like these Stewarts; only the Campbells were barbarians on the right side, and the Stewarts were barbarians on the wrong' (246).

A primitive clansman, Stevenson suggests, lurks inside the most cultivated exterior. Thus the lawyer Charles Stewart appears a peaceable character: he confides that he is not much of a Jacobite, is fond of chatting with colleagues in Parliament House, and playing a bit of golf (229). Even he, though, is atavistically drawn into the conflict, and asks in helpless self-justification, '[w]hat can I do? I'm a Stewart, ye see, and must fend for my clan and family' (230). Witnessing his reaction to the trial, David realizes that

> this, that had the externals of a sober process of law, was in its essence a clan battle between savage clans. I thought my friend the Writer [Charles Stewart] none of the least savage. Who, that had only seen him at a counsel's back before the Lord Ordinary or following a golf ball and laying down his clubs on Bruntsfield links, could have recognized for the same person this voluble and violent clansman? (346)

Stewart's regression from sedate professional to 'voluble and violent clansman' recalls Stevenson's description, in *A Footnote to History*, of how the apparently civilized white settlers in Apia 'fell to on the street like rival clansmen', and intimates the belief in inner savagery which connects his Scottish and Polynesian work.[109]

Catriona's treatment of superstition also figures the endurance of a supposedly primitive past. David's encounter with Auld Merren, a 'weird old wife' sitting under two corpses hanging from a gibbet, enacts the irruption of folklore into the present, echoing his vision of the gallows in *Kidnapped* (234).[110] Significantly, David is on his way to meet the laird of Pilrig, a refined gentleman surrounded by 'learned works and musical instruments'; when Merren offers to tell his fortune, he announces his dislike of the 'unco [uncanny]', and flees from 'the eldritch [frightful] creature' (235, 234). The gallows, however, cast a long shadow of superstition over his story: 'the shackles of the gibbet clattered in my head; and the mops and mows of the old witch . . . hag-rode my spirits' (235).

The past's ability to haunt the present is similarly dramatized in 'Black Andie's Tale of Tod Lapraik', a story which his captor relates during David's imprisonment on Bass Rock. This tale of diabolic possession, of a weaver illuminated by 'the joy o' hell', conjures up many dualities – most notably the imbrication of superstitious past and emancipated present (334). The tale's framing initially appears to support the notion of superstition as peculiar to what contemporaries saw as primitive societies: it is introduced and spoken in broad Scots. (Stevenson was proud of his mastery of dialect in the tale, declaring that it was 'a piece of living Scots' and that 'if I had never writ anything but that and "Thrawn Janet", still I'd have been a writer'.)[111] Significantly, David 'can find no word' for the island's eeriness 'in the English', but his Lowland captor is able to supply 'an expression for it in the Scots': '*unco*' (327). David imagines his Gaelic-speaking guards – 'ignorant, barbarous Highlanders', 'tractable, simple creatures' – as representing a still more irrational culture (319, 326). Even before the story is told, he remarks that 'I perceived in them . . . the effects of superstitious fear' (326). Yet the framing narrative also questions the complacent reading of superstition as limited to primitive society. David admits the Highlanders' 'uneasiness' was 'catching', noting his own susceptibility to the uncanny sound of the sea: 'a man could daunt himself with listening – not a Highlandman only' (327). A primitive past, this suggests, persists and frequently erupts within the apparently enlightened present.

Most damningly for the narrative of progress, the Lord Advocate himself is instrumental in the prosecution of the vindictive conspiracy. As the representative of royal power in Scotland after the '45, responsible for promoting order in the Highlands through the revenues gained from the Forfeited Estates, Prestongrange is part of the new, supposedly civilized order, yet he repeatedly perverts the course of justice, being complicit in kidnapping David and securing a false conviction.[112] Stevenson's Prestongrange is a charismatic but treacherous figure, whose diplomatic arts are no less dangerous though they are the mark of a cultivated and professional member of the ruling élite. In fact, his persuasive and sophistical rhetoric renders him a more perilous enemy – as he inadvertently admits of himself and Argyll, their inner savagery is masked by a disarming veneer of urbanity: 'we are Highlanders civilised' (246). He recalls Stevenson's engagement with late-Victorian anxieties about whether the 'persuasive tongue and the skilful pen' were necessarily an improvement on the 'bare fist and the stone-weapon'.[113] Thus Prestongrange's moments of utmost duplicity are often associated with writing: David describes a meeting during which

> [h]e smiled upon me like a father as he spoke, playing the while with a new pen; methought it was impossible there could be any shadow of deception in the man: yet when he drew to him a sheet of paper, dipped his pen among the ink, and began to address me, I was somehow not certain, and fell instinctively into an attitude of guard. (273)

Catriona, in common with Stevenson's Polynesian writing, represents the anglicized written word critically and valorizes local dialects and oral cultures. The formal English of the court proceedings contrasts unfavourably with the Lallans songs satirizing the trial's injustice (357–8).[114] Like the marriage certificate in 'The Beach of Falesá', written documents are associated with corruption and conspiracy: the charges against James Stewart are printed but not circulated to the defence, and David notes the 'insidious device' whereby evidence 'was handed round . . . in court; passed through the jury-box . . . and disappeared again (as though by accident) before it reached the counsel for the prisoner' (284, 358). The narrative also pits artificially refined language against natural, local dialects. With Catriona, David is able to 'la[y] aside my high, clipped English . . . and forg[et] to make my Edinburgh bows and scrapes', but he stresses the powerful impetus towards linguistic refinement: his residence with Prestongrange, whose daughter Barbara mocks his 'countrified' accent, gives him 'an address a little more genteel' (390, 367, 375). Gaelic is another casualty of this allegedly ameliorative process of anglicization. Catriona describes it to David as 'your own tongue that you forget', explaining that 'it was sung about the cradles before you or me were ever dreamed of; and your name remembers it still' (291). She figures the obsolescence of Gaelic as a loss of spontaneity and sincerity: '[t]he heart speaks in that tongue' (291). In terms which echo contemporary Gaelic Revivalist rhetoric, the narrative indicates that a predominantly oral Highland culture is dying, its songs irrevocably set in the past (Alan's airs are 'about the ancient old chiefs that are all by with it lang syne') (304).[115]

The novel's representation of superstition and oral culture thus unsettles the idea of progress from a barbaric Highland past to an enlightened modernity, resonating with the exposure of primitive clan mentalities at the heart of Edinburgh's legal and political establishment. Yet when the action shifts to Holland, where David plans to study law, these serious concerns are apparently abandoned. He renounces his earlier rebellion against the unscrupulous Hanoverian establishment. Sparing few thoughts for the man who has just been condemned to death, he is preoccupied by his developing relationship with Catriona, who is in exile on the Continent; after a protracted courtship, he eventually marries her. This change of register is intriguing. For critics including Noble, the second part obliterates Stevenson's earlier, more radical concerns, its ending indicating 'a marriage of the two Scotlands'.[116] Certainly, David opts back into the ruling order. He becomes a lawyer and landed proprietor in the Lowlands, where his adornment of his estate with 'plantations, parterres, and a terrace' signals his status as an improving landowner, perhaps suggesting an attempt to recover an uncomplicated Whig identity (377). His union with the Jacobite heroine could be interpreted as marking a retreat from the earlier exposure of political corruption, and an acceptance, much in the style of Scott, that Scotland's future lies within Britain.

However, rather than symbolically defusing the remaining threat to political stability and representing the harmonious reconciliation of Scotland's warring factions, David's retreat from a public sphere of action into a private, romantic rôle arguably inscribes a deeply pessimistic recognition that he is powerless to intervene in the confrontation between cultures. Quiller-Couch described readers' 'shock of disappointment' when 'David fails after all to save James Stewart of the Glens', but their rapid recognition of 'how inevitable was the issue when this stripling engaged to turn back the great forces of history'.[117] At the close of the novel's first part, after the execution of James Stewart, David sorrowfully reflects that '[t]ill the end of time young folk . . . will struggle as I did, and make heroical resolves, and take long risks; and the course of events will push them upon the one side and go on like a marching army' (382). This mournful sense of the inexorably brutal nature of cultural conflict suggests that the second part of *Catriona* should be read not as comedy but as tragedy.

David's disillusionment appears an inevitable effect of attaining maturity: 'young folk' always find their 'heroical resolves' thwarted. Like so many of Stevenson's romance heroes, he retreats from action to passivity. In David's case, his idealism is eroded by the pressures of adulthood, and specifically those of adult heterosexuality. Adult ambitions undermine his heroism and moral certainty. Even as he opposes Prestongrange's corruption, he agrees to stay with him because he intends 'to be called to the Bar, where your lordship's countenance would be invaluable' – a decision which disturbs his 'conscience' (355, 356). The demands of heterosexuality also impel David's retreat from the public to the private sphere, from idealism to moral compromise. Far from providing the 'conventional marriage conclusion of comedy' which Eigner describes, the second part of *Catriona* charts David's troubled negotiation of the transition from adolescence to heterosexual adulthood, as he attempts to win Catriona and, by extension, his manhood.[118] Significantly, David retreats to his Lowland estate immediately after he wounds Catriona in his final embroilment in contemporary political struggles: his 'horror' at this symbolic injury underlies his repudiation of politics (469). David's ownership of Shaws – soon the couple's family home – is founded, moreover, on his acceptance of corrupt patronage. Indeed, the narrative repeatedly associates moral compromise with the demands of family: David realizes that the 'villains of that horrid plot [to execute James Stewart] were decent, kind, respectable fathers of families' (382–3).

The final picture of life at Shaws emphasizes disenchantment and withdrawal: the estate is sheltered from the contaminating world of politics, as David avoids entanglement with both Whigs and Jacobites. In Susan Gannon's words, it is 'safely sequestered from the world'.[119] The household occasionally indulges in a whiff of Jacobitism, but as David's amused description of the 'strange doings in a good Whig house' makes clear, this does not signify Noble's 'marriage of the two Scotlands' (474). Rather, it indicates the inability of exiled Jacobitism to pose a threat to the comfortable, and compromised, Hanoverian establishment. Despite its 'romance' ending, then, *Catriona* concludes on a note of inglorious retreat: like the earlier part of the novel, it unsettles the notion of progress from Highland savagery to Lowland civilization. The narrative exposes how the ruling élite crushes a weaker culture; and the hero's helplessness in the face of this brutal 'course of events' echoes the vision of inexorable conflict and conquest at the heart of Stevenson's Polynesian writings.

Weir of Hermiston, the novel on which Stevenson was working when he died in 1894, shares this perception of an inevitably recurring struggle for power and intimates that true cross-cultural understanding and sympathy may prove elusive. Like 'Thrawn Janet' and *Heathercat, Weir* is set in the fictional Borders village of Balweary. Together, the three narratives trace a community's cultural evolution across the centuries. *Heathercat* opens with the late-seventeenth-century royalist persecution of the Covenanters; 'Thrawn Janet', set in the early eighteenth century, shows how Janet's dalliances with royalist dragoons, mentioned in *Heathercat,* still haunt her; and *Weir* evokes the village in the early nineteenth century, unable to escape a heritage of intolerance and violence.[120] Set during the Napoleonic Wars, its narrative centres on the confrontation between young Archie Weir and his father Lord Hermiston, the 'hanging judge'. Archie is banished by his father to Balweary for his public denunciation of capital punishment, and begins a doomed love affair with a local girl. The novel breaks off just as Archie ends the affair, but Stevenson's notes indicate that a rival, Frank Innes, was to seduce his sweetheart, and Archie was to kill him and be convicted of murder by his own father.[121]

For many critics, Stevenson's last novel, written from an exotic exile, was a nostalgic testament to Scottishness, drained of any contemporary pungency. Stevenson himself fed this myth, with a dedication which described how 'here afar, / Intent on my own race and place, I wrote'.[122] Even before *Weir*'s publication, Stevenson had been associated with Kailyard writers such as J. M. Barrie, S. R. Crockett, and Ian Maclaren, whose novels evoked a bygone Scotland, pastoral and organic: Maclaren hailed him as a fellow spirit, writing that '[t]he mists of his native lands and its wild traditions passed into [Stevenson's] blood . . . Never did he weary us with the pedantry of modern problems'.[123] Reviewers were quick to read *Weir* as a Kailyard novel, largely owing to its abundant use of Scots dialect. Joseph Jacobs complained that 'the whole book carries the licence of the "kailyard" to an extreme. We can scarcely have half the book before us, yet already the glossary, which is eminently necessary, deals with over a couple of hundred words . . . in short, the book is not for the Southron'.[124]

Yet the characters' use of dialect is not a straightforward mark of nostalgic romanticism, but articulates complex linguistic and cultural tensions. Indeed, whereas Kailyard novels, in Eric Anderson's words, 'ignored' the 'sadness of change and the collision of cultures', *Weir* clearly scrutinizes the painful dynamics of cultural conflict.[125] Modern critics have recognized the novel's concern with discord, but have usually read its father–son conflict in terms of psychology or autobiography. For Fielding and Sandison, *Weir* dramatizes Archie's 'Oedipal' struggle.[126] Karl Miller judges that Stevenson uses ideas about 'the religion and the law of his land' primarily to 'exhibit the power of its authoritarian fathers', while K. G. Simpson interprets the narrative in yet more plainly autobiographical terms, as exposing the 'tension between [Stevenson's] impulse towards . . . narratorial experimentation and the awe of authority with which Calvinism endowed him'.[127] Despite this critical emphasis on psychological tensions, I shall argue, all the novel's conflicts – narratorial, filial, linguistic, religious, and legal – ultimately coalesce around the idea of confrontation between cultures. Envisioning recurrent cultural encounter, the novel participates in *fin-de-siècle* doubts about progress, and resists the anthropological belief in steady evolutionary advance.

Weir's narrative method draws attention to social and cultural variance, creating a sense of disjunction as the late-nineteenth-century narrator comes into contact with the Napoleonic era during which his story is set. The narrator's contemporary allusions jar with the events narrated (describing Frank Innes's cunning, he notes that '[t]hey knew nothing of Sherlock Holmes in these days, but there was a good deal said of Talleyrand').[128] As Penny Fielding judges, the narrator's encounters with an archaic moorland world embody the opposition between psychological realism and oral narration.[129] Thus while the love between Archie and Christina appears to the latter as the workings of 'a pagan Fate', the narrator interprets it almost scientifically: 'even that phenomenon of love at first sight', he pronounces, 'which . . . seems so simple and violent, like a disruption of life's tissue, may be decomposed into a sequence of accidents happily concurring' (133). He views Borders culture according to a condescending evolutionist model of survivals, noting that the 'high, false note of barbarous mourning . . . still lingers modified among Scots heather' (67). The novel, Peter Zenzinger argues, pits the narrator's 'progressive Victorian attitude' against the supernatural fatalism of the Balweary folk.[130] Indeed, the introduction, in which the narrator describes the place where Archie was later to kill Frank, emphasizes the unreliable distortions of oral memory:

> [f]or a while it was told that Francie [Frank] walked . . . He pursued Rob Todd (if any one could have believed Robbie) . . . But the age is one of incredulity; these superstitious decorations speedily fell off; and the facts of the story itself, like the bones of a giant buried there and half dug up, survived, naked and imperfect, in the memory of the scattered neighbours. (55)

For Zenzinger, this modern faith in 'facts' indicates the narrator's awareness of the 'mental distance of his own period from that which he is describing' and his confident belief that the 'ballad world' is 'outdated'.[131]

Yet although Zenzinger emphasizes the narrator's disdain for the 'uncultured country people', equally striking is his sense of modern decline.[132] He frequently undercuts his own realism, protesting for example that, in his depiction of Christina's psychology, 'I have been painting chaos and describing the inarticulate. Every lineament that appears is too precise, almost every word used too strong' (132). His omniscience is further destabilized by his personalization: like Archie, and Stevenson himself, the narrator belongs to Edinburgh University's Speculative Society (in an earlier draft he resembled Stevenson more clearly, recounting the tale 'in as far a place and before so great an audience') (79).[133] Moreover, far from being supercilious, the narrator is attracted by a spirited folk culture. The Elliotts, a rustic family native to the moorlands, appear to exemplify traditional oral culture at its most potent. Kirstie Elliott tells epic tales of her ancestors ('[l]ike so many people of her class, she was a brave narrator'), and her rendering of the legend of the 'Four Black Brothers' is one of the novel's vernacular triumphs (104). Revealingly, the narrator himself starts but is unable to complete this tale of heroic barbarism. He passes the narration deferentially to 'my author, Kirstie, whom I but haltingly follow, for she told the tale like one inspired' (108).

Archie's banishment to the Borders initially appears to figure the regenerative power of native oral culture, as he leaves his reclusive life in Edinburgh for the invigorating moorlands. At the *fin de siècle*, critics regarded the ballad as, in Andrew Lang's words, the 'early expression of a people's life', and hailed it as a curative for the morbid introspection of modernity.[134] John Veitch concluded *The History and Poetry of the Scottish Border* (1878) with the admonition that

> [w]e need . . . some reminder of the grandeur of a simple life, of the instinctive character of high motives and noble deeds, of the self-satisfying sense of duty done; and the close work-shops of our literary manufactures would be all the better for a good fresh breeze from the hills and the holms of the Teviot and the Yarrow.[135]

Stevenson, incidentally, owned a copy of this book, and the Elliott family recalls the historical Elliots, described by Veitch as a 'remarkable family group, who have contributed to the minstrelsy of the Borders'.[136] Inspired by Kirstie's epic storytelling and expressive vernacular, Archie occasionally slips from genteel anglicization into the native dialect – a transition figured as a movement towards authenticity (the narrator describes him as 'profoundly moved, and lapsing into the broad Scots') (166). However, as Penny Fielding argues, *Weir* undercuts the idea that the ballad tradition can provide a stimulating antidote to modern morbidity.[137] The 'return to the voice' which was so enthusiastically affirmed at the *fin de siècle* provides no solutions for Archie.[138] He finds the traditional, oral culture of the ballad world is decaying, offering him no alternative to his isolated Edinburgh life: soon known as 'the Recluse of Hermiston', he is quick to 'retire into solitude' (100, 101).

Weir, indeed, is imbued with regret for the imminent passing of the ballad world. The bardic tradition survives in Kirstie's nephew Dand, yet the narrator hints that he is already obsolescent: 'though not printed himself, he was recognized by others who were and who had become famous. Walter Scott owed to Dandie the text of the "Raid of Wearie" in the *Minstrelsy*' (114). The association with Scott recalls nineteenth-century apprehensions that the Shirra's achievement in committing ballads to print might actually extinguish the oral culture from which they sprang.[139] Moreover, even Kirstie is threatened by encroaching silence and imagines 'the day over for her old-world tales and local gossip' (161). In one of the novel's most powerful passages, the pain and loss suffered in the process of cultural extinction is evoked in Kirstie's fear that '[t]alk is the last link, the last relation' (104). Kirstie's lapses into silence suggest the expiring of the ballad tradition, and the narrator laments that this 'degenerate' age is unable to give due heroic treatment to the exploits of the Elliotts: '[s]ome century earlier the last of the minstrels might have fashioned the last of the ballads out of that Homeric fight and chase; but the spirit was dead, or had been reincarnated already in Mr Sheriff Scott, and the degenerate moorsmen must be content to tell the tale in prose' (110). With the 'last of the ballads' and the 'last of the minstrels' already extinct, the narrator suggests, native poetic tradition is now obsolete.

The novel's central symbol, the Weaver's Stone, intensifies this sense that traditional cultures face decline, obliteration, and oblivion. Equally importantly, it represents the relentless process of violent confrontation between cultures. The Stone, a monument to the fictional Covenanting martyr known as the Praying Weaver, is an emblem of oral culture and collective memory: Archie's mother sits here as she tells the child folktales of the Covenanters' persecution 'till their tears ran down' (61). The narrator's claim that 'the chisel of Old Mortality has clinked on that lonely gravestone' recalls the historical figure of 'Old Mortality', whose faithful tending of Covenanters' gravestones was commemorated in Walter Scott's *Old Mortality* (1816). The inscription, though, is 'half defaced' and illegible, symbolizing, as Sandison notes, the transience of folk-memory and oral culture (55).[140] Although the tombstone inscriptions in Scott's novel are also obliterated, in this case by 'moss, lichen, and deer-hair', the accent is different: *Old Mortality* indicates that Scotland's heritage of violence is safely buried in the past and that social conflict has been superseded by the supposed consensus of Scott's time.[141] The Weaver's Stone in Stevenson's novel, by contrast, is haunted by discord: it was to be revisited by tragedy, as the scene for Archie's projected murder of Frank. In the novel's opening chapter, the narrator ominously warns readers that '[p]ublic and domestic history have . . . marked with a bloody finger this hollow among the hills; and since the Cameronian [the Praying Weaver] gave his life there, two hundred years ago . . . the silence of the moss has been broken once again by the report of fire-arms and the cry of the dying' (55). With its image of the 'bloody finger' suggesting an unavoidable destiny, this passage conjures up a bleak vision of inexorably recurring violence.

The novel's central conflict, between father and son, represents a clash between old and new social orders, and questions the forward-moving narrative of cultural evolution. Just as Stevenson's Pacific writings scrutinize the damaging impact of colonialism on native cultures, *Weir* registers the trauma suffered by Scotland when it adapted to union with a more powerful neighbour. It undercuts the notion that the Union helped to civilize the Scots, and like Stevenson's Jacobite novels emphasizes instead the cultural conflict which it inaugurates. Archie's rebellion against his father is precipitated by his desire to adapt to new cultural *mores*, linguistic and political. Hermiston, with his pithy vernacular, evokes Scots' alienation from their own cultural history, as Lord Braxfield, on whom he was based, was the last judge to employ pure Scotch idiom.[142] Archie's repugnance for his father's coarse language and 'low, gross accent' represents the hostility of a newly anglicized Scottish gentry towards its less refined progenitors (70). Stevenson had always mistrusted anglicization (in an 1876 review, he celebrated a supposedly primitive Scottish poetic tradition, condemning as artificial poets who 'aped the English manner'), but his preference for native dialect was intensified by his Pacific experiences.[143] The collision between father and son also represents the clashing of traditional, anti-radical beliefs with the new Romantic emphasis on personal freedom. As Hermiston declares, there is no room for delicate notions of individual liberty 'under the fower quarters of John Calvin' (86). An earlier draft highlights still more the divergence of manners and language, with Archie mentally censuring his father: '[h]e was coarse and cruel; he talked a shambling homespun, without /grace or\ beauty'.[144] Hermiston's reproof to his son, in this draft, further emphasizes the conflict generated by class mobility, as he laments that 'I've made a gentleman of ye – there was my mistake; – ye're spun so fine, ye're fit niether [*sic*] for warp nor woof'.[145]

The power clash between old and new social orders is not limited to that between Archie and his father, but – as indicated by the reiterated 'cry of the dying' at the Weaver's Stone – is unremitting. References to the French Revolution, Napoleonic Wars, and local insurrections evoke widespread upheaval, while in the earlier period of the Praying Weaver Covenanters challenge royalists (58, 65, 86). The fortunes of the Elliott family suggest the rapidly changing nature of political and social orders. Gib was formerly involved in radical politics, 'embrac[ing] with enthusiasm the principles of the French Revolution'; chastened by Hermiston's 'furious onslaught . . . upon the Liberals', he now contents himself with 'pray[ing] for a blessing on the arms of Bonaparte' (111–12). Clem, though born a humble countryman, has profited by his 'spirit of innovation', becoming a wealthy and successful Glasgow businessman (113). Throughout the novel, violence simmers just below the surface, ready to erupt even in apparently civilized characters. Hob Elliott, otherwise 'a stiff and rather graceless model of the rustic proprieties', avenges his father's death in a sudden resurgence of 'barbarity': the narrator reports that '[t]he transfiguration had been for the moment only; some Barbarossa, some old Adam of our ancestors, sleeps in all of us till the fit circumstance shall call it into action', and contrasts this 'formidable' deed with its incongruous setting, 'a country gagged and swaddled with civilisation' (110–11).

At every turn, then, the turbulent narrative destabilizes the belief in progressive and steady cultural evolution. It also radically undermines the possibility of cross-cultural sympathy. *Weir*'s serialization in *Cosmopolis* sheds intriguing light on the preoccupation with communication between cultures.[146] The journal was founded in 1896, in the hope that it might 'by its independence and impartiality . . . help to bring about a sense of closer fellowship between the nations – a larger sympathy making, slowly, no doubt, but effectually, for the far-off goal of perfect culture: peace and concord'.[147] This invitation to a 'larger sympathy' chimes with evolutionary anthropologists' belief in the natural upward movement of human spiritual life. Yet while *Cosmopolis*'s contributors aimed to promote cultural exchange and thus transcend national cultures, they also sensed that this might be an impossible feat.[148]

Stevenson's novel resonates with this *fin-de-siècle* doubt about cultural progress. Like his Pacific writings, which urge the importance of cultivating cross-cultural sympathy yet question the viability of this project, *Weir* pits empathy and communication against egoism and silence, but holds out little hope for the outcome of this contest. Archie's parents display an archetypal inability to reach out beyond themselves: '[i]ce and iron cannot be welded', the narrator observes, 'and the points of view of the Justice-Clerk and Mrs. Weir were not less unassimilable' (63).

The mother passes her animosity to the son: Archie is taught by her tales of martyred Covenanters to fear and despise his father as a 'persecutor' (61). Silence, and the lack of sympathy which it denotes, characterizes the relationship between father and son. Hermiston 'sufficed wholly and silently to himself', and Archie similarly makes 'no attempt whatsoever to understand the man with whom he dined and breakfasted' (69, 73). Father and son enjoy no mutual bonds ('there were not, perhaps, in Christendom, two men more radically strangers') (74). This solipsistic reticence is at the root of the tragedy related in *Weir*: had Archie allowed himself to talk, the narrator judges, 'there might have been no tale to write upon the Weirs of Hermiston' (72).

As this lack of sympathy and communication suggests, there is little hope for an end to the relentless cycle of violence symbolized by the Praying Weaver's Stone. Across the centuries charted by *Heathercat*, 'Thrawn Janet', and *Weir*, Balweary is unable to lay its bloody heritage to rest. Far from being a quasi-Kailyard testament to nostalgia and patriotism, *Weir* marked an engagement with *fin-de-siècle* anxieties about cultural progress. In its vision of primitive resurgence (the waking of 'some old Adam of our ancestors') and in its concern with the decline and obsolescence of traditional, oral cultures, the novel resonates with Stevenson's Pacific writing, undermining the anthropological narrative of progressive cultural evolution.

Stevenson's anthropological interest in the relations between past and present, savagery and civilization, Part III has shown, runs through his œuvre, forging surprising links between his fables, short stories, novels, and travel writing, and between his Scottish and Polynesian work. Chapter 5 argued that, although Stevenson was attracted by anthropologists' confidently secularizing line, even his early fiction such as 'Thrawn Janet' unsettles contemporary assumptions about the triumph of free thought, dramatizing the resurgence of superstition and intolerance. *Kidnapped* and *The Master of Ballantrae* extend this scepticism about anthropology's forward-moving narrative, with their portraits of an irrevocably divided nation radically undermining claims that Scotland was progressing towards civilized modernity.

From 1888, I have argued here, Stevenson's Pacific experiences intensified his mistrust of anthropology's progressivism. While recent interpretations have charged his Scottish fiction with an apolitical nostalgia, and hailed his Pacific work for its prescient multiculturalism, the two halves of his œuvre are clearly united by their critical engagement with anthropology's complacent ethnocentrism. In *Catriona* and *Weir* as much as *In the South Seas* and 'The Beach of Falesá', Stevenson proposes a bleak understanding of evolution, emphasizing the pain and violence inherent in the struggle for survival, and the tragic repercussions of the loss of tradition, custom, and belief. His writings destabilize Victorian anthropologists' hierarchical model of cultural progress and paint a more variegated picture: purportedly civilized societies harbouring hidden savageries, and indigenous cultures revealing an unsuspected sophistication. In this respect, Stevenson's work sheds light on the discipline at a pivotal stage in its development, pointing forward intriguingly to the twentieth century's more relativist anthropology and to its developing concern with cultural plurality.

Yet while his work fiercely celebrates undervalued native cultures, and seeks to mitigate the effects of the dominant cultural imperialism by eroding constricting boundaries and finding affinities between apparently incongruous cultures, it is nonetheless imbued with a melancholy scepticism about the possibility of cross-cultural understanding. An unthinking assumption of superiority characterizes many of Stevenson's characters – the American missionaries, Archie Hermiston, or the captain who thinks that after a perfunctory visit to a Pacific island he can write a 'chapter on [its] manners'. This inability to enter sympathetically into an alien culture casts doubt on the viability of the anthropological enterprise.

Conclusion

Stevenson's enduring scientific concerns – about the nature and direction of evolutionary change, and the relations of savagery and civilization, progress and degeneration, heredity and environment, and individual and race – converged in a contemplative and wide-ranging letter to his cousin Bob, written shortly before he died.[1] The letter opens by discussing the nature of Scottish racial divisions, contesting the theory that the Picts 'were blacker than other Celts' (361). Declaring that all British skins are becoming increasingly 'pigmented', Stevenson asserts that 'colour is not an essential part of a man or a race', and cites his observations of South Sea islanders:

> [t]ake my Polynesians, an Asiatic People probably from the neighbourhood of the Persian Gulf. They range through any amount of shades, from the burnt hue of the Low Archipelago islander which seems half negro, to the 'bleached' pretty women of the Marquesas (close by on the map) who come out for a festival no darker than an Italian; their colour seems to vary directly with the degree of exposure to the sun. (362)

Stevenson argues that skin colour is dependent less on birth than on 'exposure to the sun'. His evident fascination with heredity, however, undermines this emphasis on the formative influence of the environment. Describing his research into his own family history, he conveys the exhilarating sense of immortality which ancestry confers:

> [t]here is just a link wanting; and we might be able to go back to the eleventh century . . . What a singular thing is this undistinguished perpetuation of a family throughout the centuries, and the sudden bursting forth of character and capacity that began with our grandfather! (362)

Moving from the past to the future, from ancestry to progeny, Stevenson reflects on the mysteries of reproduction, inheritance, and the perpetuation of human life:

> as I go on in life, day by day, I become more of a bewildered child: I cannot get used to this world, to procreation, to heredity, to sight, to

> hearing; the commonest things are a burthen; the sight of Belle [his step-daughter] and her twelve-year-old boy, already taller than herself, is enough to turn my hair grey; as for Fanny and her brood, it is insane to think of. (362)

As the letter continues, he develops this sense of life as a mystifying spectacle. Humankind, he suggests, has not progressed steadily from savagery to civilization; rather than evolving in a unified manner, it still harbours traces of earlier developmental stages. Behind a façade of civilization, he implies, humans betray their bestial origins: he contrasts the 'conventional surface' and 'social stage-directions' of life with a 'wild' and 'simian' human nature (362–3). Stevenson claims that '[c]ivilisation has become reflex with us; you might think that hunger was the name of the best sauce', yet that the 'crowding dumb multitudes' remain 'monkeys', driven to 'do things, write able articles, stitch shoes, dig, from the purely simian impulse' (363). The equivocal representation of the 'simian impulse' (understood as both a revitalizing energy and a dumb inarticulacy) is characteristic of Stevenson's writings, in which the affirmation of primitive life is often tempered by uneasiness. Uncertainty about the nature and direction of human evolution pervades the letter. He muses, for example, on the emergence of a European anarchist movement. Perplexed by the anarchists' combination of 'dastardly' conduct and elevated 'spiritual life', he conjectures that '[t]his is just what the early Christians must have seemed to the Romans. Is this then a new *Drive* among the monkeys?' (365). Yet it is in the contrasts and incongruities of human life that Stevenson finds its fascination and appeal: '[t]he prim obliterated polite face of life, and the broad, bawdy, and orgiastic – or maenadic – foundations', he declares, 'form a spectacle to which no habit reconciles me' (362).

Indeed, as this book has shown, Stevenson's interest in life's 'broad, bawdy . . . foundations' forms a unifying preoccupation across his work. His enduring intellectual concern with the meaning and value of primitive instincts, energies, and cultures runs through his generically diverse œuvre, and unites his Scottish and Polynesian writings. Recent criticism has repeatedly cast Stevenson as a nostalgic antiquarian in his Scottish novels, and – contrastingly – an anticipator of postcolonialism in his Pacific work. These interpretations typically view Stevenson as either in advance of or behind his own historical moment. My exploration of the contemporary scientific context of his writings resituates him in the late-Victorian period and, by doing so, reconciles his Scottish and Polynesian work.

In tracing the intersections between literary and scientific discourses, I have suggested some of the ways in which evolutionary psychology and anthropology were open to interventions by literary writers. Stevenson and the scientists, I have argued, were engaged in a creative dialogue, one which amounted to a collective endeavour to understand humankind's evolutionary heritage. Despite warning that 'science carries us into zones of speculation where there is no habitable city for the mind of man', Stevenson constantly attempted to reconcile these domains of thought, to find human meaning in the evolutionary vistas opened up by psychology and anthropology.[2] His ability to participate in debate within these disciplines owed much to their unprofessionalized standing. Equally important, intellectual agendas – evolutionary psychologists' focus on the unconscious mind and creative inspiration, and anthropologists' concern with myth, legend, and folklore – conspired to accord a privileged status and special insight to fictional writers. The belief that Stevenson enjoyed unusual access to the realm of the unconscious imagination thus informed psychologists' interest in his writings, prompting F. W. H. Myers's request that he make a record of his dream-life: '*externalise* your dreams in waking hours', he implored, 'for the sake of Science'.[3]

Stevenson's engagement with science, I have revealed, was much more extensive and equivocal than has hitherto been acknowledged. It lies at the heart of the ambiguities and interpretative tensions which give his writings their imaginative power. Rather than simply reflecting scientific theories, his writings resist confident assumptions about evolutionary progress. They expose the divergent, often conflicting, nature of evolutionist thought and conduct a radical revaluation of contemporary notions of primitive life. Thus Stevenson's use of evolutionist rhetoric to celebrate romance's appeal to savage appetites paradoxically undermined a progressivist evolutionary psychology, and his early scepticism about a confident evolutionary narrative intensified under the pressure of his Pacific experiences, informing his later fiction's heightened wariness about the resurgence of romance's primitive energies. His transactions with degenerationist thought are equally unsettling. Playing on the unspoken conflict between hereditary and environmental explanations of atavism, his neo-Gothic fiction suggests that degeneracy stems not so much from biology as from the culturally informed denial of humankind's savage heritage.

Finally, and perhaps most compellingly, Stevenson questions anthropological readings of purportedly primitive cultures. His writings destabilize a hierarchical and ethnocentric evolutionism, pointing forward to the twentieth century's more relativist anthropology and to its developing concern with cultural plurality. Yet his vision is strikingly different from the cultural relativism of the late twentieth and early twenty-first centuries. Where present-day relativists emphasize 'difference', Stevenson attested to 'sameness', what humankind held in common. Beneath the cultivated veneer (the 'prim obliterated polite face of life'), he found everywhere the same primitive core: the 'simian impulse' and the 'orgiastic – or maenadic – foundations'.

Notes

Introduction: Stevenson, evolution, and the 'primitive'

1. An initial version, *The South Seas*, was published in a limited copyright edition in 1890; the material was then serialized in 1891 in *Black and White*, the New York *Sun* and the *Auckland Star*. *In the South Seas*, a compilation selected by Sidney Colvin, appeared in volume form in 1896.
2. Fanny Stevenson to Sidney Colvin, May 1889, in *The Letters of Robert Louis Stevenson*, ed. Bradford Booth and Ernest Mehew, 8 vols (New Haven, Connecticut: Yale University Press, 1994–95), 6: 303 (hereafter, *Letters*).
3. Fanny Stevenson to Colvin, May 1889, *Letters*, 6: 304, 303.
4. Fanny Stevenson to Colvin, January 1891, *Letters*, 7: 79.
5. Fanny Stevenson to Colvin, January 1891, *Letters*, 7: 79.
6. Fanny Stevenson to Colvin, January 1891, *Letters*, 7: 79.
7. Fanny wrote in the aftermath of a bruising marital tiff: Fanny Stevenson to Colvin, January 1891, *Letters*, 7: 80.
8. Fanny Stevenson to Colvin, January 1891, *Letters*, 7: 79.
9. Fanny Stevenson to Colvin, January 1891, *Letters*, 7: 80. Despite Fanny's efforts to make the work less scientific, critical reaction confirmed her fears about its aridity: see Neil Rennie, 'Introduction', in Robert Louis Stevenson, *In the South Seas* (1896; comp. Sidney Colvin) (London: Penguin, 1998), viii–xxxv, xxi.
10. Matthew Arnold, 'Literature and Science' (1882), in *The Complete Prose Works of Matthew Arnold*, ed. R. H. Super, vol. 10 (Ann Arbor, Michigan: University of Michigan Press, 1974), 53–73, 62.
11. On the Snow–Leavis contest, see Stefan Collini, 'Introduction', in C. P. Snow, *The Two Cultures* (Cambridge: Cambridge University Press, 1993), vii–lxxi; Elinor S. Shaffer, 'Introduction: The Third Culture – Negotiating the "Two Cultures"', in Elinor S. Shaffer, ed., *The Third Culture: Literature and Science* (Berlin: Walter de Gruyter, 1998), 1–12, 1–2. On the opposition of literature and science as a 'cultural artefact', see John Christie and Sally Shuttleworth, 'Introduction: Between Literature and Science', in John Christie and Sally Shuttleworth, eds, *Nature Transfigured: Science and Literature, 1700–1900* (Manchester: Manchester University Press, 1989), 1–12, 3.
12. Thomas S. Kuhn, *The Structure of Scientific Revolutions* (Chicago, Illinois: University of Chicago Press, 1962), 3–4, 151; see also George Levine, 'One Culture: Science and Literature', in George Levine, ed., *One Culture: Essays in Science and Literature* (Madison, Wisconsin: University of Wisconsin Press, 1987), 3–32, 5–22.
13. Collini, 'Introduction', liii.
14. Gillian Beer, *Open Fields: Science in Cultural Encounter* (Oxford: Oxford University Press, 1996), 173.
15. Beer, *Fields*, 173.
16. Beer, *Fields*, 173.

17. Gillian Beer, *Darwin's Plots: Evolutionary Narrative in Darwin, George Eliot and Nineteenth-Century Fiction* (1983), 2nd edn (Cambridge: Cambridge University Press, 2000).
18. George Levine, *Darwin and the Novelists: Patterns of Science in Victorian Fiction* (Cambridge, Massachusetts: Harvard University Press, 1988), 2–3, 8, 13.
19. Sally Shuttleworth, *George Eliot and Nineteenth-Century Science: the Make-Believe of a Beginning* (Cambridge: Cambridge University Press, 1984), and *Charlotte Brontë and Victorian Psychology* (Cambridge: Cambridge University Press, 1996); Peter Allan Dale, *In Pursuit of a Scientific Culture: Science, Art, and Society in the Victorian Age* (Madison, Wisconsin: University of Wisconsin Press, 1989); Laura Otis, *Organic Memory: History and the Body in the Late Nineteenth and Early Twentieth Centuries* (Lincoln, Nebraska: University of Nebraska Press, 1994).
20. Helen Small, *Love's Madness: Medicine, the Novel, and Female Insanity 1800–1865* (Oxford: Oxford University Press, 1996), 35–40.
21. The paper was published that year in *Transactions of the Royal Scottish Society of Arts*.
22. Stevenson to Sidney Colvin, November 1887, in *Selected Letters of Robert Louis Stevenson*, ed. Ernest Mehew (New Haven, Connecticut: Yale University Press, 1997), 353 (hereafter, *Selected Letters*); on his loss of faith, see Chapter 2.
23. Stevenson, 'Selections from His Notebook' (1923), in *Memories and Portraits, Memoirs of Himself, Selections from His Notebook* (London: Heinemann, 1924), 171–94, 184, 176; Stevenson to Frances Sitwell, September 1873, *Letters*, 1: 287; Stevenson to James Walter Ferrier, November 1872, *Selected Letters*, 28; on his essays, see Chapter 1.
24. On the Society for Psychical Research, see Stevenson to Arthur Conan Doyle, April 1893, *Letters*, 8: 50, 50n; on his anthropological transactions, see Chapter 6.
25. John Jay Chapman, 'Robert Louis Stevenson', in *Emerson and Other Essays* (London: David Nutt, 1898), 217–47, 223. The reference is to Hannah More's widely read novel, *Cœlebs in Search of a Wife* (1808).
26. Andrew Noble, 'Highland History and Narrative Form in Scott and Stevenson', in Andrew Noble, ed., *Robert Louis Stevenson* (London: Vision Press, 1983), 134–87; Christopher Harvie, 'The Politics of Stevenson', in Jenni Calder, ed., *Stevenson and Victorian Scotland* (Edinburgh: Edinburgh University Press, 1981), 107–25.
27. Vanessa Smith, *Literary Culture and the Pacific: Nineteenth-Century Textual Encounters* (Cambridge: Cambridge University Press, 1998), Chapters 3 to 5; Rod Edmond, *Representing the South Pacific: Colonial Discourse from Cook to Gauguin* (Cambridge: Cambridge University Press, 1997), Chapter 6; Barry Menikoff, *Robert Louis Stevenson and 'The Beach of Falesá': a Study in Victorian Publishing* (Stanford, California: Stanford University Press, 1984); Robert Hillier, *The South Seas Fiction of Robert Louis Stevenson* (New York: Peter Lang, 1989).
28. See Roslyn Jolly, 'Introduction', in Stevenson, *South Sea Tales* (Oxford: Oxford University Press, 1996), ix–xxxiii, xxxiii.
29. Alan Sandison, *Robert Louis Stevenson and the Appearance of Modernism* (Basingstoke: Macmillan, now Palgrave Macmillan, 1996), 100, 139–40, 12–13.
30. Barry Menikoff, '*New Arabian Nights*: Stevenson's Experiment in Fiction', *Nineteenth-Century Literature* 45 (1990–91), 339–62, 343.

31. Stephen Heath, 'Psychopathia Sexualis: Stevenson's *Strange Case*', in Lyn Pykett, ed., *Reading Fin de Siècle Fictions* (London: Longman, 1996), 64–79; Stephen D. Arata, 'The Sedulous Ape: Atavism, Professionalism, and Stevenson's *Jekyll and Hyde*', *Criticism: a Quarterly Journal for Literature and the Arts* 37 (1995), 233–59; Robert Mighall, *A Geography of Victorian Gothic Fiction: Mapping History's Nightmares* (Oxford: Oxford University Press, 1999), 145–53, 187–95.
32. 'Introduction', in Elazar Barkan and Ronald Bush, eds, *Prehistories of the Future: the Primitivist Project and the Culture of Modernism* (Stanford, California: Stanford University Press, 1995), 1–19, 2.
33. Beer, *Fields*, 173.
34. Elaine Showalter, *Sexual Anarchy: Gender and Culture at the Fin de Siècle* (London: Bloomsbury, 1991), 105; Roger Cooter and Stephen Pumfrey, 'Separate Spheres and Public Places: Reflections on the History of Science Popularization and Science in Popular Culture', *History of Science* 32 (1994), 237–67, 251. See also Bernard Lightman, '"The Voices of Nature": Popularizing Victorian Science', in Bernard Lightman, ed., *Victorian Science in Context* (Chicago, Illinois: University of Chicago Press, 1997), 187–211.
35. Ed Block, 'James Sully, Evolutionist Psychology, and Late Victorian Gothic Fiction', *Victorian Studies* 25 (1982), 443–67, 444.
36. Block, 'Sully', 461.
37. Ed Block, *Rituals of Dis-integration: Romance and Madness in the Victorian Psychomythic Tale* (New York: Garland, 1993), 7–8.
38. On the origin of the term 'evolution', see Peter J. Bowler, *The Invention of Progress: the Victorians and the Past* (Oxford: Basil Blackwell, 1989), 10.
39. See Peter J. Bowler, *Biology and Social Thought* (Berkeley, California: Office for History of Science and Technology, University of California at Berkeley, 1993), and *The Non-Darwinian Revolution: Reinterpreting a Historical Myth* (Baltimore, Maryland: Johns Hopkins University Press, 1988).
40. J. W. Burrow, *Evolution and Society: a Study in Victorian Social Theory* (Cambridge: Cambridge University Press, 1966), 11–14.
41. George W. Stocking, Jr., *Victorian Anthropology* (New York: Free Press, 1987), *passim*; Bowler, *Biology*, 38–9.
42. Rick Rylance, *Victorian Psychology and British Culture 1850–1880* (Oxford: Oxford University Press, 2000), 203–50; Stocking, *Anthropology*, 154–64.
43. Bowler, *Biology*, 4–7.
44. Martin Fichman, 'Biology and Politics: Defining the Boundaries', in Bernard Lightman, ed., *Victorian Science in Context* (Chicago, Illinois: University of Chicago Press, 1997), 94–118, 97.
45. On Spencer's Lamarckism, see Bowler, *Biology*, 63–9. Lamarck's theory was only undermined with the advent of genetics in the early twentieth century.
46. Beer, *Plots*, 12.
47. For the traditional view, see Jeremy MacClancy, 'Anthropology: "The latest form of evening entertainment"', in David Bradshaw, ed., *A Concise Companion to Modernism* (Oxford: Blackwell Publishers, 2003), 75–94, 82–8. Sinéad Garrigan Mattar suggests, along similar lines to my argument, that the work of W. B. Yeats and J. M. Synge foreshadows modernism's evolutionist interests: *Primitivism, Science, and the Irish Revival* (Oxford: Clarendon Press, 2004), 1–5.

48. Gregory Castle, *Modernism and the Celtic Revival* (Cambridge: Cambridge University Press, 2001), 11.
49. David Richards, *Masks of Difference: Cultural Representations in Literature, Anthropology and Art* (Cambridge: Cambridge University Press, 1994), 216.
50. Nicholas Daly, *Modernism, Romance and the Fin de Siècle: Popular Fiction and British Culture, 1880–1914* (Cambridge: Cambridge University Press, 1999), 118.
51. Peter Broks, 'Science, Media and Culture: British Magazines, 1890–1914', *Public Understanding of Science* 2 (1993), 123–39; Paul White, 'Cross-cultural Encounters: the Co-production of Science and Literature in Mid-Victorian Periodicals', in Roger Luckhurst and Josephine McDonagh, eds, *Transactions and Encounters: Science and Culture in the Nineteenth Century* (Manchester: Manchester University Press, 2002), 75–95.
52. Rylance, *Psychology*, 203–4; Stocking, *Anthropology*, 266–7.
53. Unsourced quotation, cited in Roger Lancelyn Green, *Andrew Lang: a Critical Biography with a Short-Title Bibliography of the Works of Andrew Lang* (Leicester: Edmund Ward, 1946), 115.

Part I. '[O]ur civilised nerves still tingle with . . . rude terrors and pleasures'

1. Stevenson, 'Pastoral' (1887), in *Memories and Portraits* (London: Chatto and Windus, 1904), 90–105, 102.
2. Rick Rylance, *Victorian Psychology and British Culture 1850–1880* (Oxford: Oxford University Press, 2000), 203–50, 215.
3. Herbert Spencer, *The Principles of Psychology* (1855), 2nd edn, 2 vols (London: Williams and Norgate, 1870–72), 1: 452; Laura Otis, *Organic Memory: History and the Body in the Late Nineteenth and Early Twentieth Centuries* (Lincoln, Nebraska: University of Nebraska Press, 1994), 1–40.
4. E. B. Tylor, *Primitive Culture: Researches into the Development of Mythology, Philosophy, Religion, Art, and Custom*, 2 vols (London: John Murray, 1871), 1: 27, 28, 15.
5. Spencer, *Principles*, 1: 503. See also Tylor, *Primitive Culture*, 2: 401–10; George W. Stocking, Jr., *Victorian Anthropology* (New York: The Free Press, 1987), 132–6.

1. Stevenson and the art of fiction

1. Rudyard Kipling, 'The Finest Story in the World' (1891), in *Selected Stories*, ed. Sandra Kemp (London: J. M. Dent, 1987), 54–82; Oscar Wilde, 'The Critic as Artist' (1890), in *The Artist as Critic: Critical Writings of Oscar Wilde*, ed. Richard Ellmann (New York: Vintage Books, 1969), 340–408, 384.
2. James Sully, *My Life and Friends* (London: T. Fisher Unwin, 1918), 195, 194.
3. Sully, *Life*, 215.
4. Alvin Sullivan, ed., *British Literary Magazines: the Victorian and Edwardian Age, 1837–1913* (Westport, Connecticut: Greenwood Press, 1984), 82–3.
5. Ed Block, 'James Sully, Evolutionist Psychology, and Late Victorian Gothic Fiction', *Victorian Studies* 25 (1982), 443–67, 444.
6. Herbert Spencer, *The Principles of Psychology* (1855), 2nd edn, 2 vols (London: Williams and Norgate, 1870–72), 2: 648.

7. Stevenson, 'Books Which Have Influenced Me' (1887), in *Essays Literary and Critical* (London: Heinemann et al., 1923), 62–8, 64–5. On Spencer's influence on Stevenson, see Chapter 3.
8. W. D. Howells, 'Henry James, Jr.' (1882), in *Selected Literary Criticism*, ed. Ulrich Halfmann and Christoph K. Lohmann, 3 vols (Bloomington, Indiana: Indiana University Press, 1993), 1: 317–23, 319, 323.
9. Andrew Lang, 'Realism and Romance', *Contemporary Review* 52 (1887), 683–93, 689.
10. Oscar Maurer, 'Andrew Lang and *Longman's Magazine*, 1882–1905', *University of Texas Studies in English* 34 (1955), 152–78; Marysa Demoor, 'Andrew Lang's *Causeries* 1874–1912', *Victorian Periodicals Review* 21.1 (1988), 15–22.
11. H. Rider Haggard, 'About Fiction', *Contemporary Review* 51 (1887), 172–80; Stephen D. Arata, *Fictions of Loss in the Victorian Fin de Siècle* (Cambridge: Cambridge University Press, 1996), 79–104; Peter Keating, *The Haunted Study: a Social History of the English Novel 1875–1914* (London: Secker and Warburg, 1989), 344–56.
12. Keating, *Study*, 353.
13. Discussions of the 'Art of Fiction' debate, for example, typically downplay Stevenson's contribution, comparing his 'conventional' aims to James's innovative conception of literature: see Mark Spilka, 'Henry James and Walter Besant: "The Art of Fiction" Controversy', *Novel: a Forum on Fiction* 6 (1973), 101–19, 118.
14. Stevenson, 'A Gossip on Romance' (1882), in *Memories and Portraits* (London: Chatto and Windus, 1904), 247–74, 252, 258.
15. Stevenson, 'Gossip', 255.
16. Walter Edwards Houghton, Esther Rhoads Houghton, and Jean Harris Slingerland, eds, *The Wellesley Index to Victorian Periodicals 1824–1900*, 5 vols (Toronto: Toronto University Press, 1966–89), 4: 430–3. The 1870 Elementary Education Act introduced compulsory elementary education; the 1880 Education Act, strengthening school attendance laws, effectively made the earlier provisions standard across England and Wales.
17. N. N. Feltes, *Literary Capital and the Late Victorian Novel* (Madison, Wisconsin: University of Wisconsin Press, 1993), 79.
18. Henry James, 'The Art of Fiction', *Longman's Magazine* 4 (1884), 502–21, 510.
19. Stevenson, 'A Humble Remonstrance' (1884), in *Memories and Portraits* (London: Chatto and Windus, 1904), 275–99, 281, 283.
20. Henry James to Stevenson, July 1888, in *The Letters of Henry James*, ed. Percy Lubbock, 2 vols (London: Macmillan, 1920), 1: 139; Spilka, 'James', 115.
21. Stevenson, 'Remonstrance', 286.
22. Stevenson, 'Remonstrance', 286; James, 'Art', 518.
23. James, 'Art', 518.
24. Stevenson, 'Remonstrance', 287.
25. Stevenson, 'Remonstrance', 287.
26. James Sully, 'The Undefinable in Art', *Cornhill Magazine* 38 (1878), 559–72; see also Kate Flint, *The Victorians and the Visual Imagination* (Cambridge: Cambridge University Press, 2000), 247–8.
27. Stevenson, 'On Some Technical Elements of Style' (1885), in *Essays Literary and Critical* (London: Heinemann et al., 1923), 33–50, 33.
28. Stevenson, 'Elements', 49.

29. Stevenson, 'Pastoral' (1887), in *Memories and Portraits* (London: Chatto and Windus, 1904), 90–105, 97, 102.
30. Stevenson, 'Pastoral', 102.
31. Stevenson, 'Pastoral', 102–3.
32. Laura Otis, *Organic Memory: History and the Body in the Late Nineteenth and Early Twentieth Centuries* (Lincoln, Nebraska: University of Nebraska Press, 1994), 5–6; on Spencer's Lamarckism, see Robert Nye, 'Sociology and Degeneration: the Irony of Progress', in J. Edward Chamberlin and Sander L. Gilman, eds, *Degeneration: the Dark Side of Progress* (New York: Columbia University Press, 1985), 49–71, 56–7.
33. Samuel Butler, *The Way of All Flesh* (written between 1872 and 1884 but not published until 1903), ed. Richard Hoggart (Harmondsworth: Penguin, 1966), 158–9.
34. Stevenson, 'Pastoral', 103–4. The phrase 'Probably Arboreal' was a favourite of Stevenson's, and also occurs several times in 'The Manse'. It originated with Darwin, who observed, '[w]e thus learn that man is descended from a hairy, tailed quadruped, probably arboreal in its habits': Charles Darwin, *The Descent of Man and Selection in Relation to Sex* (1871), 2nd edn (1874; London: Folio Society, 1990), 533.
35. Stevenson, 'Pastoral', 104.
36. Stevenson, 'The Manse' (1887), in *Memories and Portraits* (London: Chatto and Windus, 1904), 106–19, 112, 114.
37. Stevenson, 'Manse', 116–17.
38. Samuel Butler, *Life and Habit* (London: Trübner, 1878), 249.
39. Stevenson, 'Manse', 114.
40. Stevenson, 'Manse', 115–16. Stevenson clearly echoes Tristram Shandy's description of himself as 'The HOMUNCULUS', though Shandy employs the term in a more limited sense, as the minuscule human form believed to harbour in the spermatozoon: Laurence Sterne, *The Life and Opinions of Tristram Shandy, Gentleman* (1760), ed. Ian Campbell Ross (Oxford: Oxford University Press, 1983), 6.
41. Helen Small, 'The Unquiet Limit: Old Age and Memory in Victorian Narrative', in Matthew Campbell, Jacqueline M. Labbé, and Sally Shuttleworth eds, *Memory and Memorials 1789–1914: Literary and Cultural Perspectives* (London: Routledge, 2000), 60–79, 67–8.
42. Stevenson, 'Manse', 117.
43. Stevenson, 'Manse', 118.
44. Stevenson, 'Manse', 118.
45. Stevenson, 'Manse', 119.
46. Charles Darwin, *The Variation of Animals and Plants Under Domestication* (1868), 2nd edn, 2 vols (1875; Baltimore, Maryland: Johns Hopkins University Press, 1998), 2: 36.
47. Stevenson, 'Popular Authors' (1888), in *Essays Literary and Critical* (London: Heinemann et al., 1923), 20–32, 31, 21.
48. Stevenson to Haggard, July to August 1891, in *The Letters of Robert Louis Stevenson*, ed. Bradford Booth and Ernest Mehew, 8 vols (New Haven, Connecticut: Yale University Press, 1994–95), 7: 145 (hereafter, *Letters*); Stevenson to Edward Burlingame, November 1891, *Letters*, 7: 189. The Saga Library was translated by William Morris and Eiríkr Magnússon.

49. Linda Dowling, *Language and Decadence in the Victorian Fin de Siècle* (Princeton, New Jersey: Princeton University Press, 1986), 175–243, 181; Wilde, 'Critic', 351.
50. Dowling, *Language*, 61–7.
51. See for instance Andrew Lang, '"Kalevala": Or, the Finnish National Epic', in *Custom and Myth* (London: Longmans, Green, 1884), 156–79; Stevenson, review of James Grant Wilson, *The Poets and Poetry of Scotland, from the Earliest to the Present Time*, vol. 1, *Academy* 9 (1876), 138–9, 139.
52. Stevenson, 'Talk and Talkers: (I)' (1882), in *Essays and Poems*, ed. Claire Harman (London: J. M. Dent, 1992), 153–62, 153.
53. Penny Fielding, *Writing and Orality: Nationality, Culture, and Nineteenth-Century Scottish Fiction* (Oxford: Clarendon Press, 1996), 135.
54. Stevenson, 'Talk and Talkers: (I)', 153.
55. Stevenson, 'Talk and Talkers: (I)', 154.
56. Stevenson, 'Talk and Talkers: A Sequel', *Cornhill Magazine* 46 (1882), 151–8, 151.
57. Stevenson, 'Remonstrance', 284.
58. Nicholas Daly, *Modernism, Romance and the Fin de Siècle: Popular Fiction and British Culture, 1880–1914* (Cambridge: Cambridge University Press, 1999), 22.
59. Sigmund Freud, 'Civilization and Its Discontents' (1930), in *The Freud Reader*, ed. Peter Gay (London: Random House, 1995), 722–72, 752, 771.
60. Glenda Norquay, 'Introduction', in *R. L. Stevenson on Fiction: An Anthology of Literary and Critical Essays* (Edinburgh: Edinburgh University Press, 1999), 1–25, 11.
61. Sally Shuttleworth, 'The Psychology of Childhood in Victorian Literature and Medicine', in Helen Small and Trudi Tate, eds, *Literature, Science, Psychoanalysis, 1830–1970: Essays in Honour of Gillian Beer* (Cambridge: Cambridge University Press, 2003), 86–101, 97.
62. E. B. Tylor, *Primitive Culture: Researches into the Development of Mythology, Philosophy, Religion, Art, and Custom*, 2 vols (London: John Murray, 1871), 1: 257.
63. Tylor, *Culture*, 1: 258. Lang echoes this association between children and 'savages' in Andrew Lang, *Myth, Ritual, and Religion*, 2 vols (London: Longmans, Green, 1887), 2: 325.
64. Stevenson, 'Child's Play', *Cornhill Magazine* 38 (1878), 352–9, 356–7.
65. Stevenson, 'Play', 357.
66. Stevenson, 'Play', 357.
67. Robert Louis Stevenson, '"Rosa Quo Locorum"' (1896), in *Further Memories* (London: Heinemann et al., 1923), 1–8, 1.
68. Stevenson, '"Rosa"', 5.
69. Andrew Lang, 'At the Sign of the Ship', *Longman's Magazine* 28 (1896), 313–22, 315.
70. Tylor, *Culture*, 1: 284; see also James Sully, 'Poetic Imagination and Primitive Conception', *Cornhill Magazine* 34 (1876), 294–306, 295, 298.
71. Stevenson, 'Play', 356.
72. Sigmund Freud, 'Creative Writers and Day-dreaming' (1908), in *The Freud Reader*, ed. Peter Gay (London: Random House, 1995), 436–43, 438.
73. Spencer, *Principles*, 2: 627.
74. Spencer, *Principles*, 2: 632.

75. Stevenson, 'The Lantern-Bearers' (1888), in *Further Memories* (London: Heinemann, 1923), 29–40, 34.
76. Stevenson, 'Play', 357. Stevenson's collections of playful tales, *New Arabian Nights* (1878) and *More New Arabian Nights: The Dynamiter* (1885), the latter a collaboration with Fanny van de Grift Stevenson, are testament to his imaginative debt to the *Arabian Nights*.
77. Grant Allen, *Physiological Æsthetics* (London: H. S. King, 1877), 215–16, 276–7.
78. Stevenson, 'Gossip', 262.
79. Lang, 'At the Sign of the Ship', *Longman's Magazine* 11 (1887–88), 458–64, 458. Even before the article's publication, Lang had already repeatedly and admiringly discussed Stevenson's ideas about inspiration: 'At the Sign of the Ship', *Longman's Magazine* 7 (1885–86), 439–48, 441–2; 'At the Sign of the Ship', *Longman's Magazine* 11 (1887–88), 234–40, 235.
80. Stevenson, 'A Chapter on Dreams' (1888), in *Further Memories* (London: Heinemann, 1923), 41–53, 43.
81. Stevenson, 'Chapter', 46–7, 52–3. On dual consciousness, see Part II.
82. Stevenson, 'Chapter', 45.
83. Stevenson, 'Chapter', 47.
84. Stevenson to W. Craibe Angus, November 1891, *Letters*, 7: 208.
85. E. S. Dallas, *The Gay Science*, 2 vols (London: Chapman and Hall, 1866), 1: 201. Jenny Bourne Taylor notes the similarity in 'Obscure Recesses: Locating the Victorian Unconscious', in J. B. Bullen, ed., *Writing and Victorianism* (London: Longman, 1997), 137–79, 155–6.
86. Explaining that 'the pleasure, in one word, had become a business', Stevenson describes how he no longer sought in dreams 'amusement, but printable and profitable tales': Stevenson, 'Chapter', 46.
87. Stevenson, 'Chapter', 52.
88. Stevenson, 'Chapter', 51.
89. Stevenson, 'Chapter', 50.
90. Elaine Showalter, *Sexual Anarchy: Gender and Culture at the Fin de Siècle* (London: Bloomsbury, 1991), 105. On Stevenson's familiarity with psychological debates about 'multiplex personality', see Chapter 4.
91. F. W. H. Myers, *Human Personality and Its Survival of Bodily Death*, 2 vols (London: Longmans and Green, 1903) 1: 14–15.
92. Unpublished letter, Myers to Stevenson, 29 April 1892: Yale University, Beinecke Rare Book and Manuscript Library, Stevenson Collection, Cat. No. 5263. For Stevenson's reply, which recounts his experiences of dual consciousness while suffering from a fever, see Chapter 3.
93. Myers, *Personality*, 1: 126.
94. Myers, *Personality*, 1: 301, 90.
95. See J. P. Williams, 'Psychical Research and Psychiatry in Late Victorian Britain: Trance as Ecstasy or Trance as Insanity', in W. F. Bynum, Roy Porter, and Michael Shepherd, eds, *The Anatomy of Madness: Essays in the History of Psychiatry*, 3 vols (London: Tavistock Publications, 1985–88), 1: 233–54.
96. F. W. H. Myers, 'Multiplex Personality', *Nineteenth Century* 20 (1886), 648–66, 659.
97. Stevenson, *An Inland Voyage* (1878), in *Travels with a Donkey in the Cévennes and Selected Travel Writings* (Oxford: Oxford University Press, 1992), 1–120, 91–2.
98. Stevenson, *Voyage*, 92.

99. Sully, *Life*, 216, 194.
100. Sully, *Life*, 194–5.
101. Sully, *Life*, 196.
102. Sully, *Life*, 196.
103. Sully, *Life*, 196–7.
104. Sully, 'Imagination', 299.
105. Shuttleworth, 'Psychology', 97.

2. Romance fiction: 'stories round the savage camp-fire'

1. Stevenson, 'A Humble Remonstrance' (1884), in *Memories and Portraits* (London: Chatto and Windus, 1904), 275–99, 284.
2. W. D. Howells, 'Henry James, Jr.' (1882), in *Selected Literary Criticism*, ed. Ulrich Halfmann and Christoph K. Lohmann, 3 vols (Bloomington, Indiana: Indiana University Press, 1993), 1: 317–23, 323, 319; H. Rider Haggard, 'About Fiction', *Contemporary Review* 51 (1887), 172–80, 176.
3. Gillian Beer, *The Romance* (London: Methuen, 1970), 8.
4. Elaine Showalter, *Sexual Anarchy: Gender and Culture at the Fin de Siècle* (London: Bloomsbury, 1991), 80–2.
5. Stephen Arata, *Fictions of Loss in the Victorian Fin de Siècle* (Cambridge: Cambridge University Press, 1996), 80.
6. Andrew Lang, 'Mr. Kipling's Stories', in *Essays in Little* (London: Henry and Co., 1891), 198–205, 200.
7. Joseph Bristow, *Empire Boys: Adventures in a Man's World* (London: HarperCollins, 1991), Chapter 1, 'Reading for the Empire'.
8. Arata, *Fictions*, 80, 94–5; Peter Keating, *The Haunted Study: a Social History of the English Novel 1875–1914* (London: Secker and Warburg, 1989), 353–6.
9. Leslie A. Fiedler, 'R. L. S. Revisited', in *No! in Thunder: Essays on Myth and Literature* (London: Eyre and Spottiswoode, 1963), 77–91, 77.
10. David Daiches, *Robert Louis Stevenson* (Glasgow: William Maclellan, 1947), 55, 73.
11. Edwin Eigner, *Robert Louis Stevenson and Romantic Tradition* (Princeton, New Jersey: Princeton University Press, 1966), ix.
12. Roslyn Jolly, 'Stevenson's "Sterling Domestic Fiction": "The Beach of Falesá"', *Review of English Studies* n.s. 50 (1999), 463–82; Patrick Brantlinger, *Rule of Darkness: British Literature and Imperialism, 1830–1914* (Ithaca, New York: Cornell University Press, 1988), 41. Vanessa Smith challenges this model of Stevenson's transition from romance to realism, arguing that his texts should not be located within 'British debates about genre and authorial politics', but read as transactions between Pacific and metropolitan print cultures: *Literary Culture and the Pacific: Nineteenth-Century Textual Encounters* (Cambridge: Cambridge University Press, 1998), 15.
13. Brantlinger, *Rule*, 39.
14. Stevenson, *Treasure Island* (1881–82), ed. Emma Letley (Oxford: Oxford University Press, 1985), xxx. Subsequent page references appear in the text.
15. Stevenson to Henley, August 1881, in *The Letters of Robert Louis Stevenson*, ed. Bradford Booth and Ernest Mehew, 8 vols (New Haven, Connecticut: Yale University Press, 1994–95), 3: 224 (hereafter, *Letters*).

16. Stevenson to Henley, August 1881, *Letters*, 3: 225.
17. Stevenson, 'Remonstrance', 289.
18. Stevenson, 'Remonstrance', 288.
19. Stevenson, 'Remonstrance', 287–8.
20. Stevenson, 'Remonstrance', 288.
21. Stevenson, 'My First Book: "Treasure Island"' (1894), in *Treasure Island*, 192–200, 194.
22. Stevenson, 'A Gossip on Romance' (1882), in *Memories and Portraits* (London: Chatto and Windus, 1904), 247–74, 255.
23. Stevenson, 'Book', 196.
24. Stevenson, 'Book', 196.
25. H. Rider Haggard, *King Solomon's Mines* (1885), ed. Dennis Butts (Oxford: Oxford University Press, 1989), 1.
26. Arata, *Fictions*, 89.
27. Recalling his 'passion for maps', Marlow describes how uncharted territory fired him with the 'glories of exploration': Joseph Conrad, *Heart of Darkness* (1899, 1902), in *Heart of Darkness with The Congo Diary*, ed. Robert Hampson (London: Penguin, 1995), 3–139, 21.
28. Emma Letley, 'Introduction', in Stevenson, *Treasure Island*, ix.
29. Francis Russell Hart claims that 'the only true suspense is . . . the problem of knowing Long John Silver', in *The Scottish Novel: From Smollett to Spark* (Cambridge, Massachusetts: Harvard University Press, 1978), 156. Alastair Fowler views the narrative as 'a series of contests for power', in 'Parables of Adventure: the Debatable Novels of Robert Louis Stevenson', in Ian Campbell, ed., *Nineteenth-Century Scottish Fiction: Critical Essays* (Manchester: Carcanet, 1979), 105–29, 111.
30. Stevenson, 'Gossip', 267.
31. Bristow, *Empire Boys*, 111.
32. Stevenson, 'Book', 198.
33. Stevenson, 'The English Admirals' (1878), in *Virginibus Puerisque, The Amateur Emigrant, The Pacific Capitals, Silverado Squatters* (London: Heinemann et al., 1922), 137–55, 138.
34. Stevenson, 'Admirals', 143–4.
35. Stevenson, 'Admirals', 149–50.
36. Stevenson, 'Admirals', 139.
37. Stevenson, 'The Persons of the Tale' (1895), in *Juvenilia, Moral Emblems, Fables, and Other Papers* (London: Heinemann et al., 1923), 183–7, 184–5.
38. See the perceptive discussion in Letley, 'Introduction', xxii–xxiii.
39. Stevenson, 'Persons', 184, 183.
40. R. M. Ballantyne, *The Coral Island* (1858; London: Bloomsbury Books, 1994), 156, 197–204.
41. Robert Crawford, '"My Bed Is Like a Little Boat": Stevenson's Voyage into Masculinity', a paper delivered at the 'Stevenson, Scotland, and Samoa' conference, Stirling, 2000.
42. Robert Kiely, *Robert Louis Stevenson and the Fiction of Adventure* (Cambridge, Massachusetts: Harvard University Press, 1964), 81.
43. Bristow, *Empire Boys*, 111.
44. Eigner, *Stevenson*, 76.
45. Bristow, *Empire Boys*, 95.

46. Stevenson, *Island*, xxx; Stevenson, 'Remonstrance', 287.
47. Stevenson, 'Memoirs of Himself' (1912), in *Memories and Portraits, Memoirs of Himself, Selections from His Notebook* (London: Heinemann, 1924), 147–68, 161–2.
48. Stevenson, 'Memoirs', 161.
49. Stevenson to Frances Sitwell, June 1875, in *Selected Letters of Robert Louis Stevenson*, ed. Ernest Mehew (New Haven, Connecticut: Yale University Press, 1997), 110 (hereafter, *Selected Letters*).
50. Stevenson to Sidney Colvin, November 1890, *Selected Letters*, 436.
51. Bristow, *Empire Boys*, 123.
52. For details, see Chapter 6.
53. Stevenson, *A Footnote to History: Eight Years of Trouble in Samoa* (1892), in *Vailima Papers* (London: Heinemann et al., 1924), 67–240, 160.
54. Stevenson to Colvin, May 1892, *Letters*, 7: 282; Stevenson to Charles Baxter, November 1891, *Selected Letters*, 475.
55. Osbourne drafted the first three or four chapters, but the rest of the book was Stevenson's alone. The novel was serialized in *To-day* (1893–94), and published as a book by Heinemann in 1894: Roger G. Swearingen, *The Prose Writings of Robert Louis Stevenson: a Guide* (Hamden, Connecticut: Archon Books, 1980), 187, 186.
56. Unpublished letter, cited in Catherine Kerrigan and Peter Hinchcliffe, 'Introduction', in *The Ebb-Tide: a Trio and a Quartette*, ed. Catherine Kerrigan and Peter Hinchcliffe (Edinburgh: Edinburgh University Press, 1995), xvii–xxxi, xx.
57. At the close of *The Black Arrow*, the hero recognizes sadly that he must renounce adventure's delights and retires to live in a secluded 'green forest', far from 'the dust and blood of that unruly epoch': Stevenson, *The Black Arrow: A Tale of the Two Roses* (1883; London: Heinemann et al., 1923), 262.
58. Stevenson to Alexander Ireland, March 1882, *Letters*, 3: 302.
59. Stevenson to James, June 1893, *Letters*, 8: 107.
60. This debate, in its British context, was encouraged by James Sully's critique of pessimism: see *Pessimism: A History and A Criticism* (London: H. S. King, 1877), 357–9, 399, and *passim*. On late-Victorian pessimism, see Peter Allan Dale, *In Pursuit of a Scientific Culture: Science, Art, and Society in the Victorian Age* (Madison, Wisconsin: University of Wisconsin Press, 1989), Chapter 9.
61. Stevenson to William Archer, October 1885, *Letters*, 5: 141–2.
62. Andrew Lang, 'At the Sign of the Ship', *Longman's Magazine* 18 (1891), 215–33.
63. Andrew Lang, 'At the Sign of the Ship', *Longman's Magazine* 9 (1887), 552–9, 554.
64. Stevenson and Lloyd Osbourne, *The Ebb-Tide: A Trio and Quartette* (1893–94), in Stevenson, *South Sea Tales*, ed. Roslyn Jolly (Oxford: Oxford University Press, 1996), 123–252, 123. Subsequent page references appear in the text.
65. Stevenson, *In the South Seas* (1896; comp. Sidney Colvin), ed. Neil Rennie (London: Penguin, 1998), 5.
66. Stevenson to Colvin, April to May 1893, *Letters*, 8: 69.
67. Ballantyne, *Coral Island*, 21.
68. Brantlinger, *Rule*, 239.
69. Ballantyne, *Coral Island*, 5.
70. Smith, *Literary Culture*, 160.

71. Stevenson and Lloyd Osbourne, *The Wrecker* (1891–92; London: Heinemann et al., 1924), 119.
72. Stevenson and Osbourne, *Wrecker*, 403.
73. Fowler, 'Parables', 120; Roger Ebbatson, '*The Ebb-Tide*: Missionary Endeavour in the Islands of Light', in Andrew Dix and Jonathan Taylor, eds, *Figures of Heresy* (Brighton, East Sussex: Sussex Academic Press, 2006), 90–107, 100.
74. Fowler, 'Parables', 116. For the novel's complex engagement with religion, see Ebbatson, '*Ebb-Tide*', *passim*.
75. Conrad, *Heart of Darkness*, 49.
76. On the continuities between *fin-de-siècle* homoeroticism and romance's conservative homosocial bonds, see Arata, *Fictions*, 79; on *The Ebb-Tide*'s homoerotic resonances, see Wayne Koestenbaum, *Double Talk: the Erotics of Male Literary Collaboration* (London: Routledge, 1989), 145–8.
77. Stevenson, *In the South Seas*, 209.
78. Ebbatson, '*Ebb-Tide*', 98.
79. W. E. Henley, 'Invictus' (1875), in M. H. Abrams and Stephen Greenblatt, eds, *The Norton Anthology of English Literature*, 7th edn (New York: W. W. Norton, 2000), 2: 1747.
80. Stevenson to Charles Baxter, February 1893, *Letters*, 8: 29.

Part II 'Downward, downward lies your way': degeneration and psychology

1. Stevenson to Auguste Rodin, December 1886, in *The Letters of Robert Louis Stevenson*, ed. Bradford Booth and Ernest Mehew, 8 vols (New Haven, Connecticut: Yale University Press, 1994–95), 5: 334–5 (translated from Stevenson's French by Mehew). Hereafter, *Letters*.
2. Stevenson to Margaret Stevenson, April 1886, *Letters*, 5: 246; Stevenson to Margaret Stevenson, April 1886, *Letters*, 5: 247.
3. Henry Maudsley, *The Physiology and Pathology of Mind* (London: Macmillan, 1867); Maudsley, *The Pathology of Mind: A Study of its Distempers, Deformities, and Disorders* (London: Macmillan, 1895); Edwin Ray Lankester, *Degeneration: A Chapter in Darwinism* (London: Macmillan, 1880); for other degenerationist writings, see Jenny Bourne Taylor and Sally Shuttleworth, eds, *Embodied Selves: an Anthology of Psychological Texts 1830–1890* (Oxford: Oxford University Press, 1998), Section 5.
4. Herbert Spencer, *The Principles of Psychology* (1855), 2nd edn, 2 vols (London: Williams and Norgate, 1870–72), 1: 604–13 (this section on mental pathologies did not appear in the first edition); Herbert Spencer, *The Man Versus the State* (1884), in *Spencer: Political Writings*, ed. John Offer (Cambridge: Cambridge University Press, 1994), 59–175, 127–9. See also Robert Nye, 'Sociology and Degeneration: the Irony of Progress', in J. Edward Chamberlin and Sander L. Gilman, eds, *Degeneration: the Dark Side of Progress* (New York: Columbia University Press, 1985), 49–71, 58–9.
5. Gareth Stedman Jones, *Outcast London: a Study in the Relationship between Classes in Victorian Society* (Oxford: Clarendon Press, 1971), Chapter 16.

6. G. B. Shaw, *The Sanity of Art: An Exposure of the Current Nonsense about Artists Being Degenerate* (1895; London: The New Age Press, 1908), 104.
7. Maudsley, *Pathology*, 4.
8. Daniel Pick, *Faces of Degeneration: a European Disorder, c. 1848–1918* (Cambridge: Cambridge University Press, 1989); William Greenslade, *Degeneration, Culture and the Novel 1880–1940* (Cambridge: Cambridge University Press, 1994).
9. Stephen D. Arata, 'The Sedulous Ape: Atavism, Professionalism, and Stevenson's *Jekyll and Hyde*', *Criticism: a Quarterly Journal for Literature and the Arts* 37 (1995), 233–59, 235; Robert Mighall, *A Geography of Victorian Gothic Fiction: Mapping History's Nightmares* (Oxford: Oxford University Press, 1999), 146–7.
10. Stevenson disparagingly called *Jekyll and Hyde* a 'gothic gnome', in a letter to W. H. Low, December 1885 to January 1886, *Letters*, 5: 163.

3. 'There was less *me* and more *not-me*': Stevenson and nervous morbidity

1. Jenny Bourne Taylor, 'Obscure Recesses: Locating the Victorian Unconscious', in J. B. Bullen, ed., *Writing and Victorianism* (London: Longman, 1997), 137–79, 141.
2. Stevenson, 'Memoirs of Himself' (1912), in *Memories and Portraits, Memoirs of Himself, Selections from His Notebook* (London: Heinemann, 1924), 147–68, 154.
3. See Janet Oppenheim, *'Shattered Nerves': Doctors, Patients, and Depression in Victorian England* (Oxford: Oxford University Press, 1991), Chapter 7.
4. Oppenheim, *'Nerves'*, 235.
5. Stevenson, 'Memoirs', 157.
6. Stevenson, 'Memoirs', 155.
7. James Crichton-Browne, 'Psychical Diseases of Early Life', *Journal of Mental Science* 6 (1859), 284–320, 313.
8. Stevenson, 'Memoirs', 153–4.
9. Stevenson mentions reading Spencer 'very hard', in a letter to James Walter Ferrier, November 1872, in *Selected Letters of Robert Louis Stevenson*, ed. Ernest Mehew (New Haven, Connecticut: Yale University Press, 1997), 28 (hereafter, *Selected Letters*). Stevenson later described coming 'under the influence of Herbert Spencer' at this period, noting that '[n]o more persuasive rabbi exists, and few better . . . I should be much of a hound if I lost my gratitude to Herbert Spencer': Stevenson, 'Books Which Have Influenced Me' (1887), in *Essays Literary and Critical* (London: Heinemann et al., 1923), 62–8, 64–5. See also Stevenson's consideration of his doubts, in a letter to R. A. M. Stevenson, October 1872, in *The Letters of Robert Louis Stevenson*, ed. Bradford Booth and Ernest Mehew, 8 vols (New Haven, Connecticut: Yale University Press, 1994–95), 1: 254–6 (hereafter, *Letters*); and Bob's (largely illegible, and undated) discussion of Spencer's *Principles of Psychology* and *Principles of Biology*, and of Stevenson's conflict with his parents, in an unpublished letter, R. A. M. Stevenson to Stevenson, in Yale University, Beinecke Rare Book and Manuscript Library, Stevenson Collection, Cat. No. 5674. Stevenson's father felt that his son had been corrupted by both his cousin and Spencer's

works: see Stevenson to Frances Sitwell, September 1873, *Letters*, 1: 294–5; Thomas Stevenson to Sidney Colvin, 1879, cited in *Letters*, 1: 34.

10. Stevenson, 'The Misadventures of John Nicholson' (1887), in *Weir of Hermiston and Other Stories*, ed. Paul Binding (London: Penguin, 1979), 216–84, 219.
11. Stevenson to Charles Baxter, November 1873, *Selected Letters*, 59.
12. Stevenson to Frances Sitwell, September 1873, *Letters*, 1: 312.
13. Stevenson, *New Arabian Nights* (1878; London: Heinemann, 1923), 18, 21.
14. Stevenson to Edmund Purcell, February 1886, *Selected Letters*, 309.
15. Stevenson to Frances Sitwell, February 1874, *Selected Letters*, 80.
16. See the anxiety in J. R. Seeley, 'Ethics and Religion', in The Society of Ethical Propagandists, ed., *Ethics and Religion* (London: Swan Sonnenschein, 1900), 1–30, and among almost all the contributors to 'A Modern "Symposium." The Influence Upon Morality of a Decline in Religious Belief', *Nineteenth Century* 1 (1877), 331–58, 531–46. Leslie Stephen was relatively confident that loss of faith need not entail moral decay, although for Peter Allan Dale he was 'straining after an optimistic conclusion to the Darwinian story': Leslie Stephen, *The Science of Ethics* (1882; Bristol: Thoemmes, 1991), 457–8; Peter Allan Dale, *In Pursuit of a Scientific Culture: Science, Art, and Society in the Victorian Age* (Madison, Wisconsin: University of Wisconsin Press, 1989), 205. See also Noel Annan, *Leslie Stephen: the Godless Victorian* (London: Weidenfeld and Nicolson, 1984), Chapters 9 and 10; Bernard Lightman, *The Origins of Agnosticism: Victorian Unbelief and the Limits of Knowledge* (Baltimore, Maryland: Johns Hopkins University Press, 1987), Chapter 5.
17. Stevenson to Sidney Colvin, November 1887, *Selected Letters*, 353.
18. Stevenson, 'Pulvis et Umbra' (1888), in *Across the Plains: With Other Memories and Essays* (London: Chatto and Windus, 1907), 289–301, 290.
19. Stevenson, 'Pulvis', 293.
20. Stevenson, 'Pulvis', 293, 294.
21. Stevenson, 'Pulvis', 298.
22. Note by Thomas Hardy, transcribed in Florence Emily Hardy, *The Life of Thomas Hardy: 1840–1928* (London: Macmillan, 1962), 149.
23. Stevenson, 'Pulvis', 299, 300.
24. For Argyll's discussion of the human will as an 'image' of the 'Divine Will', see G. D. Campbell, Duke of Argyll, *The Reign of Law* (London: Alexander Strahan, 1867), 10, 20–1.
25. For Stevenson's address to the Edinburgh University debating society on 'Law and Free Will – Notes on the Duke of Argyll' (1873), see Stevenson to Frances Sitwell, September 1873, *Selected Letters*, 43. The paper was not preserved.
26. Stevenson, 'Pulvis', 301.
27. According to J. C. Furnas, Stevenson led prayers at Vailima, but still disliked organized religion: *Voyage to Windward: the Life of Robert Louis Stevenson* (London: Faber and Faber, 1952), 333–4.
28. Stevenson, 'Autobiographical Note' (undated and unpublished manuscript), in Yale University, Beinecke Rare Book and Manuscript Library, Stevenson Collection, Cat. No. 5998.
29. Stevenson, 'The Manse' (1887), in *Memories and Portraits* (London: Chatto and Windus, 1904), 106–19, 117.
30. Stevenson to R. A. M. Stevenson, September 1868, *Letters*, 1: 151; Stevenson to R. A. M. Stevenson, March 1870, *Letters*, 1: 192; Stevenson to R. A. M. Stevenson,

October 1872, *Letters*, 1: 254; Stevenson to Frances Sitwell, November 1873, *Selected Letters*, 53; Stevenson to Frances Sitwell, December 1873, *Letters*, 1: 402; Stevenson to Frances Sitwell, May 1874, *Letters*, 2: 7.

31. Stevenson to Margaret Stevenson, May 1886, *Letters*, 5: 255; Stevenson to W. E. Henley, August 1887, *Letters*, 5: 437.
32. Rudyard Kipling to Edmonia Hill, November 1889, cited in Stevenson, *Letters*, 1: 51; Stevenson to Charles Baxter, May 1889, *Letters*, 6: 294.
33. Stevenson to Henry James, July 1894, *Letters*, 8: 312.
34. Stevenson, *An Inland Voyage* (1878), in *Travels with a Donkey in the Cévennes and Selected Travel Writings* (Oxford: Oxford University Press, 1992), 1–120, 91–2; Stevenson to Myers, July 1892, rpr. in F. W. H. Myers, *Human Personality and Its Survival of Bodily Death*, 2 vols (London: Longmans and Green, 1903), 1: 301–2.
35. Oppenheim, *'Nerves'*, 141–52.
36. Oppenheim, *'Nerves'*, 151.
37. Oppenheim, *'Nerves'*, 141–8; Mark Micale, *Approaching Hysteria: Disease and Its Interpretations* (Princeton, New Jersey: Princeton University Press, 1995), 25, 161–8, 239–60.
38. Lloyd Osbourne, 'Prefatory Note', in Stevenson, *Further Memories* (London: Heinemann et al., 1923), 191–6, 191.
39. Stevenson outlined his plans for martyrdom in Ireland in a letter to Anne Jenkin, April 1887, *Selected Letters*, 333. On his enjoyment of the Samoan conflict, see Stevenson to Sidney Colvin, June to July 1893, *Selected Letters*, 551.
40. Henry Maudsley, *The Physiology and Pathology of Mind* (London: Macmillan, 1867), 204.
41. Henry Maudsley, *Responsibility in Mental Disease* (London: H. S. King, 1874), 273.
42. Robert Nye, 'Sociology and Degeneration: the Irony of Progress', in J. Edward Chamberlin and Sander L. Gilman, eds, *Degeneration: the Dark Side of Progress* (New York: Columbia University Press, 1985), 49–71.
43. Stevenson to Frances Sitwell, November 1873, *Selected Letters*, 64–5.
44. Oppenheim, *'Nerves'*, 89.
45. See for example Stevenson to Margaret Stevenson, April 1886, *Letters*, 5: 245–6.
46. Stevenson, 'Thomas Stevenson: Civil Engineer' (1887), in *Memories and Portraits* (London: Chatto and Windus, 1904), 132–43, 141.
47. [William Sharp], Fiona Macleod (pseud.), 'From Iona', in *The Sin-Eater and Other Tales* (Edinburgh: Patrick Geddes, 1895), 1–13, 8. For discussion of the *fin-de-siècle* association of Gaelicism with morbidity, see Scott Ashley, 'Primitivism, Celticism and Morbidity in the Atlantic *Fin de Siècle*', in Patrick McGuinness, ed., *Symbolism, Decadence and the Fin de Siècle: French and European Perspectives* (Exeter: University of Exeter Press, 2000), 175–93; Linda Dowling, *Language and Decadence in the Victorian Fin de Siècle* (Princeton, New Jersey: Princeton University Press, 1986), 228–9.
48. Stevenson, 'Thomas Stevenson', 143, 141, 143.
49. See for instance Stevenson to Thomas Stevenson, December 1883, *Selected Letters*, 242.
50. Francis Galton, *Records of Family Faculties: Consisting of Tabular Forms and Directions for Entering Data, with an Explanatory Preface* (London: Macmillan, 1884), 1.
51. Galton, *Records*, 13.

52. Stevenson's copy is in Yale University, Beinecke Rare Book and Manuscript Library, Stevenson Collection, Cat. No. 7298.
53. Stevenson's copy of *Records*, Beinecke Library.
54. See William Greenslade, *Degeneration, Culture and the Novel 1880–1940* (Cambridge: Cambridge University Press, 1994), 88–99.
55. Crichton-Browne, 'Diseases', 291, 290. Cited in Jenny Bourne Taylor and Sally Shuttleworth, eds, *Embodied Selves: an Anthology of Psychological Texts 1830–1890* (Oxford: Oxford University Press, 1998), 337.
56. Stevenson to Will Low, January 1894, *Selected Letters*, 603.
57. Stevenson to R. A. M. Stevenson, October 1868, *Letters*, 1: 166.
58. Stevenson to R. A. M. Stevenson, October 1868, *Letters*, 1: 165.
59. Stevenson to R. A. M. Stevenson, October 1868, *Letters*, 1: 166.
60. Stevenson to Sidney Colvin, October 1894, *Selected Letters*, 603.
61. Max Nordau, *Degeneration*, tr. from 2nd edn (London: Heinemann, 1895), vii–ix.
62. See for example James Sully, *Illusions: A Psychological Study* (London: Kegan Paul, 1881), 122–3.
63. J. M. Fothergill, *The Maintenance of Health: A Medical Work for Lay Readers* (London: Smith, Elder, 1874), 260–1.
64. Henry Maudsley, 'Hallucinations of the Senses', *Fortnightly Review* n.s. 24 (1878), 370–86, 376.
65. Maudsley, 'Hallucinations', 376.
66. Michael J. Clark, 'The Rejection of Psychological Approaches to Mental Disorder in Late Nineteenth-Century Psychiatry', in Andrew Scull, ed., *Madhouses, Mad-doctors, and Madmen: the Social History of Psychiatry in the Victorian Era* (London: Athlone Press, 1981), 271–312, 274.
67. James Sully, 'Genius and Insanity', *Nineteenth Century* 10 (1881), 573–87. Cited in Ed Block, 'James Sully, Evolutionist Psychology, and Late Victorian Gothic Fiction', *Victorian Studies* 25 (1982), 443–67, 452.
68. Karl Miller, *Doubles: Studies in Literary History* (Oxford: Oxford University Press, 1985), 22.
69. James Crichton-Browne, 'Dreamy Mental States', in *Stray Leaves from a Physician's Portfolio* (London: Hodder and Stoughton, [1927]), 1–42.
70. Crichton-Browne, 'States', 7–8.
71. Crichton-Browne, 'States', 5.
72. James Sully, 'Poetic Imagination and Primitive Conception', *Cornhill Magazine* 34 (1876), 294–306, 299; Sully, *Illusions*, 224–7. See Ed Block's discussion of the similarities between Stevenson's and Sully's treatments of dual consciousness, in Block, 'Sully', 451, and *passim*.
73. For his mother's response, see *Letters*, 2: 2n.
74. Stevenson, 'Ordered South' (1874), in *Travels*, 249.
75. Stevenson, 'Ordered South', 245–6.
76. Stevenson, 'Ordered South', 245.
77. Stevenson, *An Inland Voyage* (1878), in *Travels*, 91–2. See Chapter 1.
78. Stevenson, *Voyage*, 91.
79. Stevenson, 'Ordered South', 250.
80. Stevenson, 'A Chapter on Dreams' (1888), in *Further Memories* (London: Heinemann, 1923), 41–53, 43.
81. Stevenson, 'Chapter', 52.

82. See Chapter 1.
83. Stevenson to Myers, July 1892, rpr. in Myers, *Human Personality*, 1: 301–2.
84. Myers, *Human Personality*, 1: 301.
85. Stevenson, 'Dunoon: Visit in 1870 at a House where RLS Had Spent a Week in Childhood' (unpublished manuscript, written in the early 1870s), in Yale University, Beinecke Rare Book and Manuscript Library, Stevenson Collection, Cat. No. 6174.
86. Stefan Collini, *Public Moralists: Political Thought and Intellectual Life in Britain 1850–1930* (Oxford: Clarendon Press, 1991), 65.
87. Stevenson to R. A. M. Stevenson, November 1868, *Selected Letters*, 169.
88. Stevenson to R. A. M. Stevenson, October 1872, *Letters*, 1: 254.
89. Stevenson, 'The Day After Tomorrow' (1887), in *Ethical Studies, Edinburgh: Picturesque Notes* (London: Heinemann et al., 1924), 113–23, 120.
90. Stevenson, *Nights*, 103; Stevenson, 'The Pavilion on the Links' (1880), in *New Arabian Nights and Other Tales* (London: Heinemann et al., 1922), 249–343, 253–4; Stevenson, 'Thrawn Janet' (1881), in *Weir of Hermiston and Other Stories*, ed. Paul Binding (London: Penguin, 1979), 203–15, 206.
91. James Sully, 'The Dream as a Revelation', *Fortnightly Review* n.s. 53 (1893), 354–69, 364.
92. Stevenson to W. E. Henley, November 1885, *Selected Letters*, 311; Stevenson to Thomas Stevenson, December 1883, *Selected Letters*, 242.
93. Stevenson, 'A Gossip on Romance' (1882), in *Memories and Portraits* (London: Chatto and Windus, 1904), 247–74, 258–9.
94. Stevenson, 'A Humble Remonstrance' (1884), in *Memories and Portraits* (London: Chatto and Windus, 1904), 275–99, 286.
95. Kate Flint, *The Woman Reader 1837–1914* (Oxford: Oxford University Press, 1993), 90; Stephen Arata, 'Close Reading and Contextual Reading in *Dr Jekyll and Mr Hyde*', a paper delivered at the 'Stevenson, Scotland and Samoa' conference, Stirling, 2000.
96. Flint, *Reader*, 58.
97. Flint, *Reader*, Chapter 1 and *passim*.
98. Kelly Mays, 'The Disease of Reading and Victorian Periodicals', in John O. Jordan and Robert L. Patten, eds, *Literature in the Marketplace: Nineteenth-Century British Publishing and Reading Practices* (Cambridge: Cambridge University Press, 1995), 165–94, 179.
99. Patrick Brantlinger, *The Reading Lesson: the Threat of Mass Literacy in Nineteenth-Century British Fiction* (Bloomington, Indiana: Indiana University Press, 1998), 15–24.
100. Stevenson to Edmund Gosse, January 1886, *Letters*, 5: 171.
101. Several other neo-Gothic tales are considered in later chapters: for 'Thrawn Janet' (1881) and *The Master of Ballantrae* (1888–89), see Chapter 5, and for 'The Beach of Falesá' (1892) and 'Black Andie's Tale of Tod Lapraik', in *Catriona* (1892–93), see Chapter 6.
102. Stevenson refers to his 'crawlers' in a letter to W. E. Henley, August 1881, *Letters*, 3: 224; Fanny Stevenson recounts how she awoke Stevenson from a dream which inspired him with the central scene for *Jekyll and Hyde*, to be indignantly reprimanded, 'I was dreaming a fine bogey tale': Graham Balfour, *The Life of Robert Louis Stevenson*, 2 vols (London: Methuen, 1901), 2: 13.
103. Lady Taylor to Stevenson, February 1887, cited in *Letters*, 5: 365.

104. Stevenson to Lady Taylor, February 1887, *Letters*, 5: 365.
105. Stevenson to Colvin, July 1881, *Letters*, 3: 204.
106. Stevenson to Henry James, January 1888, *Selected Letters*, 357; Stevenson to Colvin, September 1891, *Selected Letters*, 467.
107. Thomas Bodley Scott, 'Memories', in Rosaline Orme Masson, ed., *I Can Remember Robert Louis Stevenson* (Edinburgh: Chambers, 1922), 212–14, 213.
108. Stevenson to Edmund Gosse, November 1884, *Letters*, 5: 33.
109. ('The Body Snatcher' was eventually substituted, as 'Markheim' was under length.) *Pall Mall Gazette*, 22 November 1884, cited in *Letters*, 5: 33n.
110. Stevenson to Gosse, November 1884, *Letters*, 5: 33.

4. 'Gothic gnomes': degenerate fictions

1. Stevenson described *Jekyll and Hyde* as a 'gothic gnome', in a letter to W. H. Low, December 1885 to January 1886, in *The Letters of Robert Louis Stevenson*, ed. Bradford Booth and Ernest Mehew, 8 vols (New Haven, Connecticut: Yale University Press, 1994–95), 5: 163 (hereafter, *Letters*).
2. Robert Mighall, *A Geography of Victorian Gothic Fiction: Mapping History's Nightmares* (Oxford: Oxford University Press, 1999), xviii–xxiii.
3. Stevenson to Colvin, July 1881, in *Letters*, 3: 204–5.
4. Stevenson, 'The Merry Men' (1882), in *Dr. Jekyll and Mr. Hyde, The Merry Men, and Other Tales* (London: J. M. Dent, 1925), 63–106, 65. Subsequent page references appear in the text.
5. Ed Block, 'James Sully, Evolutionist Psychology, and Late Victorian Gothic Fiction', *Victorian Studies* 25 (1982), 443–67, 458.
6. Block, 'Sully', 458.
7. Stevenson, *Travels with a Donkey in the Cévennes* (1879), in *Travels with a Donkey in the Cévennes and Selected Travel Writings* (Oxford: Oxford University Press, 1992), 121–231, 209.
8. Edwin M. Eigner, *Robert Louis Stevenson and Romantic Tradition* (Princeton, New Jersey: Princeton University Press, 1966), 142.
9. E. B. Tylor, *Primitive Culture: Researches into the Development of Mythology, Philosophy, Religion, Art, and Custom*, 2 vols (London: John Murray, 1871), 1: 258.
10. James Sully, 'Poetic Imagination and Primitive Conception', *Cornhill Magazine* 34 (1876), 294–306, 296–8; *Illusions: A Psychological Study* (London: Kegan Paul, 1881), 224–7.
11. Tylor, *Primitive Culture*, 1: 141–4, 144; Henry Maudsley, *Natural Causes and Supernatural Seemings* (1886), 3rd edn (London: Kegan Paul, Trench, Trübner and Co., 1897), 106–7.
12. Block, 'Sully', 458–9.
13. Stevenson, 'The Merry Men', *Cornhill Magazine* 46.1 (July 1882), 56–73, 62.
14. See Kenneth Gelder's discussion of this version in 'Robert Louis Stevenson's Revisions to "The Merry Men"', *Studies in Scottish Literature* 21 (1986), 262–87, 285.
15. J. R. Moore, 'Stevenson's Source for "The Merry Men"', *Philological Quarterly* 23 (1944), 135–40, 140.
16. Honor Mulholland, 'Robert Louis Stevenson and the Romance Form', in Andrew Noble, ed., *Robert Louis Stevenson* (London: Vision Press, 1983), 96–117, 109, 111.

17. Stevenson, 'The Merry Men', *Cornhill Magazine*, 46.1 (July 1882), 71.
18. Eigner, *Stevenson*, 137–8.
19. Tom Shearer, 'A Strange Judgement of God's? Stevenson's *The Merry Men*', *Studies in Scottish Literature* 20 (1985), 71–85, 74, 78.
20. Nicholas Phillipson, 'Providence and Progress: an Introduction to the Historical Thought of William Robertson', in Stewart J. Brown, ed., *William Robertson and the Expansion of Empire* (Cambridge: Cambridge University Press, 1997), 55–73.
21. Moore, 'Stevenson's Source', 140.
22. Block, 'Sully', 459.
23. Stevenson, *An Inland Voyage* (1878), in *Travels*, 91–2.
24. Eigner, *Stevenson*, 140–1.
25. Stevenson, 'Olalla' (1885), in *Dr. Jekyll and Mr. Hyde, The Merry Men, and Other Tales* (London: J. M. Dent, 1925), 157–93, 157. Subsequent page references appear in the text.
26. Ed Block, *Rituals of Dis-integration: Romance and Madness in the Victorian Psychomythic Tale* (New York: Garland, 1993), 150; Claire Harman, *Robert Louis Stevenson: a Biography* (London: HarperCollins, 2005), 308.
27. Eigner, *Stevenson*, 197.
28. Stevenson, 'Et Tu in Arcadia Vixisti', in *Underwoods* (1887), rpr. in *Collected Poems*, ed. Janet Adam Smith (London: Rupert Hart-Davis, 1950), 109–77, 125.
29. Arthur Machen, *The Great God Pan* (1894; Salem, New Hampshire: Ayer, 1970); Vernon Lee (pseud. of Violet Paget), 'Marsyas in Flanders' (1900), in *For Maurice: Five Unlikely Stories* (London: Bodley Head, 1927), 71–92; Walter Pater, 'Apollo in Picardy' (1893), in *Miscellaneous Studies* (1895; London: Macmillan, 1910), 142–71.
30. J. G. Millingen, *Mind and Matter: Illustrated by Considerations on Hereditary Insanity, and the Influence of Temperament in the Development of the Passions* (London: H. Hurst, 1847), 157. Cited in Jenny Bourne Taylor and Sally Shuttleworth, eds, *Embodied Selves: An Anthology of Psychological Texts 1830–1890* (Oxford: Oxford University Press, 1998), 169.
31. See Mighall, *Geography*, 158–64.
32. Mighall, *Geography*, 164.
33. Stevenson, 'Pastoral' (1887), in *Memories and Portraits* (London: Chatto and Windus, 1904), 90–105, 90.
34. Block, *Rituals*, 150, 155, 154.
35. Arthur Conan Doyle, *The Hound of the Baskervilles* (1901–2), ed. W. W. Robson (Oxford: Oxford University Press, 1993), 139; Dorian recognizes himself in his ancestor Philip Herbert's portrait: Oscar Wilde, *The Picture of Dorian Gray* (1890, revised 1891), in *The Major Works*, ed. Isobel Murray (Oxford: Oxford University Press, 1989), 47–214, 154. See the discussion in Mighall, *Geography*, 159–63.
36. Block, *Rituals*, 140, 151–2.
37. Mighall, *Geography*, 158.
38. Eigner similarly interprets Olalla's theology as 'twisted': *Stevenson*, 211.
39. 'Olalla' was published in the Christmas number of Charles Gray Robertson's *Court and Society Review* (1885), 3–15.
40. In the event, for reasons of length, 'The Body Snatcher' was substituted, and 'Markheim' was published instead in Unwin's 1885 Christmas Annual: 'The

Body Snatcher', *Pall Mall Christmas 'Extra'* 13 (December 1884), 3–12; 'Markheim', *The Broken Shaft: Tales in Mid-Ocean* [Unwin's Christmas Annual], ed. Henry Norman (London: T. Fisher Unwin, December 1885), 27–38.

41. Stevenson to Charles Morley, November 1884, *Letters*, 5: 34.
42. Colvin, headnote to Stevenson's letter to Edmund Gosse, 15 November 1884, in *The Letters of Robert Louis Stevenson*, ed. Sidney Colvin, 5 vols (London: Heinemann et al., 1924), 3: 21.
43. Stevenson, *Letters*, 5: 35n.
44. Stevenson to Morley, November 1884, *Letters*, 5: 35.
45. Stevenson, review of *The Works of Edgar Allan Poe*, vols 1 and 2 (1875), in *Essays Literary and Critical* (London: Heinemann et al., 1923), 178–85, 181.
46. Edgar Allan Poe, 'The Tell-Tale Heart' (1843), in *Selected Tales*, ed. David van Leer (Oxford: Oxford University Press, 1998), 193–7; Stevenson, review of *The Works of Edgar Allan Poe*, 181.
47. Fyodor Dostoevky, *Crime and Punishment* (1866), tr. Jessie Coulson (Oxford: Oxford University Press, 1995). Stevenson mentions reading the French translation, *Le Crime et Le Châtiment* (1884), in a letter to W. E. Henley, November 1885, *Letters*, 5: 151.
48. Dostoevsky, *Crime and Punishment*, 76, 79.
49. Stevenson, 'Markheim' (1885), in *Dr. Jekyll and Mr. Hyde, The Merry Men, and Other Tales* (London: J. M. Dent, 1925), 131–45, 134. Subsequent page references appear in the text.
50. Joseph Egan, '"Markheim": a Drama of Moral Psychology', *Nineteenth-Century Fiction* 20 (1966), 377–84, 382.
51. James Hogg, *The Private Memoirs and Confessions of a Justified Sinner* (1824), ed. John Carey (Oxford: Oxford University Press, 1995), 121.
52. Stevenson mentions Poe's tale in a letter to Andrew Lang, December 1885, *Letters*, 5: 158; Edgar Allan Poe, 'William Wilson' (1839), in *Selected Tales*, ed. David van Leer (Oxford: Oxford University Press, 1998), 66–83, 81.
53. Jenni Calder, *RLS: a Life Study* (London: Hamish Hamilton, 1980), 221.
54. Irving Saposnik, 'Stevenson's "Markheim": a Fictional "Christmas Sermon"', *Nineteenth-Century Fiction* 21 (1966), 277–82, 278.
55. Forbes Winslow, *On the Obscure Diseases of the Brain, and Disorders of the Mind* (1860), 4th edn (London: John Churchill, 1868), 234, 299, 234.
56. See F. W. H. Myers, 'Multiplex Personality', *Nineteenth Century* 20 (1886), 648–66.
57. Stevenson, 'A Chapter on Dreams' (1888), in *Further Memories* (London: Heinemann, 1923), 41–53, 42. This passage echoes the mental physiologist W. B. Carpenter's belief that 'Consciousness of Agreement between our present and our past Mental experiences, constitutes the basis of our feeling of *personal identity*': W. B. Carpenter, *Principles of Mental Physiology: With Their Applications to the Training and Discipline of the Mind, and the Study of its Morbid Conditions* (London: H. S. King, 1874), 455. The resonances with Sully's discussion of memory are even more striking: Sully notes that '[o]ur sense of personal identity may be said to be rooted in that special side of the mnemonic process which consists in the linking of all sequent events together by means of a thread of common consciousness'. Indeed, Sully's location of identity in memory leads directly on to a discussion of dual consciousness, as he describes how a rupture in one's mental life may lead to

such a violent contrast between 'old and new feelings' that the subject (now pathologized as a 'patient') may experience an 'imaginative fission or cleavage of self', often regarding the 'new feelings as making up another self, a foreign *Tu*, as distinguished from the familiar *Ego*': Sully, *Illusions*, 286, 289.

58. Dostoevsky, *Crime and Punishment*, 505, 526–7; see Eigner, *Stevenson*, 129–30.
59. Eigner, *Stevenson*, 128; Saposnik, '"Markheim"', 278.
60. Egan, '"Markheim"', 384.
61. Richard Boyle and Patrick Brantlinger, 'The Education of Edward Hyde: Stevenson's "Gothic Gnome" and the Mass Readership of Late-Victorian England', in Gordon Hirsch and William Veeder, eds, *Dr. Jekyll and Mr. Hyde after One Hundred Years* (London: University of Chicago Press, 1988), 265–82, 266.
62. Gavin Ogilvy, 'Robert Louis Stevenson', *British Weekly*, 2 November 1888, rpr. in Stevenson, *Strange Case of Dr. Jekyll and Mr. Hyde* (1886), ed. Katherine Linehan (New York: W. W. Norton, 2003), 120.
63. Stevenson to Fanny Stevenson, October 1885, *Letters*, 5: 135; Stevenson to Colvin, September to October 1885, *Letters*, 5: 128.
64. Julia Wedgwood, review in *Contemporary Review* (April 1886), rpr. in Stevenson, *Strange Case*, ed. Linehan, 100.
65. James Ashcroft Noble, review in *Academy* (23 January 1886), rpr. in Paul Maixner, ed., *Robert Louis Stevenson: the Critical Heritage* (London: Routledge and Kegan Paul, 1981), 203.
66. Noble, review, 203.
67. Stevenson, 'Chapter', 51.
68. Stevenson, 'Chapter', 52.
69. Stevenson, 'Chapter', 43.
70. Stevenson, 'Chapter', 44.
71. Mrs R. L. Stevenson, 'Note', in Stevenson, *The Strange Case of Dr Jekyll and Mr Hyde, Prince Otto*, Skerryvore Edition, vol. 4 (London: Heinemann et al., 1924), xvii–xxi, xix–xxi.
72. 'The Rev. Dr. Nicholson on "Dr. Jekyll and Mr. Hyde"', *Leamington Spa Courier* (24 November 1888), rpr. in Stevenson, *Strange Case*, ed. Linehan, 102–4.
73. Graham Balfour, *The Life of Robert Louis Stevenson*, 2 vols (London: Methuen, 1901), 2: 12.
74. Marie-Christine Leps, *Apprehending the Criminal: the Production of Deviance in Nineteenth-Century Discourse* (Durham, North Carolina: Duke University Press, 1992), 205–20; Block, 'Sully'; Mary Rosner, '"A Total Subversion of Character": Dr Jekyll's Moral Insanity', *Victorian Newsletter* 93 (1998), 27–31; Stephen Heath, 'Psychopathia Sexualis: Stevenson's *Strange Case*', in Lyn Pykett, ed., *Reading Fin de Siècle Fictions* (London: Longman, 1996), 64–79; Robert Mighall, 'Diagnosing Jekyll: the Scientific Context of Dr Jekyll's Experiment and Mr Hyde's Embodiment', in Stevenson, *The Strange Case of Dr Jekyll and Mr Hyde and Other Tales of Terror*, ed. Robert Mighall (London: Penguin, 2002), 145–61.
75. Stephen D. Arata, 'The Sedulous Ape: Atavism, Professionalism, and Stevenson's *Jekyll and Hyde*', *Criticism: a Quarterly Journal for Literature and the Arts* 37 (1995), 233–59; Mighall, *Geography*, 145–53, 187–95. For Daniel Pick too, *Jekyll and Hyde*, among other neo-Gothic novels, 'implicitly interrogated the validity of any determinist methodology': Daniel Pick, *Faces of*

Degeneration: a European Disorder, c. 1848–1918 (Cambridge: Cambridge University Press, 1989), 163.

76. Maudsley, *The Pathology of Mind: A Study of its Distempers, Deformities, and Disorders* (London: Macmillan, 1895), 540.
77. Stevenson, *The Strange Case of Dr Jekyll and Mr Hyde* (1886), in *The Strange Case of Dr Jekyll and Mr Hyde and Other Stories*, ed. Jenni Calder (London: Penguin, 1979), 27–97, 81–2. Subsequent page references appear in the text.
78. Romans 7.23, 22.
79. Stevenson, 'Pulvis et Umbra' (1888), in *Across the Plains: With Other Memories and Essays* (London: Chatto and Windus, 1907), 289–301, 300.
80. Myers, 'Personality', 648.
81. John Herdman, *The Double in Nineteenth-Century Fiction* (Basingstoke: Macmillan, now Palgrave Macmillan, 1990), 132.
82. Myers to Stevenson, February 1886, rpr. in Maixner, *Stevenson*, 215.
83. Myers to Stevenson, March 1886, rpr. in Maixner, *Stevenson*, 220.
84. Myers, 'Personality'; Mighall, 'Diagnosing', 146–7; Karl Miller, *Doubles: Studies in Literary History* (Oxford: Oxford University Press, 1985), 209–15.
85. Mrs R. L. Stevenson, 'Note', xviii; Roger G. Swearingen, *The Prose Writings of Robert Louis Stevenson: a Guide* (Hamden, Connecticut: Archon Books, 1980), 101. The paper was probably Myers's 'Multiplex Personality', which appeared in November 1886.
86. Richard Proctor, 'Dual Consciousness', *Cornhill Magazine* 35 (1877), 86–105, 91–2; Stevenson, 'On Falling in Love', *Cornhill Magazine* 35 (1877), 214–20.
87. Proctor, 'Consciousness', 91–2.
88. See Henry Maudsley, *Responsibility in Mental Disease* (London: H. S. King, 1874), *passim*.
89. Smith Baker, 'Etiological Significance of Heterogeneous Personality', *Journal of Nervous and Mental Disease* 20 (1893), 664–74, 671.
90. Janet Oppenheim, *'Shattered Nerves': Doctors, Patients, and Depression in Victorian England* (Oxford: Oxford University Press, 1991), 272–80; Robert Nye, 'Sociology and Degeneration: the Irony of Progress', in J. Edward Chamberlin and Sander L. Gilman, eds, *Degeneration: the Dark Side of Progress* (New York: Columbia University Press, 1985), 49–71, 59.
91. For moral insanity, see for instance George H. Savage, 'Moral Insanity', *Journal of Mental Science* 27 (1881), 147–55.
92. T. H. Huxley, 'Biogenesis and Abiogenesis. (The Presidential Address to the British Association for the Advancement of Science, 1870)', in *Critiques and Addresses* (London: Macmillan, 1873), 218–50, 239. Huxley acknowledged the monstrosity of his vision, describing it as 'a land flowing with the abominable': 'Biogenesis', 248. For a consideration of the 'gothicity' of *fin-de-siècle* sciences, see Kelly Hurley, *The Gothic Body: Sexuality, Materialism, and Degeneration at the Fin-de-Siècle* (Cambridge: Cambridge University Press, 1996), 5.
93. H. Rider Haggard, *She* (1887; Oxford: Oxford University Press, 1991), 293; Machen, *Pan*, 80–1.
94. Stevenson, *New Arabian Nights* (1878; London: Heinemann, 1923), 18.
95. Edwin Ray Lankester, *Degeneration: A Chapter in Darwinism* (London: Macmillan, 1880), 33.
96. Stevenson, 'The Day After Tomorrow' (1887), in *Ethical Studies, Edinburgh: Picturesque Notes* (London: Heinemann et al., 1924), 113–23, 120. As Wells's

Time-Traveller says, '[s]trength is the outcome of need; security sets a premium on feebleness': H. G. Wells, *The Time Machine* (1895), ed. John Lawton (London: J. M. Dent, 1995), 27.
97. Stevenson, 'Day', 121.
98. Stevenson, 'Day', 120.
99. Arata, 'Ape', 239.
100. Heath, 'Psychopathia', 71.
101. Edward Charles Spitzka, 'Cases of Masturbation (Masturbatic Insanity)', *Journal of Mental Science* 34 (April 1888), 52–61, 53, 52. See Mighall's discussion of this analogy in *Geography*, 192–5.
102. Baker, 'Significance', 672–3.
103. Elaine Showalter, *Sexual Anarchy: Gender and Culture at the Fin de Siècle* (London: Bloomsbury, 1991), 107.
104. Showalter, *Anarchy*, 112. Sodomy, of course, was already a criminal offence.
105. Significant manuscript variations are reprinted in Stevenson, *Case*, ed. Linehan, 66–72.
106. Stevenson, *Case*, ed. Linehan, 68.
107. Stevenson, *Case*, ed. Linehan, 71, 70.
108. Stevenson, *Case*, ed. Linehan, 70.
109. Stevenson to John Paul Bocock, November 1887, *Letters* 6: 56.
110. Heath, 'Psychopathia', 65.
111. Arata, 'Ape', 236.
112. M. Kellen Williams, '"Down with the Door, Poole": Designating Deviance in Stevenson's *Strange Case of Dr. Jekyll and Mr. Hyde*', *English Literature in Transition* 39 (1996), 412–29.
113. Stevenson, 'A Note on Realism' (1883), in *Essays in the Art of Writing* (London: Chatto and Windus, 1908), 93–107, 105.
114. Arata, 'Ape', 235–6; Mighall, *Geography*, 145–6.
115. Heath, 'Psychopathia', 65.
116. Mighall, *Geography*, 191.
117. Hurley, *Body*, 101–2.
118. Havelock Ellis, *The Criminal* (London: Walter Scott, 1890), 78–9; Hurley, *Body*, 101. For a discussion of women's instinctive ability to sense danger, see Grant Allen, 'Woman's Intuition', *Forum (and Century)* 9 (1890), 333–40.
119. Eigner, *Stevenson*, 158.
120. For the increasing interest in suggestion and imitation, see Athena Vrettos, *Somatic Fictions: Imagining Illness in Victorian Culture* (Stanford, California: Stanford University Press, 1995), 84.
121. Sully, *Illusions*, 277; Daniel Hack Tuke, *Illustrations of the Influence of the Mind Upon the Body in Health and Disease Designed to Elucidate the Action of the Imagination*, 2nd edn, 2 vols (London: J. and A. Churchill, 1884), 1: 108–10.
122. Gustave Le Bon, *The Crowd: A Study of the Popular Mind* (London: Fisher Unwin, 1896), 31.
123. Unsigned review, *The Times* (25 January 1886), rpr. in Maixner, *Stevenson*, 205.
124. Review, *Birmingham Daily Post* (19 January 1886), rpr. in Stevenson, *Case*, ed. Linehan, 94–5.
125. Mighall, 'Diagnosing', 157.
126. 'The Whitechapel Murder', *East London Advertiser* (8 September 1888), http://www.casebook.org/press_reports/east_london_advertiser/ela880908.html

(accessed 16 May 2005); 'Here and There', *East London Advertiser* (13 October 1888), http://www.casebook.org/press_reports/east_london_advertiser/ela 881013. html (accessed 16 May 2005).

127. 'A Serious Question', in *Punch* (15 September 1888), rpr. in Stevenson, *The Strange Case of Dr Jekyll and Mr Hyde* (1886), ed. Martin A. Danahay (Peterborough, Ontario: Broadview, 1999), 187.
128. 'Dramatic and Musical', *Daily Telegraph* (12 October 1888), 3.
129. Donald Rumbelow, *The Complete Jack the Ripper* (London: W. H. Allen, 1979), 77.
130. J. A. Symonds to Stevenson, 3 March 1886, in *The Letters of John Addington Symonds*, ed. Herbert M. Schueller and Robert L. Peters, 3 vols (Detroit, Michigan: Wayne State University Press, 1968–69), 3: 121.
131. Symonds, Letters, 3: 120–1.
132. Symonds, *Letters*, 3: 121.
133. Symonds, *Letters*, 3: 121.
134. Oscar Wilde, 'The Decay of Lying' (1889), in *The Artist as Critic: Critical Writings of Oscar Wilde*, ed. Richard Ellmann (New York: Vintage, 1969), 290–320, 295.

Part III Stevenson as anthropologist: culture, folklore, and language

1. Stevenson, *In the South Seas* (1896; comp. Sidney Colvin), ed. Neil Rennie (London: Penguin, 1998), 13.
2. Vanessa Smith, *Literary Culture and the Pacific: Nineteenth-Century Textual Encounters* (Cambridge: Cambridge University Press, 1998), 110; Rod Edmond, *Representing the South Pacific: Colonial Discourse from Cook to Gauguin* (Cambridge: Cambridge University Press, 1997), 163.
3. Penny Fielding, *Writing and Orality: Nationality, Culture, and Nineteenth-Century Scottish Fiction* (Oxford: Clarendon Press, 1996), 132–207; David Daiches, 'Stevenson and Scotland', in Jenni Calder, ed., *Stevenson and Victorian Scotland* (Edinburgh: Edinburgh University Press, 1981), 11–32; Caroline McCracken-Flesher, 'Thinking Nationally/Writing Colonially? Scott, Stevenson, and England', *Novel: a Forum on Fiction* 24 (1990–91), 296–318; Kenneth Gelder, 'Stevenson and the Covenanters: "Black Andie's Tale of Tod Lapraik" and "Thrawn Janet"', *Scottish Literary Journal* 11 (1984), 56–70.
4. Andrew Noble, 'Highland History and Narrative Form in Scott and Stevenson', in Andrew Noble, ed., *Robert Louis Stevenson* (London: Vision Press, 1983), 134–87; Christopher Harvie, 'The Politics of Stevenson', in Calder, ed., *Stevenson and Victorian Scotland*, 107–25.
5. Smith, *Literary Culture*; Roslyn Jolly, 'South Sea Gothic: Pierre Loti and Robert Louis Stevenson', *English Literature in Transition 1880–1920* 47 (2004), 28–49; Barry Menikoff, *Robert Louis Stevenson and 'The Beach of Falesá': a Study in Victorian Publishing* (Stanford, California: Stanford University Press, 1984).
6. Roslyn Jolly, 'Introduction', in Stevenson, *South Sea Tales* (Oxford: Oxford University Press, 1996), ix–xxxiii, xxxiii.
7. J. W. Burrow, *Evolution and Society: a Study in Victorian Social Theory* (Cambridge: Cambridge University Press, 1966), 11–14; David Spadafora,

The Idea of Progress in Eighteenth-Century Britain (New Haven, Connecticut: Yale University Press, 1990), 253–320.

8. Peter J. Bowler, *Biology and Social Thought* (Berkeley, California: Office for History of Science and Technology, University of California at Berkeley, 1993), 38–43; George W. Stocking, Jr., *Victorian Anthropology* (New York: Free Press, 1987), *passim*.
9. See Burrow, *Evolution*, 11–14, 233, 248–9; Robert Crawford, *Devolving English Literature* (Oxford: Clarendon Press, 1992), 152–4; Peter J. Bowler, *The Invention of Progress: the Victorians and the Past* (Oxford: Blackwell, 1989), 33.
10. E. B. Tylor, *Primitive Culture: Researches into the Development of Mythology, Philosophy, Religion, Art, and Custom*, 2 vols (London: John Murray, 1871), 1: 28.
11. Tylor, *Culture*, 1: 15.
12. Tylor, *Culture*, 2: 100.
13. Tylor, *Culture*, 2: 409–10; 1: 453.
14. Andrew Lang, *Myth, Ritual, and Religion*, 2 vols (London: Longmans, Green, 1887), 1: 28.
15. The claim for the Darwinian foundation of anthropology is made, for example, in Richard M. Dorson, *The British Folklorists: a History* (London: Routledge and Kegan Paul, 1968), 160. For a perceptive account which contests this assumption, see Adam Kuper, *The Invention of Primitive Society: Transformations of an Illusion* (London: Routledge, 1988), 1–8.
16. Herbert Spencer, *The Principles of Sociology*, vol. 1 (London: Williams and Norgate, 1876), 83.
17. Stocking, *Anthropology*, 228.
18. Gillian Beer, *Darwin's Plots: Evolutionary Narrative in Darwin, George Eliot and Nineteenth-Century Fiction* (1983), 2nd edn (Cambridge: Cambridge University Press, 2000), 12.

5. 'The Foreigner at Home': Stevenson and Scotland

1. On the dissolution of Scottish literary culture, see Ian Duncan, 'North Britain, Inc.', *Victorian Literature and Culture* 23 (1995), 339–50, 339–44.
2. Robert Crawford, *Devolving English Literature* (Oxford: Clarendon Press, 1992), 156 and *passim*.
3. John Sutherland Black and George Chrystal, *The Life of William Robertson Smith* (London: Adam and Charles Black, 1912), 116, 140.
4. Black and Chrystal, *Life*, 139, 116, 140.
5. Black and Chrystal, *Life*, 140–1.
6. Adam Kuper, *The Invention of Primitive Society: Transformations of an Illusion* (London: Routledge, 1988), 4.
7. George W. Stocking, Jr., *Victorian Anthropology* (New York: Free Press, 1987), 297.
8. On Smith, see Kuper, *Invention*, 82–8; George W. Stocking, Jr., *After Tylor: British Social Anthropology 1888–1951* (London: Athlone Press, 1995), 63–81.
9. On *Essays and Reviews*, the work of Anglican Liberals who proposed a similarly developmental view of human religious thought, see Josef L. Altholz, *Anatomy of a Controversy: the Debate over 'Essays and Reviews' 1860–1864* (Aldershot, Hampshire: Scolar Press, 1994).

10. Cargill Gilston Knott, *Life and Scientific Work of Peter Guthrie Tait: Supplementing the Two Volumes of Scientific Papers Published in 1898 and 1900* (Cambridge: Cambridge University Press, 1911), 72. (Murray, a fellow student, became an eminent marine scientist.)
11. Black and Chrystal, *Life*, 140.
12. Adrian Desmond, *Huxley: From Devil's Disciple to Evolution's High Priest* (London: Penguin, 1997), 406, 370.
13. Desmond, *Huxley*, 370. On Fleeming Jenkin, subsequently Stevenson's friend, see Stevenson, 'Memoir of Fleeming Jenkin' (1888), in *The Merry Men and Other Tales, Memoir of Fleeming Jenkin* (London: Heinemann et al., 1922), 337–562.
14. Balfour Stewart and Peter Guthrie Tait, *The Unseen Universe or Physical Speculations on a Future State* (London: Macmillan, 1875), 46, 64.
15. Thomas Stevenson, *Christianity Confirmed by Jewish and Heathen Testimony and Deductions from Physical Sciences, etc.* (1877), 2nd edn (Edinburgh: David Douglas, 1879), 108–20.
16. Thomas Stevenson, *Christianity*, 108, 114–15.
17. On Stevenson's loss of faith, see Chapter 3.
18. Stevenson to Charles Baxter, February 1873, in *The Letters of Robert Louis Stevenson*, ed. Bradford Booth and Ernest Mehew, 8 vols (New Haven, Connecticut: Yale University Press, 1994–95), 1: 173 (hereafter, *Letters*); Stevenson to Frances Sitwell, September 1873, *Letters*, 1: 312.
19. Stevenson to Frances Sitwell, September 1873, *Letters*, 1: 312.
20. G. D. Campbell, Duke of Argyll, *The Reign of Law* (London: Alexander Strahan, 1867), 30–46, 10.
21. See *Selected Letters of Robert Louis Stevenson*, ed. Ernest Mehew (New Haven, Connecticut: Yale University Press, 1997), 43n (hereafter, *Selected Letters*). As the address was not preserved, the details of Stevenson's position in the debate about scientific determinism are unclear. However, an undated notebook entry echoes the terms of the debate, observing that 'we claim as against current orthodoxy . . . the exclusion of free will . . . our thought and lives are as completely governed by what appear to be laws, as is the course of a river or the direction of the wind': Stevenson, 'Selections from His Notebook' (1923), in *Memories and Portraits, Memoirs of Himself, Selections from His Notebook* (London: Heinemann, 1924), 171–94, 187.
22. Stevenson to Frances Sitwell, September 1873, *Letters*, 1: 312.
23. Campbell, *Reign*, 16, 24.
24. Campbell, *Reign*, 21.
25. Stevenson to James Walter Ferrier, November 1872, *Selected Letters*, 28.
26. Stevenson, 'Memoirs of Himself' (1912), in *Memories*, 147–68, 166–7.
27. Stevenson to Frances Sitwell, June 1875, *Letters*, 2: 141.
28. Stevenson, 'Selections', 182–3.
29. Stevenson, 'Selections', 183.
30. Stevenson, 'Selections', 184.
31. Edwin M. Eigner, *Robert Louis Stevenson and Romantic Tradition* (Princeton, New Jersey: Princeton University Press, 1966), 111, 114, and *passim*. *The Strange Case of Dr. Jekyll and Mr. Hyde* has frequently been read in these terms, and the interpretation has been extended convincingly to other works such as *The Ebb-Tide* and *Weir of Hermiston*: see, for example, Joseph Bristow,

Empire Boys: Adventures in a Man's World (London: HarperCollins, 1991), 122; Andrew Noble, 'Highland History and Narrative Form in Scott and Stevenson', in Andrew Noble, ed., *Robert Louis Stevenson* (London: Vision Press, 1983), 134–87, 145; Peter Zenzinger, 'The Ballad Spirit and the Modern Mind: Narrative Perspective in Stevenson's *Weir of Hermiston*', in Horst W. Drescher and Joachim Schwend, eds, *Studies in Scottish Fiction: Nineteenth Century* (Frankfurt am Main: Verlag Peter Lang, 1985), 233–51, 246–7.

32. Stevenson, 'The House of Eld' (1895), in *Weir of Hermiston and Other Stories*, ed. Paul Binding (London: Penguin, 1979), 285–92. Page references appear in the text.
33. Honor Mulholland, 'Robert Louis Stevenson and the Romance Form', in Noble, ed., *Stevenson*, 96–117, 96–104.
34. Stevenson to Frances Sitwell, October 1873, *Letters*, 1: 341.
35. Stevenson to Charles Baxter, February 1873, *Letters*, 1: 173.
36. T. H. Huxley, 'Prologue', in *Collected Essays*, 9 vols (London: Macmillan, 1894–1908), 5: 1–58, 13.
37. Unpublished letter, Thomas Stevenson to Stevenson, 5 September 1877, in Yale University, Beinecke Rare Book and Manuscript Library, Stevenson Collection, Cat. No. 5672.
38. Thomas Stevenson to Stevenson, 5 September 1877, Beinecke Library.
39. E. B. Tylor, *Primitive Culture: Researches into the Development of Mythology, Philosophy, Religion, Art, and Custom*, 2 vols (London: John Murray, 1871), 1: 15.
40. For the growing belief that the individual was conditioned by language, see Peter Allan Dale, *In Pursuit of a Scientific Culture: Science, Art, and Society in the Victorian Age* (Madison, Wisconsin: University of Wisconsin Press, 1989), Chapters 7 and 8.
41. Stevenson, 'Thrawn Janet' (1881), in *Weir of Hermiston and Other Stories*, ed. Paul Binding (London: Penguin, 1979), 203–15. Page references appear in the text.
42. Stevenson, 'Note for "The Merry Men"' (1921), in *Miscellanea* (London: Heinemann et al., 1923), 477–8, 477; Kenneth Gelder, 'Stevenson and the Covenanters: "Black Andie's Tale of Tod Lapraik" and "Thrawn Janet"', *Scottish Literary Journal* 11 (1984), 56–70.
43. T. C. Smout, *A History of the Scottish People 1560–1830* (London: Collins, 1969), 198–207, 228–39.
44. Penny Fielding, *Writing and Orality: Nationality, Culture, and Nineteenth-Century Scottish Fiction* (Oxford: Clarendon Press, 1996), 27, 151–2.
45. Caroline McCracken-Flesher, 'Thinking Nationally/Writing Colonially? Scott, Stevenson, and England', *Novel: a Forum on Fiction* 24 (1990–91), 296–318, 313. See also Paul Binding, 'Introduction', in Stevenson, *Weir*, 7–48, 24–8.
46. Fred B. Warner, Jr., 'Stevenson's First Scottish Story', *Nineteenth-Century Fiction* 24 (1969), 335–44, 344.
47. Stevenson, 'Note', 477.
48. David Richards, *Masks of Difference: Cultural Representations in Literature, Anthropology and Art* (Cambridge: Cambridge University Press, 1994), 125–36; Colin Kidd, '*The Strange Death of Scottish History* Revisited: Constructions of the Past in Scotland, c. 1790–1914', *Scottish Historical Review* 76.1 (1997), 86–102, 87–8; Noble, 'History', 153–63.
49. Peter D. Garside, 'Scott and the "Philosophical" Historians', *Journal of the History of Ideas* 36 (1975), 497–512.

50. See for instance the execution of Fergus Mac-Ivor, in Walter Scott, *Waverley; or, 'Tis Sixty Years Since* (1814), ed. Claire Lamont (Oxford: Oxford University Press, 1986), 319–29. On Scott's progressive Unionism, see McCracken-Flesher, 'Thinking Nationally', 308–10; Peter Womack, *Improvement and Romance: Constructing the Myth of the Highlands* (Basingstoke: Macmillan, now Palgrave Macmillan, 1988), 144–7. Scott's reading of history, of course, was complex: as Kathryn Sutherland judges, an 'awareness of loss' was 'inseparable' from his belief in 'historical progress': 'Introduction', in Walter Scott, *Redgauntlet* (Oxford: Oxford University Press, 1985), vii–xxiii, viii.
51. Noble, 'History', 135.
52. T. M. Devine, *The Scottish Nation 1700–2000* (London: Penguin, 1999), 233.
53. Charles Withers, 'The Historical Creation of the Scottish Highlands', in Ian Donnachie and Christopher Whatley, eds, *The Manufacture of Scottish History* (Edinburgh: Polygon, 1992), 143–56, 151.
54. Tylor, *Culture*, 1: 40.
55. Tylor, *Culture*, 1: 40–1.
56. J. W. Burrow, *Evolution and Society: a Study in Victorian Social Theory* (Cambridge: Cambridge University Press, 1966), 11–14.
57. Tylor, *Culture*, 2: 195.
58. Andrew Lang, 'At the Sign of the Ship', *Longman's Magazine* 9 (1886–87), 105–12, 109; 'At the Sign of the Ship', *Longman's Magazine* 16 (1890), 234–40, 236.
59. Kidd, *'Death'*, 93–4.
60. R. G. Cant, *The Writing of Scottish History in the Time of Andrew Lang: Being the Andrew Lang Lecture Delivered before the University of St. Andrews 8 February 1978* (Edinburgh: Scottish Academic Press, 1978), 11.
61. J. H. Burton, *History of Scotland from Agricola's Invasion to the Extinction of the Last Jacobite Insurrection*, 2nd edn, 8 vols (Edinburgh: Blackwood, 1873), 1: viii.
62. Stevenson to Thomas Stevenson, December 1880, *Letters*, 3: 139; Stevenson to his parents, December 1880, *Letters*, 3: 145.
63. Stevenson to Sidney Colvin, December 1880, *Letters*, 3: 149.
64. Stevenson to Frances Sitwell, February 1874, *Letters*, 1: 475.
65. Devine, *Scottish Nation*, 425–35.
66. Stevenson to his parents, December 1880, *Letters*, 3: 145. Stevenson's sympathies were reversed by the Fenian terrorist campaign, which led him to contemplate fighting on the side of the Unionists in Ireland: Stevenson to Anne Jenkin, April 1887, *Selected Letters*, 333.
67. Noble, 'Highland History', 138–9, 141–51.
68. Stevenson, 'Dedication', in *Kidnapped* (1886), ed. Donald McFarlan (London: Penguin, 1994), 3.
69. Noble, 'Highland History', 145.
70. Noble, 'Highland History', 139.
71. [R. H. Hutton], unsigned review, the *Spectator* (24 July 1886), rpr. in Paul Maixner, ed., *Robert Louis Stevenson: the Critical Heritage* (London: Routledge, Kegan, Paul, 1981), 235–7.
72. Unsigned review, *Saturday Review* (7 August 1886), rpr. in Maixner, *Stevenson*, 239; see also unsigned review, *St. James's Gazette* (19 July 1886), rpr. in Maixner, *Stevenson*, 234–5.

73. James Buzard, *Disorienting Fiction: the Autoethnographic Work of Nineteenth-Century British Novels* (Princeton, New Jersey: Princeton University Press, 2005), 8.
74. Buzard, *Disorienting Fiction*, 67.
75. Buzard, *Disorienting Fiction*, 68.
76. Stevenson to Baxter, February 1886, *Letters*, 5: 206. The same wariness about linguistic dilution figures in Stevenson's caustic observation that English literature was 'principally the work of venal Scots': Stevenson to Edmund Gosse, July 1879, *Letters*, 2: 328.
77. Stevenson, 'The Foreigner at Home' (1882), in *Memories and Portraits* (London: Chatto and Windus, 1904), 1–23, 6, 23.
78. *Kidnapped* evolved out of Stevenson's study of the murder, which he intended to submit in support of his (unsuccessful) application for Edinburgh University's Chair of History and Constitutional Law in 1881: Emma Letley, 'Introduction', in Stevenson, *Kidnapped and Catriona* (Oxford: Oxford University Press, 1986), vii–xxviii, xii.
79. Stephen Shapiro, 'Mass African Suicide and the Rise of Euro-American Sentimentalism: Equiano's and Stevenson's Tales of the Semi-Periphery', in W. M. Verhoeven and Beth Dolan, eds, *Revolutions and Watersheds: Transatlantic Dialogues, 1775–1815* (Amsterdam: Rodopi, 1999), 123–44, 132.
80. Shapiro, 'Suicide', 133.
81. On the affinity between twentieth-century ethnography and the Victorian novel, see Buzard, *Disorienting Fiction*, 7, 38.
82. On Robin Oig, Rob Roy's son, see Stevenson, 'Young Rob Roy' (1881), in W. B. Cook, ed., *Local Notes and Queries: Reprinted from the Stirling Observer*, 2 vols (Stirling: Duncan and Jamieson, 'Observer' Office, 1883–86), 1: 287–8.
83. Susan R. Gannon, 'Repetition and Meaning in Stevenson's David Balfour Novels', *Studies in the Literary Imagination* 18 (1985), 21–33, 26.
84. Stevenson to J. M. Barrie, February 1892, *Letters*, 7: 238–9.
85. Donald McFarlan, 'Introduction', in Stevenson, *Kidnapped* (1886) (London: Penguin, 1994), vii–xvi, xii.
86. Scott, *Rob Roy*, 244.
87. Shapiro, 'Suicide', 133.
88. Gannon, 'Repetition', 22.
89. Scott, *Waverley*, 329–39.
90. [William Archer], unsigned review, *Pall Mall Gazette* (14 September 1889), rpr. in Maixner, *Stevenson*, 342.
91. Unsigned review, *Glasgow Herald* (17 October 1889), rpr. in Maixner, *Stevenson*, 353; Margaret Oliphant, 'The Old Saloon', *Blackwood's Magazine* 146 (November 1889), rpr. in Maixner, *Stevenson*, 360.
92. [W. E. Henley], unsigned review, *Scots Observer* (12 October 1889), rpr. in Maixner, *Stevenson*, 350.
93. The novel's fragmentation was probably exacerbated by its composition, under pressure, during its serialization in *Scribner's Magazine*: Roger Swearingen, *The Prose Writings of Robert Louis Stevenson: a Guide* (Hamden, Connecticut: Archon Books, 1980), 119–22.
94. On the Tullibardine case, see Stevenson, 'Note to "The Master of Ballantrae"' (1921), in Stevenson, *The Master of Ballantrae: a Winter's Tale*, ed. Adrian Poole (London: Penguin, 1996), 224–6, 225.

95. Douglas Gifford, 'Stevenson and Scottish Fiction: the Importance of *The Master of Ballantrae*', in Jenni Calder, ed., *Stevenson and Victorian Scotland* (Edinburgh: Edinburgh University Press, 1981), 62–87, 66, 84–5.
96. Joseph Egan, 'From History to Myth: a Symbolic Reading of *The Master of Ballantrae*', *Studies in English Literature, 1500–1900* 8 (1968), 699–710, 704–5.
97. Douglas Gifford, 'Myth, Parody and Dissociation: Scottish Fiction 1814–1914', in Douglas Gifford, ed., *The History of Scottish Literature*, vol. 3: *Nineteenth Century* (Aberdeen: Aberdeen University Press, 1988), 217–59, 249.
98. Stevenson, *The Master of Ballantrae: a Winter's Tale* (1888–89), ed. Adrian Poole (London: Penguin, 1996), 125. Subsequent page references appear in the text.
99. Adrian Poole, 'Introduction', in Stevenson, *Master*, vii–xxvi, xiv. References to the *Aeneid* are scattered through the narrative: see Stevenson, *Master*, 143, 180. On the Jacobite use of the Virgilian code, see Murray Pittock, *Poetry and Jacobite Politics in Eighteenth-Century Britain and Ireland* (Cambridge: Cambridge University Press, 1994), 38.
100. Rory Watson, '"You cannot fight me with a word": *The Master of Ballantrae* and the Wilderness beyond Dualism', a paper delivered at the 'Stevenson, Scotland and Samoa' conference, Stirling, 2000.
101. Stevenson, 'Preface' (1898), in Stevenson, *Master*, 5–8. After writing this Preface, Stevenson decided that it was 'a little too like Scott', though he later included it in the Edinburgh Edition of his collected works: Stevenson to Baxter, May 1894, *Letters*, 8: 290.
102. Fielding, *Writing*, 156–73; Alan Sandison, *Robert Louis Stevenson and the Appearance of Modernism* (Basingstoke: Macmillan, now Palgrave Macmillan, 1996), 270–312.
103. For a stimulating reading of James's association with the supernatural and folk tradition, see J. M. Harris, 'Robert Louis Stevenson: Folklore and Imperialism', *English Literature in Transition 1880–1920* 46 (2003), 382–99, 392–6.
104. Harris, 'Stevenson', 394.
105. Stevenson, 'Note to "The Master of Ballantrae"', 226; see also Carol Mills, '*The Master of Ballantrae*: an Experiment with Genre', in Noble, ed., *Stevenson*, 118–33, 118, 123–4, 131.
106. Alexander B. Clunas, '"A Double Word": Writing and Justice in *The Master of Ballantrae*', *Studies in Scottish Literature* 28 (1993), 55–74, 74.
107. Fielding, *Writing*, 161.
108. His sympathetic knowledge of the Iroquois is also indicated by his paper on 'Languages, Customs, and Manners of the Indian Six Nations' (1772): H. Manners Chichester, 'Sir William Johnson', in Leslie Stephen and Sidney Lee, eds, *Dictionary of National Biography*, vol. 30 (London: Smith, Elder, 1892), 50–2, 51.
109. Adrian Poole, 'Notes', in Stevenson, *Master*, 232n; Chichester, 'Johnston', 50–2.
110. Stevenson, 'The Genesis of "The Master of Ballantrae"' (1896), in Stevenson, *Master*, 221–4, 222.
111. Eigner, *Stevenson*, 181.
112. Swearingen, *Writings*, 119–22; Stevenson, *Master*, 125; Stevenson, 'Preface', 5.

6. '[T]he clans disarmed, the chiefs deposed': Stevenson in the South Seas

1. Henry James, *Notes on Novelists: With Some Other Notes* (London: J. M. Dent and Sons, 1914), 16–18.
2. Oscar Wilde to Robert Ross, April 1897, in *The Selected Letters of Oscar Wilde*, ed. Rupert Hart-Davis (Oxford: Oxford University Press, 1979), 246.
3. Christopher Harvie, 'The Politics of Stevenson', in Jenni Calder, ed., *Stevenson and Victorian Scotland* (Edinburgh: Edinburgh University Press, 1981), 107–25, 124.
4. Leslie Stephen, *The Science of Ethics* (1882; Bristol: Thoemmes, 1991), 120.
5. Jonathan Lamb, Vanessa Smith, and Nicholas Thomas, 'Introduction', in Jonathan Lamb, Vanessa Smith, and Nicholas Thomas, eds, *Exploration and Exchange: a South Seas Anthology 1680–1900* (Chicago, Illinois: University of Chicago Press, 2000), xiii–xxv, xxii–xxv.
6. Paul M. Kennedy, *The Samoan Tangle: a Study in Anglo-German-American Relations 1878–1900* (Dublin: Irish University Press, 1974), Chapters 2 and 3.
7. Stevenson, *A Footnote to History: Eight Years of Trouble in Samoa* (1892), in *Vailima Papers* (London: Heinemann et al., 1924), 67–240; Stevenson to the editor of *The Times*, June and July 1892, in *The Letters of Robert Louis Stevenson*, ed. Bradford Booth and Ernest Mehew, 8 vols (New Haven, Connecticut: Yale University Press, 1994–95), 7: 320–2, 338 (hereafter, *Letters*); Stevenson to the editor of *The Times*, February 1893, in *Selected Letters of Robert Louis Stevenson*, ed. Ernest Mehew (New Haven, Connecticut: Yale University Press, 1997), 526–8 (hereafter, *Selected Letters*).
8. On Vailima, see Stevenson to W. H. Triggs, December 1893, *Letters*, 8: 200; on the consulship, see Stevenson to Colvin, May to June 1892, *Letters*, 7: 311; Stevenson to Colvin, September to October 1892, *Letters*, 7: 386–7.
9. Stevenson to Colvin, June to July 1891, *Selected Letters*, 461.
10. Robert Hillier, 'Folklore and Oral Tradition in Stevenson's South Seas Narrative Poems and Short Stories', *Scottish Literary Journal* 14 (1987), 32–47, 32.
11. Grant Allen, 'Sacred Stones', *Fortnightly Review* 53 (1890), 96–116.
12. Andrew Lang, 'Was Jehovah a Fetish Stone?', *Contemporary Review* 57 (1890), 353–65, 355–6.
13. Stevenson to Lang, August 1890, *Letters*, 6: 416. Stevenson's letter was published, with an introduction by Lang, in the *Athenæum* 96 (1890), 516.
14. Stevenson to Lang, August 1890, *Letters*, 6: 416.
15. Stevenson to Lang, August 1890, *Letters*, 6: 417.
16. Unpublished letter, Joseph Jacobs to Stevenson, 22 August 1893, in Yale University, Beinecke Rare Book and Manuscript Library, Stevenson Collection, Cat. No. 4904.
17. Jacobs to Stevenson, 22 August 1893, Beinecke Library.
18. Jacobs to Stevenson, 22 August 1893, Beinecke Library. The reference is to Stevenson's *Ballads* (London: Chatto and Windus, 1890), a collection of his Scottish and Polynesian narrative poems.
19. Scott Ashley, 'The Poetics of Race in 1890s Ireland: an Ethnography of the Aran Islands', *Patterns of Prejudice* 35 (2001), 5–18, 18.
20. George W. Stocking, Jr., *Victorian Anthropology* (New York: Free Press, 1987), 267.
21. For a survey of the debate, see James Buzard and Joseph Childers, 'Introduction: Victorian Ethnographies', *Victorian Studies* 41.3 (1998), 351–3;

James Buzard, *Disorienting Fiction: the Autoethnographic Work of Nineteenth-Century British Novels* (Princeton, New Jersey: Princeton University Press, 2005), 5–11.

22. Stocking, *Anthropology*, 287–93.
23. Adam Kuper, *Culture: the Anthropologists' Account* (Cambridge, Massachusetts: Harvard University Press, 1999), 60–7.
24. Christopher Herbert, *Culture and Anomie: Ethnographic Imagination in the Nineteenth Century* (Chicago, Illinois: University of Chicago Press, 1991), 28–9.
25. Stocking, *Anthropology*, 289.
26. Carlo Ginzburg, 'Tusitala and His Polish Reader', in *No Island Is an Island: Four Glances at English Literature in a World Perspective* (New York: Columbia University Press, 2000), 69–88, 79; David Richards, *Masks of Difference: Cultural Representations in Literature, Anthropology and Art* (Cambridge: Cambridge University Press, 1994), 191.
27. For a critique of the emphasis on cultural difference, see Kuper, *Culture*, 218–46.
28. Buzard, *Disorienting Fiction*, 7.
29. An initial version, *The South Seas*, was published as a copyright edition of 22 copies in 1890; the material was then serialized in 1891 in *Black and White*, the New York *Sun*, and the *Auckland Star*. *In the South Seas*, a compilation selected and edited by Sidney Colvin, first appeared in volume form in 1896: Swearingen, *Writings*, 134–43. Citations are to *In the South Seas*, ed. Neil Rennie (London: Penguin, 1998).
30. Fanny Stevenson to Sidney Colvin, January 1891, *Letters*, 7: 79.
31. Neil Rennie, 'Introduction', in Stevenson, *In the South Seas*, viii–xxxv, xxv.
32. Rod Edmond, *Representing the South Pacific: Colonial Discourse from Cook to Gauguin* (Cambridge: Cambridge University Press, 1997), 167–8.
33. Roslyn Jolly, 'Robert Louis Stevenson and Samoan History: Crossing the Roman Wall', in Bruce Bennett, Jeff Doyle, and Satendra Nandan, eds, *Crossing Cultures: Essays on Literature and Culture of the Asia-Pacific* (London: Skoob Books, 1996), 113–20, 115.
34. Gillian Beer, *Darwin's Plots: Evolutionary Narrative in Darwin, George Eliot and Nineteenth-Century Fiction* (1983), 2nd edn (Cambridge: Cambridge University Press, 2000), 12.
35. This *laissez-faire* evolutionism became popularly known as 'Social Darwinism', but as Peter Bowler points out this was a misnomer, as it was largely based on biological theories which were 'non-Darwinian in origin': *Biology and Social Thought* (Berkeley, California: Office for History of Science and Technology, University of California at Berkeley, 1993), 61.
36. Vanessa Smith, *Literary Culture and the Pacific: Nineteenth-Century Textual Encounters* (Cambridge: Cambridge University Press, 1998), 130, 134.
37. F. Max Müller, 'Preface', in W. W. Gill, ed., *Myths and Songs from the South Pacific* (London: H. S. King, 1876), v–xviii, vi–vii.
38. Edmond, *Representing the South Pacific*, 160–8.
39. Herman Melville, *Typee: A Peep at Polynesian Life During a Four Months' Residence in a Valley of the Marquesas* (1846), ed. Harrison Hayford (New York: New American Library, 1964), 221, and *Omoo: A Narrative of Adventures in the South Seas* (1847), ed. Harrison Hayford and Walter Blair (New York: Hendricks House, 1969), 123, 185–9.
40. Arthur Johnstone, *Recollections of Robert Louis Stevenson in the Pacific* (London: Chatto and Windus, 1905), 293, 148.

41. Johnstone, *Recollections*, 8, 6.
42. Charles Darwin, *The Descent of Man and Selection in Relation to Sex* (1871), 2nd edn (1874; London: Folio Society, 1990), 158.
43. Edmond, *Representing the South Pacific*, 167.
44. O. Plumacher, 'Pessimism', *Mind: A Quarterly Review of Psychology and Physiology* 4 (1879), 68–89, 85–6.
45. Richards, *Masks*, 175, 151–2, 177.
46. Grant Allen, *The Great Taboo* (London: Chatto and Windus, 1890), 280.
47. Allen, *Taboo*, 1–7.
48. Stevenson, 'The Foreigner at Home' (1882), in *Memories and Portraits* (London: Chatto and Windus, 1904), 1–23, 3–5.
49. Stevenson to Adelaide Boodle, July 1894, *Letters*, 8: 326. However, Ann Colley notes Stevenson's admiration for some missionaries, and his belief that they might now help to preserve native traditions against the more formal incursions of colonial power: Ann Colley, *Robert Louis Stevenson and the Colonial Imagination* (Aldershot, Hampshire: Ashgate, 2004), 11, 28, 34.
50. Stevenson, undated entry, 'Selections from His Notebook' (1923), in *Memories and Portraits, Memoirs of Himself, Selections from His Notebook* (London: Heinemann, 1924), 171–94, 190.
51. Stevenson, 'Selections', 190.
52. Kirsti Wishart, '*Kidnapped* in Samoa: David Balfour and the Unsuccessful Anthropologist', a paper delivered at the 'Stevenson, Scotland and Samoa' conference, Stirling, 2000.
53. Stevenson, 'Selections', 175–6.
54. Stevenson, 'Selections', 176. Stevenson's note is followed by the citation 'Tzlai's Prin. Cult. II. 79', clearly a misreading for Tylor's *Primitive Culture*, which describes the 'rude Tupinambas of Brazil' as equating those who 'had lived virtuously' with those 'who have well avenged themselves and eaten many of their enemies': E. B. Tylor, *Primitive Culture: Researches into the Development of Mythology, Philosophy, Religion, Art, and Custom*, 2 vols (London: John Murray, 1871), 2: 79. Stevenson's accent on cultural variance is notably absent from Tylor's account.
55. Colvin to Stevenson, March 1894, cited in *Letters*, 8: 279.
56. Stevenson to Colvin, October 1894, *Selected Letters*, 605.
57. Mary Louise Pratt, *Imperial Eyes: Travel Writing and Transculturation* (London: Routledge, 1992), 6.
58. Stevenson, 'The Isle of Voices' (1893), in *South Sea Tales*, ed. Roslyn Jolly (Oxford: Oxford University Press, 1996), 103–22; Stevenson, 'The Bottle Imp' (1891), in *South Sea Tales*, 72–102.
59. Stevenson, 'Isle', 116.
60. Stevenson, 'The Beach of Falesá' (1892), in *South Sea Tales*, 3–71. Page references appear in the text.
61. Patrick Brantlinger, *Rule of Darkness: British Literature and Imperialism, 1830–1914* (Ithaca, New York: Cornell University Press, 1988), 39.
62. Roslyn Jolly, 'Stevenson's "Sterling Domestic Fiction": "The Beach of Falesá"', *Review of English Studies* n.s. 50 (1999), 463–82, 463.
63. Edmond, *Representing the South Pacific*, 176.
64. Roslyn Jolly, 'South Sea Gothic: Pierre Loti and Robert Louis Stevenson', *English Literature in Transition 1880–1920* 47 (2004), 28–49; Jason Marc

Harris, 'Robert Louis Stevenson: Folklore and Imperialism', *English Literature in Transition 1880–1920* 46 (2003), 382–99.

65. For Rod Edmond, who argues that Stevenson elsewhere perpetuates the analogy between Polynesians and children, the critical rendering of Wiltshire is 'a subtle exercise in authorial self-exploration': *Representing the South Pacific*, 174.
66. Brantlinger, *Rule*, 229–30.
67. Jolly, 'Introduction', in Stevenson, *South Sea Tales*, xiv–xv.
68. Harris, 'Stevenson', 387.
69. Tylor, *Primitive Culture*, 1: 141, 144.
70. For a similar reading which examines the representation of supernatural fear as a 'tool of British imperialism', see Harris, 'Stevenson', 396.
71. Stevenson to Colvin, November 1890, *Letters*, 7: 25.
72. Stevenson to Colvin, November 1890, *Letters*, 7: 27.
73. Edmond, *Representing the South Pacific*, 192.
74. Jolly, 'South Sea Gothic', 42.
75. Barry Menikoff, *Robert Louis Stevenson and 'The Beach of Falesá': a Study in Victorian Publishing* (Stanford, California: Stanford University Press, 1984), 16–22.
76. Stevenson, *In the South Seas*, 23; Stevenson's copy of Herman Melville's *Typee* is in Yale University, Beinecke Rare Book and Manuscript Library, Stevenson Collection, Cat. No. 7918.
77. Linda Dowling, *Language and Decadence in the Victorian Fin de Siècle* (Princeton, New Jersey: Princeton University Press, 1986), 61–7, 175–243.
78. For Lang's ambivalent combination of nostalgia and progressivism, see 'Introduction', in Lang, ed., *The Blue Fairy Book* (London: Longmans, Green, 1889), xi–xxii, xi.
79. Flora Masson, 'Louis Stevenson in Edinburgh', in Rosaline Orme Masson, ed., *I Can Remember Robert Louis Stevenson* (Edinburgh: Chambers, 1922), 125–36, 128.
80. Stevenson, *In the South Seas*, 10.
81. Katherine Bailey Linehan, '"Taking Up with Kanakas": Stevenson's Complex Social Criticism in "The Beach of Falesá"', *English Literature in Transition 1880–1920* 33 (1990), 407–22, 412.
82. By contrast with this collaborative language, the language of the imperial adventurer Case is one of appropriation. Case's ability to command different linguistic registers is clearly represented as a key to power: '[h]e could speak, when he chose, fit for a drawing-room; and when he chose he could blaspheme worse than a Yankee boatswain, and talk smart to sicken a kanaka' (5).
83. For Tylor's discussion of the degenerative direction of miscegenation, see Tylor, *Culture*, 1: 41. Stevenson's understanding of 'Beach-la-Mar' resonates with postcolonial theories of hybridity and creolization: see Bill Ashcroft, Gareth Griffiths, and Helen Tiffin, eds, *The Post-Colonial Studies Reader* (London: Routledge, 1995), 183–209. Robert Young discusses the persistence, throughout the twentieth century, of nineteenth-century metaphors of hybridity, in *Colonial Desire: Hybridity in Theory, Culture and Race* (London: Routledge, 1995), Chapter 1.
84. Menikoff, *Stevenson*, 4–8, 35–6, 53–71, 97–8, 59.

85. See Dowling's discussion of linguistic relativism and related anxieties about imperialism, in *Language*, 93–101.
86. Jolly, 'South Sea Gothic', 37.
87. Stevenson, 'Address to Native Students at the London Missionary School at Malua, Samoa' (delivered in 1889 or 1890), unpublished manuscript, in Yale University, Beinecke Rare Book and Manuscript Library, Stevenson Collection, Cat. No. 5940.
88. William Thomson, 'On the Age of the Sun's Heat', *Macmillan's Magazine* 5 (1862), 388–93, 393. P. G. Tait used the theory in Balfour Stewart and Peter Guthrie Tait, *The Unseen Universe or Physical Speculations on a Future State* (London: Macmillan, 1875), 64, 91. On Tait, see Chapter 5. For discussion of the 'death of the sun', see Gillian Beer, *Open Fields: Science in Cultural Encounter* (Oxford: Oxford University Press, 1996), 219–41.
89. See also Edmond, *Representing the South Pacific*, 165–6.
90. Stevenson to R. A. M. Stevenson, June 1894, *Selected Letters*, 584.
91. Stevenson to William Low, January 1894, *Letters*, 8: 235.
92. Stevenson to R. A. M. Stevenson, September 1894, *Selected Letters*, 599.
93. Stevenson to R. A. M. Stevenson, June 1894, *Selected Letters*, 583.
94. Gillian Beer, 'Origins and Oblivion in Victorian Narrative', in R. B. Yeazell, ed., *Sex, Politics, and Science in the Nineteenth-Century Novel* (Baltimore, Maryland: Johns Hopkins University Press, 1986), 63–87, 85.
95. Edwin M. Eigner, *Robert Louis Stevenson and Romantic Tradition* (Princeton, New Jersey: Princeton University Press, 1966), 97.
96. Andrew Noble, 'Highland History and Narrative Form in Scott and Stevenson', in Andrew Noble, ed., *Robert Louis Stevenson* (London: Vision Press, 1983), 134–87, 139.
97. Serialized in the girls' magazine, *Atalanta*, *Catriona* was hailed by reviewers for its engaging heroine, a departure within Stevenson's œuvre (unlike *Weir of Hermiston*, though, this novel never portrays its heroine's inner life): A. T. Quiller-Couch, review of *Catriona*, *Speaker* (9 September 1893), rpr. in Paul Maixner, ed., *Robert Louis Stevenson: the Critical Heritage* (London: Routledge and Kegan Paul), 428; [T. Watts-Dunton], unsigned review, *Athenæum* (16 September 1893), rpr. in Maixner, *Stevenson*, 433.
98. Quiller-Couch, review, 427.
99. Stevenson to Colvin, February to March 1892, *Letters*, 7: 241.
100. Emma Letley, 'Introduction', in Stevenson, *Kidnapped and Catriona*, ed. Emma Letley (Oxford: Oxford University Press, 1986), vii–xxviii, xx.
101. Letley, 'Introduction', xx.
102. Stevenson, *Catriona* (1892–93), in *Kidnapped and Catriona*, ed. Emma Letley (Oxford: Oxford University Press, 1986), 209–475, 249. Subsequent page references appear in the text.
103. Walter Scott, 'Author's Introduction' (1829), in *Rob Roy* (London: David Campbell, 1995), 409–66, 463.
104. The novel's hero, Frank Osbaldistone, describes himself, in words which are also apposite to Scott, as 'a supporter of the present [Hanoverian] government upon principle' but 'disposed to think with pity on those who opposed it on a mistaken feeling of loyalty and duty': Walter Scott, *Rob Roy* (1817; London: David Campbell, 1995), 37.
105. Scott, 'Author's Introduction', 409.

106. Noble, 'History', 145.
107. See Chapter 5.
108. Romans 13.4.
109. Stevenson, *Footnote*, 160.
110. Stevenson, *Kidnapped* (1886), ed. Donald McFarlan (London: Penguin, 1994), 125. See Chapter 5.
111. Stevenson to Sidney Colvin, April 1893, *Letters*, 8: 38.
112. See Paul Maharg, 'Lorimer, Inglis and R. L. S.: Law and the Kailyard Lockup', *Juridical Review* (1995), 280–91.
113. Plumacher, 'Pessimism', 86.
114. See Letley, 'Introduction', xxiv–xxv.
115. See Scott Ashley, 'Primitivism, Celticism and Morbidity in the Atlantic *Fin de Siècle*', in Patrick McGuinness, ed., *Symbolism, Decadence and the Fin de Siècle: French and European Perspectives* (Exeter: University of Exeter Press, 2000), 175–93, 182.
116. Noble, 'History', 176.
117. Quiller-Couch, review, 427.
118. Eigner, *Stevenson*, 97–8; see Alan Sandison, *Robert Louis Stevenson and the Appearance of Modernism* (Basingstoke: Macmillan, now Palgrave Macmillan, 1996), 210.
119. Susan R. Gannon, 'Repetition and Meaning in Stevenson's David Balfour Novels', *Studies in the Literary Imagination* 18 (1985), 21–33, 29.
120. Stevenson, *Heathercat: A Fragment* (1897), in *The Ebb-Tide, Weir of Hermiston, Heathercat, The Young Chevalier* (London: Heinemann et al., 1922), 435–72, 461; Stevenson, 'Thrawn Janet' (1881), in *Weir of Hermiston and Other Stories*, ed. Paul Binding (London: Penguin, 1979), 203–15, 207.
121. Sidney Colvin, 'Editorial Note' (1896), rpr. in Stevenson, *Weir of Hermiston and Other Stories*, ed. Paul Binding (London: Penguin, 1979), 293.
122. Stevenson, 'To My Wife', in *Weir of Hermiston and Other Stories*, ed. Paul Binding (London: Penguin, 1979), 53.
123. Ian Maclaren [pseud. of John Watson], 'In Memoriam', *The Bookman: An Illustrated Monthly Journal for Bookreaders, Bookbuyers, and Booksellers* 7 (1895), 111.
124. [Joseph Jacobs], unsigned review of *Weir*, *Athenæum* no. 3578 (23 May 1896), 673.
125. Eric Anderson, 'The Kailyard Revisited', in Ian Campbell, ed., *Nineteenth-Century Scottish Fiction* (Manchester: Carcanet, 1979), 130–47, 144, 146.
126. Penny Fielding, *Writing and Orality: Nationality, Culture, and Nineteenth-Century Scottish Fiction* (Oxford: Clarendon Press, 1996), 184–5; Sandison, *Stevenson*, 381.
127. Karl Miller, 'Introduction', in Stevenson, *Weir of Hermiston*, ed. Karl Miller (London: Penguin, 1996), vii–xxiv, xvi; K. G. Simpson, 'Author and Narrator in *Weir of Hermiston*', in Noble, ed., *Stevenson*, 202–27, 226.
128. Stevenson, *Weir of Hermiston* (1896), in *Weir of Hermiston and Other Stories*, ed. Paul Binding (London: Penguin, 1979), 53–172, 152. Subsequent page references appear in the text.
129. Fielding, *Writing*, 196.
130. Peter Zenzinger, 'The Ballad Spirit and the Modern Mind: Narrative Perspective in Stevenson's *Weir of Hermiston*', in Horst W. Drescher and

Joachim Schwend, eds, *Studies in Scottish Fiction: Nineteenth Century* (Frankfurt am Main: Verlag Peter Lang, 1985), 233–51, 238.

131. Zenzinger, 'Spirit', 239, 240.
132. Zenzinger, 'Spirit', 238.
133. Stevenson, draft of 'Introductory' and part of Chapter 1 of *Weir of Hermiston,* Yale University, Beinecke Rare Book and Manuscript Library, Stevenson Collection, Cat. No. 7118.
134. Andrew Lang, '"Kalevala"; Or, the Finnish National Epic', in *Custom and Myth* (London: Longmans, Green, 1884), 156–79, 158.
135. John Veitch, *The History and Poetry of the Scottish Border: Their Main Features and Relations* (Glasgow: James Maclehose, 1878), 556.
136. Veitch, *History*, 458. On Stevenson's annotated copy of the 1893 edition, see State University of New York, *Robert Louis Stevenson: a Catalogue of His Works and Books relating to Him in the Rare Book Collection* (Buffalo, New York: State University of New York at Buffalo, 1972), 61.
137. Fielding, *Writing*, 180.
138. Oscar Wilde, 'The Critic as Artist' (1890), in *The Artist as Critic: Critical Writings of Oscar Wilde,* ed. Richard Ellmann (New York: Vintage Books, 1969), 340–408, 351.
139. David Vincent, 'The Decline of Oral Tradition in Popular Culture', in Robert D. Storch, ed., *Popular Culture and Custom in Nineteenth-Century England* (London: Croom Helm, 1982), 20–47.
140. Sandison, *Stevenson*, 371.
141. Walter Scott, *Old Mortality* (1816), ed. Jane Stevenson and Peter Davidson (Oxford: Oxford University Press, 1993), 32–4, 33, 376–7.
142. See Catherine Kerrigan, 'Introduction', in Stevenson, *Weir of Hermiston,* ed. Catherine Kerrigan (Edinburgh: Edinburgh University Press, 1995), xvii–xxxvi, xx.
143. Stevenson, review of James Grant Wilson, *The Poets and Poetry of Scotland, from the Earliest to the Present Time,* vol. 1, *Academy* 9 (1876), 138–9, 139.
144. Stevenson, draft of part of Chapter 3, Yale University, Beinecke Rare Book and Manuscript Library, Stevenson Collection, Cat. No. 7120.
145. Stevenson, draft of part of Chapter 3, Beinecke Library.
146. Stevenson had contemplated publishing the novel in *Blackwood's Magazine,* but this came to nothing: Stevenson to Charles Baxter, December 1892, *Letters* 7: 441. On *Cosmopolis: An International Review,* edited by the unidentified Felix Ortmans, see Alvin Sullivan, ed., *British Literary Magazines: the Victorian and Edwardian Age, 1837–1913* (Westport, Connecticut: Greenwood Press, 1984), 91.
147. *Cosmopolis: An International Review* 1.2 (February 1896), front cover facing (unattached sheet).
148. Each issue was trilingual, and articles opened up international perspectives: see Edouard Rod's celebration of foreign influences on French literature, in 'Le Mouvement des Idées en France', *Cosmopolis* 1 (1896), 142–53, 447–57 447. However, a sense of imminent violence haunted the periodical, as contributors felt that 'Europe is in an electric condition': Henry Norman, 'The Globe and the Island', *Cosmopolis* 2 (1896), 88–100, 99.

Conclusion

1. Stevenson to R. A. M. Stevenson, September 1894, in *The Letters of Robert Louis Stevenson*, ed. Bradford Booth and Ernest Mehew, 8 vols (New Haven, Connecticut: Yale University Press, 1994–95), 8: 361–6. Page references appear in the text.
2. Stevenson, 'Pulvis et Umbra' (1888), in *Across the Plains: With Other Memories and Essays* (London: Chatto and Windus, 1907), 289–301, 290.
3. Unpublished letter, F. W. H. Myers to Stevenson, 29 April 1892: Yale University, Beinecke Rare Book and Manuscript Library, Stevenson Collection, Cat. No. 5263.

Works Cited

The date of first publication (in serial or volume form) appears in parentheses after the title, where a later edition has been used.

Manuscript and Archival Material: Yale University, Beinecke Rare Book and Manuscript Library, Stevenson Collection

Galton, Francis, *Records of Family Faculties: Consisting of Tabular Forms and Directions for Entering Data, with an Explanatory Preface* (London: Macmillan, 1884), annotated copy from Stevenson's library, Cat. No. 7298.

Jacobs, Joseph, unpublished letter to Robert Louis Stevenson, 22 August 1893, Cat. No. 4904.

Melville, Herman, *Typee; or, A Narrative of a Four Months' Residence among the Natives of a Valley of the Marquesas Islands, or, A Peep at Polynesian Life* (1846; London: John Murray, 1861), annotated copy from Stevenson's library, Cat. No. 7918.

Myers, F. W. H., unpublished letter to Robert Louis Stevenson, 29 April 1892, Cat. No. 5263.

Stevenson, R. A. M., unpublished letter to Robert Louis Stevenson, 187[?], Cat. No. 5674.

Stevenson, Robert Louis, 'Address to Native Students at the London Missionary School at Malua, Samoa', unpublished manuscript, Cat. No. 5940.

______, 'Autobiographical Note', unpublished manuscript, Cat. No. 5998.

______, Draft of 'Introductory' and part of Chapter 1 of *Weir of Hermiston*, unpublished manuscript, Cat. No. 7118.

______, Draft of part of Chapter 3 of *Weir of Hermiston*, unpublished manuscript, Cat. No. 7120.

______, 'Dunoon: Visit in 1870 at a House where RLS Had Spent a Week in Childhood', unpublished manuscript, Cat. No. 6174.

Stevenson, Thomas, unpublished letter to Robert Louis Stevenson, 5 September 1877, Cat. No. 5672.

Primary Sources

Allen, Grant, *Physiological Æsthetics* (London: H. S. King, 1877).

______, *The Great Taboo* (London: Chatto and Windus, 1890).

______, 'Sacred Stones', *Fortnightly Review* 53 (1890), 96–116.

______, 'Woman's Intuition', *Forum (and Century)* 9 (1890), 333–40.

[Anon.], 'Dramatic and Musical', *Daily Telegraph* (12 October 1888), 3.

Arnold, Matthew, 'Literature and Science' (1882), in *The Complete Prose Works of Matthew Arnold*, ed. R. H. Super, vol. 10 (Ann Arbor, Michigan: University of Michigan Press, 1974), 53–73.

Baker, Smith, 'Etiological Significance of Heterogeneous Personality', *Journal of Nervous and Mental Disease* 20 (1893), 664–74.
Ballantyne, R. M., *The Coral Island* (1858; London: Bloomsbury Books, 1994).
Bon, Gustave Le, *The Crowd: A Study of the Popular Mind* (London: Fisher Unwin, 1896).
Burton, J. H., *History of Scotland from Agricola's Invasion to the Extinction of the Last Jacobite Insurrection*, 2nd edn, 8 vols (Edinburgh: Blackwood, 1873).
Butler, Samuel, *Life and Habit* (London: Trübner, 1878).
______, *The Way of All Flesh* (1903), ed. Richard Hoggart (Harmondsworth: Penguin, 1966).
Campbell, G. D., Duke of Argyll, *The Reign of Law* (London: Alexander Strahan, 1867).
______, R. H. Hutton, James Martineau, et al., 'A Modern "Symposium." The Influence Upon Morality of a Decline in Religious Belief', *Nineteenth Century* 1 (1877), 331–58, 531–46.
Carpenter, W. B., *Principles of Mental Physiology: With Their Applications to the Training and Discipline of the Mind, and the Study of its Morbid Conditions* (London: H. S. King, 1874).
Chapman, John Jay, 'Robert Louis Stevenson', in *Emerson and Other Essays* (London: David Nutt, 1898), 217–47.
Conrad, Joseph, *Heart of Darkness* (1899, 1902), in *Heart of Darkness with The Congo Diary*, ed. Robert Hampson (London: Penguin, 1995), 3–139.
Cosmopolis: An International Review 1.2 (February 1896).
Crichton-Browne, James, 'Psychical Diseases of Early Life', *Journal of Mental Science* 6 (1859), 284–320.
______, 'Dreamy Mental States', in *Stray Leaves from a Physician's Portfolio* (London: Hodder and Stoughton, [1927]), 1–42.
Dallas, E. S., *The Gay Science*, 2 vols (London: Chapman and Hall, 1866).
Darwin, Charles, *The Origin of Species by Means of Natural Selection or the Preservation of Favoured Races in the Struggle for Life* (1859), ed. J. W. Burrow (London: Penguin, 1968).
______, *The Variation of Animals and Plants Under Domestication* (1868), 2nd edn, 2 vols (1875; Baltimore, Maryland: Johns Hopkins University Press, 1998).
______, *The Descent of Man and Selection in Relation to Sex* (1871), 2nd edn (1874; London: Folio Society, 1990).
Dostoevky, Fyodor, *Crime and Punishment* (1866), tr. Jessie Coulson (Oxford: Oxford University Press, 1995).
Doyle, Arthur Conan, *The Hound of the Baskervilles* (1901–2), ed. W. W. Robson (Oxford: Oxford University Press, 1993).
Ellis, Havelock, *The Criminal* (London: Walter Scott, 1890).
Fothergill, J. M., *The Maintenance of Health: A Medical Work for Lay Readers* (London: Smith, Elder, 1874).
Freud, Sigmund, 'Creative Writers and Day-dreaming' (1908), in *The Freud Reader*, ed. Peter Gay (London: Random House, 1995), 436–43.
______, 'Civilization and Its Discontents' (1930), in *The Freud Reader*, ed. Peter Gay (London: Random House, 1995), 722–72.
Galton, Francis, *Records of Family Faculties: Consisting of Tabular Forms and Directions for Entering Data, with an Explanatory Preface* (London: Macmillan, 1884).
Gill, W. W., ed., *Myths and Songs from the South Pacific* (London: H. S. King, 1876).

Haggard, H. Rider, *King Solomon's Mines* (1885), ed. Dennis Butts (Oxford: Oxford University Press, 1989).
______, 'About Fiction', *Contemporary Review* 51 (1887), 172–80.
______, *She* (1887; Oxford: Oxford University Press, 1991).
Henley, W. E., 'Invictus' (1875), in M. H. Abrams and Stephen Greenblatt, eds, *The Norton Anthology of English Literature*, 7th edn (New York: W. W. Norton, 2000), 2: 1747.
Hogg, James, *The Private Memoirs and Confessions of a Justified Sinner* (1824), ed. John Carey (Oxford: Oxford University Press, 1995).
Howells, W. D., 'Henry James, Jr.' (1882), in *Selected Literary Criticism*, ed. Ulrich Halfmann and Christoph K. Lohmann, 3 vols (Bloomington, Indiana: Indiana University Press, 1993), 1: 317–23.
Huxley, T. H., 'Biogenesis and Abiogenesis. (The Presidential Address to the British Association for the Advancement of Science, 1870)', in *Critiques and Addresses* (London: Macmillan, 1873), 218–50.
______, 'Prologue', in *Collected Essays*, 9 vols (London: Macmillan, 1894–1908), 5: 1–58.
[Jacobs, Joseph], anonymous review of Robert Louis Stevenson, *Weir of Hermiston*, *Athenæum* no. 3578 (23 May 1896), 673.
James, Henry, 'The Art of Fiction', *Longman's Magazine* 4 (1884), 502–21.
______, *Notes on Novelists: With Some Other Notes* (London: J. M. Dent and Sons, 1914).
______, *The Letters of Henry James*, ed. Percy Lubbock, 2 vols (London: Macmillan, 1920).
Jefferies, Richard, *After London; or, Wild England* (London: Cassell, 1885).
Johnstone, Arthur, *Recollections of Robert Louis Stevenson in the Pacific* (London: Chatto and Windus, 1905).
Kipling, Rudyard, 'The Finest Story in the World' (1891), in *Selected Stories*, ed. Sandra Kemp (London: J. M. Dent, 1987), 54–82.
Lang, Andrew, '"Kalevala"; Or, the Finnish National Epic', in *Custom and Myth* (London: Longmans, Green, 1884), 156–79.
______, 'At the Sign of the Ship', *Longman's Magazine* 7 (1885–86), 439–48.
______, 'At the Sign of the Ship', *Longman's Magazine* 9 (1886–87), 105–12, 552–9.
______, *Myth, Ritual, and Religion*, 2 vols (London: Longmans, Green, 1887).
______, 'Realism and Romance', *Contemporary Review* 52 (1887), 683–93.
______, 'At the Sign of the Ship', *Longman's Magazine* 11 (1887–88), 234–40, 458–64.
______, 'Introduction', in *The Blue Fairy Book*, ed. Andrew Lang (London: Longmans, Green, 1889), xi–xxii.
______, 'At the Sign of the Ship', *Longman's Magazine* 16 (1890), 234–40.
______, 'Was Jehovah A Fetish Stone?', *Contemporary Review* 57 (1890), 353–65.
______, 'At the Sign of the Ship', *Longman's Magazine* 18 (1891), 215–33.
______, 'Mr. Kipling's Stories', in *Essays in Little* (London: Henry and Co., 1891), 198–205.
______, 'At the Sign of the Ship', *Longman's Magazine* 28 (1896), 313–22.
Lankester, Edwin Ray, *Degeneration: A Chapter in Darwinism* (London: Macmillan, 1880).
Lee, Vernon (pseud. of Violet Paget), 'Marsyas in Flanders' (1900), in *For Maurice: Five Unlikely Stories* (London: Bodley Head, 1927), 71–92.
Machen, Arthur, *The Great God Pan* (1894; Salem, New Hampshire: Ayer, 1970).

Maclaren, Ian (pseud. of John Watson), 'In Memoriam', *The Bookman: An Illustrated Monthly Journal for Bookreaders, Bookbuyers, and Booksellers* 7 (1895), 111.

Maixner, Paul, ed., *Robert Louis Stevenson: the Critical Heritage* (London: Routledge and Kegan Paul, 1981).

Maudsley, Henry, *The Physiology and Pathology of Mind* (London: Macmillan, 1867).

______, *Responsibility in Mental Disease* (London: H. S. King, 1874).

______, 'Hallucinations of the Senses', *Fortnightly Review* n.s. 24 (1878), 370–86.

______, *Natural Causes and Supernatural Seemings* (1886), 3rd edn (London: Kegan Paul, Trench, Trübner and Co., 1897).

______, *The Pathology of Mind: A Study of its Distempers, Deformities, and Disorders* (London: Macmillan, 1895).

Melville, Herman, *Typee: A Peep at Polynesian Life During a Four Months' Residence in a Valley of the Marquesas* (1846), ed. Harrison Hayford (New York: New American Library, 1964).

______, *Omoo: A Narrative of Adventures in the South Seas* (1847), ed. Harrison Hayford and Walter Blair (New York: Hendricks House, 1969).

Millingen, J. G., *Mind and Matter: Illustrated by Considerations on Hereditary Insanity, and the Influence of Temperament in the Development of the Passions* (London: H. Hurst, 1847).

Müller, F. Max, 'Preface', in W. W. Gill, ed., *Myths and Songs from the South Pacific* (London: H. S. King, 1876), v–xviii.

Myers, F. W. H., 'Multiplex Personality', *Nineteenth Century* 20 (1886), 648–66.

______, *Human Personality and Its Survival of Bodily Death*, 2 vols (London: Longmans and Green, 1903).

Nordau, Max, *Degeneration*, tr. from 2nd edn (London: Heinemann, 1895).

Norman, Henry, 'The Globe and the Island', *Cosmopolis* 2 (1896), 88–100.

Osbourne, Lloyd, 'Prefatory Note', in Robert Louis Stevenson, *Further Memories* (London: Heinemann et al., 1923), 191–6.

Pater, Walter, 'Apollo in Picardy' (1893), in *Miscellaneous Studies* (1895; London: Macmillan, 1910), 142–71.

Plumacher, O., 'Pessimism', *Mind: A Quarterly Review of Psychology and Physiology* 4 (1879), 68–89.

Poe, Edgar Allan, 'William Wilson' (1839), in *Selected Tales*, ed. David van Leer (Oxford: Oxford University Press, 1998), 66–83.

______, 'The Tell-Tale Heart' (1843), in *Selected Tales*, ed. David van Leer (Oxford: Oxford University Press, 1998), 193–7.

Proctor, Richard, 'Dual Consciousness', *Cornhill Magazine* 35 (1877), 86–105.

Rod, Edouard, 'Le Mouvement des Idées en France', *Cosmopolis* 1 (1896), 142–53, 447–57.

Savage, George H., 'Moral Insanity', *Journal of Mental Science* 27 (1881), 147–55.

Scott, Walter, *Waverley; or, 'Tis Sixty Years Since* (1814), ed. Claire Lamont (Oxford: Oxford University Press, 1986).

______, *Old Mortality* (1816), ed. Jane Stevenson and Peter Davidson (Oxford: Oxford University Press, 1993).

______, *Rob Roy* (1817; London: David Campbell, 1995).

______, 'Author's Introduction' (1829), in *Rob Roy* (London: David Campbell, 1995), 409–66.

Seeley, J. R., 'Ethics and Religion', in The Society of Ethical Propagandists, ed., *Ethics and Religion* (London: Swan Sonnenschein, 1900), 1–30.

[Sharp, William], Macleod, Fiona (pseud.), 'From Iona', in *The Sin-Eater and Other Tales* (Edinburgh: Patrick Geddes, 1895), 1–13.

Shaw, G. B., *The Sanity of Art: An Exposure of the Current Nonsense about Artists Being Degenerate* (1895; London: The New Age Press, 1908).

The Society of Ethical Propagandists, ed., *Ethics and Religion* (London: Swan Sonnenschein, 1900).

Spencer, Herbert, *The Principles of Psychology* (1855), 2nd edn, 2 vols (London: Williams and Norgate, 1870–72).

______, *The Principles of Sociology*, vol. 1 (London: Williams and Norgate, 1876).

______, *The Man Versus the State* (1884), in *Spencer: Political Writings*, ed. John Offer (Cambridge: Cambridge University Press, 1994), 59–175.

Spitzka, Edward Charles, 'Cases of Masturbation (Masturbatic Insanity)', *Journal of Mental Science* 34 (April 1888), 52–61.

Stephen, Leslie, *The Science of Ethics* (1882; Bristol: Thoemmes, 1991).

Sterne, Laurence, *The Life and Opinions of Tristram Shandy, Gentleman* (1760), ed. Ian Campbell Ross (Oxford: Oxford University Press, 1983).

Stevenson, Fanny van de Grift, 'Note', in Robert Louis Stevenson, *The Strange Case of Dr Jekyll and Mr Hyde, Prince Otto*, Skerryvore Edition (London: Heinemann et al., 1924), xvii–xxi.

Stevenson, Robert Louis, 'Ordered South' (1874), in *Travels with a Donkey in the Cévennes and Selected Travel Writings* (Oxford: Oxford University Press, 1992), 243–54.

______, review of *The Works of Edgar Allan Poe*, vols 1 and 2 (1875), in *Essays Literary and Critical* (London: Heinemann et al., 1923), 178–85.

______, review of James Grant Wilson, *The Poets and Poetry of Scotland, from the Earliest to the Present Time*, vol. 1, *Academy* 9 (1876), 138–9.

______, 'On Falling in Love', *Cornhill Magazine* 35 (1877), 214–20.

______, 'Child's Play', *Cornhill Magazine* 38 (1878), 352–9.

______, 'The English Admirals' (1878), in *Virginibus Puerisque, The Amateur Emigrant, The Pacific Capitals, Silverado Squatters* (London: Heinemann et al., 1922), 137–55.

______, *An Inland Voyage* (1878), in *Travels with a Donkey in the Cévennes and Selected Travel Writings* (Oxford: Oxford University Press, 1992), 1–120.

______, *New Arabian Nights* (1878; London: Heinemann, 1923).

______, *Travels with a Donkey in the Cévennes* (1879), in *Travels with a Donkey in the Cévennes and Selected Travel Writings* (Oxford: Oxford University Press, 1992), 121–231.

______, 'The Pavilion on the Links' (1880), in *New Arabian Nights and Other Tales* (London: Heinemann et al., 1922), 249–343.

______, 'Thrawn Janet' (1881), in *Weir of Hermiston and Other Stories*, ed. Paul Binding (London: Penguin, 1979), 203–15.

______, 'Young Rob Roy' (1881), in W. B. Cook, ed., *Local Notes and Queries: Reprinted from the Stirling Observer*, 2 vols (Stirling: Duncan and Jamieson, 'Observer' Office, 1883–86), 1: 287–8.

______, *Treasure Island* (1881–82), ed. Emma Letley (Oxford: Oxford University Press, 1985).

______, 'The Foreigner at Home' (1882), in *Memories and Portraits* (London: Chatto and Windus, 1904), 1–23.

______, 'A Gossip on Romance' (1882), in *Memories and Portraits* (London: Chatto and Windus, 1904), 247–74.

______, 'The Merry Men' (1882), *Cornhill Magazine* 45.6 (June 1882), 676–95, and 46.1 (July 1882), 56–73.
______, 'The Merry Men' (1882), in *Dr. Jekyll and Mr. Hyde, The Merry Men, and Other Tales* (London: J. M. Dent, 1925), 63–106.
______, 'Talk and Talkers: (I)' (1882), in *Essays and Poems*, ed. Claire Harman (London: J. M. Dent, 1992), 153–62.
______, 'Talk and Talkers: A Sequel', *Cornhill Magazine* 46 (1882), 151–8.
______, *The Black Arrow: A Tale of the Two Roses* (1883; London: Heinemann et al., 1923).
______, 'A Note on Realism' (1883), in *Essays in the Art of Writing* (London: Chatto and Windus, 1908), 93–107.
______, 'The Body Snatcher', *Pall Mall Christmas 'Extra'* 13 (December 1884), 3–12.
______, 'A Humble Remonstrance' (1884), in *Memories and Portraits* (London: Chatto and Windus, 1904), 275–99.
______, 'Markheim', *The Broken Shaft: Tales in Mid-Ocean* [Unwin's Christmas Annual], ed. Henry Norman (London: T. Fisher Unwin, December 1885), 27–38.
______, 'Markheim' (1885), in *Dr. Jekyll and Mr. Hyde, The Merry Men, and Other Tales* (London: J. M. Dent, 1925), 131–45.
______, 'Olalla' (1885), in *Dr. Jekyll and Mr. Hyde, The Merry Men, and Other Tales* (London: J. M. Dent, 1925), 157–93.
______, 'On Some Technical Elements of Style' (1885), in *Essays Literary and Critical* (London: Heinemann et al., 1923), 33–50.
______, *Kidnapped* (1886), ed. Donald McFarlan (London: Penguin, 1994).
______, *The Strange Case of Dr Jekyll and Mr Hyde* (1886), in *The Strange Case of Dr Jekyll and Mr Hyde and Other Stories*, ed. Jenni Calder (London: Penguin, 1979), 27–97.
______, *The Strange Case of Dr Jekyll and Mr Hyde* (1886), ed. Martin A. Danahay (Peterborough, Ontario: Broadview, 1999).
______, *The Strange Case of Dr. Jekyll and Mr. Hyde* (1886), ed. Katherine Linehan (New York: W. W. Norton, 2003).
______, 'Books Which Have Influenced Me' (1887), in *Essays Literary and Critical* (London: Heinemann et al., 1923), 62–8.
______, 'The Day After Tomorrow' (1887), in *Ethical Studies, Edinburgh: Picturesque Notes* (London: Heinemann et al., 1924), 113–23.
______, 'The Manse' (1887), in *Memories and Portraits* (London: Chatto and Windus, 1904), 106–19.
______, 'The Misadventures of John Nicholson' (1887), in *Weir of Hermiston and Other Stories*, ed. Paul Binding (London: Penguin, 1979), 216–84.
______, 'Pastoral' (1887), in *Memories and Portraits* (London: Chatto and Windus, 1904), 90–105.
______, 'Thomas Stevenson: Civil Engineer' (1887), in *Memories and Portraits* (London: Chatto and Windus, 1904), 132–43.
______, *Underwoods* (1887), in *Collected Poems*, ed. Janet Adam Smith (London: Rupert Hart-Davis, 1950), 109–77.
______, 'A Chapter on Dreams' (1888), in *Further Memories* (London: Heinemann, 1923), 41–53.
______, 'The Lantern-Bearers' (1888), in *Further Memories* (London: Heinemann, 1923), 29–40.
______, 'Memoir of Fleeming Jenkin' (1888), in *The Merry Men and Other Tales, Memoir of Fleeming Jenkin* (London: Heinemann et al., 1922), 337–562.

______, 'Popular Authors' (1888), in *Essays Literary and Critical* (London: Heinemann et al., 1923), 20–32.
______, 'Pulvis et Umbra' (1888), in *Across the Plains: With Other Memories and Essays* (London: Chatto and Windus, 1907), 289–301.
______, *The Master of Ballantrae: A Winter's Tale* (1888–89), ed. Adrian Poole (London: Penguin, 1996).
______, *Ballads* (1890; London: Chatto and Windus).
______, 'The Bottle Imp' (1891), in *South Sea Tales*, ed. Roslyn Jolly (Oxford: Oxford University Press, 1996), 72–102.
______, with Lloyd Osbourne, *The Wrecker* (1891–92; London: Heinemann et al., 1924).
______, 'The Beach of Falesá' (1892), in *South Sea Tales*, ed. Roslyn Jolly (Oxford: Oxford University Press, 1996), 3–71.
______, *A Footnote to History: Eight Years of Trouble in Samoa* (1892), in *Vailima Papers* (London: Heinemann et al., 1924), 67–240.
______, *Catriona* (1892–93), in *Kidnapped and Catriona*, ed. Emma Letley (Oxford: Oxford University Press, 1986), 209–475.
______, 'The Isle of Voices' (1893), in *South Sea Tales*, ed. Roslyn Jolly (Oxford: Oxford University Press, 1996), 103–22.
______, with Lloyd Osbourne, *The Ebb-Tide: A Trio and Quartette* (1893–94), in *South Sea Tales*, ed. Roslyn Jolly (Oxford: Oxford University Press, 1996), 123–252.
______, 'My First Book: "Treasure Island"' (1894), in *Treasure Island*, ed. Emma Letley (Oxford: Oxford University Press, 1985), 192–200.
______, 'The House of Eld' (1895), in *Weir of Hermiston and Other Stories*, ed. Paul Binding (London: Penguin, 1979), 285–92.
______, 'The Persons of the Tale' (1895), in *Juvenilia, Moral Emblems, Fables, and Other Papers* (London: Heinemann et al., 1923), 183–7.
______, 'The Genesis of "The Master of Ballantrae"' (1896), in *The Master of Ballantrae: A Winter's Tale*, ed. Adrian Poole (London: Penguin, 1996), 221–4.
______, *In the South Seas* (1896; comp. Sidney Colvin), ed. Neil Rennie (London: Penguin, 1998).
______, '"Rosa Quo Locorum"' (1896), in *Further Memories* (London: Heinemann et al., 1923), 1–8.
______, *Weir of Hermiston* (1896), in *Weir of Hermiston and Other Stories*, ed. Paul Binding (London: Penguin, 1979), 53–172.
______, *Weir of Hermiston* (1896), ed. Catherine Kerrigan (Edinburgh: Edinburgh University Press, 1995).
______, *Heathercat: A Fragment* (1897), in *The Ebb-Tide, Weir of Hermiston, Heathercat, The Young Chevalier* (London: Heinemann et al., 1922), 435–72.
______, 'Preface' (1898), in *The Master of Ballantrae: A Winter's Tale*, ed. Adrian Poole (London: Penguin, 1996), 5–8.
______, 'Memoirs of Himself' (1912), in *Memories and Portraits, Memoirs of Himself, Selections from His Notebook* (London: Heinemann, 1924), 147–68.
______, 'Note for "The Merry Men"' (1921), in *Miscellanea* (London: Heinemann et al., 1923), 477–8.
______, 'Note to "The Master of Ballantrae"' (1921), in *The Master of Ballantrae: A Winter's Tale*, ed. Adrian Poole (London: Penguin, 1996), 224–6.
______, 'Selections from His Notebook' (1923), in *Memories and Portraits, Memoirs of Himself, Selections from His Notebook* (London: Heinemann, 1924), 171–94.

______, *The Letters of Robert Louis Stevenson*, ed. Sidney Colvin, 5 vols (London: Heinemann et al., 1924).

______, *The Letters of Robert Louis Stevenson*, ed. Bradford Booth and Ernest Mehew, 8 vols (New Haven, Connecticut: Yale University Press, 1994–95).

______, *Selected Letters of Robert Louis Stevenson*, ed. Ernest Mehew (New Haven, Connecticut: Yale University Press, 1997).

Stevenson, Thomas, *Christianity Confirmed by Jewish and Heathen Testimony and Deductions from Physical Sciences, etc.* (1877), 2nd edn (Edinburgh: David Douglas, 1879).

Stewart, Balfour, and Peter Guthrie Tait, *The Unseen Universe or Physical Speculations on a Future State* (London: Macmillan, 1875).

Sully, James, 'Poetic Imagination and Primitive Conception', *Cornhill Magazine* 34 (1876), 294–306.

______, *Pessimism: A History and A Criticism* (London: H. S. King, 1877).

______, 'The Undefinable in Art', *Cornhill Magazine* 38 (1878), 559–72.

______, 'Genius and Insanity', *Nineteenth Century* 10 (1881), 573–87.

______, *Illusions: A Psychological Study* (London: Kegan Paul, 1881).

______, 'The Dream as a Revelation', *Fortnightly Review* n.s. 53 (1893), 354–69.

______, *My Life and Friends* (London: T. Fisher Unwin, 1918).

Symonds, John Addington, *The Letters of John Addington Symonds*, ed. Herbert M. Schueller and Robert L. Peters, 3 vols (Detroit, Michigan: Wayne State University Press, 1968–69).

Taylor, Jenny Bourne, and Sally Shuttleworth, eds, *Embodied Selves: An Anthology of Psychological Texts 1830–1890* (Oxford: Oxford University Press, 1998).

Thomson, William, 'On the Age of the Sun's Heat', *Macmillan's Magazine* 5 (1862), 388–93.

Tuke, Daniel Hack, *Illustrations of the Influence of the Mind Upon the Body in Health and Disease Designed to Elucidate the Action of the Imagination*, 2nd edn, 2 vols (London: J. and A. Churchill, 1884).

Tylor, E. B., *Primitive Culture: Researches into the Development of Mythology, Philosophy, Religion, Art, and Custom*, 2 vols (London: John Murray, 1871).

Veitch, John, *The History and Poetry of the Scottish Border: Their Main Features and Relations* (Glasgow: James Maclehose, 1878).

Wells, H. G., *The Time Machine* (1895), ed. John Lawton (London: J. M. Dent, 1995).

Wilde, Oscar, 'The Decay of Lying' (1889), in *The Artist as Critic: Critical Writings of Oscar Wilde*, ed. Richard Ellmann (New York: Vintage, 1969), 290–320.

______, 'The Critic as Artist' (1890), in *The Artist as Critic: Critical Writings of Oscar Wilde*, ed. Richard Ellmann (New York: Vintage, 1969), 340–408.

______, *The Picture of Dorian Gray* (1890, revised 1891), in *The Major Works*, ed. Isobel Murray (Oxford: Oxford University Press, 1989), 47–214.

______, *The Selected Letters of Oscar Wilde*, ed. Rupert Hart-Davis (Oxford: Oxford University Press, 1979).

Winslow, Forbes, *On the Obscure Diseases of the Brain, and Disorders of the Mind* (1860), 4th edn (London: John Churchill, 1868).

Secondary Sources

Altholz, Josef L., *Anatomy of a Controversy: the Debate over 'Essays and Reviews' 1860–1864* (Aldershot, Hampshire: Scolar Press, 1994).

Anderson, Eric, 'The Kailyard Revisited', in Ian Campbell, ed., *Nineteenth-Century Scottish Fiction* (Manchester: Carcanet, 1979), 130–47.
Annan, Noel, *Leslie Stephen: the Godless Victorian* (London: Weidenfeld and Nicolson, 1984).
Arata, Stephen D., 'The Sedulous Ape: Atavism, Professionalism, and Stevenson's *Jekyll and Hyde*', *Criticism: a Quarterly Journal for Literature and the Arts* 37 (1995), 233–59.
______, *Fictions of Loss in the Victorian Fin de Siècle* (Cambridge: Cambridge University Press, 1996).
Ashcroft, Bill, Gareth Griffiths, and Helen Tiffin, eds, *The Post-Colonial Studies Reader* (London: Routledge, 1995).
Ashley, Scott, 'Primitivism, Celticism and Morbidity in the Atlantic *Fin de Siècle*', in Patrick McGuinness, ed., *Symbolism, Decadence and the Fin de Siècle: French and European Perspectives* (Exeter: University of Exeter Press, 2000), 175–93.
______, 'The Poetics of Race in 1890s Ireland: an Ethnography of the Aran Islands', *Patterns of Prejudice* 35 (2001), 5–18.
Balfour, Graham, *The Life of Robert Louis Stevenson*, 2 vols (London: Methuen, 1901).
Barkan, Elazar, and Ronald Bush, 'Introduction', in Elazar Barkan and Ronald Bush, eds, *Prehistories of the Future: the Primitivist Project and the Culture of Modernism* (Stanford, California: Stanford University Press, 1995), 1–19.
Barkan, Elazar, and Ronald Bush, eds, *Prehistories of the Future: the Primitivist Project and the Culture of Modernism* (Stanford, California: Stanford University Press, 1995).
Beer, Gillian, *The Romance* (London: Methuen, 1970).
______, *Darwin's Plots: Evolutionary Narrative in Darwin, George Eliot and Nineteenth-Century Fiction* (1983), 2nd edn (Cambridge: Cambridge University Press, 2000).
______, 'Origins and Oblivion in Victorian Narrative', in R. B. Yeazell, ed., *Sex, Politics, and Science in the Nineteenth-Century Novel* (Baltimore, Maryland: Johns Hopkins University Press, 1986), 63–87.
______, *Open Fields: Science in Cultural Encounter* (Oxford: Oxford University Press, 1996).
Bennett, Bruce, Jeff Doyle, and Satendra Nandan, eds, *Crossing Cultures: Essays on Literature and Culture of the Asia-Pacific* (London: Skoob Books, 1996).
Binding, Paul, 'Introduction', in Robert Louis Stevenson, *Weir of Hermiston and Other Stories*, ed. Paul Binding (London: Penguin, 1979), 7–48.
Black, John Sutherland, and George Chrystal, *The Life of William Robertson Smith* (London: Adam and Charles Black, 1912).
Block, Ed, 'James Sully, Evolutionist Psychology, and Late Victorian Gothic Fiction', *Victorian Studies* 25 (1982), 443–67.
______, *Rituals of Dis-integration: Romance and Madness in the Victorian Psychomythic Tale* (New York: Garland, 1993).
Bowler, Peter J., *The Non-Darwinian Revolution: Reinterpreting a Historical Myth* (Baltimore, Maryland: Johns Hopkins University Press, 1988).
______, *The Invention of Progress: the Victorians and the Past* (Oxford: Basil Blackwell, 1989).
______, *Biology and Social Thought* (Berkeley, California: Office for History of Science and Technology, University of California at Berkeley, 1993).
Boyle, Richard, and Patrick Brantlinger, 'The Education of Edward Hyde: Stevenson's "Gothic Gnome" and the Mass Readership of Late-Victorian England', in

Gordon Hirsch and William Veeder, eds, *Dr. Jekyll and Mr. Hyde after One Hundred Years* (Chicago, Illinois: University of Chicago Press, 1988), 265–82.

Bradshaw, David, ed., *A Concise Companion to Modernism* (Oxford: Blackwell Publishers, 2003).

Brantlinger, Patrick, *Rule of Darkness: British Literature and Imperialism, 1830–1914* (Ithaca, New York: Cornell University Press, 1988).

______, *The Reading Lesson: the Threat of Mass Literacy in Nineteenth-Century British Fiction* (Bloomington, Indiana: Indiana University Press, 1998).

Bristow, Joseph, *Empire Boys: Adventures in a Man's World* (London: HarperCollins, 1991).

Broks, Peter, 'Science, Media and Culture: British Magazines, 1890–1914', *Public Understanding of Science* 2 (1993), 123–39.

Brown, Stewart J., ed., *William Robertson and the Expansion of Empire* (Cambridge: Cambridge University Press, 1997).

Bullen, J. B., ed., *Writing and Victorianism* (London: Longman, 1997).

Burrow, J. W., *Evolution and Society: a Study in Victorian Social Theory* (Cambridge: Cambridge University Press, 1966).

Buzard, James, *Disorienting Fiction: the Autoethnographic Work of Nineteenth-Century British Novels* (Princeton, New Jersey: Princeton University Press, 2005).

______, and Joseph Childers, 'Introduction: Victorian Ethnographies', *Victorian Studies* 41.3 (1998), 351–3.

Bynum, W. F., Roy Porter, and Michael Shepherd, eds, *The Anatomy of Madness: Essays in the History of Psychiatry*, 3 vols (London: Tavistock Publications, 1985–88).

Calder, Jenni, *RLS: a Life Study* (London: Hamish Hamilton, 1980).

______, ed., *Stevenson and Victorian Scotland* (Edinburgh: Edinburgh University Press, 1981).

Campbell, Ian, ed., *Nineteenth-Century Scottish Fiction: Critical Essays* (Manchester: Carcanet, 1979).

Campbell, Matthew, Jacqueline M. Labbé, and Sally Shuttleworth, eds, *Memory and Memorials 1789–1914: Literary and Cultural Perspectives* (London: Routledge, 2000).

Cant, R. G., *The Writing of Scottish History in the Time of Andrew Lang: Being the Andrew Lang Lecture Delivered before the University of St. Andrews 8 February 1978* (Edinburgh: Scottish Academic Press, 1978).

Castle, Gregory, *Modernism and the Celtic Revival* (Cambridge: Cambridge University Press, 2001).

Chamberlin, J. Edward, and Sander L. Gilman, eds, *Degeneration: the Dark Side of Progress* (New York: Columbia University Press, 1985).

Chichester, H. Manners, 'Sir William Johnson', in Leslie Stephen and Sidney Lee, eds, *Dictionary of National Biography*, vol. 30 (London: Smith, Elder, 1892), 50–2.

Christie, John, and Sally Shuttleworth, 'Introduction: Between Literature and Science', in John Christie and Sally Shuttleworth, eds, *Nature Transfigured: Science and Literature, 1700–1900* (Manchester: Manchester University Press, 1989), 1–12.

Christie, John, and Sally Shuttleworth, eds, *Nature Transfigured: Science and Literature, 1700–1900* (Manchester: Manchester University Press, 1989).

Clark, Michael J., 'The Rejection of Psychological Approaches to Mental Disorder in Late Nineteenth-Century Psychiatry', in Andrew Scull, ed., *Madhouses, Mad-doctors, and Madmen: the Social History of Psychiatry in the Victorian Era* (London: Athlone Press, 1981), 271–312.

Clunas, Alexander B., '"A Double Word": Writing and Justice in *The Master of Ballantrae*', *Studies in Scottish Literature* 28 (1993), 55–74.
Colley, Ann, *Robert Louis Stevenson and the Colonial Imagination* (Aldershot, Hampshire: Ashgate, 2004).
Collini, Stefan, *Public Moralists: Political Thought and Intellectual Life in Britain 1850–1930* (Oxford: Clarendon Press, 1991).
——, 'Introduction', in C. P. Snow, *The Two Cultures* (Cambridge: Cambridge University Press, 1993), vii–lxxi.
Cooter, Roger, and Stephen Pumfrey, 'Separate Spheres and Public Places: Reflections on the History of Science Popularization and Science in Popular Culture', *History of Science* 32 (1994), 237–67.
Crawford, Robert, *Devolving English Literature* (Oxford: Clarendon Press, 1992).
Daiches, David, *Robert Louis Stevenson* (Glasgow: William Maclellan, 1947).
——, 'Stevenson and Scotland', in Jenni Calder, ed., *Stevenson and Victorian Scotland* (Edinburgh: Edinburgh University Press, 1981), 11–32.
Dale, Peter Allan, *In Pursuit of a Scientific Culture: Science, Art, and Society in the Victorian Age* (Madison, Wisconsin: University of Wisconsin Press, 1989).
Daly, Nicholas, *Modernism, Romance and the Fin de Siècle: Popular Fiction and British Culture, 1880–1914* (Cambridge: Cambridge University Press, 1999).
Demoor, Marysa, 'Andrew Lang's *Causeries* 1874–1912', *Victorian Periodicals Review* 21.1 (1988), 15–22.
Desmond, Adrian, *Huxley: From Devil's Disciple to Evolution's High Priest* (London: Penguin, 1997).
Devine, T. M., *The Scottish Nation 1700–2000* (London: Penguin, 1999).
Dix, Andrew, and Jonathan Taylor, eds, *Figures of Heresy* (Brighton, East Sussex: Sussex Academic Press, 2006).
Donnachie, Ian, and Christopher Whatley, eds, *The Manufacture of Scottish History* (Edinburgh: Polygon, 1992).
Dorson, Richard M., *The British Folklorists: a History* (London: Routledge and Kegan Paul, 1968).
Dowling, Linda, *Language and Decadence in the Victorian Fin de Siècle* (Princeton, New Jersey: Princeton University Press, 1986).
Drescher, Horst W., and Joachim Schwend, eds, *Studies in Scottish Fiction: Nineteenth Century* (Frankfurt am Main: Verlag Peter Lang, 1985).
Duncan, Ian, 'North Britain, Inc.', *Victorian Literature and Culture* 23 (1995), 339–50.
Ebbatson, Roger, '*The Ebb-Tide*: Missionary Endeavour in the Islands of Light', in Andrew Dix and Jonathan Taylor, eds, *Figures of Heresy* (Brighton, East Sussex: Sussex Academic Press, 2006), 90–107.
Edmond, Rod, *Representing the South Pacific: Colonial Discourse from Cook to Gauguin* (Cambridge: Cambridge University Press, 1997).
Egan, Joseph, '"Markheim": a Drama of Moral Psychology', *Nineteenth-Century Fiction* 20 (1966), 377–84.
——, 'From History to Myth: a Symbolic Reading of *The Master of Ballantrae*', *Studies in English Literature, 1500–1900* 8 (1968), 699–710.
Eigner, Edwin, *Robert Louis Stevenson and Romantic Tradition* (Princeton, New Jersey: Princeton University Press, 1966).
Feltes, N. N., *Literary Capital and the Late Victorian Novel* (Madison, Wisconsin: University of Wisconsin Press, 1993).

Fichman, Martin, 'Biology and Politics: Defining the Boundaries', in Bernard Lightman, ed., *Victorian Science in Context* (Chicago, Illinois: University of Chicago Press, 1997), 94–118.

Fiedler, Leslie A., 'R. L. S. Revisited', in *No! in Thunder: Essays on Myth and Literature* (London: Eyre and Spottiswoode, 1963), 77–91.

Fielding, Penny, *Writing and Orality: Nationality, Culture, and Nineteenth-Century Scottish Fiction* (Oxford: Clarendon Press, 1996).

Flint, Kate, *The Woman Reader 1837–1914* (Oxford: Oxford University Press, 1993).

______, *The Victorians and the Visual Imagination* (Cambridge: Cambridge University Press, 2000).

Fowler, Alastair, 'Parables of Adventure: the Debatable Novels of Robert Louis Stevenson', in Ian Campbell, ed., *Nineteenth-Century Scottish Fiction: Critical Essays* (Manchester: Carcanet, 1979), 105–29.

Furnas, J. C., *Voyage to Windward: the Life of Robert Louis Stevenson* (London: Faber and Faber, 1952).

Gannon, Susan R., 'Repetition and Meaning in Stevenson's David Balfour Novels', *Studies in the Literary Imagination* 18 (1985), 21–33.

Garside, Peter D., 'Scott and the "Philosophical" Historians', *Journal of the History of Ideas* 36 (1975), 497–512.

Gelder, Kenneth, 'Stevenson and the Covenanters: "Black Andie's Tale of Tod Lapraik" and "Thrawn Janet"', *Scottish Literary Journal* 11 (1984), 56–70.

______, 'Robert Louis Stevenson's Revisions to "The Merry Men"', *Studies in Scottish Literature* 21 (1986), 262–87.

Gifford, Douglas, 'Stevenson and Scottish Fiction: the Importance of *The Master of Ballantrae*', in Jenni Calder, ed., *Stevenson and Victorian Scotland* (Edinburgh: Edinburgh University Press, 1981), 62–87.

______, 'Myth, Parody and Dissociation: Scottish Fiction 1814–1914', in Douglas Gifford, ed., *The History of Scottish Literature*, vol. 3: *Nineteenth Century* (Aberdeen: Aberdeen University Press, 1988), 217–59.

______, ed., *The History of Scottish Literature*, vol. 3: *Nineteenth Century* (Aberdeen: Aberdeen University Press, 1988).

Ginzburg, Carlo, 'Tusitala and His Polish Reader', in *No Island Is an Island: Four Glances at English Literature in a World Perspective* (New York: Columbia University Press, 2000), 69–88.

Green, Roger Lancelyn, *Andrew Lang: a Critical Biography with a Short-Title Bibliography of the Works of Andrew Lang* (Leicester: Edmund Ward, 1946).

Greenslade, William, *Degeneration, Culture and the Novel 1880–1940* (Cambridge: Cambridge University Press, 1994).

Hardy, Florence Emily, *The Life of Thomas Hardy: 1840–1928* (London: Macmillan, 1962).

Harman, Claire, *Robert Louis Stevenson: a Biography* (London: HarperCollins, 2005).

Harris, Jason Marc, 'Robert Louis Stevenson: Folklore and Imperialism', *English Literature in Transition 1880–1920* 46 (2003), 382–99.

Hart, Francis Russell, *The Scottish Novel: From Smollett to Spark* (Cambridge, Massachusetts: Harvard University Press, 1978).

Harvie, Christopher, 'The Politics of Stevenson', in Jenni Calder, ed., *Stevenson and Victorian Scotland* (Edinburgh: Edinburgh University Press, 1981), 107–25.

Heath, Stephen, 'Psychopathia Sexualis: Stevenson's *Strange Case*', in Lyn Pykett, ed., *Reading Fin de Siècle Fictions* (London: Longman, 1996), 64–79.
Herbert, Christopher, *Culture and Anomie: Ethnographic Imagination in the Nineteenth Century* (Chicago, Illinois: University of Chicago Press, 1991).
Herdman, John, *The Double in Nineteenth-Century Fiction* (Basingstoke: Macmillan, now Palgrave Macmillan, 1990).
Hillier, Robert Irwin, 'Folklore and Oral Tradition in Stevenson's South Seas Narrative Poems and Short Stories', *Scottish Literary Journal* 14.2 (1987), 32–47.
______, *The South Seas Fiction of Robert Louis Stevenson* (New York: Peter Lang, 1989).
Hirsch, Gordon, and William Veeder, eds, *Dr. Jekyll and Mr. Hyde after One Hundred Years* (Chicago, Illinois: University of Chicago Press, 1988).
Houghton, Walter Edwards, Esther Rhoads Houghton, and Jean Harris Slingerland, eds, *The Wellesley Index to Victorian Periodicals 1824–1900*, 5 vols (Toronto: Toronto University Press, 1966–89).
Hurley, Kelly, *The Gothic Body: Sexuality, Materialism, and Degeneration at the Fin-de-Siècle* (Cambridge: Cambridge University Press, 1996).
Jolly, Roslyn, 'Introduction', in Robert Louis Stevenson, *South Sea Tales* (Oxford: Oxford University Press, 1996), ix–xxxiii.
______, 'Robert Louis Stevenson and Samoan History: Crossing the Roman Wall', in Bruce Bennett, Jeff Doyle, and Satendra Nandan, eds, *Crossing Cultures: Essays on Literature and Culture of the Asia-Pacific* (London: Skoob Books, 1996), 113–20.
______, 'Stevenson's "Sterling Domestic Fiction": "The Beach of Falesá"', *Review of English Studies* n.s. 50 (1999), 463–82.
______, 'South Sea Gothic: Pierre Loti and Robert Louis Stevenson', *English Literature in Transition 1880–1920* 47 (2004), 28–49.
Jones, Gareth Stedman, *Outcast London: a Study in the Relationship between Classes in Victorian Society* (Oxford: Clarendon Press, 1971).
Jordan, John O., and Robert L. Patten, eds, *Literature in the Marketplace: Nineteenth-Century British Publishing and Reading Practices* (Cambridge: Cambridge University Press, 1995).
Keating, Peter, *The Haunted Study: a Social History of the English Novel 1875–1914* (London: Secker and Warburg, 1989).
Kennedy, Paul M., *The Samoan Tangle: a Study in Anglo-German-American Relations 1878–1900* (Dublin: Irish University Press, 1974).
Kerrigan, Catherine, 'Introduction', in Robert Louis Stevenson, *Weir of Hermiston*, ed. Catherine Kerrigan (Edinburgh: Edinburgh University Press, 1995), xvii–xxxvi.
______, and Peter Hinchcliffe, 'Introduction', in Robert Louis Stevenson, *The Ebb-Tide: A Trio and a Quartette*, ed. Catherine Kerrigan and Peter Hinchcliffe (Edinburgh: Edinburgh University Press, 1995), xvii–xxxi.
Kidd, Colin, '*The Strange Death of Scottish History* Revisited: Constructions of the Past in Scotland, c. 1790–1914', *Scottish Historical Review* 76.1 (1997), 86–102.
Kiely, Robert, *Robert Louis Stevenson and the Fiction of Adventure* (Cambridge, Massachusetts: Harvard University Press, 1964).
Knott, Cargill Gilston, *Life and Scientific Work of Peter Guthrie Tait: Supplementing the Two Volumes of Scientific Papers Published in 1898 and 1900* (Cambridge: Cambridge University Press, 1911).

Koestenbaum, Wayne, *Double Talk: the Erotics of Male Literary Collaboration* (London: Routledge, 1989).
Kuhn, Thomas S., *The Structure of Scientific Revolutions* (Chicago, Illinois: University of Chicago Press, 1962).
Kuper, Adam, *The Invention of Primitive Society: Transformations of an Illusion* (London: Routledge, 1988).
______, *Culture: the Anthropologists' Account* (Cambridge, Massachusetts: Harvard University Press, 1999).
Lamb, Jonathan, Vanessa Smith, and Nicholas Thomas, 'Introduction', in Jonathan Lamb, Vanessa Smith, and Nicholas Thomas, eds, *Exploration and Exchange: a South Seas Anthology 1680–1900* (Chicago, Illinois: University of Chicago Press, 2000), xiii–xxv.
Leps, Marie-Christine, *Apprehending the Criminal: the Production of Deviance in Nineteenth-Century Discourse* (Durham, North Carolina: Duke University Press, 1992).
Letley, Emma, 'Introduction', in Robert Louis Stevenson, *Treasure Island* (Oxford: Oxford University Press, 1985), vii–xxiii.
______, 'Introduction', in Robert Louis Stevenson, *Kidnapped and Catriona* (Oxford: Oxford University Press, 1986), vii–xxviii.
Levine, George, 'One Culture: Science and Literature', in George Levine, ed., *One Culture: Essays in Science and Literature* (Madison, Wisconsin: University of Wisconsin Press, 1987), 3–32.
______, *Darwin and the Novelists: Patterns of Science in Victorian Fiction* (Cambridge, Massachusetts: Harvard University Press, 1988).
______, ed., *One Culture: Essays in Science and Literature* (Madison, Wisconsin: University of Wisconsin Press, 1987).
Lightman, Bernard, *The Origins of Agnosticism: Victorian Unbelief and the Limits of Knowledge* (Baltimore, Maryland: Johns Hopkins University Press, 1987).
______, '"The Voices of Nature": Popularizing Victorian Science', in Bernard Lightman, ed., *Victorian Science in Context* (Chicago, Illinois: University of Chicago Press, 1997), 187–211.
______, ed., *Victorian Science in Context* (Chicago, Illinois: University of Chicago Press, 1997).
Linehan, Katherine Bailey, '"Taking Up with Kanakas": Stevenson's Complex Social Criticism in "The Beach of Falesá"', *English Literature in Transition 1880–1920* 33 (1990), 407–22.
Luckhurst, Roger, and Josephine McDonagh, eds, *Transactions and Encounters: Science and Culture in the Nineteenth Century* (Manchester: Manchester University Press, 2002).
MacClancy, Jeremy, 'Anthropology: "The latest form of evening entertainment"', in David Bradshaw, ed., *A Concise Companion to Modernism* (Oxford: Blackwell Publishers, 2003), 75–94.
McCracken-Flesher, Caroline, 'Thinking Nationally/Writing Colonially? Scott, Stevenson, and England', *Novel: a Forum on Fiction* 24 (1990–91), 296–318.
McFarlan, Donald, 'Introduction', in Robert Louis Stevenson, *Kidnapped* (London: Penguin, 1994), vii–xvi.
McGuinness, Patrick, ed., *Symbolism, Decadence and the Fin de Siècle: French and European Perspectives* (Exeter: University of Exeter Press, 2000).

Maharg, Paul, 'Lorimer, Inglis and R. L. S.: Law and the Kailyard Lockup', *Juridical Review* (1995), 280–91.
Masson, Flora, 'Louis Stevenson in Edinburgh', in Rosaline Orme Masson, ed., *I Can Remember Robert Louis Stevenson* (Edinburgh: Chambers, 1922), 125–36.
Masson, Rosaline Orme, ed., *I Can Remember Robert Louis Stevenson* (Edinburgh: Chambers, 1922).
Mattar, Sinéad Garrigan, *Primitivism, Science, and the Irish Revival* (Oxford: Clarendon Press, 2004).
Maurer, Oscar, 'Andrew Lang and *Longman's Magazine*, 1882–1905', *University of Texas Studies in English* 34 (1955), 152–78.
Mays, Kelly, 'The Disease of Reading and Victorian Periodicals', in John O. Jordan and Robert L. Patten, eds, *Literature in the Marketplace: Nineteenth-Century British Publishing and Reading Practices* (Cambridge: Cambridge University Press, 1995), 165–94.
Menikoff, Barry, *Robert Louis Stevenson and 'The Beach of Falesá': a Study in Victorian Publishing* (Stanford, California: Stanford University Press, 1984).
——, '*New Arabian Nights*: Stevenson's Experiment in Fiction', *Nineteenth-Century Literature* 45 (1990–91), 339–62.
Micale, Mark, *Approaching Hysteria: Disease and Its Interpretations* (Princeton, New Jersey: Princeton University Press, 1995).
Mighall, Robert, *A Geography of Victorian Gothic Fiction: Mapping History's Nightmares* (Oxford: Oxford University Press, 1999).
——, 'Diagnosing Jekyll: the Scientific Context of Dr Jekyll's Experiment and Mr Hyde's Embodiment', in Robert Louis Stevenson, *The Strange Case of Dr Jekyll and Mr Hyde and Other Tales of Terror*, ed. Robert Mighall (London: Penguin, 2002), 145–61.
Miller, Karl, *Doubles: Studies in Literary History* (Oxford: Oxford University Press, 1985).
——, 'Introduction', in Robert Louis Stevenson, *Weir of Hermiston*, ed. Karl Miller (London: Penguin, 1996), vii–xxxiv.
Mills, Carol, '*The Master of Ballantrae*: an Experiment with Genre', in Andrew Noble, ed., *Robert Louis Stevenson* (London: Vision Press, 1983), 118–33.
Moore, J. R., 'Stevenson's Source for "The Merry Men"', *Philological Quarterly* 23 (1944), 135–40.
Mulholland, Honor, 'Robert Louis Stevenson and the Romance Form', in Andrew Noble, ed., *Robert Louis Stevenson* (London: Vision Press, 1983), 96–117.
Noble, Andrew, 'Highland History and Narrative Form in Scott and Stevenson', in Andrew Noble, ed., *Robert Louis Stevenson* (London: Vision Press, 1983), 134–87.
——, ed., *Robert Louis Stevenson* (London: Vision Press, 1983).
Norquay, Glenda, 'Introduction', in *R. L. Stevenson on Fiction: an Anthology of Literary and Critical Essays* (Edinburgh: Edinburgh University Press, 1999), 1–25.
Nye, Robert, 'Sociology and Degeneration: the Irony of Progress', in J. Edward Chamberlin and Sander L. Gilman, eds, *Degeneration: the Dark Side of Progress* (New York: Columbia University Press, 1985), 49–71.
Oppenheim, Janet, *'Shattered Nerves': Doctors, Patients, and Depression in Victorian England* (Oxford: Oxford University Press, 1991).
Otis, Laura, *Organic Memory: History and the Body in the Late Nineteenth and Early Twentieth Centuries* (Lincoln, Nebraska: University of Nebraska Press, 1994).

Phillipson, Nicholas, 'Providence and Progress: an Introduction to the Historical Thought of William Robertson', in Stewart J. Brown, ed., *William Robertson and the Expansion of Empire* (Cambridge: Cambridge University Press, 1997), 55–73.

Pick, Daniel, *Faces of Degeneration: a European Disorder, c. 1848–1918* (Cambridge: Cambridge University Press, 1989).

Pittock, Murray, *Poetry and Jacobite Politics in Eighteenth-Century Britain and Ireland* (Cambridge: Cambridge University Press, 1994).

Poole, Adrian, 'Introduction', in Robert Louis Stevenson, *The Master of Ballantrae: A Winter's Tale* (London: Penguin, 1996), vii–xxvi.

Pratt, Mary Louise, *Imperial Eyes: Travel Writing and Transculturation* (London: Routledge, 1992).

Pykett, Lyn, ed., *Reading Fin de Siècle Fictions* (London: Longman, 1996).

Rennie, Neil, 'Introduction', in Robert Louis Stevenson, *In the South Seas* (London: Penguin, 1998), viii–xxxv.

Richards, David, *Masks of Difference: Cultural Representations in Literature, Anthropology and Art* (Cambridge: Cambridge University Press, 1994).

Rosner, Mary, '"A Total Subversion of Character": Dr Jekyll's Moral Insanity', *Victorian Newsletter* 93 (1998), 27–31.

Rumbelow, Donald, *The Complete Jack the Ripper* (London: W. H. Allen, 1979).

Rylance, Rick, *Victorian Psychology and British Culture 1850–1880* (Oxford: Oxford University Press, 2000).

Sandison, Alan, *Robert Louis Stevenson and the Appearance of Modernism* (Basingstoke: Macmillan, now Palgrave Macmillan, 1996).

Saposnik, Irving, 'Stevenson's "Markheim": a Fictional "Christmas Sermon"', *Nineteenth-Century Fiction* 21 (1966), 277–82.

Scott, Thomas Bodley, 'Memories', in Rosaline Orme Masson, ed., *I Can Remember Robert Louis Stevenson* (Edinburgh: Chambers, 1922), 212–14.

Scull, Andrew, ed., *Madhouses, Mad-doctors, and Madmen: The Social History of Psychiatry in the Victorian Era* (London: Athlone Press, 1981).

Shaffer, Elinor S., 'Introduction: The Third Culture – Negotiating the "Two Cultures"', in Elinor S. Shaffer, ed., *The Third Culture: Literature and Science* (Berlin: Walter de Gruyter, 1998), 1–12.

______, ed., *The Third Culture: Literature and Science* (Berlin: Walter de Gruyter, 1998).

Shapiro, Stephen, 'Mass African Suicide and the Rise of Euro-American Sentimentalism: Equiano's and Stevenson's Tales of the Semi-Periphery', in W. M. Verhoeven and Beth Dolan, eds, *Revolutions and Watersheds: Transatlantic Dialogues, 1775–1815* (Amsterdam: Rodopi, 1999), 123–44.

Shearer, Tom, 'A Strange Judgement of God's? Stevenson's *The Merry Men*', *Studies in Scottish Literature* 20 (1985), 71–85.

Showalter, Elaine, *Sexual Anarchy: Gender and Culture at the Fin de Siècle* (London: Bloomsbury, 1991).

Shuttleworth, Sally, *George Eliot and Nineteenth-Century Science: the Make-Believe of a Beginning* (Cambridge: Cambridge University Press, 1984).

______, *Charlotte Brontë and Victorian Psychology* (Cambridge: Cambridge University Press, 1996).

______, 'The Psychology of Childhood in Victorian Literature and Medicine', in Helen Small and Trudi Tate, eds, *Literature, Science, Psychoanalysis, 1830–1970: Essays in Honour of Gillian Beer* (Cambridge: Cambridge University Press, 2003), 86–101.

Simpson, K. G., 'Author and Narrator in *Weir of Hermiston*', in Andrew Noble, ed., *Robert Louis Stevenson* (London: Vision Press, 1983), 202–27.

Small, Helen, *Love's Madness: Medicine, the Novel, and Female Insanity 1800–1865* (Oxford: Oxford University Press, 1996).

______, 'The Unquiet Limit: Old Age and Memory in Victorian Narrative', in Matthew Campbell, Jacqueline M. Labbé, and Sally Shuttleworth, eds, *Memory and Memorials 1789–1914: Literary and Cultural Perspectives* (London: Routledge, 2000), 60–79.

______, and Trudi Tate, eds, *Literature, Science, Psychoanalysis, 1830–1970: Essays in Honour of Gillian Beer* (Cambridge: Cambridge University Press, 2003).

Smith, Vanessa, *Literary Culture and the Pacific: Nineteenth-Century Textual Encounters* (Cambridge: Cambridge University Press, 1998).

Smout, T. C., *A History of the Scottish People 1560–1830* (London: Collins, 1969).

Snow, C. P., 'The Two Cultures' (1959), in *The Two Cultures*, intro. by Stefan Collini (Cambridge: Cambridge University Press, 1993), 1–51.

Spadafora, David, *The Idea of Progress in Eighteenth-Century Britain* (New Haven, Connecticut: Yale University Press, 1990).

Spilka, Mark, 'Henry James and Walter Besant: "The Art of Fiction" Controversy', *Novel: a Forum on Fiction* 6 (1973), 101–19.

State University of New York, *Robert Louis Stevenson: a Catalogue of His Works and Books relating to Him in the Rare Book Collection* (Buffalo, New York: State University of New York at Buffalo, 1972).

Stocking, George W., Jr., *Victorian Anthropology* (New York: Free Press, 1987).

______, *After Tylor: British Social Anthropology 1888–1951* (London: Athlone Press, 1995).

Storch, Robert D., ed., *Popular Culture and Custom in Nineteenth-Century England* (London: Croom Helm, 1982).

Sullivan, Alvin, ed., *British Literary Magazines: the Victorian and Edwardian Age, 1837–1913* (Westport, Connecticut: Greenwood Press, 1984).

Sutherland, Kathryn, 'Introduction', in Walter Scott, *Redgauntlet* (Oxford: Oxford University Press, 1985), vii–xxiii.

Swearingen, Roger G., *The Prose Writings of Robert Louis Stevenson: a Guide* (Hamden, Connecticut: Archon Books, 1980).

Taylor, Jenny Bourne, 'Obscure Recesses: Locating the Victorian Unconscious', in J. B. Bullen, ed., *Writing and Victorianism* (London: Longman, 1997), 137–79.

Verhoeven, W. M., and Beth Dolan, eds, *Revolutions and Watersheds: Transatlantic Dialogues, 1775–1815* (Amsterdam: Rodopi, 1999).

Vincent, David, 'The Decline of Oral Tradition in Popular Culture', in Robert D. Storch, ed., *Popular Culture and Custom in Nineteenth-Century England* (London: Croom Helm, 1982), 20–47.

Vrettos, Athena, *Somatic Fictions: Imagining Illness in Victorian Culture* (Stanford, California: Stanford University Press, 1995).

Warner, Fred B., Jr., 'Stevenson's First Scottish Story', *Nineteenth-Century Fiction* 24 (1969), 335–44.

White, Paul, 'Cross-cultural Encounters: The Co-production of Science and Literature in Mid-Victorian Periodicals', in Roger Luckhurst and Josephine McDonagh, eds, *Transactions and Encounters: Science and Culture in the Nineteenth Century* (Manchester: Manchester University Press, 2002), 75–95.

Williams, J. P., 'Psychical Research and Psychiatry in Late Victorian Britain: Trance as Ecstasy or Trance as Insanity', in W. F. Bynum, Roy Porter, and

Michael Shepherd, eds, *The Anatomy of Madness: Essays in the History of Psychiatry,* 3 vols (London: Tavistock Publications, 1985–88), 1: 233–54.

Williams, M. Kellen, '"Down with the Door, Poole": Designating Deviance in Stevenson's *Strange Case of Dr. Jekyll and Mr. Hyde*', *English Literature in Transition* 39 (1996), 412–29.

Withers, Charles, 'The Historical Creation of the Scottish Highlands', in Ian Donnachie and Christopher Whatley, eds, *The Manufacture of Scottish History* (Edinburgh: Polygon, 1992), 143–56.

Womack, Peter, *Improvement and Romance: Constructing the Myth of the Highlands* (Basingstoke: Macmillan, now Palgrave Macmillan, 1988).

Yeazell, R. B., ed., *Sex, Politics, and Science in the Nineteenth-Century Novel* (Baltimore, Maryland: Johns Hopkins University Press, 1986).

Young, Robert, *Colonial Desire: Hybridity in Theory, Culture and Race* (London: Routledge, 1995).

Zenzinger, Peter, 'The Ballad Spirit and the Modern Mind: Narrative Perspective in Stevenson's *Weir of Hermiston*', in Horst W. Drescher and Joachim Schwend, eds, *Studies in Scottish Fiction: Nineteenth Century* (Frankfurt am Main: Verlag Peter Lang, 1985), 233–51.

Conference papers

Arata, Stephen, 'Close Reading and Contextual Reading in *Dr Jekyll and Mr Hyde*', a paper delivered at the 'Stevenson, Scotland and Samoa' conference, Stirling, 2000.

Crawford, Robert, '"My Bed Is Like a Little Boat": Stevenson's Voyage into Masculinity', a paper delivered at the 'Stevenson, Scotland, and Samoa' conference, Stirling, 2000.

Watson, Rory, '"You cannot fight me with a word": *The Master of Ballantrae* and the Wilderness beyond Dualism', a paper delivered at the 'Stevenson, Scotland and Samoa' conference, Stirling, 2000.

Wishart, Kirsti, '*Kidnapped* in Samoa: David Balfour and the Unsuccessful Anthropologist', a paper delivered at the 'Stevenson, Scotland and Samoa' conference, Stirling, 2000.

Online sources

[Anon.], 'The Whitechapel Murder', *East London Advertiser* (8 September 1888), http://www.casebook.org/press_reports/east_london_advertiser/ela880908.html (accessed 16 May 2005).

[Anon.], 'Here and There', *East London Advertiser* (13 October 1888), http:// www.casebook.org/press_reports/east_london_advertiser/ela881013.html (accessed 16 May 2005).

Index

References to illustrations are printed in bold.

adventure fiction, *see* romance
æsthetics, evolutionist, 15, 16–20, 25–6
agnosticism, 118
Allen, Grant, 11, 15, 25, 140
  The Great Taboo, 148
altered mental states, *see* mental states, altered
ancestry, 20–2, 62–3, 64–8
Anderson, Eric, 166
anglicization, 123, 157, 163–4, 168, 170
  see also Union, the Anglo-Scottish
animism, 24, 78, 82
anthropology, 7, 9, 108–10, 111–37, 139–73, 176
  criminal, 94, 95, 102
  secularizing mission of, 108–9, 112–22
Arabian Nights, 25–6, 48, 133
Arata, Stephen, 5, 32, 35, 57, 94, 98, 100, 101
Archer, William, 131
Arnold, Matthew, 2
'Art of Fiction' debate, 18
artistic decadence, 57, 68–72
Ashley, Scott, 141

Baker, Smith, 96, 99
Balfour, Graham, 93–4
ballad tradition, 168–9
Ballantyne, R. M., 33, 42
  The Coral Island, 39, 41, 42, 46, 47, 49
Barkan, Elazar, 5
Barrie, J. M., 166
Beer, Gillian, 3, 6, 8, 31, 109, 143
  Darwin's Plots, 3
Besant, Walter, 'The Art of Fiction', 18
Block, Ed, 6, 16, 78, 79, 81, 82, 83, 87, 88
Boas, Franz, 142
Bowler, Peter, 7
Boyle, Richard, 92
Brantlinger, Patrick, 32, 47, 92, 151, 152
Bristow, Joseph, 32, 37, 41
Broks, Peter, 9
Brontë, Charlotte, 3
Burton, J. H., *History of Scotland*, 124
Bush, Ronald, 5
Butler, Samuel, 14, 19, 21
  The Way of All Flesh, 20
Buzard, James, 125, 142

Calder, Jenni, 90
Campbell, G. D., Duke of Argyll, 62
  The Reign of Law, 62, 113
Castle, Gregory, 8
Celticism, 158–9
  see also Gaelic Revival
Chapman, John Jay, 4
Charcot, Jean-Martin, 63
childhood imagination, *see* imagination, childhood
civilization and savagery, *see* savagery and civilization
class, 50–1, 56–7, 94, 170
Clifford, W. K., 114
Clunas, Alexander, 134
Collini, Stefan, 3, 72
colonialism, *see* evangelical colonialism; imperialism
Colvin, Sidney, 1, 43, 45, 61, 63, 89, 124, 140, 150
Conrad, Joseph, 47, 151
  Heart of Darkness, 35, 50
Cooper, James Fenimore, 33
Cooter, Roger, 5
Cornhill Magazine, 9, 15–16, 79–80, 96, 119
Cosmopolis, 171
Covenanters, 78, 119–22, 166, 169–72

Crawford, Robert, 39, 111
creativity, *see* imagination, creative
Crichton-Browne, James, 60, 65, 68
'On Dreamy Mental States', 69, 71
Criminal Law Amendment Act (1885), 99
criminology, 57, 94, 95, 100, 102
Crockett, S. R., 166
crowd theory, 102
Cummy [Stevenson's nurse], 60

Daiches, David, 32
Dale, Peter Allan, 3
Dallas, E. S., *The Gay Science*, 27
Daly, Nicholas, 8, 24
Darwin, Charles, 1, 3, 4, 7, 8, 20, 22, 56, 61, 62, 109, 113, 115–16, 142, 143, 147, 149
The Descent of Man, 146
The Origin of Species, 7
'Death of the Sun', 158
decadence, *see* artistic decadence
Defoe, Daniel, *Robinson Crusoe*, 48, 49
degeneration, 8, 44–53, 56–8, 59–76, 77–105, 152–3, 153–4, 157, 161–2, 169
tensions within theories of, 64, 69–70, 72, 104–5, 176
see also environment; heredity; will
Desmond, Adrian, 113
determinism, hereditary, 83–8
see also environment; heredity; will
Dickens, Charles, 69
divided consciousness, 26–9, 55–6, 69–72, 89–92, 93, 96–8, 101–2
Dostoevsky, Fyodor, 73
Crime and Punishment, 89, 92
Dowling, Linda, 23, 156
Doyle, Arthur Conan, 17, 57
The Hound of the Baskervilles, 86, 87
dreaming, 15, 26–9, 93
dual consciousness, *see* divided consciousness

Ebbatson, Roger, 49, 51
Edinburgh Evening Club, 111–13
Edmond, Rod, 5, 107, 143, 146, 147, 151, 155
Egan, Joseph, 90, 92
Eigner, Edwin, 32, 41, 78, 80, 82, 84, 92, 102, 116, 159, 165
Eliot, George, 4
Eliot, T. S., 8
Ellis, Havelock, 95
The Criminal, 102
Englishness, 35, 37–8, 40, 41, 42, 85
environment, 56, 58, 60, 64, 68–76, 94–5, 97–105, 174
see also heredity
ethnography, 126, 127–9, 137, 141–2, 149–50
ethnology, 124
evangelical colonialism, 49–52
evolutionism, 6, 7–9
evolutionary hierarchies, 9, 11, 30, 46, 108–9, 110, 116, 123, 132, 134–6, 137, 141–2, 146, 148, 149–50, 152, 153, 157, 173, 176
evolutionary meliorism, 7–8, 11, 14, 16, 20, 25, 30, 108–37, 139–73, 176
sociocultural, 108–9
tensions within, 6, 7–9, 143, 176
see also under individual evolutionary sciences

Feltes, N. N., 18
Ferguson, Adam, 108
Fichman, Martin, 7
Fiedler, Leslie, 32
Fielding, Penny, 23, 119, 135, 166, 167, 168–9
Flint, Kate, 74
folklore, 23, 82, 107–8, 109, 121, 123, 128, 140–1, 151, 154–5, 158–9, 162, 168
see also rational emancipation; rationality; superstition
Fothergill, J. M., 69
Fowler, Alastair, 49, 50
Frazer, J. G., 8, 111, 148
The Golden Bough, 112
free will, *see* will
Freud, Sigmund, 6, 25
'Civilization and Its Discontents', 24

Gaelic Revival, 64–5, 164
see also Celticism
Galton, Francis, 65, 69, 83, 86–7
Inquiries into Human Faculty and Its Development, 65
Records of Family Faculties, 65, **66–7**
Gannon, Susan, 129, 130, 165
Gelder, Kenneth, 119
gender, 31–2, 35, 51, 98, 160
see also heterosexuality; homosexuality; homosociality; masculinity
genius, 2, 27, 28, 57, 65–8, 69, 71
Gifford, Douglas, 131
Gill, W. W., *Myths and Songs from the South Pacific*, 145
Gissing, George, 57
Gosse, Edmund, 74
Greenslade, William, 57

Haggard, H. Rider, 8, 11, 17, 23, 31, 44
King Solomon's Mines, 35
She, 97
Hardy, Thomas, 4, 57, 61
Harman, Claire, 83
Harris, J. M., 133, 152
Harvie, Christopher, 4, 139
Heath, Stephen, 5, 99, 100, 101
Henley, W. E., 33, 131
'Invictus', 51–2
Henty, G. A., 32
Herbert, Christopher, 142
Herdman, John, 96
heredity, 10–11, 13, 14, 19–22, 56, 58, 60, 64–70, 72, 83–8, 94–105, 158–9, 174–5
see also determinism, hereditary; environment; will
heterosexuality, 31–2, 99, 165
Hillier, Robert, 5, 140
history of science, 2–3
Hogg, James, *The Private Memoirs and Confessions of a Justified Sinner*, 90, 119
homosexuality, 99
homosociality, 51
Hope, Anthony, 17, 32
Howells, W. D., 16, 29, 31
Hutton, R. H., 125
Huxley, T. H., 2, 97, 113, 118
hysteria, 63, 73–4, 79, 95

imagination
childhood, 22, 24–5
creative, 15, 26–9, 68–72
imperialism, 8, 11, 31–2, 33, 35, 37–8, 40–1, 42–53, 129, 135–6, 137, 139–57, 173
see also anglicization; South Seas; Union, the Anglo-Scottish
India, 133–6
inheritance, of acquired characteristics, 7, 20, 64
see also heredity
Innes, Cosmo, 124
insanity, 10, 57, 77–80, 95, 96, 97
inspiration, *see* imagination, creative
interdisciplinarity, *see* science, and literature
introspection, 56, 72–3
Ireland, 124–5

'Jack the Ripper', 103
Jacobitism, 124, 129–37, 159–65
Jacobs, Joseph, 141, 166
James, Henry, 16, 18, 43, 44, 139
'The Art of Fiction', 18
Jefferies, Richard, *After London*, 158
Jenkin, Fleeming, 113
Johnstone, Arthur, 146–7
Jolly, Roslyn, 32, 143, 151, 153, 155, 157
Jowett, Benjamin, et al., *Essays and Reviews*, 112
Jung, Carl Gustav, 6

Kailyard, 166, 172
Keating, Peter, 17
Keats, John, 68
Kiely, Robert, 40
Kingston, W. H. G., 33
Kipling, Rudyard, 8, 15, 17, 63
Krafft-Ebing, Richard von, 99
Kuhn, Thomas, *The Structure of Scientific Revolutions*, 3

Labouchère Amendment, 99
Laing, R. D., 6
Lamarck, Jean-Baptiste, 7, 20, 64, 95
Lang, Andrew, 9, 15–18, 23, 25, 26, 31, 32, 35, 37, 44, 47, 109, 111, 114, 140, 141, 156, 168
language, 23, 50–1, 79–80, 100–1, 126, 135, 150, 156–7, 162, 163–4, 168–9, 170
  see also orality; print culture
Lankester, Edwin Ray, 8, 56, 98
Le Bon, Gustave, *The Crowd*, 102
Leavis, F. R., 2
Lee, Vernon, 'Marsyas in Flanders', 84
Letley, Emma, 160
Levine, George, 3
Linehan, Katherine, 156
linguistic science, 23, 156
literature
  decadence of, 68–73
  popular, 15, 16–18, 19–20, 22, 30, 73–5, 77, 92–3, 102–5
  and science, *see* science, and literature
Lombroso, Cesare, 65, 95
Longman's Magazine, 9, 17, 18, 19
Longmans, 92

McCracken–Flesher, Caroline, 120
McFarlan, Donald, 129
Machen, Arthur, *The Great God Pan*, 84–5, 97
Maclaren, Ian, 166
McLennan, J. F., 108, 111, 112
Malinowski, Bronislaw, 142
Mansfield, Richard, 100, 103
masculinity
  anxieties about, 10, 62–4, 68, 75
  ideal of heroic, 23, 31–3, 35–53
Maudsley, Henry, 8, 28, 56, 57, 64, 69, 72, 79, 95
Mays, Kelly, 74
meliorism, *see* evolutionism, evolutionary meliorism
Melville, Herman, 44, 49, 155
  Omoo, 49, 146
  Typee, 146, 155
Menikoff, Barry, 5, 155, 157
mental states, altered, 27–9, 59–60, 69–72
  see also genius; imagination; unconscious mind
Mighall, Robert, 5, 57, 77, 86, 87, 94, 101, 103
Millar, John, 108
Miller, Karl, 69, 166–7
Millingen, J. M., 86
Modernism, 8–9
modernity, 16–17, 23–4, 30, 32, 35, 68, 98, 168
  see also overcivilization
Moore, J. R., 80
Morel, Bénédict-Augustin, 56
Morley, Charles, 75, 89
Mulholland, Honor, 80
Müller, Friedrich Max, 145
multiple personality, *see* divided consciousness
Murray, John, 112
Myers, A. T., 16
Myers, F. W. H., 5, 6, 9, 15–16, 27–9, 63, 71, 96, 176
  Human Personality and Its Survival of Bodily Death, 28, 71

Native Americans, 134–6
natural selection, 7, 56, 98, 115–16, 143, 147
naturalism, 43, 47, 48
Neo-Gothic fiction, 74–5, 77
nervous morbidity, *see* psychological disorders
New Imperialism, 32, 52
Nicholson, Rev. Dr, 93
Noble, Andrew, 4, 125, 159, 160–1, 164, 165
Nordau, Max, 57, 68
Norquay, Glenda, 24

Oppenheim, Janet, 63, 64
orality, 22, 23–4, 119–20, 132–4, 152, 155–7, 163–4, 167, 168–70
  see also print culture
organic memory, 13, 14, 19–22
Osbourne, Lloyd, 33, 43, 63
Otis, Laura, 3

Outcast London, 94, 98
overcivilization, 16–18, 30, 35, 52, 98
see also modernity

Pall Mall Gazette, 75, 89
Pan myth, 84–5, 86
Pater, Walter, 'Apollo in Picardy', 84
periodical press, 9, 114, 140
pessimism, 44, 147
Pick, Daniel, 57
Plumacher, O., 147
plurality, cultural, 142–57, 173, 176–7
see also relativism, cultural
Poe, Edgar Allan, 89
'The Tell-Tale Heart', 89
'William Wilson', 90
Poole, Adrian, 132
postcolonialism, 5, 108, 139, 175
Pratt, Mary Louise, 150
primitive consciousness, survival of, 10–12, 13–14, 15–30, 31, 32–3, 37, 41, 52–3, 69–70, 71–2, 73, 77–86, 93, 95–105, 122, 132–4, 162, 176
see also primitive resurgences; rational emancipation; rationality; savagery and civilization; superstition
primitive resurgences, 10, 11, 13, 20, 22, 29, 32–3, 37, 41, 45–6, 52–3, 56, 69, 77–88, 95–105, 119–22, 131, 134, 137, 153–5, 161–2, 171, 172
see also primitive consciousness, survival of; savagery and civilization
primitivism, 5, 8–9
print culture, 23, 132–3, 152, 155–7, 163, 169–70
see also orality
Proctor, Richard, 'Dual Consciousness', 96
progress, *see* evolutionism, evolutionary meliorism
psychiatry, evolutionist, 64, 65, 68–70, 71, 94, 95–7
psychical research, 4, 15
see also spiritualism
psychological disorders, 10, 59–76, 77–105
see also hysteria; insanity; introspection
psychology, evolutionary, 7, 9, 14, 15–30, 56, 64–74, 77–105, 175–6
Pumfrey, Stephen, 5

Quiller-Couch, Arthur, 159, 164

'race', 14, 15, 19, 21, 24–5, 43, 46, 47–8, 64–5, 83–8, 124, 129, 135, 146, 152, 157–9, 174
rational emancipation, 109, 114–15, 116–22, 131–7, 152–7, 162
see also rationality; superstition
rationality, 80–3, 84, 85, 100–2, 131–7, 152–7, 162, 176–8
see also rational emancipation; superstition
reading, 72–5, 102–5
realism, 16–18, 31–2, 37, 43–4, 47, 53, 74, 101, 133–4, 138–9, 151, 167, 168
see also romance
Reid, Henry Mayne, 39, 42
relativism, cultural, 142–57, 173, 176–7
see also plurality, cultural
religion, 49–52, 59–62, 78–83, 88, 109, 111–22, 149, 154, 175
Rennie, Neil, 143
Ribot, Théodule, 56
Richards, David, 8
Robertson, William, 81, 123
Rodin, Auguste, 55
romance, 8, 14, 16–30, 31–53, 70, 73–4, 133–4, 139, 142, 151–7, 159, 165, 176
see also realism
Royal Scottish Society of Arts, 4

Saintsbury, George, 17
Sandison, Alan, 5, 166, 169
Saposnik, Irving, 90, 92
savagery and civilization, 6, 8–12, 13–14, 15, 19, 20, 22, 25, 30, 42–3, 44, 46, 52–3, 77, 80–3, 94, 95, 97–8, 100, 102, 105, 107–8,

109–10, 116, 120, 122, 123, 125, 129, 131–7, 140, 146, 152, 153–4, 157, 160–2, 164, 170–1, 173, 175, 177
see also evolutionism, evolutionary hierarchies; evolutionism, evolutionary meliorism; primitive consciousness, survival of; primitive resurgences
Savile Club, 9, 15–16
science, history of, 2–3
and literature: interdisciplinary studies of, 3–4; relations of, 3–4, 6, 27–30, 108, 140–1, 175–6
Scotland, 107–8, 111–13, 114, 116, 119–37, 138–9, 146, 157–73, 174, 175
as divided nation, 125–37, 164–5
Highlands, 123–31, 146, 159–65
Lowlands, 123–31, 160–5
Scott, Walter, 73, 119, 123, 124, 125, 131, 146, 164, 169
Old Mortality, 169
Redgauntlet, 119
Rob Roy, 130, 160
Waverley, 126, 130
Scottish Enlightenment, 7, 81, 108, 109, 123, 133, 134
sexology, 57, 94, 96, 99
sexuality, 84–5, 86, 96, 99–100, 101
Shapiro, Stephen, 127, 130
Sharp, William, 65
Shaw, George Bernard, 57
Shearer, Tom, 80
Showalter, Elaine, 6, 27, 31, 51
Shuttleworth, Sally, 3, 24, 29
Simpson, K. G., 167
Small, Helen, 3
Smith, Adam, 108
Smith, Vanessa, 5, 48, 107, 144
Smith, William Robertson, 111, 112
Snow, C. P., 2
Society for Psychical Research, 4, 28
South Seas, 42–53, 107–8, 126, 138–58, 160, 162, 163, 165, 170, 172, 175
speech, *see* language; orality
Spencer, Herbert, 4, 7, 15, 16, 19, 20, 21, 22, 25, 56, 60, 108, 109, 113, 140, 143
The Principles of Psychology, 14, 56
spiritualism, 4, 153–4
see also psychical research
Spitzka, Edward Charles, 99
Stephen, Leslie, 118, 119, 139
Stevenson, Fanny van de Grift, 1, 65, 93, 96, 142
Stevenson, R. A. M. [Bob], 60, 68
Stevenson, Robert Louis
ancestry and family background, 4, 62–3, 158–9, 174
anti-imperialism, 33, 42–3, 53, 139–40, 157
childhood, 21, 59–60
critical reputation, 4, 5, 32, 108, 138–9, 166, 172, 175
education and youth in Edinburgh, 4, 111–14
family relationships, 60–2, 113–19
psychological morbidity, 55–8, 59–76
religious crisis, 60–2, 113–19
scientific interests and transactions, 4, 5–6, 8–9, 15–16, 27–9, 140–1, 174
Scottishness, 4, 107–8, 166, 175
South Seas life, 1–2, 42–3, 45, 53, 107–8, 138–9, **138**, 140–1, 142–50, **144–5**, 154–5, 160, 170, 174, 175, 176
Stevenson, Robert Louis, *works*
Ballads, 23
'The Beach of Falesá', 11, 32, 39, 43, 47, 74, 75, 142, 151–7, 163
The Black Arrow, 9, 37, 43, 63, 125
'The Body Snatcher', 74, 75
'The Bottle Imp', 151
Catriona, 11, 159–65
'A Chapter on Dreams', 26–30, 71, 89, 93, 94
'Child's Play', 22, 24–5, 39
'The Day After Tomorrow', 72, 98
The Dynamiter, 9
The Ebb-Tide, 10, 14, 32, 33, 43–53, **46**, 61
'The English Admirals', 37–8

Stevenson, Robert Louis, *works – continued*
'Et Tu in Arcadia Vixisti', 84, 86
A Footnote to History, 43, 139, 143, 160, 162
'The Foreigner at Home', 127
'A Gossip on Romance', 17–18, 37, 48
Heathercat, 159, 166, 172
'The House of Eld', 11, 116–19, 122
'A Humble Remonstrance', 17, 18, 24, 34
In the South Seas, 1, 11, 45, 51, 107, 142–50, **144–5**, 155, 156, 157–8, 173
An Inland Voyage, 28, 63, 70–1, 82
'The Isle of Voices', 151
Kidnapped, 4, 11, 125–31, 132, 146, 150, 159, 162
'The Lantern-Bearers', 22, 25
'The Manse', 19, 20–2, 41, 63
'Markheim', 10, 74, 88–92, 93, 105
The Master of Ballantrae, 11, 39, 74, 75, 125, 131–7, 139
'Memoirs of Himself', 59–60
'The Merry Men', 10, 77–83, 85, 90, 92, 105, 122
'The Misadventures of John Nicholson', 60
New Arabian Nights, 9, 61, 73, 97
'Olalla', 10, 26, 83–8, 91, 92, 95, 104, 105, 122
'On Some Technical Elements of Style', 19
'Ordered South', 70, 71
'Pastoral', 13, 19–20, 22, 87
'The Pavilion on the Links', 73
'The Persons of the Tale', 39
'Popular Authors', 22
'Pulvis et Umbra', 4, 61–2, 95
Records of a Family of Engineers, 158
'"Rosa Quo Locorum"', 25
The Strange Case of Dr. Jekyll and Mr. Hyde, 5, 6, 10, 26, 27, 29, 55–6, 57, 74, 75, 90, 92–105, 125
'Talk and Talkers', 22, 23–4, 155–6
'Talk and Talkers: A Sequel', 22, 23–4, 155–6
'Thrawn Janet', 11, 73, 74, 119–22, 154, 156, 162, 165, 172
Treasure Island, 4, 10, 14, 18, 32, 33–42, **36**, 43, 52, 53, 63, 92, 125
Underwoods, 9
Weir of Hermiston, 11, 32, 51, 159, 165–72, 173
The Wrecker, 43, 47, 49
The Young Chevalier, 159
Stevenson, Thomas, 64, 65, 111, 112–14, 118, 156
Christianity Confirmed, 113
Stewart, Balfour, *see* Tait, P. G.
Stocking, George, 109, 142
Sullivan, T. R., 100, 103
Sully, James, 6, 9, 15–16, 19, 25, 27, 29–30, 69, 71, 72, 73, 79, 102, 114
'Poetic Imagination and Primitive Conception', 29
superstition, 80–3, 101–2, 116–24, 131–7, 148, 149–50, 151–5, 162–4, 167–8
see also folklore; rational emancipation; rationality
'survivals', 13, 14, 17, 98, 109, 116, 120, 123, 137, 143, 148, 154, 167
see also primitive consciousness, survival of; primitive resurgences; savagery and civilization
Symonds, J. A., 64, 103–4, 105
sympathy, cross-cultural, 11, 148–50, 171–2, 173
Synge, J. M., 141

Tait, P. G., 111, 112–13
and Balfour Stewart, *The Unseen Universe*, 113, 114
Taylor, Jenny Bourne, 59
Taylor, Lady Theodosia Alice, 74
Tembinoka, King of Apemama, 51, 140
Thackeray, William Makepeace, *Vanity Fair*, 73
Thomson, William, Lord Kelvin, 113, 158
Tuke, Daniel Hack, 102
Tylor, E. B., 4, 7, 24, 25, 79, 108, 115, 118, 123, 141, 143, 148, 150, 153–4
Primitive Culture, 14, 109
'two cultures' 1–3, 6

unconscious mind, 15, 18–30, 176
see also imagination; mental states, altered; organic memory
Union, the Anglo-Scottish, 122, 123, 125–31, 132, 170
see also anglicization; imperialism

Veitch, John, *The History and Poetry of the Scottish Border*, 168
Virgil, *Aeneid*, 132

Warner, Fred, 120
Watson, Rory, 132
Wedgwood, Julia, 92
Wells, H. G., 57
The Time Machine, 98
Weyman, Stanley, 32
Whigs, 127–37, 159–65
White, Paul, 9
Wilde, Oscar, 15, 23, 139
'The Decay of Lying', 105
The Picture of Dorian Gray, 86, 87
will, 27, 58, 64, 69–72, 83–8, 90–2, 97, 103–4, 113–14
see also determinism, hereditary; environment; heredity
Williams, M. Kellen, 101
Wilson, Daniel, 124
Winslow, Forbes, 91
Wishart, Kirsti, 150
written word, *see* print culture

Young Folks, 33, 37

Zenzinger, Peter, 167
Zola, Émile, 43–4, 47